SNAKES ON A PLANE

When Hawaiian surfer Sean Jones witnesses a murder by a Triad gangster, the FBI want him safe in LA to testify in court. The problem is that Eddie Kim, the gangster in question, is a resourceful man and will do anything to stop himself going to prison. As the witness begins the flight to LA with his FBI chaperone, he's blissfully unaware of the pallet full of deadly snakes in the cargo hold. As the snakes are unleashed, all hell breaks loose and it falls to Sean and Agent Neville Flynn to stop the snakes and land the plane!

D0723395

SNAKES ON A PLANE

A NOVEL BY
CHRISTA FAUST

BLACK FLAME

This book is dedicated to all the usual suspects. You know who you are and you know what you did.

A Black Flame Publication
www.blackflame.com

First published in 2006 by BL Publishing, Games Workshop Ltd., Willow Road, Nottingham NG7 2WS, UK.

Distributed in the US by Simon & Schuster, 1230 Avenue of the Americas, New York, NY 10020, USA.

10 9 8 7 6 5 4 3 2 1

ISBN 13: 978 1 84416 381 6
ISBN 10: 1 84416 381 4

A CIP record for this book is available from the British Library.

Printed in the UK by Bookmarque, Surrey, UK.

ONE

Sean Jones was seventeen, handsome and tan with a sturdy surfer's build and an easy smile. He was born and grew up in Waimea Bay, Oahu and considered himself Hawaiian, nearly native, even though he was about as physically far from a Pacific Islander as he could be. He loved his home island, with all its flaws and all its contradictions. The tourists and pro surfers, cantankerous locals and hippies, tattoo artists, frat boys and hula girls. The beauty and the poverty, the unspoiled natural vistas and the non-stop sleazy human hustle. Lush jungle and bare, unwelcoming rock. Monstrous all-inclusive resorts like walled cities and tumble-down trailers full of single mothers and their naked, unwashed children. Riotous nightlife and serene waterfalls. Pickpockets and poi, orchids and corruption. Everything. Sean couldn't imagine living anywhere else.

He hurtled down one of his favorite secret local trails on his brand new 2006 Yamaha TT-R125E Off Road dirt bike, savoring the hot adrenaline roaring through his veins and the thrill of catching air off the jumps while feeling everything else in his life just slip away. All the worries, the responsibilities, the day-to-day headaches just seemed to get lost in the dust and he could live purely in that moment without a care in the world.

This was the first time since the confirmation of Mel's death that Sean had been able to really let go and enjoy himself. Mel, his mother (though she'd always hated being called mom or mommy or anything but Mel), had been more like a child than Sean, and he had been the one taking care of her for as long as he could remember. She had been beautiful once, with an exotic, fine-boned model's face and a taut, tanned and flawless body, but she'd been utterly incapable of anything tedious and mundane like housekeeping or paying bills. In the last five years or so, her beauty had been rapidly fading as the partying, the drugs and the care-free living started catching up with her in spades. Ever since she was eighteen, her wealthy parents back on the mainland had shelled out ten thousand dollars every quarter to Melissa "Mel" Dayton, in order to make sure their wayward run-away embarrassment of a daughter never darkened their doorstep again. They did not know about Mel's three month marriage to celebrity surfer Jasper Jones or the subsequent birth of Sean, six months after Jasper took off for Bali. Sean, in turn, knew next to nothing about his maternal grandparents, other than the fact that they were, according to Mel, total stuck up assholes who only wanted to control Mel and make her into a debutante robot that would have nice manners and look good in a cocktail frock. Sean only knew his grandfather's first name because he had finally forced Mel to put Sean's name on her bank account so he could make sure all the bills got paid. Mel often forgot, or lost the bill or was just too lazy. There would be eight grand in the bank, yet Sean would come home from school to find the electricity or the hot water shut off. When Sean took over the finances at age fifteen, everything got straightened out and he started to realize how things worked. Every three months, there would be a transfer from someone named David Dayton—his grandfather, presumably. Out of curiosity, Sean had once tried looking David Dayton up on the internet, but the name was too common and he could not tell which one was his grandfather. He sometimes entertained childish fantasies of meeting David Dayton and finding out that he was a really cool guy who was actually thrilled to meet his grandson, just like he imagined going to Bali to find his father Jasper, who, unlike his grandfather, was all over the internet and had apparently founded a surf school in Kuta Beach. Jasper Jones was handsome and roguish, with striking, pale green eyes two or three shades lighter than Sean's. He had a big crescent-shaped scar on his left thigh where a tiger shark had taken a bite out of him, and he liked showing it off at every opportunity. He was a legend.

Sean had been saving up for a surfing trip to Bali for nearly a year, but he told himself over and over that it was just a trip, that his buddies had picked Bali, not him, and anyway it *was* a great place to surf. His wanting to go there really had nothing to do with wanting to meet Jasper.

Besides, the idea of finally meeting the man whose DNA contributed to Sean's existence made Sean feel sick, excited and terrified. What could he possibly say to Jasper? Hey, what's up, dude, I'm your kid. Or how about, Why did you leave us? Honestly, Sean could see how someone could get sick of Mel pretty fast, but didn't Jasper even want to be part of Sean's life, watch him grow up, teach him to surf and be a dad and a role model to someone who would have worshiped the ground he walked on? Did he even know Sean existed? Every time Sean transferred a few more dollars into his savings account for the trip, he found himself swamped with contradictory emotions.

Of course, the spur of the moment purchase of the kick-ass new dirt bike had set him back a few bucks, but since Mel's death had put an end to her irresponsible spending, Sean's expenses had dropped to nearly nothing and he really needed to do something just for himself for once.

Mel had been missing in action for eight months. This was no big deal, as she often took off whenever a whim struck her. She had been gone for nearly a year when she first put Sean's name on the bank account. Sean guessed she must have figured he no longer needed her around. When she eventually came back, he found out that she had been to Australia and gotten remarried to some rich exotic bird smuggler, had then divorced again. She did that sort of thing all the time. Sean figured she'd be back when she ran out of safety nets and men to pick up the check. This time was different though. This time cops showed up at the apartment with serious faces and a sheaf of paperwork. Partial remains had been found on the beach. One of the local surfers recognized a necklace that Mel always wore, a linked chain of silver hibiscus. The official cause of death was determined to be drowning, though it was not entirely clear if foul play was involved or not. Tests indicated a very high concentration of several drugs, including ecstasy, marijuana and Vicodin, along with a staggering amount of alcohol. The two detectives informed the numb and silent Sean that they would continue to investigate to see if they could turn up any leads, but that it would more than likely be ruled an accidental death.

That had been three months earlier. Although he had essentially been living on his own since he was fifteen, it felt very strange to know for sure that Mel would never be coming back. He had always resented her for her blasé, noncommittal attitude towards child-rearing and her profound, nearly autistic level of selfishness, but Sean still loved her. His life felt empty without someone to take care of.

He found himself becoming involved with a string of girls—beautiful, selfish girls just like Mel, who liked that he had money and strung him along, making him jump through hoops for them until they tired of him and moved on without saying goodbye. Having just been dumped by his latest Mel substitute, a stunning Eurasian surfer girl named Tegan, Sean found himself staring at his bank statement, listing the most recent ten grand transfer from David Dayton. He wondered if he ought to try to contact the Daytons and let them know about Mel's death, but he also feared that if he did, the transfers would stop, and he would have to get some crummy job for minimum wage just to get by. So, rather than think about such things, he made the mature and carefully considered decision to buy a new dirt bike.

As Sean hit the last and highest jump before the bridge, he threw his bike sideways, letting out a joyous, unselfconscious whoop, seeming to float, suspended in the warm, humid air, before landing perfectly and skidding to a stop inches from the rusted steel legs of the old forgotten bridge. He pushed his dusty goggles up on his forehead, pulled his T-shirt off and used it to wipe the sweat from his face. He patted the pockets of his safety orange cargo shorts until he found the can of Red Bull he had stashed away. He popped open the can and took a long, deep drink.

His mouth full of Red Bull, Sean cocked his head up to a faint shuffling sound on the bridge above. When nothing happened, he swallowed and tilted the nearly empty can up to his lips, shaking it to coax out the last few drops.

Suddenly there was a blurred rush of movement less than ten feet in front of him. He flinched and gripped his handlebars, letting the empty Red Bull can tumble to the ground. To his utter astonishment, it was a man, hanging upside down by his ankles. Typical tourist duds: pineapple patterned shirt, white linen shorts, expensive leather sandals. Sean had never heard of anyone bungee jumping off this crumbling old bridge, but he figured it wasn't out of the question until he looked a little closer. He could see that the rope cinched tightly around the man's bleeding ankles was rough manila line, not elastic rubber mil spec bungee cord, and his hands were also tied, bound behind his back. More than that, the guy's face was unbelievably battered—nose mashed into a formless red mess like a dropped tomato, eyes swollen nearly shut and brow studded with lumpy contusions. The lips were split and the teeth broken and jagged. Almost inhuman, masked in trauma, only the desperate pleading eyes reminded Sean that he was looking at something real. Not a monster mask, not something on television, but a real living human being.

"Get out of here," the man whispered with a kind of terrified urgency.

Sean made a move to dismount and help the man, to do something, anything, but the man shook his head, eyes bright with fear.

"No!" the man said. "Go on, get the hell out of here while you still can."

Sean stood astride his bike, frozen, brain struggling to process this shocking turn of events, when he heard the distinct sound of a motor. Not another bike, but a car, an SUV by the sound of it, heading up the road. In a few seconds, the vehicle would be coming around the bend, and whoever was inside would see Sean. There was no time to think.

"Go!" urged the hanging man.

Sean nodded and swiftly backed his bike behind one of the massive bridge pylons with only a second to spare as the SUV came lumbering around the corner.

It was an ostentatious silver Lincoln Navigator, pimped up and blacked out, and looking like trouble. The door opened and disgorged a man from its cool, luxurious interior. From his hiding place, Sean could not see the man's face, only his expensive suit, his expensive hair and the nicked and hard-used Louisville slugger he clutched in one ring-heavy hand.

Sean heard a rustle and crunch of multiple footsteps and three Asian men appeared from the trail that lead up to the left side of the bridge, heading over to join in the grisly ball game. The men were all dressed in identical black suits and looked as if they had been ordered at bulk discount from the same Asian Henchman catalog used for cheap action movies. The oldest of the three had longish, thinning hair and a wispy goatee, a dead ringer for that one stunt man who always gets killed in the first five minutes of every movie fight scene ever filmed. The two younger guys were as similar as brothers, except that one was sporting preposterously bleached blond *Dragon Ball Z* hair and the other was totally bald.

"They say the higher you aim, the farther you fall," a warm and almost cheerful voice told the hanging man, "and look at you now, Mr Prosecutor." The man from the Navigator knelt down and touched his victim's bloody cheek. "Not so high and mighty anymore."

The hanging man's face hardened beneath the blood and bruises and he let fly with a gob of scarlet saliva, hitting his tormentor dead in the face. "Fuck you, Kim!"

The three underlings all took a step back, faces trying for deadpan badass but betraying a powerful underlying anxiety. Clearly they were amazed that anyone would have the balls to do what the hanging man had just done, and were waiting for the inevitable shit storm such an action would bring about. Several endless seconds passed and nothing happened. The boss, Kim presumably, was casually fishing in an inner pocket for a monogrammed silk handkerchief. He unfolded the hankie carefully, used it to wipe his face, and let it drop to the dirt like a used tissue.

"That was a very noble gesture," Kim said thoughtfully. "I'm impressed, really. I never thought a pretty boy like you would have that kind of balls. I'll be sure to tell your son Eric all about it."

Sean saw Kim's face clearly in that moment. A wide, blocky face with pockmarked skin and close-set eyes beneath thick, nearly connected brows, Sean thought he looked more Korean, while the henchmen were all clearly Chinese. And wasn't Kim a Korean name? Sean pressed his lips together. He should not be thinking about any of this. He should be concentrating on forgetting. There was no way that seeing something like this could possibly be good for him. Why couldn't he just be like most Westerners and think all Asians look alike? Because whoever these particular Asians were, it was abundantly clear that Sean did *not* want to know them. He covered his mouth, horrified, wanting desperately to do something to help, to call the police, anything, but he was paralyzed with fear. He felt a fierce empathy for that kid, for Eric. A boy who *had* a father and was about to lose him.

"I'll say to your son," Kim continued, "'Eric, the reason you get to grow up without a father is because of how goddamn noble that fucker was.'"

Kim cocked back the bat and planted his feet firmly in the dust.

"Then again, I was raised by a single mom," Kim said, swinging the bat like he was aiming for the cheap seats.

The bat connected with the hanging man's skull and made a horrible, dull and yet somehow juicy sound that Sean would never forget. Sean wanted to cover his eyes or look away, but he couldn't. He just watched with a kind of dreamy horror as the man's body swung and twisted like a broken piñata beneath the rain of blows.

"I didn't turn out so bad," Kim was saying. "Did I?"

The hanging man did not answer and Kim went to town on the helpless, dangling body, beating him long after he ceased to struggle. The bat struck its target again and again. Sean could practically feel every single blow. He was sure he was going to puke and give himself away, but somehow he was able to keep it together, to stay silent and motionless as the atrocity unfolded before him.

Eventually, Kim seemed to tire of beating the lifeless side of beef before him and took a step back. He was streaked from head to toe with thick, clotted gore. His expensive suit was ruined, expensive hair jeweled with congealing droplets that glistened like corrupt garnets in the oblivious Hawaiian sun. He looked utterly insane—not wild-eyed movie-crazy, but a strange kind of dull, emotionless, unplugged crazy, head tilted slightly and eyes as shallow and inhuman as the glass eyes of dolls. He just stood that way, unmoving, unplugged and utterly disconnected for what felt to Sean like centuries. The scene was silent except for the gentle patter of dripping blood hitting the hard packed dirt. The three underlings looked everywhere but at their boss, shuffling and impatient as children in church. Eventually, something happened. Sean watched, amazed, as happy, cheerful animation flowed into Kim's empty face like water filling a glass.

"Well," he said suddenly, like a man who has just finished his breakfast, "I'm going back to Los Angeles." He strolled over to his car, tossing the bloody bat at one of his underlings. "Clean this mess up," Kim said over his shoulder as he opened the Navigator's door.

Suddenly, Sean knew that he could not stand to be there to watch them cut down and dispose of the man's battered body. He had to get away, right now. All thought left his mind except the instinct to run. He kick-started his bike and peeled out, speeding away as fast as he could push the little machine between his legs.

He could feel the swift turn of predatory eyes following him as he sped away. As he went screaming around the bend, he had a sudden vision, as clear and pure as some kind of psychic message. He saw the can, that Red Bull can, tumbling to the dirt when he first saw the hanging man. The can that he had been holding... In his fingers.

His fingerprints were all over it.

But only cops had the kind of technology to find someone from their fingerprints, right? Only cops, not some Asian mafia guys. Criminals couldn't possibly use fingerprints to find him. Could they?

TWO

It was just after dawn. Sean was wide awake and owl-eyed in front of the television set in his dim apartment. He had not slept. His surfboard was propped forgotten in a corner, plans to catch a few early morning waves abandoned in the wake of yesterday's hideous events. All he could do was hug his knees and watch brain-dead morning programming, waiting out the endless minutes until it was time for the morning news.

There had been nothing yesterday, not on the evening or the eleven o'clock reports, and Sean was starting to wonder if maybe the thugs had done too good of a job disposing of the body. Perhaps the man would never be found. Sean had tossed and turned all night in his sweat-soaked bed, sleepless and wracked with guilt. Should he call the cops? What about that guy's family, his

17

son Eric? Did they know what had happened yet? Sean knew that getting involved was just asking for trouble, but what about the Red Bull can? Could they find him? Could the cops find him? Maybe he ought to get out of town or something, but where could he go? They were on an island, after all. There weren't all that many places to hide.

All these yammering and competing thoughts abruptly vanished when KHNL Channel 8 anchor Minna Sugimoto appeared on the screen, broadcasting live from the foot of the abandoned bridge. Behind her, yellow crime scene tape wound around the steel pylons, blocking off an area of black, blood-soaked dirt. The manila rope had been severed and swung ominously unburdened in the morning breeze.

"Details remain sketchy regarding the brutal slaying yesterday of Los Angeles Prosecutor Daniel Hayes, who had been vacationing here in Waimea Bay," Minna told the camera with earnest concern. "Hayes has been in the news quite a bit recently for his high profile pursuit of reputed Triad gangster Edward Kim. Mr Kim's representatives have issued a statement of condolence to Mr Hayes's family and claim absolutely no involvement in what they called quote 'a hideous act of violence' unquote. The ongoing saga in the criminal investigation of Mr Kim has involved charges of murder, torture and racketeering, as well as police corruption at the highest level, both here in Hawaii and on the mainland."

The story wrapped up with the other anchors commenting on how awful it all was, followed by a report on the ongoing legal battle over allowing non-Hawaiian students into Kamehameha schools. Sean stared unthinking at the screen for a few moments, and then reached for the remote and shut the television off.

Running his fingers through his tousled hair, he wondered what in the hell he was supposed to do. Before he could come up with anything brilliant, he was interrupted by the low whine of a power drill. Justin and Cory, his neighbors to the left, would be passed out cold from last night's wild party, since Sean had heard them stumble in drunkenly about an hour earlier. They would not be doing any home improvements at six o'clock in the morning. The apartment to the right was currently empty, since the espresso-fueled New Yorker who had rented it had finally had enough of laid back Hawaii. Mrs Kame'eleihiwa, the landlady, might conceivably be putting up more hanging baskets for her orchids in the breezeway outside Sean's door, but even she was not that much of a morning person. Surely Sean was just being paranoid?

He crept over to the door as the sound intensified. Sucking in a deep breath, he bent to look through the peep hole. He was treated to a fish-eye view of the spiky blond explosion covering the head of one of Kim's underlings from the day before. Standing behind him were the two other goons. Their suits were clean, but otherwise identical to the ones they had been wearing the last time Sean had seen them. The blond was busily drilling through the inexpensive deadbolt in Sean's door.

Sean inhaled more than spoke a breathless curse and backed away from the door like it was on fire. "Shit," he whispered. "Shit shit shit shit!"

He turned and ran to the sliding glass door that led to the balcony on the far side of the living room. Throwing a glance over his shoulder at the front door, he pushed aside the vertical blinds, shouldered open the glass door and slipped out into the humid morning. He peered over the railing at Mrs Kame'eleihiwa's garden two storeys down. He could try to make it over the cement patio and into the dirt, but it would be tricky. Why the hell did Mrs Kame'eleihiwa plant all those big, prickly, dangerous and alien-looking flowers anyway? Why couldn't she have put in something softer, like petunias?

The goons were nearly in. There was no time to think. Trying for courage and getting something more like desperation, he swung one leg up onto the railing of the balcony, ready to make the jump, when a huge black hand wrapped suddenly around his face, trapping his surprised yell inside his mouth.

"Do as I say, you'll live," a voice said. Deep and commanding, it gave Sean no choice.

Sean nodded desperately against the iron grip of the fingers across his face as the front door exploded violently open, rebounding loudly against the wall. Sean had no idea who this inexplicable savior might be, but he had no other options. He nodded again, indicating his willingness to do exactly as the man said.

"Flat against the wall," the voice said. "Don't even breathe."

Slowly the big, scarred fingers released their grip on Sean's face and he spun around, pressing his back to the wall as he finally got a look at the owner of the voice.

Well over six feet tall, black and bald with a kind of infinite calm in his dark eyes, he looked like exactly the sort of person you wanted to show up when pissed off gangsters were busting down your front door at six o'clock in the morning. He drew a nasty-looking Glock from a shoulder holster and crouched down by the open sliding glass door with a smooth, effortless grace that seemed impossible from such a large man.

Sean stood still, willing his body to become one with the pink stucco against his back as footsteps moved rapidly across his living room and towards the partially open sliding glass door.

The sound of the gun spitting out three rapid shots was louder and flatter than Sean had expected and he jumped in spite of himself. He could hear two thugs fall to the carpet, screaming and clutching at shattered kneecaps. The calm black man stepped into the doorway and squeezed off another shot that was answered by several others with a deeper, throatier report. Sean threw his arms over his face as the sliding glass door shattered in a spray of glittering shards. He could feel the flying glass slicing into his forearms as he let out his breath in a terrified yelp that he was too deaf to hear.

There were more shots traded back and forth, then the big man reappeared on the balcony, unruffled and cool as ever. He pushed Sean towards the railing. "Move it," he said.

He didn't have to ask twice. Sean leapt awkwardly over the railing without a second thought, missing the cement by inches and rolling into the spiky jumble of Mrs Kame'eleihiwa's heliconias. He barely got to his feet before the man was down, landing like a cat beside him and gripping his shoulder.

"Go," he said. "This way."

He more threw than helped Sean over the back fence and dragged him into a waiting Mustang, illegally parked in the alley behind the complex. His mysterious savior cranked the engine, threw the car into reverse and squealed into a backward one-eighty. Suddenly the older thug, the one who looked like the guy who always gets killed in the movies, dropped over the top of the fence and opened fire on the car. Clearly this guy had much better luck than the guy in the movies. He was still alive and he was *pissed*.

Covering his head with his hands and trying to sink into the bucket seat, Sean thought he might be screaming but could still barely hear anything but the flat crack of gunshots. His savior stomped on the accelerator and tore off down the alley, knocking down garbage cans and scaring feral cats as they went.

"What the hell is going on?" Sean wailed.

The man did not take his eyes off the road. His voice was calm, still weirdly muffled in Sean's deafened ears. "You witnessed a murder," the man said. "You didn't tell anyone. Why?"

"I meant to, honest," Sean spluttered. "I just... I mean... I..."

"Why didn't you call the cops?" the man asked.

Was not reporting a murder a crime? Was he under arrest? Why hadn't he called the cops? Flipping through all possible excuses and apologies, he simply gave up and told the truth. "The news said the cops were corrupt!" Sean said. "I was afraid they'd be in on it."

The man nodded. "Smart kid."

"Who are you anyway?" Sean asked. "Are you a cop?"

The man extended his massive hand. "FBI agent Neville Flynn. Pleased to meet you."

Sean reached out to take the man's offered hand when he suddenly realized that he was wearing nothing but black boxer shorts with yellow smiley faces all over them. The man seemed to note Sean's realization and the tiniest rind of a smile appeared in the corner of his mouth.

THREE

In a crummy downscale safe house near the Honolulu Airport, Sean sat in a rickety folding chair with his arms wrapped defensively around his body. He had been given clothes: an appalling, rainbow-colored airport gift shop T-shirt that said "Aloha" and a pair of uncomfortably tight white Bermuda shorts, but he still felt as defenseless as if he was naked.

On the other side of the cheap desk was a man who had introduced himself as Agent John Sanders. He was blond and beefy, younger than Flynn and utterly opposite in his demeanor, intense and aggressive where Flynn was cool and laconic. This Sanders guy was currently hell-bent on breaking Sean down and was doing a pretty good job of it. Sean was scared, unsure and anxious as he tapped his fingers against his knee and kept his head down against Sanders's verbal onslaught.

"God damnit!" Sanders was saying. "You left the scene of a crime. Don't you realize that you had a responsibility?"

Flynn picked that moment to enter the room. He held two cans of Dr Pepper and gave Sanders a look that seemed to tell him to back off. Sanders narrowed his eyes at Sean and then stood and stalked out of the room like a sulky kid.

"Look, Sean," Flynn said, handing him one of the Dr Peppers. It was wonderfully cool and Sean pressed it to his sweating forehead. "I've been doing this for a while now and I've picked up all kinds of nifty tricks. Good cop..." He gestured towards the closed door with his chin. "Bad cop." He opened his own soda and took a drink. "Reverse psychology, stare down contests, threats... you name it, I've done it." He took another swig and shrugged. "So why don't we just fast forward through all those potential scenarios and save ourselves a busload of aggravation and time—of which we have close to zero—and I tell you the truth. What do you say?"

Sean frowned, unsure. He looked down at his unopened Dr Pepper.

"Truth is," Flynn continued, "I'm not worried about you if you testify. At all. I'm worried about you if you *don't*."

Flynn's words hung in the air between them, slowly sinking in.

"But what if I didn't see him clearly? I wouldn't be a very credible witness, would I? If I can't identify him—"

Flynn cut Sean neatly off. "What did I just tell you about saving ourselves time and aggravation?" he asked. "He *knows* you saw him. That's why his thugs were at your apartment. Make no mistake, Eddie Kim *will* kill you." He paused, eyebrows drawn together. "If you let him."

It was almost too much to process. Sean's life had just been coming back together after Mel's death and now this. It seemed so unfair. "I just can't believe this," he said softly. "I mean... last week I was planning a surfing trip to Bali, and now..."

"Planning to try and meet up with your father?" Flynn asked.

Sean stared at Flynn, slack jawed. "My..." He wiped the back of his hand across his mouth and then opened the Dr Pepper and took a drink. "How do you know about my father?"

"If I know about him," Flynn asked, "don't you think Eddie Kim knows about him too?"

Sean's eyes went wide. "What are you saying?" he asked.

Flynn looked away, non-committal. "I don't know," he said. "I just know that as long as Eddie Kim is a free man, he will find a way to get to you, and if he can't find a way to get you, he'll get people you care about. You don't seem to have much in the way of family, but that won't stop our pal Eddie from tracking down Jasper Jones and David and Serena Dayton, and your third grade teacher and every little wahine that ever let you put your hands under her bikini. Am I starting to make my point?"

Sean frowned. "You make it sound like I have no choice," he said.

"Oh, you have choices," Flynn said. "We all have choices, but only one choice is the right one."

This whole ugly mess was piling up like a train wreck inside Sean's head. He didn't know what the right choice was. He didn't know anything anymore.

"Come with me to Los Angeles," Flynn continued. "Testify against Eddie Kim and put that son of a bitch away for life."

Flynn drained his Dr Pepper and set the can on the cheap desk. "Think it through," he told Sean as he turned to leave. "I'll be outside."

Sean stared down into the dark mouth of his Dr Pepper can, silent and anxious. It was all too much to grasp and he was tired, scared and uncertain, but he knew in his heart that Flynn was right. There was no way around it. There *was* only one correct choice. No matter how hard he tried, there just didn't seem to be any other way to go on this. He had to testify against Kim, for Eric's sake. He knew that it was probably crazy to risk his life for the sake of a kid he'd never met, but his life would be at risk no matter what. That guy Kim was obviously dangerously insane. He would stop at nothing to get Sean. Sean knew what he had to do.

"Agent Flynn?" Sean called cautiously into the hallway.

He heard echoing steps and then the big man appeared from a shadowed doorway. "Yeah?"

"I'll do it," Sean said, before he could lose his nerve.

"I knew you were a smart kid," Flynn replied, smiling.

"But you guys are going to protect me, right?" Sean said. "You'll be with me the whole way to Los Angeles and all the way through to the trial."

"I'm your new best friend," Flynn said. "I'm on you like white on rice. By the time the trial rolls around, you're gonna be sick to death of me hanging around all the time."

"Will I be able to come home?" Sean asked cautiously. "After the trial, I mean. I won't have to move to Idaho or something, will I?"

Flynn's face went suddenly serious. "I can't answer that," he said quietly. "Not yet."

Sean looked over at the window. The blinds were closed and even if they weren't, the tiny window afforded only a grim industrial view of the ass end of the airport. The thought of being a permanent exile from his beloved island made him feel physically ill. But it was like Flynn said, only one choice was the right one.

"Okay," Sean said, "but listen, I gotta have some decent clothes. I can't let anyone see me in this goofy get up."

Flynn nodded and smiled. "You got it, kid," he said.

FOUR

Flight attendant Claire Miller headed along the airport concourse, the soft drone of the wheels on her compact roller case playing against the counterpoint clack of her conservative navy blue heels. She was thirty-two, tall and pale with an abundance of tight raven curls begrudgingly corralled into a loose updo by a huge blue plastic clip. Beneath the chaotic mass of glossy hair was a feline, heart shaped face with arresting hazel eyes and a wide, mischievous mouth. With long legs and lean hips beneath her tight blue skirt, she could easily have been a model or an actress. She was a Gemini and a notorious heartbreaker, not out of malice or desire to inflict emotional trauma, but just because she was an unapologetic free spirit. Men were drawn like moths to a flame to her refreshingly honest "no strings" approach to dating and her unwillingness to be confined to a conventional relationship, but they were invariably crushed when they discovered that she really meant it too. Each one thought that somehow, he would be the one to tame her and make her his own. She would just laugh and fly away into the sunset, always leaving them wanting more.

She turned her head as the rolling sound of her wheeled case suddenly doubled. Beside her was fellow flight attendant, Tiffany Engelhard. Tiffany was a skinny, energetic little thing who looked just like her name—blonde, blue-eyed, too flat chested for *Playboy*, and too short for *Vogue*, but she might get a spread in Maxim if she was willing to pose in a bikini. She wasn't a bad kid, if a little over-sexed and manic. Her big ambition in life was to be discovered and become a star, though what she planned to do as a star—sing, act, model—wasn't exactly clear. She did, however, already have her stage name picked out. Tiffany Hart. She had spent the majority of the previous flight practicing her autograph on SPA napkins, dotting the "I" in Tiffany with a fat heart. She claimed to be working as a flight attendant to save up for breast implants.

"Hey, Tiff," Claire said. "What's up?"

"Same shit, different flight," Tiffany replied. "How about you? You dump that cute tennis player yet?"

"Like a used rubber," Claire said, grinning. "He had a great bod and all, but he was just way too clingy for my taste, always wanting to talk about our 'relationship.' Please. We slept together less than a dozen times. Hardly what I would call a relationship."

"The only relationship you have is with your Hitachi Magic Wand," Tiffany joked, "and only because it doesn't cry when you leave it under the bed for three weeks."

Claire stifled a giggle as they passed a big burly soldier with an M-16 slung over his massive shoulder. "Why does seeing more security make me more afraid, not less?" Claire asked, glancing at the soldier.

Tiffany gave the grunt a flirtatious smile, throwing a little more swing into her walk as they moved away from him. "Me," Tiffany stage whispered, "I'm just afraid I'll have to take one home."

Claire rolled her eyes.

"Oh come on, Claire," Tiffany said. "You've never wanted to play with GI Joe?"

Claire laughed and shook her head. "Down, Barbie, down," she said.

Tiffany giggled and together they headed towards the departure gate.

"So," Tiffany said, "any special requests for your final flight?"

For some reason, that innocent question sent a cold shiver down Claire's spine. Sure, she was planning to leave the flight attendant game and finally go to law school like she had always wanted. She would become a lawyer like her dad and make a difference in the world that went beyond dispensing peanuts and lemon-scented towelettes, and showing people how a seat belt works. But something about the way Tiffany said "final flight" made it sound dark and ominous. A lot of flight attendants were extremely superstitious, but Claire had never been that way. Sure, a crash was possible, but you were more likely to die in your car on your freeway commute to your soul-killing cubicle job than on an airplane. All the terror scares and steroidal security and everything made it next to impossible for anything bad to happen in the air. So why did Claire suddenly feel so anxious?

"I only want what every flight attendant wants," Claire forced herself to say, burying her anxiety.

Tiffany looked up at her, smiled and spoke in unison with Claire as she finished her request.

"Low maintenance passengers!"

When they arrived at the gate, they saw immediately that there would be no such luck. There was a huge crowd of people with flashing cameras, and bobbing above the sea of reaching hands were two stony black faces, eyes hidden behind expensive sunglasses and big hands spread wide to keep back the crowd.

"Oh great," Claire said. "What member of Hollywood royalty will be gracing us with their illustrious famousness this evening?"

"It's not an actor," Tiffany said, going all goo-goo eyed. "It's that rapper Three Gs. You know…" She broke out into an appallingly white version of the booty girl shake, wiggling her meager posterior and chanting in a deep voice, "Make that booty jump! Yeah! Pump that rump! Pump that rump! I wanna see them cheeks flutter, smooth like butter, did I stutter? Hell no! You heard me bitch, pump that rump! Pump that rump!"

"Oh my," Claire said, arching a dark eyebrow. "I must have missed that one."

As if summoned by Tiffany's little performance, the man himself suddenly appeared between his two massive bodyguards, arms wide and magnanimous. He was tall and handsome, but not breathtakingly so, with a long, lanky basketball player's physique. Claire thought she could sense some element of tightly wrapped anxiety in his eyes as he faced his fans.

"Troy, Leroy," he said. "It's cool."

Claire smirked. Troy and Leroy? Were they twins? Did all bodyguards have rhyming names or was it some sort of rap-related policy that required everything to rhyme? They sure didn't look like twins. Both were huge, but one was also enormously fat. The other was much better looking, also heavy and thickly built, but with a hint of sardonic humor beneath his professional bad-ass front.

A busty blonde suddenly bullied her way through the crowd towards the rapper. She was dressed in a skin-tight pink velour tracksuit with the jacket unzipped down to her pierced navel and nothing beneath. She was thrusting a piece of paper at the rapper to sign. He icily disdained her little scrap, but her pout soon transformed to delirious fan ecstasy as he took a Sharpie marker from one of his bodyguards and signed the exposed silicone cleavage of her breasts.

"Wow," Tiffany said, eyes far away and thoughtful. "I wonder if she has a card."

"A business card?" Claire asked. "Why?"

"Not for her," Tiffany said dismissively. "For the doctor that did her boobs!"

"Oh, of course," Claire replied. "Silly me."

A little eight year-old white kid in full mini-gangsta get up sashayed over and reached up high to slap the rapper's hand. The rapper looked down at the kid and forced a smile.

"Keep it real," he told the kid.

"Hell yeah!" the kid replied.

The kid smiled and turned to go, and Claire saw the rapper twist his body away from the crowd and pull a small bottle from his pocket, pouring its contents into his cupped palm and then vigorously rubbing his hands together. He then pushed the empty bottle into the hand of one of his guards, speaking low out of the corner of his mouth.

Claire shrugged and navigated deftly through the crowd towards the gate.

"Ladies and gentleman," a thick, nasal voice announced over the loudspeaker. "We regret to inform you that South Pacific Air Flight 121 has been delayed. The projected delay at this time is thirty minutes."

A shared groan of dismay rippled through the passengers waiting in line by the gate.

"We apologize for the inconvenience," the voice continued, "and we will begin boarding as soon as possible. Thank you."

Claire and Tiffany exchanged a look as they hustled past the fretting passengers.

"Excuse me, miss," said a pink-faced fat woman. "What seems to be the problem? When will we be able to get on the plane?"

"I'm sorry, ma'am," Claire said as she and Tiffany wheeled towards the jet way. "We know as much as you guys right now. As soon as there is more information available, we'll be sure to pass it on, okay?"

The woman looked doubtful and crossed her thick arms across her heroic bosom.

"Miss," another passenger was saying.

"Oh, miss," said another.

"Let's go," Claire whispered to Tiffany as they opened the barrier to slip into the jetway. "Pretty soon they're gonna be screaming for blood!"

The humming quiet of the long, carpeted jetway was a wonderful relief as the two flight attendants hustled towards the aircraft door. Claire motioned for Tiffany to go ahead and then followed her down the aisle to the galley.

"Surprise!" shouted tandem voices as two other flight attendants appeared in the galley door holding mini bottles of champagne.

Grace Bresson was the den mother of South Pacific Airlines. In her early fifties, she was a seasoned veteran, well versed in dealing with unruly passengers and all manner of in-flight disturbances. She had been more of a mother to Claire than her own self-centered bitch of a mom ever was. She was smiling gently at Claire and peeling the foil from the neck of a baby-sized bottle of champagne. The other flight attendant was Ken Cosette. Prettier than all three of them combined, Ken had big blue eyes fringed with thick dark lashes, a sensuous mouth and a large, incongruously heroic chin. His spiky hair was heavily frosted and he had a tendency to throw his muscular dancer's body around in an exaggeratedly feminine manner. He had the thin, overly plucked eyebrows and shiny skin of a drag queen without makeup. When asked about his sexual orientation, he would invariably answer "slut." He liked to joke that he was every straight man's worst nightmare, a fag who wants to steal your girlfriend. In spite of his self-proclaimed proclivity to hump anything that moved, he had recently amazed them all by apparently falling in love, rhapsodizing endlessly about his spectacularly gorgeous and perfect soul mate.

"Claire," Ken said. "Don't go! The last thing this world needs is another lawyer. I mean really..." He gestured around at the narrow confines of the galley. "How could you leave all this?"

Claire looked at him with an arched brow, silent, until he broke.

"Oh what am I talking about?" he said. "Take me with you, you bitch!"

They all chuckled as Grace poured little shots of champagne into flimsy plastic cups emblazoned with hibiscus and the SPA logo.

"Kanpai!" Grace said, clicking her cup to Claire's. "May your objections never be overruled."

"Break a leg, sweetie," Ken said. "We'll miss the hell out of you."

"Yeah," Tiffany said. "I'll be calling you when I get my first celebrity divorce or I need to sue my manager for embezzling my millions."

"Your first divorce?" Grace asked. "You're only twenty-three and you're already planning on having more than one divorce?" Grace shook her head. "Christ, when I was twenty-three, I thought I was going to meet Prince Charming, fall madly in love and live happily ever after in the suburbs with two point five kids. Needless to say, that didn't happen."

Tiffany laughed and tossed her blonde hair. "I *am* gonna meet Prince Charming," she said. "We'll fall madly in love, have a huge wedding on television and then, when I find out he's been chasing the chambermaids, I'll take half his castle and his riches and run off with one of his hot young knights."

"You go girl," Ken said, high-fiving Tiffany.

"What about you, Claire?" Grace asked. "Now that you're planning on sleeping in the same time zone every night, think you might settle down with Mr Right?"

"Oh, I don't know," Claire said, sipping her champagne. "I never could get the hang of the whole relationship thing. It always seemed like more trouble than it's worth."

"You know, I always thought that too," Ken said, warming to the girl-talk. "Until I met Kitty. She's like, totally unconventional and never lays a heavy relationship trip on me. I mean, really, who would have thought a tramp like me would be in the same bed twice? But honestly, I know that Kit is my true soul mate! Now I can't imagine ever wanting to be with anyone else. We've even been talking the M word, can you believe it? Although honestly there may be a cat fight over who gets to wear the big white dress."

Grace shot Claire a look. They had heard so much about the mythical Kitty over the past six months and yet none of them had ever met her. Was she for real? Was Ken really gonna settle down in the suburbs and have two point five kids? Somehow the idea of a person like Ken settling down and getting married made Claire feel ancient and weirdly out of sync with the universe.

"Well," Claire said. "Finding Mr Right is not a real high priority for me at the moment."

"Yeah," Tiffany said. "Claire is only interested in Mr Right Now."

The flight attendants finished their champagne, tossed their cups, and went to work prepping for the flight. Less than five minutes later, Claire had stowed her suitcase and turned from tying her apron to see two regal German shepherds barreling down the aisle, followed by two dead-eyed, Kevlar-clad FBI agents. Before she could say anything about this strange intrusion, Captain Sam McKeon appeared in the doorway. He grinned sardonically beneath his thick moustache.

"FBI's escorting some guy to LA," McKeon said. "They just took over all of First Class."

"What?" Claire watched the dogs going row by row and sniffing each seat. "Can they do that?"

"Apparently so," McKeon said. "FAA Section 108 states that if deemed necessary, they can pretty much do any damn thing they want."

"Lovely," Claire said, seeing her nice calm, quiet last flight going rapidly to hell in a hand basket. "So who gets to tell the paying First Class passengers that they'll be flying Coach?"

"That'd be you, kid," McKeon said, winking at her and turning to slip into the cockpit.

Claire shook her head. She just had to keep on telling herself that it was only five short hours. Only five hours and she would never need to deal with this kind of shit ever again. Five hours wasn't all that long. It was less than a quarter of a day. This would all be over soon and then she would be moving on to start a whole new life. Just five more hours.

As if all this wasn't enough, the co-pilot for the flight picked that moment to arrive and it was none other than SPA's own "most likely to be sued for sexual harassment" Rick "Arch" Archibald. All Texas swagger and florid testosterone, Arch was the kind of man who would have smacked all the stew's asses twenty years earlier. He was not unattractive, but his unshakable confidence in his own appeal to the weaker sex had the exact opposite effect on Claire. His regulation navy uniform fit snugly over his ostentatious muscles and his feet were clad in distinctly non-regulation pointy-toed cowboy boots made of gaudy silver snakeskin.

"Well hello, darlin'," Arch drawled. "I was hoping you'd be the sky candy on this flight. And can I say that you are looking especially delicious this evening."

"I love it when you demean me, Arch," Claire said, smirking. "Makes me feel like a real woman."

"My pleasure, little missy," Arch replied, touching the bill of his cap. "And would you be so kind as to rustle us up a couple a black coffees while you're at it? There's a good girl."

He did not slap Claire's ass, but he might as well have.

"What a jerk," she said to Tiffany as she went to get the coffee.

"Isn't he smooth?" Grace replied. "God's gift to womankind."

"I'd do him," Tiffany said, taking the two cups of coffee from Claire and sashaying off towards the cockpit.

Claire and Grace exchanged knowing grins.

"She is totally incorrigible," Grace said, pouring herself a cup of coffee. "Want some?"

"Sure," Claire said, grabbing a paper cup and allowing Grace to fill it. She dumped in three packets of sugar, but no cream.

"Are you okay, kid?" Grace asked. "You seem... I don't know, edgy."

"I'm fine," Claire said, sipping her coffee. "I just know it's gonna be a bad flight."

"Yeah," Grace replied. "Not much we can do about being commandeered by the FBI."

"Do you know what it's all about?" Claire asked.

Grace shrugged. "Beats me," she said, pouring a second cup of coffee. "I just work here. I'll just be glad when it's over."

"I'll drink to that," Claire said, draining her own cup.

FIVE

Mercedes Harbont stood in the midst of the confusion by the gate, talking loudly into her Treo. She was tall, blonde and sleek with a kind of racehorse elegance in her long legs and aristocratic profile. Immaculately coiffed, swaddled in couture and balanced on sky-high, steel heeled peep-toe mules by Lola Ciabara, Mercedes was the pampered daughter of communications mogul Armand Harbont and former supermodel Fiona. She was a magnet for the surreptitious glances of every male around her, but she was used to that sort of thing and concentrated on giving her new assistant the business.

"Did we ask for Bruno from Simply Corporate?" she asked, glancing down at her French manicured nails. "Alana, when I say we, I mean you." She toyed with a stack of slender platinum rings on her left index finger. "No, all drivers are not the same, that's my point. Last thing I need is some loser droning on about whatever for the whole ride home. I want you to ask for Bruno. Just do it."

A muffled yelp sounded from inside her Fendi purse and she ended her call and slipped her hand into the bag. "Hush, Mary-Kate," she said softly.

A tiny, thin and shivering fawn chihuahua poked her nose out of the bag, ears down and huge, runny brown eyes taking up most of her tiny apple head. She was wearing a pink patent leather harness and what looked like a diamond tennis bracelet around her scrawny neck. She yipped anxiously.

"It's okay, sugarbaby," Mercedes cooed. She turned to the young couple behind her in line. "She gets nervous flying."

The couple behind her were obviously newly-weds, earnest yuppies with matching carry-on bags and matching sunburns. She was plain and blonde with a short, pixie haircut and environmentally friendly shoes. He was dark-haired with a wide mouth and knitted brows. He was clearly more nervous than Mary-Kate.

"Boy," the young man said. "I sure know how she feels." He held out an orange prescription bottle. "Does she need some Xanax?"

"No, no," Mercedes said. "She'll be fine."

"She's a real cutie," the woman said, reaching out a hand towards Mary-Kate. "Is she a tea-cup?"

Mary-Kate growled defensively and the woman pulled her hand away.

"Young lady!" Mercedes said sternly to Mary-Kate. "Sorry," she said to the woman. "She can be a total bitch sometimes."

"I have a chihuahua too," the woman said. "A tea-cup just like her, but with long hair. I totally understand that they can be a little defensive sometimes, especially in scary, unfamiliar situations like this." The woman slowly held out her hand again for Mary-Kate to sniff. The dog sniffed twice and then licked the woman's fingers with a tiny pink tongue. "Where did you get her?"

"I was at this mall in Vegas," Mercedes said. "And I saw her in the window of this pet shop. Even though she was the smallest, she was the most expensive one, weren't you sugarbaby? I just had to have her."

"Honey…" the man said softly to the woman, a warning tone in his voice.

"I see," said the woman. "Would you like to see some pictures of my chihuahua? Her name is Esperanza. It means Hope in Spanish."

"Sure," Mercedes said.

"Come on, honey," the man said, putting his hand on the woman's arm.

The woman shook off his touch and fished in her purse for her day planner. Inside the planner was a laminated photo. She took the photo out and handed it to Mercedes.

The photo showed a filthy, skeletal white dog cowering in a wire cage. Her raw pink skin was covered with sores and her eyes were swollen nearly shut. You could tell she was a long-haired chihuahua because she still had some long matted

fur on her head, but the rest of her body was bald
and mangy. One of her front legs was bent at an
unnatural angle. There were two puppies in the
cage with her, but they were bloated and covered
with flies.

"Oh my God," Mercedes said. "Gross! What's
wrong with her? Are those puppies dead?"

"That photo was taken the day that the police
raided and shut down the puppy mill where she
was kept as a prisoner for the first three years of
her life," the woman said. "Having litter after litter
of puppies to supply mall pet stores like the one
where you bought Mary-Kate."

Mercedes's eyes went wide.

"Her cage was on the bottom of a stack of three,
and all the urine and feces from the dogs above her
just fell down on top of her and her puppies," the
woman continued. "She had been 'de-barked' by
having a metal rod shoved down her throat and hit
with a hammer to destroy her vocal cords, so that
she would not annoy her captors with her miserable and desperate cries. Of course, this procedure
is performed without any sort of anesthesia. She
also had to have one of her front legs removed,
after it was permanently damaged when she
caught it in the chicken wire beneath her and
received no veterinary care for months."

"Jesus, Ashley," the man said and walked over to
the window to look out at the arriving planes.

"You may think something like this harsh or
ugly," Ashley said to the incredulous Mercedes,
"and you'd be right, it *is* ugly, but pretending that
the cute little puppies you see in pet stores are

brought by the stork or found in cabbage patches is just as bad or worse. They come from puppy mills like the one where I rescued Esperanza, and every time you buy one of those puppies, you are paying for thousands of dogs just like her to remain captive and unloved, prisoners of greed. Over five hundred thousand puppies are born in these inhumane conditions every year. I know you love Mary-Kate, and I'm sure she loves you, but how would you feel if someone locked Mary-Kate in a dark lonely cage for the rest of her life with no toys, no bed and no love?"

"That's awful," Mercedes said, eyes glistening with tears. "Isn't that just awful, sugarbaby? Those poor, poor puppies!"

"When you first brought Mary-Kate home from the pet store," Ashley asked, "she was real sick, wasn't she?"

Mercedes nodded, lower lip quivering. "She had this awful... you know..." Mercedes dropped her voice to a whisper to say the word. "*Diarrhea*." She continued solemnly. "She wouldn't eat for three days, not even the special pâté I ordered for her from Bastide. Even after she started eating, she still had to have surgery on her little knees because the vet said they were, like, sliding around."

"That's called luxating patella," Ashley said. "A lot of badly bred small dogs have that problem. Mary-Kate is very lucky that she had someone like you to pay for all the care she needed because of her poor breeding, but many others like her aren't so lucky and wind up dumped in shelters or put to sleep instead."

"Put to sleep?" Mercedes said, eyes seeming to grow wider and wider.

"Luckily," Ashley continued, clearly on a roll, "there are rescue organizations to help dogs like Esperanza and their less fortunate puppies."

Ashley took out a second photo. It pictured the same little white dog, only now she was clean and healthy, missing a front leg, but plump, and sporting a full long coat of soft fur and a silly doggy smile.

"Here's Esperanza now," Ashley said. "She will never be able to bark or eat solid food and she still gets scared by loud noises or fast hand movements, but she is happy and safe, and she likes her new job as a poster girl for Chihuahua Rescue."

"Chihuahua Rescue?" Mercedes asked.

"That's right," Ashley said, handing Mercedes a folded pamphlet. "I've been a foster mom for Chi Rescue for five years, ever since Esperanza came into my life. Most people think of chihuahuas as rich people's dogs and think they don't need to be rescued, but these little guys are abandoned and dumped in shelters every day all over the country by people who don't understand their feisty temperaments. They think they are just like a cute stuffed toy they can carry around in their designer handbag, instead of a living, breathing being with needs and feelings just like you or me."

"Oh," Mercedes said softly, eyes traveling over the before and after photos in the pamphlet.

"We are always looking for donations," Ashley said, "to help pay for vet care and neutering, and shelter fees, and all the other expenses we have in our battle to put a stop to puppy mills in the United States."

"Will you excuse me," Mercedes said, clutching Mary-Kate tightly against her breasts, pulling out her Treo and turning away. "Alana?" she said into the phone. "I want you to make out a check for five thousand dollars to Chihuahua Rescue. That's right. Chihuahua Rescue." She looked down at the pamphlet. "Send it care of Susan Marlowe, 8913 West Olympic Boulevard, number 205, Beverly Hills, California, 90211." She paused. "No, that's not true; they *do* need rescuing. See, there's these terrible places called puppy mills..."

Ashley smiled to herself and walked over to join her husband Tyler by the window.

"I wish you wouldn't do that," Tyler said, "beating everyone over the head all the time with the rescue thing."

"What's the harm in educating people?" Ashley asked, sliding her arms around Tyler from behind. "Besides, that silly girl just called in a nice fat donation! We'll be able to pay for Cookie's jaw reconstruction surgery, and maybe have enough left over to finally reimburse Janice for all the gas she had to burn doing transports and home-checks last month. Besides..." She kissed the back of his neck. "You knew what you were getting into when you agreed to marry me, didn't you? Rescue has always been my number one priority."

"I know baby," Tyler said. "I'm just all wound up about the flight, that's all."

"Why don't you do that thing the doctor taught you, remember?" Ashley said, massaging Tyler's shoulders. "The visualizations?"

"Because, honey," Tyler replied, muscles clenching as a massive 747 roared off into the night sky. "My visualizations scare the hell out of me."

Ashley turned him to face her, hands cupping his cheeks. "Look at me," she said, planting a small kiss on his lips. "You're gonna be fine, doggy daddy."

"Sure," he said, obviously not even remotely fine.

A pretty young mother walked past them, soothing her fretting infant. Ashley smiled at her and she smiled back, and the baby, suddenly calm, smiled too. Ashley wondered if she and Tyler would ever decide to have a baby. She always had it somewhere in the back of her mind that she wanted kids someday, but she was constantly fostering difficult dogs that needed extra TLC and would not be able to tolerate the noisy chaos of children. Of course, any child of Ashley's would be taught to respect and cherish animals from birth and never to tease or pull tails. Still, her dogs were her life and it seemed almost out of the realm of possibility to bring a baby into the picture.

But that little baby sure was sweet. It raised a chubby hand to bat the mother's lips, and the mother smiled indulgently and made a wet raspberry against the baby's palm. The baby giggled and cooed.

Tyler noted the direction of Ashley's gaze and arched an eyebrow. "You're not thinking..." he said.

Ashley shrugged. "Oh, I don't know," she said. "I mean, I figured we'd start a family eventually but..." she trailed off and looked back at the baby. "It seems so totally unrealistic. Still..."

"They are cute little bastards," Tyler said, yelping as Ashley slapped his arm. "No seriously, I could see having a little Tyler Junior around some day. Teach him to play the guitar. Go to ball games."

"I was thinking of a little girl," Ashley said, "but you can still teach her to play guitar and take her to ball games."

Tyler smiled at Ashley and slid his arm around her waist. "I think we should get started right away," he said, kissing her neck.

"You're crazy!" Ashley said, pushing him away and laughing.

The same nasal voice came over the intercom again, interrupting them. "Your attention please," the voice said. "South Pacific Air Flight 121 is still experiencing an unexpected delay. Estimated departure time is now ten fifteen pm. Thank you for your patience."

Tyler's cheerful randiness melted away and his face went pale. "Shit," he said. "Why do they keep prolonging the agony?"

Ashley pushed his hair back from his forehead. "Just stay cool, doggy daddy," she said. "We'll be home soon."

"Why are they doing this?" Tyler continued. "Is there something wrong with the plane?"

"There's nothing wrong with the plane," Ashley said. "You know how they're all crazy with security now because of nine-eleven."

"Right," Tyler said, eyes down. "Right."

"Honey," Ashley said. "You told me you were afraid of flying, but I had no idea it was really this bad. Why did you let me pick Hawaii for our honeymoon if you were so scared?"

"Because you told me that you'd always dreamed of a romantic Hawaiian honeymoon and I wanted you to have it," he said. "I wasn't gonna let my silly irrational fear deprive my baby of her dream vacation."

"I love you," Ashley said. "You're the best."

"Yeah," Tyler said, wiping sweat from his brow on the back of his hand. "Love you too, baby, and this was a fantastic trip. Really, just perfect. I'll just be glad when we are back home in Los Angeles."

"I know," Ashley said. "Why don't you take another Xanax once we get on the plane?"

Tyler nodded and looked back out on the runway.

SIX

Sean sat in a tiny locked room in the airport that felt more like a prison than a security measure: beige carpet, beige upholstery and dreary beige music drizzling from recessed beige speakers. At least Flynn had managed to get Sean some new clothes. Sean didn't know what he'd expected Flynn to come back with—maybe a no-nonsense suit like his own or something—but instead he'd brought Sean a nice, comfortably loose pair of black board shorts and a simple gray, oversized T-shirt. Flynn had also provided a small carry-on bag filled with similar clothes, fresh underwear and socks, and a travel kit with toothpaste and a tooth-brush, deodorant, a razor, everything. Somehow, looking at that neat little bag made the reality of the situation finally sink in for Sean. He was really leaving Oahu. Leaving his little apartment and his things and his life and going thousands of miles away to testify against a mad man who would stop at nothing to kill Sean if he could. Sean had visited some of the other islands once or twice, but he had never actually left Hawaii in his life. How long would he be gone? Would he ever be back? Would Mrs Kame'eleihiwa keep his apartment for him? More importantly, would she be okay? Would those thugs hurt her, do things to her to see if she knew where Sean had gone? She wasn't the friendliest landlady on earth, but she had always been decent to him and never evicted them even when Mel used to get several months behind on the rent. Sean could not stand the thought of anything happening to the old bird because of him.

He watched through the large bulletproof window as cops and FBI agents swarmed ant-like all over a sleek chartered jet with the Federal Bureau of Investigations logo on the side. They sure seemed to know what they were doing, but Sean could not help but feel anxious and jittery. Could they really protect him? He trusted Flynn, but he kept thinking of the dead, unplugged expression on Kim's face after he had murdered that district attorney. Sean suspected that nobody alive had ever seen that awful expression. Nobody but him, anyway.

The locked door buzzed open, startling Sean. He tried to play it cool as Flynn entered the little room holding a plastic shopping bag.

"Ready for this?" Flynn asked.

Sean nodded, trying to force his dry throat to swallow. "Yeah," he lied. "Absolutely. You bet."

Flynn looked at Sean thoughtfully as if he was well aware of the lie and had decided not to comment.

"Is that our plane?" Sean asked, pointing out at the chartered jet.

Flynn shook his head. "No, but every cop in Honolulu thinks it is."

Sean nodded, wide-eyed and mystified by all the intrigue as Flynn set the plastic bag on the table between them.

"I need you to put this stuff on," Flynn said.

Sean, who had just changed into the clothes he was currently wearing, peered doubtfully into the plastic bag. It contained a navy blue coverall with the South Pacific air logo on the back, just like the ones the various mechanics and technicians out on the airstrip wore. There was a cap too, along with a pair of aviator-style mirrored sunglasses and a Kevlar bullet-proof vest.

"Just put the vest and the jumpsuit on over your clothes," Flynn said. "You can take the suit off as soon as you are onboard the aircraft, though we'll need you to keep the Kevlar on until we get you to the safe house in LA."

"Okay," Sean said cautiously, opening the Velcro fasteners on the vest and pulling it on over his head. "If you say so."

Flynn watched Sean slip into the coverall and then put the cap on Sean's head and handed him the glasses.

"Perfect," he said, reaching to hit the button that unlocked the door. "Let me introduce Agents Gage, San Marco and Tokushima."

Two men and a woman entered the room. All three were dressed in coveralls just like Sean. The woman was tall and blonde with a severe face and eyebrows so pale they were nearly invisible. The men were both large and stern-looking, Italian and Japanese respectively, but otherwise essentially identical.

"They will be escorting you to the plane," Flynn said. "Don't worry, these guys are good. You're safe with them. In fact…" He indicated the blonde woman with his chin. "Gage here is way tougher than I am. Aren't you, Gage?"

The blonde gave an almost imperceivable nod and the corner of her mouth twitched slightly in a move that was more of a facial tic than a smile.

"Remind me on the flight to tell you the story of the time when Agent Gage stitched up her own knife wound in the back of a moving jeep on the road to Mykolayiv," Flynn said. "Ever been to the Ukraine?"

Sean shook his head.

"Let me tell you," Flynn continued. "They have a whole lot of potholes over there."

"What about you?" Sean asked, trying very hard not to sound too anxious. "I thought you said you were gonna be on me like white on rice."

"I'll be watching your every move," Flynn said, "and I'll meet you on the plane. It's just that Eddie's goon saw me save your ass this morning. If they see me get on a plane with anybody but Sanders, they're gonna assume it's you."

Sean looked at the three agents and then down at his feet, still incongruously clad in rubber flip-flops.

"Okay," he said quietly.

"This way," the humorless woman said.

Sean cast an anxious glance over his shoulder at Flynn.

The big man nodded encouragingly. "I told you," he said. "Sanders and I are gonna meet you there. Go."

Sean nodded and followed the blonde woman out the door.

Out on the tarmac, a man named Billy Yip was dressed in a jumpsuit just like the one Sean had just put on and was just as out of place. He watched silently as a pair of uniformed men with bomb sniffing dogs exited the cargo hold of the 747 aircraft scheduled for South Pacific Air Flight 121. There had been quite a bit of action around this particular plane and the flight had been delayed, even though none of the local mechanics had been allowed anywhere near it. The bomb sniffing dogs and the security people had just let four maintenance workers on board, including, Billy had noticed, one wearing rubber flip flop sandals. Billy had a hunch. He pulled his cellphone from one of the many pockets in the navy coverall and hit a number on the speed dial.

Lulu Fang sat on a tall stool at the Starbucks counter, sipping an iced latte and crossing and uncrossing her nylon-clad legs. She was a dangerous vixen with a severe bob haircut, blood-red lipstick and a tight white leather suit. When her cellphone tinkled its gentle wind chime ring tone, she pulled it from her tiny purse and flipped it open.

"*Wei?*" she said into the little phone, nodded twice and hung up without another word.

Sliding off the stool and onto her killer stiletto heels, she tugged the hem of her skin-tight white leather skirt down so it just barely covered the tops of her silvery stockings, and strode purposefully towards the crowd around the gate for departing Flight 121. There were a lot of angry people milling around the desk, but Lulu skirted the mob and made a beeline for a geeky-looking security guy standing by an adjacent door.

"I don't suppose you have any idea what's going on with my flight?" Lulu purred. "I'm dying for a cigarette."

"Don't know ma'am," he said, skittish eyes locked on her high-heeled shoes.

"Mmmmmm," she said, reaching in her purse for a tin of cinnamon-flavored candies. She opened the tin and picked up one of the candies between two long, glossy red nails and placed it on her outstretched tongue. "Want one?"

The guard shook his head.

"I guess you could say I have an oral fixation," she said, sucking on the candy. "I just have to have something in my mouth all the time."

The guard nodded and swallowed nervously.

"It's so unfair that they don't let you smoke on the plane," she said. "They hardly let you smoke anywhere these days. Pretty soon the only place you will be able to smoke is at home, and honestly what's the point of that? I only want to smoke in places where men can watch me. It's very sexy, don't you think? A woman smoking, I mean. It's so... naughty." She licked her lips. "I swear I'm just dying for a cigarette. Do you think it will be much longer?"

"I don't know, ma'am," he said.

"I saw those police dogs on the plane," she said, making her eyes big and liquid. "There isn't some kind of bomb threat, is there?"

"No, ma'am, nothing like that," the guard said. "It's just some sort of FBI business. Nothing dangerous."

"I see," Lulu said, smiling. "Well in that case, I better go have a cigarette after all. We might be here all night."

She walked away, feeling the guard's gaze following her down the concourse. When she reached the awful little glassed-in, roofless smoking prison, she pushed open the double doors and placed a cigarette between her lips. The crowd of chain-smoking Asian business men around her nearly started a riot elbowing each other out of the way to be first to offer her a light. She accepted one from the gold lighter of a distinguished-looking older Chinese man and pulled out her cellphone.

"South Pacific Air Flight 121," she said into the phone.

A large van pulled up beside the belly of the plane scheduled for Flight 121. A colorful logo on the side read *Aloha Kingdom Flowers and Gifts*. A pair of workers got out and one went around back to get the forklift while the other approached the security men with a clipboard.

"What have you got there?" one of the guards asked.

"Orchid plants," the driver said in a thick Chinese accent.

"Why didn't you put them in regular cargo?" he asked.

The driver shook his head emphatically. "No," he said. "Not cut flowers. Whole plant. Orchid roots die in cold. Very delicate, just like cat." He pointed to a cat carrier with a very unhappy cat inside being loaded into the special pressurized hold for pets.

"Right," the security guard said, taking the clipboard from the driver and fishing for a pen to sign the form. "Bring them around this way."

The second man had loaded up the forklift with large boxes from the back of the truck and was bringing them around to the hold.

"Who knew flowers would be so heavy you'd need a forklift to move 'em?" the guard said.

"Now that's what I call lazy," the other said, laughing as the two oblivious men loaded the large boxes onto the plane.

Useen by the two security guards, the Asian driver pulled a cellphone from his overall pocket and rapidly punched in a number. While he waited for the call to connect, the driver opened one of the flower boxes and used a spray bottle to shower the contents. The call connected.

"Yes, sir. I'm soaking the leis with it. The pheremones will make the snakes go fuckin' crazy."

"How much longer do you think they'll be?" the first guy asked again. "I'm frickin starving."

"You're always starving," his buddy replied. "Look at you, you lucky fuck, you're skinny as a rail and always stuffing your face. Me, I tried Slim Fast, Atkins, Grapefruit Diet, every damn diet in the book and I still can't shake that last fifteen pounds."

"I could go for a nice pastrami sandwich," the first guy said.

"Fuck you and your nice pastrami sandwich," the second guy said. "You see this?" He pulled a foil wrapped diet bar from his pocket. "This is my fucking dinner, so do me a favor and keep your nice pastrami sandwich to yourself."

"Look, they're done," the first guard said, as the two Asian men got back into the Aloha Kingdom truck and drove away. "Better get this closed up and ready to go."

"Right," the second guy said.

SEVEN

Claire and Tiffany were standing by the stairs that led up to the first class cabin when two men in dark suits, one black and bald and one white and blond, entered the plane, striding purposefully down the aisle.

"I'm sorry," Claire said, frowning. "I don't know how you got in here, but boarding will not begin for another fifteen minutes."

The black man pulled a leather bi-fold from an inner pocket in his jacket and flipped it open, revealing a photo ID card and a badge. "FBI, ma'am," he said.

"Right," Claire said. "Okay."

"Welcome aboard, gentlemen," Tiffany said with a wolfish smile.

"Thank you, ma'am," the man replied.

When he returned his badge to the inner pocket of his jacket, Claire caught a glimpse of the black nylon straps of a shoulder holster against his clean white shirt. She shuddered. Whatever was going on here was clearly no joke.

The two men headed up the stairs to the cabin and Tiffany arched a brow, clearly chomping at the bit. "Did I ever tell you how much I love men in positions of authority?" she asked.

"I don't know," Claire replied. "I prefer to be on top myself."

Tiffany giggled. "Come on," she begged. "Let me take First tonight? Pretty please? With Sweet and Low on top?"

Claire shrugged and gave Tiffany a lopsided grin. "Okay, okay," Claire said. "It's all yours. But only because we are so light on passengers tonight and not until after all the other passengers are seated."

"You're in my will!" Tiffany said, lifting up her navy blue SPA blouse to fold over the waistband of her skirt, pulling the hemline two inches higher up her long slender thighs.

When Sean arrived with his three escorts in the cabin, which was apparently upstairs from all the lowly peasants in the rest of the plane, he found Flynn and his cranky partner already there. The seats were huge and covered with soft blue leather and there were little televisions in the back of each seat. While he was marveling over all of the ostentatious luxuries, Gage and Flynn were quietly conferring.

"I saw an Asian mechanic making a cellphone call," she said. "Probably nothing, since there is no other indication that this flight has been compromised, but keep your guard up."

"My guard is always up," Flynn replied.

"Right," Gage said. "Like that time with the beer girl in Battambang."

"That was fifteen years ago, Gage," Flynn said, grinning. "You're just jealous because she didn't want you."

"I prefer the Tiger girls," she said. "Never trust a 33 girl."

"You hear that, Sean?" Flynn asked. "That's some sound advice. Keep that in mind the next time you're working an undercover operation in a Cambodian dive bar."

Sean looked up from fiddling with the air-phone in his seat.

"Uh, right," Sean said.

"Take care, kid," Gage said. "I'd say good luck, but I don't believe in luck. Anyway, you're in good hands."

"Thanks," Sean said, but the three agents slipped away without another word.

Flynn took a seat across the aisle from Sean. "You can take that jumpsuit off now if you like."

"Oh yeah, right," Sean said, stepping out into the aisle and peeling off the coverall.

"Leave the vest!" Flynn said as Sean's fingers tugged at the Velcro fasteners on the left side of the Kevlar vest.

"I just want to loosen it up a little," Sean said defensively. "It's hot."

"No," Flynn said, leaving no room for discussion. "I said leave it."

"Okay, fine," Sean said, stashing the jumpsuit in his carry-on, which he found stowed beneath his seat. "Man, these seats are huge. My first big plane flight and I get to fly first class."

"See?" Flynn said. "Things are looking up already."

Sean looked up over the top of the seat in front of him and saw the bulky, blond Sanders hunched over an air-phone at the forward bulkhead. He had the phone jammed between his ear and shoulder and was methodically checking and rechecking his handgun while he spoke. Sean figured these FBI guys must get special permission to have guns on a plane, but it was still weird to see one handled so casually out in the open.

"So," Sean said, turning his gaze back to Flynn. "How long have you guys been working together?"

"Five years," Flynn replied. "Two blown marriages, one each. In fact, we've been partners longer than either one of us managed to stay married. When my wife left me, she told me I oughta just marry Sanders, since I spent more time with him than I ever had with her." Flynn let out a low chuckle. "He's the toughest son of a bitch I ever met. Smart too. He speaks six languages, is a champion Go player and a master of hung gar kung fu. What he lacks in charm, he makes up in ass kicking. I trust him with my life."

"Wow," Sean said. "What about you?"

"What about me?" Flynn asked.

"What special, cool, kick-ass skills do you have?"

Flynn smirked. "I'm really good at Monopoly."

"Monopoly?" Sean smiled.

"Yup," Flynn said. "I get Boardwalk every time."

"Flynn," Sanders called. "Captain's patching us through to Harris for the flight."

"All right," Flynn said. "Give me a minute, kid."

"Sure," Sean said.

He watched the big man unfold his long legs into the aisle and head up toward the front. Sanders handed him the phone and came back down the aisle to take a seat behind Sean. Sean twisted around in his seat and looked over at the blond man. He had taken a paperback book out of his briefcase, but opened it backward and started reading the last page. That's when Sean noticed that it was not English; it was little vertical rows of characters, either in Chinese or Japanese. Sean couldn't tell the difference.

"Hey," Sean said.

"What?" Sanders said, not looking up.

"Flynn said you like to play Go," Sean said.

Sanders looked up at him, dark eyes unreadable. He nodded.

"Well," Sean said, "I tried to learn the simple capturing game a few years back, but I just couldn't get the hang of it and I couldn't find anyone with the patience to teach me. Maybe when we are all cooped up together and bored to death during the trial, we could get a Go set and you could show me some new strategies."

Sanders frowned at him. "I don't know. You seem more like the Monopoly type to me."

"I'll play Monopoly with Flynn," Sean said, "but I'd rather play Go with you."

Sanders made a gruff noise that was sort of a laugh. "We'll see," he said, and Sean figured that was the best he could hope for.

Hank Harris was still not used to spending his days behind a desk. He was in his early forties with thick dark hair and heavy eyebrows and he had a fit, active build that seemed to resent its imprisonment in the ergonomic desk chair. The desk top before him was immaculate and he had already rearranged its sparse collection of items several times. Whistling tunelessly, he scooched a glass paperweight with the Federal Bureau of Investigation logo etched into its surface a few inches to the left, and then moved it back to its original position and sighed. His wife Ana Luisa was thrilled that he had been promoted and it made his home life much smoother to have her happy, but this even, uneventful life was making him stir-crazy.

He pulled a pair of takeout menus from a drawer in the desk and was weighing Thai against Italian when the brand new phone on his desk rang, making him jump a little. He grabbed it and stuffed the handset between his shoulder and his ear. "Harris."

"Hey buddy," said the deep, distinct voice of Neville Flynn. "How are you enjoying your promotion?"

"Love it," Harris replied, stashing the menus and moving the paperweight to the left again.

"You said that a little too quickly," Flynn said. "Try again."

"I swear to you, man," Harris said. "No more junk food hangovers from all night surveillance. I am in bed every night with Ana Luisa and she's been letting me know how happy that makes her. She loves living in Los Angeles and the kids do too. I've actually spent time with my kids, while they are awake no less. I'm even starting to be able to tell them apart. There's three of them, you know, and they're actually kinda fun. Who knew?"

"Stop it, Hank," Flynn said. "This is me you're talking to. Admit it, you're bored to tears. You miss the action, don't you?"

"Nah," Harris said, reaching out to move the paperweight again and then pulling his hand back.

"What do you even do with your time?" Flynn asked.

"I've been surfing the net," Harris said.

"Our tax dollars at work," Flynn said. "Porn, no doubt."

"On eBay, my cynical-minded friend," Harris replied. "I am smack in the middle of a furious bidding war with some punk from Iowa over a black velvet Billy Idol portrait."

"You need help," Flynn said. "How's our pal Mr Kim?"

"Don't worry about Eddie," Harris said. "He's not going anywhere. If he moves, we have three units on him." He glanced over at a wall of surveillance monitors keeping a close watch over Eddie Kim's Bel Aire estate. "He so much as sneaks out a fart and we've got it on tape."

"Good," Flynn said. "We should be hitting LAX at eight thirty in the morning. Stay in touch."

"You bet," Harris said.

"Don't work too hard," Flynn said and rang off.

Harris looked briefly back up at the monitors and then pulled out the Thai menu again.

EIGHT

When Eddie Kim bought his Bel Air mansion, he had the cavernous art-deco ballroom converted into a dojo. That's where Mr Alexander Gong sat on an uncomfortable wooden bench, watching the young Kim sparring with a partner who was clearly better than Kim and was doing everything in his power to hide that fact. Kim was far too aggressive. All offense and anger, like so many of the younger ones. Mr Gong was nearly seventy years old, and had been a part of the Triad organization since birth. He had seen hundreds of men like Eddie Kim. Men who thought all problems could be solved with aggression.

Mr Gong sipped the cup of ginseng tea provided by a pretty young girl who had slipped away without a word. It was ludicrous and rude, making him wait until this foolish display of testosterone was finished. Mr Gong would have been much happier sitting out on the patio where he could see the fountain and warm his old bones in this lovely California sun. His son James had very much wanted to attend this meeting, but the elder Mr Gong had asked him to wait in the car. James was a good and trustworthy man, but he was clearly put out by being treated like a child. The elder Mr Gong knew that it could not be helped. He needed to meet with Eddie Kim alone.

This Eddie Kim was becoming quite a loose cannon. He was half Korean and half Chinese, but his mother was Mr Gong's niece May. May had been a terribly rebellious child and she had infuriated her father by running off with that Korean actor, but she was family, and when that actor deserted her, leaving her pregnant, broke and alone in New Orleans, the Gongs had wired her money and taken her back into the fold.

Eddie had grown up angry. Angry that the family would not allow him to take the Gong name, but instead made him keep the name of his thoughtless Korean father as a reminder of the circumstances of his inauspicious birth. Angry that he did not get the preferential treatment awarded to James's first born son Steven, who was the same age, but cool-headed and intelligent where Eddie was volatile and impulsive. Eddie Kim was a true sadist, unstable but useful and willing to do jobs with relish that few other men would touch. He had his place in the organization, but Mr Gong feared that Kim was becoming less and less sane each day. Kim was very close to becoming a liability.

As he watched, Kim delivered a powerful but sloppy punch to the head of his opponent. The opponent did not block the blow and went down in a crumpled heap on the expensive parquet floor. Mr Gong wondered if the man liked his job. It was probably much easier than the job of the girl who brought the tea. She probably had to accept sexual advances from Kim as well.

Kim trotted over to where Mr Gong sat, wiping his sweaty face on a towel. He was wearing only loud Day-Glo green and yellow track pants. His physique was that of a racing dog, wiry and sculpted from tension. His large feet were bare and very clean.

"Mr Gong," Kim said in his rough Americanized Chinese. "How was your flight from Hong Kong?"

"Fine, thank you," Mr Gong said in English. "This tea is excellent."

"I am glad you enjoyed it," Kim said. "If you would like another cup, I will join you."

"That would be very nice, thank you," Mr Gong said.

Kim pushed a silent button and the pretty girl reappeared.

"Only the finest for the illustrious head of the Gong household," Kim said as the girl poured a second cup. "Naturally."

Mr Gong chose to ignore the thinly veiled hostility in that statement and instead smiled at the girl. Her quick gaze darted up at him and then away. Kim waved a hand to dismiss her and she vanished like smoke.

"I very much enjoy returning to Los Angeles after being away for so long," Mr Gong said. "The weather is so agreeable, perfect for a man my age. Also, I want to go back to Universal Studios. Have you been there?"

"Sure," Kim said. "It's not bad."

"I would like to go on that new 'Revenge of the Mummy' ride," Mr Gong said, sipping thoughtfully at his tea. "Of course, James feels that I am too old for that sort of thing, and my dear departed wife would probably concur, but I believe that one must live one's life to the fullest at any age, don't you agree?"

"Yes," Kim said. "I could not agree more."

Mr Gong could feel the younger man bristling with impatience. Such was the way of all young people these days. Mr Gong sighed heavily and put his cup down on a small table to his left. It was a terrible table—some crudely-made Warring States reproduction that was blocky and unharmonious in shape, burdened with a rash of unnecessary gold leaf decoration. Beside his cup, there was an equally appalling vase filled with blameless orchids that seemed to hang their pure white faces in shame to be part of such an egregious display of poor taste.

"Edward," Mr Gong said eventually, thumbing the switch on a tiny scrambling device in his left pocket, just in case any FBI listening devices were present in the room. "We in the organization are quite concerned about this Hawaiian business."

Kim opened his mouth, but Mr Gong held up a hand to silence him.

"I feel certain that you will have no problem taking care of the situation," Mr Gong continued. "However, there are those who feel that your chosen method for handling this problem is…" Mr Gong narrowed his eyes. "…somewhat uncertain. I have been asked to remind you that failure to adequately handle this problem would not bode well for your position in the organization."

"I assure you…" Kim began.

"You needn't assure me, Edward," Mr Gong said with a chilly smile. "I have every confidence in you." He laid an arthritic hand on Kim's bare shoulder. "I am sure that you are well aware of what is at stake here," Mr Gong said. "Isn't that right?"

"Look, accidents happen," Kim said. "You think I didn't exhaust every other option? That kid *saw* me."

"Of course," Mr Gong said. "I know that you will not fail."

"The kid won't make it to LAX alive," Kim said. "That's a promise."

"Excellent," Mr Gong said, getting slowly to his feet and thumbing off the scrambling device. "I knew there was nothing to be concerned about. Tell me, Edward. How is your mother?"

"Fine," Kim said. "She's fine."

"I understand the doctors have agreed that she has been making significant improvement with this new round of medications," Mr Gong said.

"I suppose," Kim said. "She has more than one hour a day during which she stops screaming, if you want to call that an improvement."

"Edward," Mr Gong said, chiding gently. "You mustn't be so negative. May has had a very difficult life. She needs support from her family. We all do. Family is everything, you know. If there is a problem in the family, we solve it. It's that simple."

Mr Gong gave Kim a significant look and the younger man scowled and looked away.

"Thank you for the tea," Mr Gong said. "And for your hospitality."

"You are always welcome in my house, Mr Gong," Kim said. "Enjoy 'Revenge of the Mummy.'"

Mr Gong smiled. "I certainly will."

NINE

Paul Oswald had had a bad feeling about this trip from the beginning. For one thing, he'd always hated Hawaii. If he wanted to do the tropics, he much preferred somewhere like Nicaragua or Sulawasi. Someplace with fewer humans, fewer McDonalds. Hawaii was everything that sucked about the mainland tourist traps, only hotter. Paul cherished being alone, and nothing made him happier than spending time in which he could be totally removed from the clamor and whining of his fellow Americans. His cabin in Big Bear, a remote jungle resort in which the only human presence consisted of silent servants who spoke no English.

This trip, on the other hand, had been exactly the opposite.

Paul had been attending a mandatory "Vision and Values" Offsite for senior level managers in the computer hardware company he worked for. It had been a weekend of insipid focus groups in which he had been forced to think of ten words that best evoked the vision and values of the corporation and play humiliating games designed to promote teamwork. The whole tedious affair was overseen by a gaggle of relentlessly chipper women with ergonomic hair and flip charts.

Paul did not want to be incentivized. He wanted to be left alone. Instead, he had been forced to listen to the importance of Work-Life Balance and promoting a Family-Friendly workplace. Paul had never understood why all the happy little yuppie breeders were allowed to take off every five minutes because Junior stubbed his toe or won an award for nose picking, while their single coworkers were expected to cheerfully pick up the slack. His own lonely little Post-it note suggestion that they focus on "Excellence in Product" was thoughtlessly pushed aside while all the cooing women gushed about the importance of FAMILY and the need for everyone to kowtow to the almighty babies. What the hell did babies have to do with computers anyway?

Paul was not allowed to take off work to play computer chess or read a book or do a little extra cardio at the gym, so why were these tyrannical little DNA packets allowed to intrude into their parents' work schedules at the drop of a hat?

At least it was over now. He'd bitten the bullet and survived, and if he could just make it through the flight home with minimal fuss, he would be back in Los Angeles, back in his serene, quiet house, mercifully alone.

But apparently, that just wasn't possible. As soon as they made the call to board First Class passengers, Paul had been the first in line, in front of a bimbo, a fat lady and some rich yo with his two heavies. Before they could make it to the stairs leading up to the first class cabin, they were met by a shopworn slut with a big phony smile and too much kinky black hair.

"Unfortunately," she said, full of unctuous sympathy, "First Class has been overbooked, but there's plenty of room to stretch out in Coach, which is less than half full. For the inconvenience, we'll be giving each one of you a free travel coupon good on any South Pacific Air Flight."

Paul took the coupon and scowled. "A free travel coupon doesn't help me get to my meeting on time, now does it?"

"Sir," the smug little bitch replied, "I'm pretty sure Coach will get to Los Angeles about the same time as First Class."

"Very funny," Paul replied. "Does my Platinum Awards Membership include free sarcasm or should I take that up with your supervisor..." He looked at the plastic name tag pinned above her less-than-impressive A-cup breast. "Claire?"

He pushed past her, ignoring her bitchy little aside to her fellow stewardess, a used up old relic that she obviously hung around with to make herself look younger.

Behind him, the bimbo chimed up. "No First Class? You can't be serious!"

"I'm afraid only Coach is available," the bitchy stewardess replied.

"Coach?" the horrified bimbo repeated. "Is it safe there?"

"I assure you, miss," the stewardess said, "it's completely safe."

Paul grumbled to himself as he stalked down the aisle, looking for a seat as far away from anyone else as possible. Then, as he folded himself into his paperback-sized seat and set up his laptop on the tiny tray table, the bimbo plopped herself down in the seat directly across the aisle from him and a shaky little chihuahua in a diamond collar popped up out of her handbag like a jack-in-the-box. The ratty little dog sneezed twice, then turned its runny gaze to Paul and started yipping like its tail was on fire. The bimbo seemed to think this was cute and snapped a photo of the thing with her Treo.

Paul rolled his eyes dramatically. "Oh, beautiful. First they stick me in Coach and then I get a god-damn dog next to me. What the hell's next? A screaming baby?"

As if cued, a smug blonde woman with an infant came parading like Miss America down the aisle, fawningly accompanied by the used-up older stewardess to whom the kinky-haired, bitchy one had made her little comment. Paul tried to concentrate all his will on making the woman sit as far away as possible, but of course the older stewardess led her right to the row in front of Paul.

The two women spent another full minute in high-pitched baby-talk worship over the oblivious infant.

"She's eight months old," the mother said. "Her name is Isabella."

"Oooooh," the stewardess cooed. "Such a beautiful name for a beautiful little angel. Yes you are. Is this her first plane flight?"

"Yes," the mother said. "I have to admit I'm a little nervous."

"I remember when I took my oldest son on a plane to see his grandparents for the first time," the stewardess said. "I was a total basket case for days and he wound up sleeping through the whole flight. He's twenty-two now. Is she your first?"

"My first and only," the mother said, kissing the baby's big, veiny head. "She's my whole world."

"Yeah," the stewardess said wistfully. "I remember how that was. You can't help but feel so protective with the first one." She smiled. "Then by the time I had my youngest daughter, I pretty much let them all juggle chainsaws on the freeway."

The women tittered and giggled. The baby squirmed and yawned and shook its little pink fists.

"Great!" Paul said, finally, unable to contain himself any longer. "Fucking wonderful."

The baby started to howl as if it had been personally offended by Paul's annoyance. The woman turned on him with a burning self-righteous glare. "Is there a problem, mister?" she asked.

"What do you think?" he replied sullenly.

She bounced the screaming brat up and down on her hip and made her eyes really big in a parody of earnest politeness. "I think sometimes babies misbehave during flights," she said. "And that can be a nightmare for the passengers around them."

He frowned. Where was she going with this? People with babies never acknowledge how annoying they are. They always think the little beasts are perfect angels and that everyone ought to worship the brats as blindly as they do.

"Exactly," he said cautiously. "So what are you going to do about it?"

She flashed a smug grin. "I'm going to kindly ask you to stop misbehaving," she said, "so that you don't become a nightmare for the rest of us."

Paul took in a deep breath and started to count to ten. There was no point in even engaging people like her. What, did she read that lame little zinger in the latest issue of *Baby Fetish Weekly*? The used-up old stewardess gave the triumphant madonna a supportive smile and everyone nodded like the brainwashed robots they were. Paul struggled to keep his cool. That's what he got for speaking out loud to idiots. These yuppie mommies were the new Inquisitors of our time and anyone who didn't buy the Babies Are Perfect religion was burned at the stake as a mean, nasty old sorcerer.

Like having a baby was so fucking special. Being proud of having made a baby was like being proud of taking a shit after you ate a sandwich. It's biology, people, cause and effect. It just happens. Rats do it. Roaches do it. How can you be proud of something that will happen automatically unless you take specific steps to prevent it?

It's bad enough that people choose to give up their autonomy and freedom to become valets for some squalling shit-machine, they also want to inflict the damn things on the rest of us. Paul would be willing to pay a thousand dollars extra just to guarantee a baby-free flight. That was part of the reason why he always flew First Class. Most baby slaves were too broke from spending all their money on designer diapers and organic nipples to afford to fly First Class. As if there weren't enough reasons not to have kids, there was the financial aspect. Why not just take all your money and throw it off a bridge? You spend hundreds of thousands of dollars on the brat so they can grow up, get on drugs, drop out of the college you paid for and run away to join a punk rock band. Not a sound investment in Paul's opinion. He would rather spend his money on rare and fragile items that would shatter if a child even looked at them, trips to exotic and dangerous places where all manner of dire fates could befall a helpless infant, or top drawer call girls that had more interest in his wallet than his reproductive capacities.

Of course, just to add to the racket, the ratty little dog started up again, harmonizing with the shrieking baby to create a migraine-inducing cacophony.

"Can you at least get that vermin to shut up?" Paul asked, massaging his temples.

"Don't worry, Mary-Kate," the bimbo said to the shuddering dog. "His hair plugs can't hurt you."

Paul snapped his laptop shut and stood, wrenching his carry-on from beneath the seat. He'd had more than enough of this bullshit. He stormed down the aisle, hunting for a seat as far away from the brat as possible.

TEN

Tiffany hiked up the hem of her skirt another quarter inch and arranged her legs so that the calf muscles stood out nicely as Three Gs and his two bodyguards came towards her down the narrow aisle. The rapper handed her his boarding pass and she smiled, lashes fluttering.

"I'm really sorry about the whole First Class thing," she said. "Let me help you find some seats."

She handed the boarding pass back to Three Gs and her fingers brushed against his. To her surprise, he hissed between his teeth and pulled his hand back as if scalded. The two guards stepped between Tiffany and the rapper.

"Please," the handsome guard said. "Don't touch the Man."

"The Man don't like to be touched," the heavier guard said.

Behind the guards, Three Gs stumbled back down the aisle towards the bathroom.

"Gosh," Tiffany said, brows knitted with confused concern. "I'm real sorry. Is he gonna be okay?"

"He's fine, honey," the handsome guard said. "Don't you worry about it. He just has a lot on his mind is all."

"Okay," Tiffany said, looking down the aisle at the lighted sign that read "OCCUPIED". "If you say so."

In the tiny closet-sized restroom, Three Gs was washing his hands. The water dribbling from the tap was only lukewarm and the liquid soap in the cheap, clotted dispenser was not anti-bacterial. Three Gs felt a kind of bright, jagged panic tearing its way out of his churning stomach as he scrubbed and rinsed, scrubbed and rinsed. He had been cool until that little boy touched him in the airport. Since then, he'd kept his left hand jammed deep into the pocket of his pants, tapping a pattern of repetitive even numbers against his leg and battling to crush down the mounting anxiety that gripped him, squeezing his heart until he could feel it skip inside his chest. His mind had seized on the skip like a dog with a bone and he was caught in a vicious cycle of obsessive thought patterns, afraid that he was having a heart attack, afraid that he would get sick and die because he'd was out of hand sanitizer, afraid that the plane would crash if he stopped the tapping even for a second. Then the stupid white girl had touched his hand and he just lost it. He barely made it into the bathroom before he burst into angry, frustrated tears. Hunched over the little sink, tortured and humiliated, he scrubbed and rinsed six more times before he was finally able to turn off the water with a paper towel and suck in a deep shaky breath. He could not let his fans see him like this.

Three Gs had always been fastidious and neat and he had always had his little quirky rituals when he was on tour. In fact, part of his mad flow as a rapper stemmed from his lifelong obsession with rhymes and matching words and counting syllables. He could create improvised, on the fly rhymes better and faster than anyone and his vocabulary was immense and legendary. But over the past year, his obsessive-compulsive fixations had been getting steadily worse and worse. The rituals were taking up more and more of his waking hours, becoming more and more involved and complicated and the fear of germs and contamination had gotten more powerful than ever. Worse than that, worst of all, was the deep, gut-wrenching shame he felt over his increasing obsessions.

Everyone who knew him knew he did not like to be touched and was funny about hand washing and things like that, but no one knew how deep it really ran and how he tortured himself about it every single day. How he lived his life as a virtual slave to these overwhelming thoughts and impulses, fighting a never-ending invisible war. He knew that there were certain drugs that could help to curb these thoughts and feelings, but he had never used any kind of drug in his life and he did not want to start. He had made a promise to his mama before she died that he would never take drugs. When he'd become involved in the music scene, he had taken a lot of ribbing for his straight-edge ways, but he'd stuck to his guns and eventually people accepted him and respected him despite his quirks for the simple reason that he was good. Damn good. But there were plenty of people out there who would love to see him fall. Jealous, vindictive people with agendas. People who seemed to think their own success was riding on his failure. On his worst days, days when he was unable to leave the bathroom for hours, the only thing that stopped him from putting a bullet in his howling brain and ending the madness once and for all was the idea that his death, his disintegration, would allow those jackals to win. He could not let them win.

He needed to get a handle on this right fucking now. There was no way he was gonna let this shit get out of control, especially not on a plane, in full view of all those people. The claustrophobic, trapped feeling made one more play for him, crushing him down, and he fought it, clenching his teeth and squeezing his eyes shut. When he opened his eyes and regarded himself in the spotted mirror, he looked almost calm.

"You're cool," he told himself. "Absolute motherfucking zero."

He used one paper towel to slide the lock open and another to turn the handle and open the door. When he made his way to the seats that Troy and

Leroy had claimed, his mask felt solid again. No one would know. As he eased himself into the chosen seat, the harsh smell of the disinfectant spray that Troy had used to clean the cushions while Three Gs was having his moment in the bathroom wrapped around him, comforting him. He looked up and down the aisle, trying to spot the blonde stewardess that had touched him. He felt a powerful need to speak to her, flirt with her and show her and everyone around him that he was alright, but she was nowhere to be found. He surveyed the single women around him, not liking the options but feeling that he had to do some kind of damage control. There was another blonde sitting a few rows back, pretty but bony with very high heels and a smell of money around her. She would have to do for now. He put on his best, most charming smile and motioned for her to join him.

Navy diver Brett Jesperson stood at the gate with his two sons, nine year-old Curtis and seven year-old Tommy. He wore his dress whites and was doing everything in his power to keep it together, to not let the boys know how upset he was. They needed him to be strong, but all he wanted was to pull them close and never let them go. They were smart kids, and they knew something was up, especially Tommy, who from the day he was born had seemed to have an almost psychic ability to key in on the emotions of those around him. Tommy's big brown eyes, eyes just like Brett's, were looking up at him, anxious and unsure. Brett swore that the boy could see right into his heart.

"Daddy," Tommy said, "why can't you come with us?"

Was there any way to answer that question? He could barely find a way to explain everything that he had been through with Kara in the past year to himself, let alone to a sensitive seven year-old. The lies, the tears, the bitter silences and finally, her decision to leave him and the boys and go off to Los Angeles so that she could pretend that she was twenty-one again and be free of tedious responsibilities like fidelity and motherhood. When Brett had received word that he was being shipped out to perform a very tricky underwater recovery mission in the Caspian Sea, he had called Kara in Hollywood and told her that she would have to take the boys for six months, maybe longer. She was furious, resentful and had accused

Brett of planning this on purpose to punish her for leaving. Brett loved his boys more than anything in the world and it made him furious that she would think of spending time with them as a punishment. They loved her and missed her and had no idea of what she had put Brett through, and Brett wanted to keep it that way. If he could have come up with anywhere else for them to go, he would not have sent them to stay with Kara. But Brett's mother was in the hospital again for emphysema and both of Kara's parents were dead. Sharee, the boys' regular sitter, had been willing to stay with them for a few weeks, but she was going back to the mainland to get married at the beginning of next month. If there had been any other option, Brett would have taken it.

"Because," Brett said, "Daddy has to go on a very important mission halfway around the world, that's why."

"Is it dangerous?" Tommy asked.

More than you want to know, kid, Brett thought, but instead he said, "Nah. It's no big deal."

"Will there be sharks?" Tommy asked.

"If there are," Brett replied, "they know better than to mess with me."

Tommy wasn't buying it.

"Listen, Tiger," Brett said. "You guys are gonna be just fine. Bet you'll even have fun."

"He's just being a baby," Curtis said.

Curtis was having an even harder time with Kara's desertion than Tommy but he was trying very hard to put on a mask of worldly indifference. Brett could see that Curtis needed to act tough and grown up and feel like he was in charge of the situation. It was just his way of coping with the loss.

"Curtis," Brett said, putting a hand on his eldest son's shoulder. "I'm counting on you to be a man."

Curtis nodded, face grim and serious.

"Now what does a man do?" Brett asked.

"He looks out for his family," Curtis replied.

"That's right," Brett said. "That's your job, okay? You watch out for Tommy."

"But what's my job?" Tommy asked.

"Your job is to have fun and write me letters to tell me all about your adventures," Brett said. "Think you can handle it?"

Tommy nodded, lower lip quivering. "But what about Mr Wong?" Tommy asked. "Is he going to be okay on the plane?"

Mr Wong was their fat, ornery Siamese cat. Tommy loved that cranky old cat more than anything and he had insisted that Mr Wong accompany them on their trip to Los Angeles. Brett knew that Mr Wong hated nearly everyone except Tommy and he would be miserable if they put him in some cattery somewhere. Mr Wong had put up a hell of a fight when Brett tried to get him into the carrier. You'd think Brett was trying to shove Mr Wong into a blender. In the end, he'd had to trick the cat into the carrier with sardines, but it had worked, and in less than six hours, Mr Wong would be in Hollywood, sharpening his claws on Kara's trendy new furniture.

"Mr Wong is going to be just fine," Brett said. "And so are you."

At that point, a pretty brunette flight attendant appeared at the gate. Brett handed her their gate pass.

"Sorry to be holding things up," Brett said. "My…" He swallowed, choking up on the word. "My ex-wife will be meeting them in Los Angeles. It's their first time flying solo."

"Is that right?" the flight attendant asked, kneeling down between the boys. "Can I tell you a secret?"

The boys nodded, Tommy looking up at Brett and back at the kneeling woman.

"Guess who's on the plane?" she said.

The boys looked at each other and shrugged.

"Three Gs," she whispered. "I bet you can meet him."

"For real?" Curtis asked, eyes lighting up.

The flight attendant nodded and smiled. "For real," she replied.

"Cool!" Curtis said. "Come on, Tommy, let's go!"

Tommy watched Curtis take off down the jetway with his red knapsack bouncing on his back, and then Tommy turned and threw himself into Brett's arms.

"Bye, Daddy," Tommy said into Brett's lapel.

"Bye, Tiger," Brett said, feeling a wave of sorrow and anxiety wash over him as he pressed his lips to Tommy's clean blond hair. "I love you both very much. Remember that."

"I love you too, Daddy," Tommy said.

"Ready?" the flight attendant said.

Brett nodded and watched Tommy take the woman's hand with a lump in his throat. "Thanks," Brett said to the flight attendant.

"My pleasure," she replied.

As he watched the door swing shut behind them, he had to stifle an urge to call them back. He was the one being a big baby. They were going to be just fine. Smiling to himself, Brett turned and headed back down the concourse.

Viola Bova hated flying. Planes were just not built for a woman of generous proportions such as herself. She was five feet eleven inches tall and just over two hundred eighty-five pounds with G cup breasts and thighs the circumference of the average fashion model's ribcage. Her waist-length black hair was wound into a sleek bun and her upturned nose had a pink mask of sunburn across the bridge. Her abundant curves were draped in a tropical fruit-patterned sarong and matching halter top that showed off acres of pink cleavage.

For most of her life, Vi had despised her body and battled endlessly with her weight, shedding pounds and backsliding again and again. She had starved herself down to two hundred pounds to fit into her mother's wedding dress, but her husband Ron had lost interest in her less than six months later and it just wasn't worth fighting anymore.

When flying could not be avoided, she always paid the extra for First Class, just so that she could save herself the humiliation of trying to squeeze her curves into the toddler-sized seats in Coach. Unfortunately, it looked as if she would be stuck in Coach this time, although the flight did seem relatively empty. If she was lucky, she would have a pair of seats to herself and would be able to push up the arm rest and actually be semi-comfortable for the duration of the flight.

Besides, it was hard to be genuinely upset about anything at the moment. Vi had just spent the weekend at the annual Goddess Haumea Hawaiian BBW retreat and she was positively glowing with catlike satisfaction. BBW, of course, stood for "Big Beautiful Women", a term that Vi hadn't even known existed until she had stumbled across a link on a plus-sized clothing website, a link for a club called 2 Much. Curious, she clicked on the banner that featured a painting of a zaftig nude and it brought her to a website that had changed her life.

Vi's computer geek husband seemed to have married her because that's what people did when they reached a certain age and because she hadn't said no. Now that all that foolishness was over with, he didn't see any need to bother with sex or even conversation with Vi. He had been her first and only lover and left her totally confused about the fuss everyone made over the whole sex thing. It hardly seemed worth the trouble it caused on all the soap operas. Really, it was much less enjoyable than eating a hot fudge sundae. Of course, that was before she found out about 2 Much.

2 Much was short for Too Much Woman For You. It was a group of strong, sassy chicks in the Los Angeles area that were all proud of being Big Beautiful Women. Their logo was a fat and saucy fifties pin-up girl in a bikini lounging on a giant cupcake and the words "Too Much is Never Enough!" They organized parties, reviewed plus size clothing lines and traded tips on finding the best, most comfortable F Cup or higher bras. Viola lurked on the message boards and clicked with awe and astonishment through the personal ads that showed women even heavier than her in sexy, revealing lingerie. Even more shocking were the ads from handsome, normal-looking men who wanted to meet women like her. It took her nearly a month to get up the nerve to post.

She created the screen name ViVacious and fretted over what to say for hours. In the end, she finally just introduced herself and said how nice it was to meet big women who were not afraid to be themselves. She could not believe the flood of responses. Women welcomed her and congratulated her on her decision not to allow the media to poison her against her own body. Men posted eager requests for photos along with her weight and measurements. She was a little overwhelmed at first, but as she started to get to know some of the frequent posters and was able to contribute to several threads, she finally felt comfortable enough to post a profile, complete with a photo she shot of herself with her web cam. It wasn't the best picture—after all, she couldn't exactly ask Ron to take one—but it showed lots of cleavage and washed out her skin so it looked all pale and perfect.

She was not used to men flirting with her in any form, so she took an enormous amount of pleasure in basking in all the interest and compliments. While it was true that she was married, it didn't hurt to flirt a little.

One of her new online friends, a short and feisty redhead who called herself Coop Kitten and used one of the artist Coop's chubby devil girls as her icon, eventually talked Vi into attending one of the 2 Much singles mixers as a celebration for her thirtieth birthday. Vi had protested that she was not really single, but Kitten had insisted, telling Vi that if her husband wasn't taking care of her needs, she ought to find someone else who could. Or several someones. Vi had always felt that as a big girl, her options were pretty limited dating-wise. That's why she had said yes to Ron in the first place. Her mother, who was also big, had drilled it into her head from puberty that beggars can't be choosers and because she was fat she ought to consider herself lucky that anyone wanted her at all. But now that she had realized that wasn't true at all, that there were plenty of guys, young good-looking guys, who liked women with meat on their bones, she could see the potential for a fresh start. Besides, Ron had forgotten her birthday. Again. Vi was tired of being the invisible woman. It was his loss.

She bought herself a sexy new dress from Torrid and some high-heeled shoes that made her well over six feet tall. She had stopped wearing heels because Ron was only one inch taller than her and did not like her to look taller than him, but standing in front of her bedroom mirror, she felt like a statuesque goddess, truly big and beautiful. She played music Ron hated at full volume in her car the whole way to the club.

For the first time in her life, Vi felt desirable. More men came over to flirt with her in that one night than in the whole rest of her life combined. She could have her pick of dozens of men and that was like the best drug in the world. She was hooked.

She went to singles parties, weekend retreats, cruises and even a few swingers clubs. She finally understood what all the fuss was about and she could not get enough. Ron never questioned where she went or wondered what she was doing. Anything that got her out of the house was fine by him. He did not want her to have a full time job, but otherwise cared very little about what she did with her free time. It was an ideal arrangement.

Now things were changing for Vi. She had come to realize on this latest trip that she did not need Ron as much as he needed her. Sure, he made good money and it was nice not to have to work, but she knew in her heart that it couldn't last forever. The sex she was having with the men she met through 2 Much was wonderful, but eventually, she wanted to be free to fall in love, to meet someone who thought she was beautiful on the inside and out. And as hostile and frustrated as she got with Ron, she did not want to wait until she fell in love with someone else to break it off with him. She had come close several times and it would not be long before she met someone she could not keep at arm's length. She felt that she owed it to Ron to end their relationship before starting a new one.

It looked like it was going to be a quiet, relatively empty flight, and Vi was pleasantly exhausted from her adventures, but as she selected a pair of empty seats and settled in, she decided that she would need to make some kind of firm choice about Ron by the time she returned to Los Angeles. She could not just continue on like this indefinitely. Looking at her chunky, masculine watch, she told herself that she had five hours to think about it. Five hours. By the time the wheels touched down in LAX, she would know what to do.

Janine Lintree walked down the aisle with her husband Wayne behind her, searching for a pair of seats that felt safe. Janine was bony and intense with a thin, frizzy corona of burgundy hair and lots of noisy ethnic jewelry. Her eyes were half closed and her long, graceful fingers quivering like antennae, picking up signals that only she could sense. She left a thick cloud of musky sandalwood and jasmine oil trailing behind her as she went, a mini-ecosystem of sweet cloying funk that her meek, silent husband inhabited like an endangered species of one. Wayne was her third husband, third time's a charm, she liked to say, and she was convinced that he was the best of the lot. He was not much in the looks department, pale and chinless with a high forehead, thinning reddish hair and a ninety-eight pound weakling build, but he had a kind heart and infinite patience. She was the first to admit that she was not easy to live with. Her gift was not always civil and most men could not handle her constant, seizure-like visions, her sudden wide-eyed refusal to do some ordinary thing that she had done every day for years. Not to mention her celebrity.

Janine had been making a more than decent living as a professional psychic for fifteen years. Rich patrons flew her all over the world to get her "read" on things. Well-known actors sent her scripts to see which films felt like hits. Socialites queried her on the most astrologically auspicious dates to undergo plastic surgery. She had just spent several days with a real estate developer client, visiting several parcels of Hawaiian land to determine which lots had the best "psychic flow" and which were contaminated by "unharmonious resonance." The developer had put her and Wayne up in a five star hotel with all expenses paid, and except for one episode with the teriyaki salmon in the hotel restaurant (The chef... she had declared in a pinched, quavering half-whisper. The chef who touched this fish... a man with black hair... I'm getting an A... a very strong A... he is... holding a knife... he is thinking about killing his lover...), they'd had a relaxing and wonderful time.

"I don't like the rear cabin," Janine said, having walked the entire length of the plane. "It's cold. Very negative."

"How about row twelve?" Wayne asked quietly, shifting her carry-on bag to his other shoulder. "You usually like twelve."

She drifted back up the aisle to row twelve, hands out like a blind woman. She was feeling very strange tonight, uneasy and unsure about everything. Sometimes, for no reason she could fathom, she felt blocked somehow, in the same way that having a stuffy nose blocks your sense of smell. This night was one of those times and it made her feel anxious and defenseless. Wayne was right, bless his heart. Twelves were almost always safe. So why couldn't she get a good read on this row? She put her hand flat against the stiff blue and yellow cushion and got a very hazy flash of the last person who had occupied this seat, a bored child, a video game that was not working and the feel of the seat back against the toes of red sneakers. Nothing bad. Sighing dramatically, she lowered herself into the window seat and motioned for Wayne to sit beside her.

That's when it hit. A psychic thermonuclear detonation inside her skull that rocked her head back and started a hot gush of blood from her nose. Suddenly, there were snakes everywhere.

Snakes squirming over every seat, dangling from the ceiling and twining up around her legs, hissing maliciously, gaping mouths displaying hooked and wicked fangs that dribbled killing poison. Every person on the plane turned at the sound of her strangled cry and she saw that they were all walking corpses, bloated and black, faces contorted and swollen until they were barely human.

An older female flight attendant hustled down the aisle towards her. "Ma'am," she said. "Is there something wrong?"

The flight attendant's face was a nightmare rictus of pain, features twisted and distorted by a horrible and painful death. Her hair was swarming with furious black-banded rattlesnakes that coiled and snapped all around her face. She had been transformed into a hideous Medusa-like monster who, rather than turning others to stone, had been turned to stone herself, paralyzed by deadly venom.

Janine threw herself with a whimper against the bulkhead, scrambling backwards in a futile attempt to escape this nightmare vision. Then she heard Wayne's voice softly calling her name, felt his warm, familiar hands on her arms, and just like that, the vision was gone. The flight attendant bending over her seat with a concerned expression was totally normal, the curious people around her all alive and well and looking at her the way people had always looked at her, ever since she was a little girl. Like she was a freak. A nut job. Crazy.

"Wayne," she said, breathless, clutching weakly at her husband's shirt. "Get me off this plane."

"I'm sorry, ma'am," the flight attendant said. "But the ground crew has already retracted the jetway. There's really nothing to be worried about. Everything is just fine. I know we are all tired and stressed out by the delays, and we all just want to get this flight off the ground. The sooner that happens, the sooner we will be in Los Angeles."

"You have to stop this flight!" Janine cried. "There's danger. Danger!"

"Please," the flight attendant said. "You are upsetting the other passengers. I can assure you…"

"You're all going to die!" Janine said. "Don't you see? You have to stop this flight. YOU HAVE TO STOP THIS FLIGHT!"

A male flight attendant appeared beside the woman. "Ma'am," the man said. "You really need to calm down."

"You're all dead!" Janine screamed. "All DEAD!"

"Claire!" the female flight attendant called. "Tell Sam to radio the ground crew and have them reconnect the jetway. We've got a screamer."

"All right now," the male flight attendant said. "Ma'am, will you just listen to me for a second? We're going to get you off the plane, but it will take a few minutes, so in the meantime please try and remain calm."

"Wayne!" Janine called. "Wayne!"

"I'm here, honey," Wayne said, wrapping his arms around her. "We're going to get off, okay?"

"Okay," Janine said softly like a child, burying her face against Wayne's narrow chest, hiding from the eyes all around her.

What could her hellish vision possibly mean? Her visions were often heavily symbolic and interpreting them was always a tricky business. Snakes? What was the meaning of all those snakes? Snakes were considered evil in Christian mythology, symbols of the Devil, but many older religions viewed them as guardians of wisdom. She'd had visions of snakes in the past that were not always negative, but the snakes in this vision were obviously malicious, representing some terrible evil about to be unleashed. What could they be trying to show her? What did they symbolize? Some kind of terrorism? A devious and evil plot? Something to do with poison?

In her heart, she knew it made no difference. Even if she was somehow able to decode her vision and decipher the hidden meaning, no one would listen to her. They never did. What ever horrible fate awaited South Pacific Air Flight 121, it would all make sense later when she saw the reports of the disaster on the news. She had long ago given up on trying to save everyone. People died every day all across the globe and one strange lady knowing about it before it happened meant nothing in the bigger scheme of things. Death was a natural part of life and trying to stop it was like trying to stop rain or night or the tides. She knew that it was all she could do to try to stay sane and protect herself and the handful of people close to her. These people around her were already dead. There was nothing more she could do for them. So she stopped screaming, hung on to Wayne and waited for security to come and escort her off the plane. It wasn't the first time and it probably wouldn't be the last.

When the big burly security officers arrived to take her away, she walked between the two armed men without looking left or right, as if she was walking down the aisle of an overcrowded animal shelter, surrounded by cage after cage of unwanted pit bulls scheduled for euthanasia. She did not want to look into the eyes of the damned. She just wanted to get out.

ELEVEN

Takeoff had been a bone rattling, vertigo-inducing thrill ride, but now that they were up in the night sky, the big plane had smoothed out and you could barely feel it moving at all. Sean tried to peer out his little round window, but he couldn't see anything but blackness and the winking light on the tip of the plane's wing. His beloved island was gone, swallowed up by the dark night. He felt a wash of fierce homesickness, underscored by a terrible uncertainty as the plane headed for distant Los Angeles, flying into Sean's future.

"Hey, what do you know?" Flynn said, thumbing through the free in-flight magazine. "Here's an article on Bali."

Sean tried to scratch under the Kevlar vest and looked across the aisle at the open magazine in Flynn's lap. There was a photo of a beautiful woman in a complex golden headdress.

"Cool," Sean said. "I'll read it when you're finished."

"When were you planning to go?" Flynn asked. "To Bali, I mean."

Sean rubbed the back of his head and shrugged. "Next February," he said. "It would have been my first real trip. I've never really been much of anywhere before."

"Bali is really amazing," Flynn said. "I was there just after the Kuta Beach bombing in oh-two and I wound up staying for three weeks. Rented a motorbike. It was something else."

"Really?" Sean said. "You don't really strike me as a surfer. No disrespect..."

"Is that all you think about?" Flynn asked. "Surfing?" He made a small disgusted sound. "There is way more to Bali than surfing, you know. There are gorgeous temples and gamelan music and ikat textiles. It's a fascinating culture and the artwork is incredible, really breathtaking. Delicious, spicy food and some of the most beautiful women in the world. "

"Did you...?" Sean looked away. "I mean, when you were there... in Kuta Beach."

"Did I meet Jasper Jones?" Flynn asked.

Sean shrugged like it didn't really matter.

Flynn shook his head. "No," he said. "I saw him out there on the waves, doing his thing, but we were never properly introduced."

"Oh," Sean said quietly.

Flynn folded the magazine closed. "Kid," he said. "Don't take this the wrong way, but you know, you're really building this shit up way too much in your head."

Sean frowned at the big man but said nothing.

"Let me tell you something," Flynn said. "I never knew my father growing up either. He was a musician, tenor sax. Broke my mama's heart. She would never even let me say his name."

Sean listened with his whole body while trying desperately to pretend that he wasn't.

"I was curious," Flynn continued. "I had heard his records and I was secretly dying to meet him. I imagined that he was loaded and that I would go live with him in glamorous Hollywood and escape my boring broke-ass life at home on the wrong side of Atlanta. When I joined the Bureau, I looked him up. His real name was Eugene Banks and I found him living in Miami, playing a regular gig at one of those old art deco hotels. I thought about it and worried about it and built it up to this towering, earth-shattering importance in my head. I had his address and phone number for a year before I got up the nerve to try and contact him."

"So what did you do?" Sean asked. "Did you call him?"

Flynn shook his head. "I went to the gig at the hotel," he said. "Waited through four sets and finally just went over and introduced myself."

Sean was breathless, waiting to hear what happened next.

"It was awkward, but we both got through it all right I suppose," Flynn said. "He thought it was hilarious that I had become a fed and asked me if I was gonna bust him for refer. I bought him a drink and we sat and talked for about an hour. And you know what I discovered in the end?"

"What?" Sean asked.

"I found out that he was just a regular guy," Flynn said. "Not a monster or a hero, but just an ordinary joe like anybody else."

Sean nodded, thoughtful.

"We stayed in touch, but we never really got close," Flynn said. "And when he died of a stroke three years later, I inherited his saxophone, a red '59 caddy and one hundred and thirteen dollars. I never told my mama about having met him, but I gave her the car. Told her it had been repossessed in one of our cases and that I bought it cheap. She liked being able to drive to church on Sundays in style. Figured she deserved something for her broken heart." Flynn looked out his dark little window. "I still have that old saxophone. Never have been able to get the hang of the damn thing, but I just don't have the heart to get rid of it. I guess I must've taken after my mother's side of the family, musically speaking."

Sean studied the big man's flat profile and dark, distant eyes, but could not discern what might be going on behind them.

"Anyway," Flynn continued, "my point is that you can build a thing like that up too much in your mind."

"Right," Sean said. "I know. It's just... well..." He paused. "Did you... ask him why he left?"

"Nah. No point really. Men and women split up every day, hell I know that better than most. It's just the way of this bad old world."

"Do *you* have any kids?" Sean asked.

"No," Flynn replied. "That's part of the reason why I think women don't want to stay with me. Seems like they all want kids, and me, I don't want to have a kid I can't be there for. I just don't want to put someone else through that. I'm never home anyway and what if I got tagged on the job or something? I couldn't have a kid of mine growing up without a father. I keep thinking maybe when I settle down and stop doing shit like this, but then, you know, the years just keep on passing by..." He paused and chucked softly. "I can't believe I'm telling you all this shit. You oughta get a job as a psychiatrist."

Sean thought suddenly of the dead man's son Eric, and felt a cold wave of sadness.

"What?" Flynn asked.

"Do you know how old Daniel Hayes's son Eric is?" Sean asked.

Flynn's brows knitted. "Five."

"Did he have any other kids?" Sean asked.

Flynn shook his head. "Why?"

"When I saw Kim kill Daniel Hayes," Sean said, "I heard him tell the guy that his son was gonna grow up without a father." He paused, chewing his lip. "That's part of what made me decide to testify. Not because that would change the fact that the kid will never have his dad back. Just because I wanted Kim to be punished for that. Not just what he did to Hayes, but what he did to his family. You know what I mean?"

Flynn nodded that he did. Neither of them said a word for several long minutes. Eventually Flynn unfolded the magazine and held it out to Sean.

"You want to read this article about Bali?" Flynn asked.

"Yeah," Sean said, taking the magazine. "Thanks."

Flynn got up, nodded to Sanders and headed toward the stairs. Pausing at the top, he looked back over his shoulder and saw Sean, bent studiously over the magazine like it was a school textbook. Somehow that affable and goofy young surfer had really managed to get under Flynn's skin. He was a good kid, and it was starting to feel like more than just a job to make sure that he was safe.

Flynn moved silently down the spiral stairs and paused, glancing both ways down the length of the cabin before heading down the aisle towards the forward galley. He studied each passenger in turn, making a note of the very fit, muscular Chinese man who appeared to be napping with his thick arms crossed on his chest. He was clearly someone to watch. Flynn knew he could get in trouble for ethnic profiling, but when dealing with Triads, it was kind of hard not to distrust anyone Chinese, especially someone as obviously bad-ass as this guy. Better to keep an eye on him, just to be on the safe side. Sanders had done the background checks on the passenger list, so he must have thought the guy was okay, but Flynn still made a mental note to ask Sanders about the guy later.

He had been concentrating so hard on the sleeping Chinese man that he didn't notice the pretty brunette stewardess pushing a bulky service cart down the aisle until he was only a half a step from bumping into her.

"Pardon me," he said quietly.

"Can I help you with something?" the woman asked, hazel eyes a little chilly.

"Just stretching my legs," he said.

"Big plane," the woman replied. "Plenty of places to do it."

"Plenty of other places, you mean," Flynn said, narrowing his eyes. When she did not reply, he continued. "Hey look, did I do something wrong here?"

"Technically, no. But maybe next time, you people could give us a little heads up before you commandeer our plane."

"You *people*? Listen, I'm just a little cog in the wheels of justice, ma'am. Just doing my job."

"Just following orders, eh?" she asked with an arched eyebrow.

"That's about the size of it," Flynn replied.

"Are you trying to say that it wasn't up to you to take this plane in particular?" she asked. "That you were forced to do so by your evil, Machiavellian superiors."

"At ease, counselor," Flynn said, shaking his head. "You're right, I admit it. I did pick this plane."

She pressed her lips together to suppress a laugh and failed.

He smiled and extended his hand. "On behalf of the Federal Bureau of Investigation, allow me to offer you an official apology."

He could see her tense posture loosen up, a smile melting her icy gaze. "You called me counselor," she said. "How did you know I plan to go to law school?"

"I can tell by your feet," he replied.

She looked down at her plain blue heels and frowned, then slowly looked back up and smiled again. "You are completely full of it," she told him. "You did a profile on each of us, didn't you?"

Flynn put his arms up in mock surrender. "Busted."

"Look," she said, conciliatory. "You want a soda or some pretzels or something?"

He stepped into an empty row of seats and motioned for her to push the cart past him.

"That's all right," he said. "I can get it myself. Just pretend I'm not even here."

He headed down the aisle to the galley and poured himself a cup of coffee. She did not pretend he was not there. He could feel her unflinching gaze as he hunted up a small packet of creamer and dumped it into his cup, and he had no idea how to feel about that. She was really quite beautiful. Lean and feline and full of secrets. She was the last thing he needed.

TWELVE

In the pressurized cargo hold, there was a tiny sound. A muffled beep and an electronic click. A human would not have heard it, but Mr Wong the Siamese cat heard it loud and clear. Mr Wong could not see the altimeter hidden deep inside the pallet of orchids. He could not see the glowing green numerals patiently counting the feet as the plane rose higher and higher into the night sky, waiting for the magic number, the number that would trigger the mechanism to open the boxes. Even if the cat could see the device, he would not know what it meant. But he did know what was inside those boxes. To Mr Wong's sensitive nose, the musty, metallic and reptilian odor could not be disguised by the fragrant perfume of the orchids. It was a bad smell, a terrible and dangerous smell that none of the clueless humans who had loaded him onto the plane seemed to notice. Mr Wong had pushed himself far back into the far end of his crate, nervously grooming himself and never taking his sharp eyes off the dangerous boxes. But when he heard that sound, he stood, hair bristling and eyes wide in the darkness.

There was another sound of spring mechanisms releasing the metal bands that held the pallet together, and hydraulic pistons slamming open the lids of a dozen boxes. Delicate orchids and their carefully wrapped roots tumbled and scattered everywhere and for a moment, there was nothing but the soporific drone of engines.

Then, a new sound: the whisper of scaled bellies sliding over the ruptured boxes.

Mr Wong yowled in terror and distress, desperately clawing at the walls of the crate. Although Mr Wong had never seen a snake, he knew instinctively that the sleek green head, bright onyx eyes and delicate forked tongue that slid between the bars of his crate door belonged to something deadly. He hissed and the creature hissed back, muscular body coiling to strike. Mr Wong slashed at this terrible new thing, claws ripping into the cool, smooth scales and the powerful muscle beneath. The thing struck at Mr Wong and he leapt aside, sinking his teeth into the muscle behind the thing's narrow head, fighting silently for his life.

Unaware of the fatal drama inside the cat carrier, dozens of other, larger snakes scattered in all directions throughout the hold. Slender snouts poked into air ducts and found their way through grates and into crawl spaces. They had only one thing on their simple, reptilian minds: to find warm things and kill them.

Tiffany tried to flirt with the handsome, burly blond FBI guy, but got nothing except ice. He barely looked up from his Chinese novel long enough to tell her he did not want anything to drink. Stung, she moved down the aisle to easier prey.

The teenage kid in the bulletproof vest was cute in a boyish, surfer dude kind of way. Probably not even legal yet, but that didn't stop her. Younger boys could be so much fun. They were so eager. So hungry.

"Hi there," she said with a lascivious smile. "See anything you want?"

"Um…" the kid said, blushing, shy eyes stealing surreptitious glances at her legs and ass. "A Coke?"

"You got it," she said, feeling much better now that someone had noticed her and thought she was hot.

She made sure to stay bent over for a little longer than necessary while searching through the cans of soda to find a Coca-Cola. When she could no longer realistically avoid finding one, she grabbed the can and held it against her chest so that the cold metal made her braless nipples stand out beneath her blouse.

"Here you go," she said, leaning over him to set the can down on his tray table, and following it up with a glass of ice cubes and a package of honey-roasted almonds. "Anything else I can give you?"

He shook his head, a shy smile creeping across his lips.

"Can I ask you something?" Tiffany asked, pushed the cart forward and sat down on the armrest of the empty seat opposite the kid.

"Sure," he replied, popping the top on the can.

"What did you do?" she asked. "I mean, a nice, clean-cut guy like you; you don't look like an international criminal mastermind who needs two FBI agents to keep you under control. No offense."

"Oh," the kid said. "That's okay. I mean..." He paused and laughed, a little self-conscious. "I'm not a criminal. I'm a witness."

"Really," Tiffany said, leaning forward, fascinated.

The kid attempted to pour the Coke into the glass, but he poured too fast and the soda foamed up, running over the edge. "Shoot," he said, mopping up the spill with a crumpled napkin.

"Here, honey," Tiffany said, grabbing a rag from the cart. "Let me get that." She smoothly wiped the tray table and then swapped the wet rag for a clean paper towel and reached down to blot the drops of Coke on his shorts.

"Hey, whoa," he said as her hand brushed lightly over his crotch. "That's okay, I got it." He took the paper towel from her and wiped himself off, unable to meet her gaze and blushing to a shade somewhere between fuchsia and magenta.

"So," she said, backing down a bit. "What sort of crime did you witness?"

"I'm not really supposed to talk about it," the kid said, turning back to peer at the blond FBI agent behind him. It was clear that he wanted very much to talk about it. "But have you ever heard of Eddie Kim?"

"Who hasn't?" she replied. "I saw him on one of those crime shows once. You know, the ones with the hokey reenactments. They say he tortured this guy who was a witness against him and you know what he did? He gouged out the guy's eyes and then fed him to these pigs, just like in that Hannibal movie. Totally gruesome."

The kid frowned and went pale, taking a sip of his Coke. "Yeah," he said quietly. "He doesn't mess around, that guy."

"So what are you?" Tiffany asked.

"I'm a witness for the prosecution," he replied.

"You're testifying against Eddie Kim?" she asked, incredulous. "That takes a lot of balls."

This kid, this sweet-faced surfer dude with the boyish smile was actually going to testify against one of the most ruthless, sadistic gangsters of all time? Tiffany was totally blown away. The amount of courage it took to do something like that was astounding. She could not help but look at the kid in a whole new light.

"Yup," the kid said, wiping his mouth anxiously on the back of his hand.

"Wow," she said, placing her hand on his other wrist where it rested on the arm rest. "That is so *hot*!"

"Uh… thanks."

"What's your name anyway, tough guy?" she asked.

"It's Sean," the kid said.

"I'm Tiffany," she said. "If you need anything during the flight, you just let me know, okay?"

"Sean," the cranky blond agent said over the back of the kid's chair. "Enough chit chat. Miss?" He gave Tiffany a stern look. "That will be all."

Tiffany pouted prettily and when the cranky guy went back to his book, she stuck her tongue out at him. Sean laughed silently.

"See you later," she said. "Sean."

"Okay," Sean said after her as she pushed the cart away down the aisle.

She could feel his eyes on her ass as she walked away, and she smiled to herself.

Troy watched the girl with the chihuahua sashay over to join Three Gs and arched an eyebrow at Leroy. This pricey blonde number was nothing like his boss's usual type. Three Gs usually tended to go for shy, bookish girls who got dragged to the show by their more outgoing friends. He would cut through all the hoochie mamas, strippers and groupies and pick some plump, mousy little thing with glasses who could never believe her good fortune. But at least the blonde looked clean. That was always of utmost importance to Three Gs. In fact, Troy knew that part of his boss's penchant for shy, quiet girls stemmed from his fear of germy girls who looked too "experienced." These were disqualified instantly as possible disease vectors. Troy wondered what was going to happen when Three Gs noticed the chihuahua in that girl's purse.

"At the end of the day," Three Gs said to the spellbound blonde, "the music business is still a business."

Someone sneezed a few rows in front of them, and Troy could see his boss's face go hard and stiff, blowing all the air out of his lungs as he waited for the germs from the sneeze to "pass by."

"As I was saying," Three Gs continued. "I'm all about taking the music and the business to the next level. 'Cause that's when evolution becomes revolution."

He paused. Troy, who had been officially working for Three Gs for seven years and had known him since they were kids, could see that the rhyming words had set off an inexplicable resonance inside Three Gs's head that would be difficult for his boss to shake.

"Evolution," he repeated. "Becomes revolution."

The blonde nodded cluelessly, blue eyes wide.

"Evolution, revolution," Three Gs said. "Troy, write that down."

Leroy, who was new and just getting used to Three Gs and his quirks, grabbed a pen and pad from an inner pocket. "Got it, boss."

"See, I have to write down my ideas," Three Gs was telling the blonde. "A certain phrase, it's like poetry. Evolution becomes revolution. Leroy, did you get that?"

"I got it, G," Leroy said.

"Just like poetry," the blonde said, still nodding.

Leroy nudged Troy and handed him the piece of paper. It read "Bullshit!"

Troy smiled ruefully. When Leroy looked away, Troy took the pen, crossing out the word "Bullshit" and writing "Evolution becomes Revolution." He slipped the note into the pocket of his day planner that held all the other rhymes and phrases that Three Gs would have to review and say out loud again at the end of the day. If Troy failed to write even one down, the ensuing panic attack would be a nightmare for everyone. Leroy was good people, capable, loyal and totally solid, but he was new and did not understand how fragile Three Gs really was. Leroy probably thought Three Gs was just talking shit, trying to mack on the hot blonde. He had no idea how critical phrases like these were for his boss. Only when the rhyming words were safely written down and tucked into Troy's day planner would Three Gs be free to stop repeating them.

A woman Troy once dated had been previously involved with an alcoholic and claimed that Troy was "enabling" G by covering for him all the time, the way she had by calling in sick for her drunk boyfriend and fixing all his fuck-ups so he didn't get fired or evicted. She seemed to be saying that G would be better off if he admitted his problem and dealt with it, instead of hiding it all the time. Of course, she and her Adult Children of Alcoholics rhetoric were long gone and Troy was still making lists of rhyming words and telling everyone that G was fine, that he just needed a minute and he'd be ready to go on stage.

Troy tuned out Three Gs's conversation with the blonde and looked out the window at a night sky full of dark nothing. He just couldn't seem to shake this strange uneasy feeling in his gut. The delays, getting downgraded, all the hassles were irritating, sure, but they did not explain this sourceless, subsonic feeling of distress that seemed to resonate up through his bones. There was nothing wrong. Everything was just fine. So why did he feel so antsy? He was wondering if his boss's anxiety was finally starting to rub off on him, when Leroy turned to him with a quizzical look on his chubby face.

"What?" Troy asked.

"What's up with you?" Leroy asked. "You seem all... I don't know."

"It's nothing, man," Troy replied. "I'm just nervous that your mama is gonna find out I'm back in town. I tried to tell her it was just a one time thing, but the bitch keeps calling and calling."

"Uh huh," Leroy said. "So that's how you want to play it?"

"I hate for you to hear it like this," Troy said, "but better you hear from me than see the video on www dot fat ugly bitches gone wild dot com."

"Yeah?" Leroy said, holding down a grin. "I hear your mama's so fat, the body snatchers had to call for back up."

"Well, your mama's so fat," Troy replied, "when I got done fucking her, I rolled over and over again and I was still on top of the bitch."

"Your mama's so stupid," Leroy countered, "she got fired from a blow job."

"I tried to hire your mama," Troy said. "But I got picketed by People for the Ethical Treatment of

Animals, talkin' 'bout making elephants do tricks is cruel."

Leroy snickered and covered his mouth. "Your mama's so ugly, she makes blind kids cry."

"Your mama's so ugly, she has to get the baby drunk to breast feed him."

"Your mama's so stank, even dogs won't sniff her ass."

"Your mama's so nasty, I wouldn't let her sniff my dog's ass."

"Enough already," Three Gs said. "I'm trying to have a civilized conversation over here, if y'all don't mind."

"Sorry, boss," Troy said, smirking.

Chen Leong was twenty-five, born in Hong Kong and raised in Monterey Park, California from the age of nine. He had been a geeky kid, a little chubby with thick glasses and a love of American science fiction. He spoke no English, but he knew the names of every *Star Trek* and *Babylon Five* character and his new American classmates in his San Gabriel Valley school found this as good a reason as any to pick on him and beat him up every single day. A year later, sick of having his lunch stepped on and his library books tossed in the mud, he decided to study martial arts. He began with kung fu and then moved on to judo, jujitsu and eventually fell in love with the violent sport of Thai kickboxing. The baby fat came off and puberty kicked in and he went from a shy, porky outcast to a handsome, roguish loner. He gave up the coke bottle glasses for contact lenses and started lifting weights. His tongue-tied shyness was suddenly perceived as an aloof sort of cool that seemed mysterious and bad-ass. If he said nothing, girls fell all over themselves to get to know him. He competed in kickboxing tournaments, first small local ones but eventually moving up to national and international titles. He had been offered a few low-budget movie roles and he liked to tell his friends he turned them down because the scripts were terrible. For the most part, they were, but the real reason he turned down the movie roles was because he suffered from horrible stage fright. He would take an elbow to the top of the head before he would take the microphone and speak to the audience after a victory. Several of his fights had been televised, and he barely noticed the cameras when he was lost in the dynamics of fighting to win, but the idea of having to actually speak lines in front of a camera made him feel sick to his stomach. His Chinese accent was nearly gone, but he was convinced that it was still there, thick and ugly and making him trip over his words. He was a great fighter but he knew he would never be any good as an actor.

Chen leaned forward in his seat and removed his long-sleeved outer shirt, revealing a tight tank top and thick, muscular arms crawling with tattoos. It seemed hotter than normal on the plane and he felt irritable and stifled. He couldn't wait to get back home to Los Angeles. He missed his family and his dog, an ugly but sweet one-eyed pit-bull that had been beaten and left for dead as a puppy. Chen had found him in the alley behind his house.

This trip to Hawaii had been bad in many ways, and he just wanted to be home.

"In Hawaii for vacation?" the fey male flight attendant asked, eyeing Chen's tattoos, or more likely his build.

"Kickboxing tournament," Chen replied.

"Ohmigod!" the guy replied, all breathy and overreacting. "You're a kick boxer? That's so totally rad. I LOVE muy thai! I've been taking muy thai for six months now. It's an awesome workout! I even got my girlfriend to start taking it too. She doesn't live in the best neighborhood, you know, and I can't always be around to protect her."

Chen wished he had pretended not to speak English. If this guy really had a "girlfriend" and he was all she had to protect her, she'd *better* be taking muy thai lessons. Then the guy started talking about the film *Ong-Bak*. If he mentioned *Beautiful Boxer*, Chen was going to have to punch him in the throat.

"Right," Chen said, looking away and trying not to encourage him.

"I used to box back in college," the guy said. "But muy thai is just so much more dynamic and exciting, don't you think?"

Chen kept his gaze on the black nothingness outside his window, burning with embarrassment. How much longer was this conversation going to continue? Chen had not had a good tournament. He'd come in third place and was feeling depressed and exhausted. He had made several mistakes during critical rounds, mistakes he would never normally make. His own girlfriend Cynthia had sworn that she would be there for the tournament, but at the last minute she had called and told him that she could not make it. Something had come up, she said. He loved her with a kind of painful determination that felt like getting in the ring and fighting in spite of an injury, but it was becoming clearer every day that she was not faithful. She was so gorgeous and perfect, a beautiful ABC girl from a good family that his parents loved and pressured him to marry every day, but there'd been something hidden and deceitful about her from the start. He loved her, but he knew in his heart that he was already losing her.

The fey guy finally seemed to notice that Chen was ignoring him and went away. Chen crossed his arms back over his chest and leaned his head back, closing his eyes. He was beginning to fear that he might have torn a rotator cuff in the last round of his last fight. His left shoulder felt like someone was digging a hot knife into the muscle just above the shoulder blade, but it still didn't hurt as much as thinking about Cynthia, about the feel of her supple skin against his in the dark, about her innocent eyes and her sweet, lying mouth. He knew that he would spend the whole flight planning how he would tell her off, how he would confront her and make her admit that she was a deceitful bitch and apologize to him for not being there when he needed her, but when he got home, she would show up on his doorstep with a tight dress and a big smile. She would throw her arms around him and smell so clean and good and he would say nothing, like always.

Chen wished he had thought to ask for a drink, but he did not want to deal with another gushing conversation with the Beautiful Boxer so he just concentrated on his breathing and tried to think of nothing.

THIRTEEN

When guitarist Kelly Mack met street skate-boarding champ Kyle "Chocodile" Cho, it was lust at first sight. Kelly was a thin, leggy girl with big, kohl-ringed brown eyes mostly hidden by a ragged mop of bleached rocker-chick hair that tumbled down over her face. The most expressive thing about her was her hands, which were long and sensitive with agile, spindly fingers like the busy legs of tarantulas. When she spoke, they moved eloquently through the air, always betraying the emotions she struggled to hide beneath her curtain of hair. Her band, Devil Girls From Mars, had a modest cult hit with their notorious cover of Love Gun, the live performance of which involved the lead singer Nyah wearing a strap-on dildo. The local indie radio station starting playing the hell out of it, along with several other tunes from their album *Harder Than You*. Next thing they knew, they had gotten their first big break playing the second stage on the Concrete Fetish Audio X tour, alongside a lineup of extreme sports contests and skateboarding demos.

Kelly had been aware of the fact that there was a sport that involved zipping around in concrete pools and flying off railings on skateboards, but she had never really given it much thought. She had never been athletic and had spent most of her angst-filled teen years locked up alone in her room, smoking pot and struggling to learn Eddie van Halen's "Cathedral" until her fingers bled. Middle child of a musical family, she had always been painfully introverted and shy, but the trial by fire of live gigs in front of often hostile audiences slowly made her braver. Brash, wild Nyah was her best friend and role model, supremely confident, fearless and always encouraging Kelly to take risks, to grab life by the balls and take no prisoners. Kelly brooded endlessly over every less-than-stellar review, whereas Nyah just assumed that the reviewer was wrong, clearly too stupid to comprehend her genius. Kelly had her heart broken again and again while Nyah took on groupies of both sexes two and three at a time and left them scattered like condom wrappers on a hotel room floor.

"Honestly, Kel," Nyah had said when they landed in Hawaii, the first stop on the Audio X tour. "We are one of only two female acts in a lineup of thirty-five bands. That's not even including the skater boys. If you don't get laid on this tour, I'm gonna have to stage some kind of intervention."

After their first wildly successful set in Honolulu, Kelly had been feeling so good about herself that she'd allowed Nyah to drag her over to the curiously constructed ramps and bowls where the skaters were doing their thing. It was really incredible to watch them fly, twist and jump, but there was one guy in particular who caught Kelly's eye.

He was devastatingly handsome, his face an exotic mash-up of Asian and black features beneath a spiky crown of black and blond dreadlocks. His body was lean and powerful, but with an amazingly loose, lanky stance that made it seem as if flying through the air forty feet above merciless concrete was totally natural; no big deal.

"If you don't go talk to him this instant," Nyah warned, "I'm going to be forced to fuck you myself."

"All right, all right," Kelly said, pushing Nyah away. "I'm going."

She had no idea what she was going to say to him, but she couldn't chicken out in front of Nyah, so she walked over to the Gatorade booth where he was standing.

"Hey," she said.

He looked up at her and she saw that he had eyes that were the oddest shade of clear, golden amber, like sunlight through a beer bottle. Animal eyes. She wondered if they were contacts of some kind, and promptly forgot whatever clever thing she had thought up to say.

"Hey," he said back. "I saw your band. Devil Girls from Mars, right? You guys rock."

She knew she had to be blushing furiously, but she tried to smile. "Thanks. You're not half bad yourself."

He smiled back and the smile was a bullet in the heart. She was hopelessly smitten.

"Name's Kyle," he said. "But the guys call me Chocodile."

"Chocodile?" she repeated like a brainless parrot.

"Yeah," Kyle said. "It's goofy, I know. How about you?"

"Kelly," she said. "Kelly Mack."

"Mack?" Kyle said. "You aren't by any chance related to old school punk legend Dickie Mack, the guitarist for the Mama's Boys and Pottymouth?"

Kelly nodded, blushing even more. "He's my dad."

"Holy crap!" Kyle said. "In that case, let me buy you a drink."

He handed her a cup of neon-blue Gatorade and then pulled a hip flask from the pocket of his cargo shorts and dumped a generous knock of something alcoholic into the plastic cup.

That's how it began. Six hours later, they were back in her hotel room, tearing each other's clothes off. Kelly was in total awe that a gorgeous specimen like Kyle would have any interest in a skinny, introverted weirdo like her, but for some reason, he could not seem to get enough of her. He wanted to listen to her album while they did it, and at first it made her feel weird and self-conscious, but she soon lost herself in him and the sheer gluttony of feasting on his flawless body. When they finally took a breather, he told her that he had never done it with a rock star before and she punched him in the arm, laughing.

They spent almost every waking minute of the rest of the Hawaiian dates together. The only time they were apart was when Kelly was on stage or Kyle was flying through some death-defying demonstration of eye-popping skate tricks. He seemed to love watching her play as much as she loved watching him skate. They had almost everything in common, loved all the same bands, all the same movies, all the same books. Even though he was from South Central LA, son of a Korean grocer and an African American postal clerk, and she'd grown up in Hollywood with her chaotic rock 'n roll family, they felt as if they had known each other all their lives.

On the last day of the tour, after Devil Girls' last show, Kelly and Kyle had made the impulsive decision to go AWOL. Their subsequent wild drunken tumble across the islands had finally ended with them declaring their eternal love for one another while having frantic sex in the tiny bathroom of a tattoo shop in Honolulu, having just had each other's names tattooed on their respective asses. When they finally bothered to look at the time, they found that they had both missed their flights back to Los Angeles. Nyah had left Kelly about forty messages on her cell and told her that she was happy that Kelly was finally getting some, but that Nyah was going to pawn Kelly's battered but beloved sunburst '68 Stratocaster that had belonged to her late grandfather if Kelly did not show up in time for the gig in Los Angeles. Kelly had been so smitten with Kyle that she had actually forgotten her guitar back at the hotel along with all her other things. Luckily for her, Nyah had packed everything up and shipped it back along with all the other equipment, but even then, Kelly found that she could not be too upset about it. Still giddy and drunk on tequila and lust, they had a huge greasy meal in the airport McDonalds and then fell asleep in each other's arms on the uncomfortable seats, waiting for the next available flight.

Now they were sore and hung over and semi-delirious, but finally on a flight back to Los Angeles. They were still unable to keep their hands off each other, clinging to each other in their seats and giggling.

"I feel like I've been run over three times," Kyle told Kelly, leaning his face against her shoulder.

"I have just the cure for you," she said, pulling a tampon out of her purse and grinning wickedly.

Kyle frowned at the feminine hygiene product. "Baby, you're scaring me a little."

She laughed and peered up at him through the tangled cascade of her ratty bleached blonde hair, peeling the paper wrapper off the cardboard tube. She slid the tube back just enough to reveal the joint hidden inside.

"I need to see a man about a horse," she said. "What do you say, Mr Ed?"

"Is that all I am to you?" Kyle asked, mock hurt.

Kelly nodded. "Yup. Pretty much."

"Oh," he replied. "Okay then."

She giggled and slipped the tampon back in her purse. "Meet me in the head in three minutes. I'll leave the door unlocked."

He nodded and pulled her close, kissing her. She kissed him back for a few molten seconds, then forced herself to pull away.

"Three minutes," she said, showing him three of her long, calloused fingers.

"Longest three minutes of my life," he replied, glancing down at his high-tech watch.

She blew him a kiss and turned down the aisle. It was really unbelievable how fast this was happening. She had never felt this kind of steamroller lust, this mad, fast-forward intimacy with someone she'd just met, and she still could not bring herself to believe he was real. He was far and away the single best-looking guy who had ever even spoken to her, and yet somehow he seemed to think she was fabulous. She couldn't help but turn it over and over in her mind, trying to find flaws. Where was the catch? There had to be one, right? Nothing could possibly be this good.

Well, there was really no point in thinking about that now. She needed to be like Nyah, to worry only about the here and now, and never mind tomorrow. The fact that her left ass cheek was still sore from the probably ill-advised tattoo was a niggling reminder that maybe being crazy and impulsive like this was not such a good idea, but what the hell. It was only four short letters, easily covered at some future date if she ever came to regret it. At least she had come to her senses at the last minute and decided against having "Chocodile" instead. She had just turned twenty-one years old. If she was gonna do crazy shit like this, she'd better do it now, before life and age and responsibility caught up with her.

She let herself into the unoccupied toilet at the rear of the cabin and began industriously prying apart the smoke detector. She almost had it completely disabled when Kyle pushed the door open, grinning.

"There's a twenty-two hundred dollar fine for that, young lady," he said. "I am afraid you are going to have to be punished."

"Oh yeah?" she said, pulling her black tank top up over her head and exposing her sheer leopard-print bra. She parked the joint in the corner of her mouth and lit up. "Do your worst!"

He removed his own shirt, revealing the wash-board abs and lean, ripped physique that had first caught her eye.

"Goddamn!" she said, whistling appreciatively. "Come here."

She took a deep hit off the joint and then grabbed Kyle by the back of his neck and exhaled into his mouth. Somewhere in the warm spiciness of the smoke, her breath became a kiss, tongue sliding and twining against his as everything else melted away. He was unhooking her bra, mouth on her nipples, and she was fighting with his belt, struggling to free him from the prison of his boxer shorts. The joint had tumbled to the floor, forgotten and still smoldering as Kelly tipped her head back, eyes closed and lost in a swirl of delicious smoky desire.

At first, Kelly thought that Kyle had slapped her face. Not hard, just a quick smack, and it felt like his hand had been wet, because her cheek seemed wet now. But he had one hand on her breast and one on the small of her back when she opened her eyes to a stoned squint. There was something dark hanging from the ceiling inches from her face. Was it a bundle of wires or a hose of some sort that had come loose?

That was when she saw the tongue.

A thin, delicate black tongue with a deep, unmistakable fork, flickering out to taste the marijuana-scented breath drifting from her open mouth. With excruciating slowness, her sluggish mind put the forked tongue together with the round, unblinking yellow eye, the sleek, scaly dark brown body. Then it clicked.

It was a snake.

Not just a snake, but an enormous snake. Christ, there were at least five coiling feet dangling from the ceiling, and who knew how much more inside the vent from which it protruded. She did not know that much about snakes, but this did not look anything like the docile boa constrictor an old boyfriend of hers had kept as a pet. It was a solid dark brown except for the paler head, which was not wide and spade-shaped and friendly-looking like that boa, but narrow and squarish and strangely hostile with its round-pupiled, aggressive eyes. Kyle must have felt her go stiff and cold against him because he stopped chewing on her nipple and looked up into her face.

"Kel," he said, "you're bleeding."

Her hand went to touch her cheek and came away wet with blood. Not just a little, but a lot, and she could feel it trickling down her neck. She tried to make her mouth form words to warn Kyle about the snake, but he saw it and made a loud, almost comical cartoon-like sound of distress, staggering back and away. But he wasn't fast enough. The dangling snake struck at Kyle, biting him just below the left ear and then immediately again on his chin. He swatted at the snake and stumbled back on his ass, making a rhythmic grunting sound as he twisted his body in revulsion and terror.

Kelly screamed and the second she opened her mouth, the muscles of her face and jaw rippled with white hot, shooting pain, all across the side of her face that was bleeding. Her voice choked up as her throat began to swell closed and she finally knew what was happening. She had not been slapped. She had been bitten.

Panic thundered through her body, racing the neurotoxic venom through her burning veins as she collapsed to her knees. As her vision went dim and swimmy, swarming with flashes of squirming color, her last thought was of Nyah. Nyah, she thought, was really gonna be pissed.

Outside the restroom door, Ken and Grace smiled knowingly at each other as they locked down the beverage cart in the galley. There was rhythmic moaning and thumping and high breathless wails coming from inside the bathroom. It was nothing the flight attendants had not heard dozens of times before.

"Mile High Club," Ken said with a wink.

"Ah," Grace replied wistfully. "Those were the days."

Another wail, winding down into low sobs.

"Damn," Grace said. "This guy is good."

An oddly constricted noise and a frenzy of thumping, then sudden silence.

"Well, maybe not that good." Grace added. "That was pretty fast."

"Poor kid just couldn't hold off anymore," Ken said, shaking his head. "I remember those teenage years all too well. I used to go off like a car alarm before I even got my pants down."

"Not like now," Grace said. "When you can give that Kitty a full two or even three whole minutes of bliss."

"Shut up, bitch!" Ken replied. "I'll have you know I've been studying tantric sex techniques that can allow a man to have an orgasm that lasts one whole hour."

"You're kidding," Grace said. "If I had an orgasm for an hour I think my clitoris would fall off."

Ken covered his mouth, snickering, and went back to cleaning out the coffee maker.

Beneath them, deep inside the infrastructure of the plane, a lone Russell's viper was traveling through a space barely larger than its slender body. Surrounded by thick wires, the agitated reptile forced its way through the electronic tangle until it came to a vertical bend in the crawlspace. Questing for purchase amid the computerized boards and winking lights, the snake wrapped its body around a thick-cabled trunk of copper and rubber. Several wires were pulled loose by its weight and there was a sudden brilliant blue-white flash of voltage followed by a shower of sparks. The snake's stunned body tumbled to the floor, twitching, and the happy, Christmas twinkle of the lights on the computer boards went suddenly gray and dead.

FOURTEEN

In the cockpit, Captain Sam McKeon and his copilot Rich Archibald were in the midst of a fierce debate on the topic of female pubic hair.

"Only hair I want to see on a woman is on her head, thank you very much," Arch was saying.

"See," McKeon replied. "You're missing the whole point of it. A nice thick silky bush is the difference between a girl and a real woman. Always has been. This new mania for shaving down to nothing is bullshit, plain and simple. It's unnatural, I tell you. These days every broad in *Playboy* has got that Barbie-doll-crotch look going on. At the very most they might have a tiny, inoffensive square of trimmed hair like a Velcro tab up on top. These days, it seems almost against the law to have any hair at all. Give me a real woman like Vanessa Del Rio or Christy Canyon any day over some skinny, tit-implanted fitness fanatic whose snatch looks like a sterile rubber sex toy fresh out of the package."

"Captain," Arch drawled. "I do believe that you have your head firmly up your ass."

"You just couldn't handle a real woman, Arch," McKeon replied. "That's why you go for these modern plastic teenage sex dolls."

"You ain't nothing but an old fart," Arch said. "Bitchin' about 'these young kids today' and how it was all so much better back in the day."

"That's not true," McKeon protested.

"Sure it is," Arch said. "Name one gal who's made a video in the last five years that you think is worth a damn."

"Well, there's that Lena Ramon. She's my favorite, a hot little girl-next-door number and she's not afraid to sport nice thick fur. Plus they're doing all that great amateur stuff where they use regular girls who look and act like humans instead of pneumatic blonde pleasure bots. In fact, if you ask me…"

That's when the entire computerized display in front of them suddenly crashed. Every digital instrument necessary to fly the plane—altitude, airspeed, heading, everything—went dead and black.

"Holy shit!" Arch said.

McKeon leaned forward, frantically flipping switches, with his eyes wide and lips pressed into a tight anxious line, all thoughts of Lena Ramon's bush rudely elbowed aside by a cold, swelling panic.

"ND. Down," he said. "EICAS. Down. I'm going to back up. May Day LAX."

Arch spoke into his headset, honey-smooth Southern voice calm and even. "LAX, Hula one-two-one," he said. "May Day. We are fifteen hundred nautical miles southwest of LAX. Repeat, May Day. We are in distress."

"Hula one-two-one," a voice over the radio replied. "LAX tower. Please state the nature of your distress."

In the Coach cabin, the lights had been dimmed so that an in-flight movie could be shown. The movie was some insipid garbage about two bimbos who try to steal each other's shoes, boyfriends and plastic surgeons. Almost no one was listening to it, but the flickering screen still mesmerized the drowsy passengers, magnetizing their gazes in the dark cabin. No one seemed to notice the dozens of cool, scaly bodies that were pushing their way through vents beneath the seats, coiling around shoes and carry-on bags, moving silently through the cabin.

Jennifer Branalin was watching the movie, but listening to her MP3 player and playing a game on her cellphone at the same time. Jen was fifteen, returning home to Los Angeles after a two week visit with her grandparents in Waikiki. It drove her mom completely nuts that Jen was constantly doing four or five things at once. Her mom just did not understand how totally boring it was to have to just stare at one thing for a million years. Jen craved stimulation and variety. She wanted to text message her best friend while checking her bids on eBay and watching three television shows at once with her own custom soundtrack banging in her ear-buds. She could not possibly concentrate on homework without the television for company and at least two other windows open on her laptop so she could check her email and chat with cute boys at the same time. She once saw a science fiction show where they implanted these special lenses into a guy's eyes so he could see his computer display superimposed over the real world at all times and do all kinds of top secret spy stuff without anyone even knowing. Jen couldn't wait for them to invent that. She would be the first in line.

In spite of Jen's self-proclaimed ability to pay attention to many things at once, there was one very important thing happening about which she was blissfully unaware. It was the presence of a very hostile, very agitated horned viper inches from her slender bare foot. She was also unaware of how close she had come to a horrible, painful and excruciatingly slow death when the viper struck at her ankle just as she casually lifted her feet and folded her long, tan legs up Indian style in the tiny seat. The snake missed and banged its wide-open mouth against the metal leg of the seat, leaving behind a trickle of brownish-yellow venom. Stunned by the unexpected impact, the snake retreated, working its unhinged jaw from side to side to realign the bones after the failed strike and coiling its body into a tight one-eighty to head back the way it had come.

* * *

Lisa Daly sat several rows down from Jen, hugging her belly and lost in her own thoughts, trying to figure out how everything had gone so utterly and completely wrong in just one short month. She was nineteen and not especially pretty—her nose was a little too big, her lips a little too thin and her lank blonde hair never seemed to want to do anything but just hang there. Her body was thin and unremarkable, but not for long. She was also pregnant, though no one could really tell just by looking at her, not yet anyway. She had missed her period and gone in for the test three weeks later. A week after that, Jeremy was telling her to get the hell out of his life and take her baby with her. That was yesterday. Today she was on a plane back home to Seattle, via Los Angeles, with nothing but the clothes on her back, the baby in her belly and a suitcase that was barely half full.

There was a lady with a baby sitting about six rows back and Lisa wanted desperately to go talk to her, to tell her that she, Lisa, was going to have a baby too. She wanted more than anything for someone to smile and say congratulations instead of screaming or calling her a scheming bitch or a dumb slut. But she was too shy, and then the movie started so she just sat there alone in her seat, going over and over the wreckage of her life like one of those forensic doctors on television, trying to figure out where it all went wrong.

When she'd first met Jeremy, he'd been so sweet and charming, always surprising her in funny ways and sending her flowers and things. He was the best-looking guy she'd ever dated, with a sexy, brooding James Dean sort of look going on and an amazing body, like an underwear model. He was impulsive, exciting and every date with him felt like some kind of grand adventure. She never really understood what he saw in her, but he looked so sincere when he told her that he loved her, that he wanted her to drop out of school and move to Hawaii with him. How could she say no?

At first it was like an amazing, crazy dream. Hawaii was dazzling and she felt gorgeous there, all tan and sun-kissed and holding a drink with an umbrella in it. He had a great job, but the funny thing was, she didn't know exactly what it was. It seemed to mostly involve hanging around in clubs, but he made tons of money and was ridiculously generous and so she never really gave it much thought.

Things were going fine until he started staying out later and later, always blaming his mysterious job and always acting like it was no big deal. She saw him talking to girls, beautiful girls with big tits who looked like models, and she started to get scared. She spent more and more time alone in their big apartment, feeling panicked and isolated and lonely and ugly. She did not have any friends in Hawaii. In fact, she didn't know anyone but Jeremy. It's not like she'd really planned to get pregnant. It was just that when her birth control pills ran out, she didn't bother to get more. A baby would be so nice, someone to keep her company in the big empty apartment, and if she was pregnant, then Jeremy would have no choice but to marry her and settle down. They could maybe buy a nice house and Jeremy could paint the nursery blue or pink, depending on if it was a boy or a girl. Anyway, it had seemed like a good idea at the time.

Boy, was she wrong. She remembered taking the bus home from the clinic and feeling all warm, womanly and happy, and thinking how she couldn't wait to tell Jeremy about his little son or daughter. Imagining how he would kiss her, touch her stomach and tell her how he would take care of her and their baby. That little fantasy ended the minute he walked in the door.

It was very late, almost dawn, and he was annoyed to find her waiting up. He told her he didn't like her waiting up because it made him feel tied down. He couldn't concentrate on his job, thinking about her moping around waiting for him like a dog. She didn't know how to tell him about the baby, so she just did, just blurted it out.

He did not kiss her and touch her stomach. He did not promise to take care of her. He was furious. He asked about her pills. She lied and said they just must not have worked somehow. He threw money at her and told her to "get rid of it" before he woke up the next day, then went into the bedroom and slammed the door. By "it" he meant their baby.

Needless to say, she did not "get rid of it." There was no way she was going to murder her baby, not for him or for anyone. The next day he was hung over and sullen and she didn't say anything about it until later.

When she brought it up a second time, he told her that he thought she'd "handled it" already. When she explained that she didn't want to "handle it," she wanted to have the baby, he flew into a rage, telling her she was a sneaky scheming bitch and telling her she was out of her tiny teenaged mind if she thought her cheap trick was going to tie him down. He told her that he didn't care about her or her baby and he never wanted to see her again. He threw her clothes into the elevator and told her he would find her and kill her if she ever tried to get even one dime out of him for child support.

Alone, broke and terrified, she called her mom from a payphone at the gas station. She had to listen to an hour-long lecture about how she was a tramp and an idiot and how she had ruined her life and they all hoped that she was proud of herself for bringing shame on her whole family. After that, her mother had begrudgingly agreed to buy her a plane ticket back home.

So that's where Lisa was headed. Back to dreary, gray Tacoma, Washington and her old tiny bedroom and her smug mother waiting with her big steaming pot of I-told-you-so and a sign for Lisa to wear around her neck that said "FAILURE." Lisa would have no choice but to stay there with her mom until the baby was old enough to go to daycare. But she swore to herself that no matter what, she would never make her own daughter or son feel so small and stupid. She would save money and get her own place where the two of them could be happy and safe. They didn't need anyone else. Her baby would grow up feeling special, loved and appreciated no matter what, and that baby would love her back every day. The baby wouldn't feel tied down. The baby would cry for her to come and hug it. The baby would need her. Together, they would have a wonderful, happy life and no one else would be able to spoil it. It was just a matter of getting through this first year. After that, she silently told the tiny twist of potential inside her, things will be different, and that's a promise.

Of course, neither Lisa nor the fetus inside her had any idea that there was six feet of cold-blooded death coiling beneath her seat, waiting to take all their problems away for good.

Back in the cockpit, Captain McKeon continued to jiggle and flip switches like someone in an old movie trying to get an operator on the line. Nothing. Arch looked out through the curved glass as the aircraft suddenly plunged into a thick roiling soup of cloud and fierce lashing rain.

"That's about right," Arch said, shaking his head.

"Wonderful," replied McKeon. "Just what we need."

"We can't climb out of this mess till we get our instruments back up," Arch said.

"Time for a little sugar," McKeon said, picking up the phone. "Gracie?" he said into the handset.

Grace held the phone to her ear with a cold dread coiling in her belly. "Okay," she replied. "Got it." She took three long, deep breaths to calm her speeding heart and then switched over to the public address system.

"Ladies and gentlemen," she said, voice calm and steady. "Please don't be alarmed by the flickering lights. We're encountering turbulence and the captain requests that you remain in your seats with your seatbelts securely fastened."

Tyler clutched Ashley's hand, face icy-pale and sheened with cold sweat.

"Turbulence?" he whispered. "Oh my God!"

"It's no big deal, honey," Ashley said. Just as the word "honey" left her mouth, the plane proved her wrong by dropping swiftly, rattling them all in their seats, lights doing a bright, seizure-quick flicker.

"Shit," Tyler spat between gritted teeth. "Shit, shit, shit."

The dark-haired, pretty flight attendant came over and crouched gracefully beside them. "Is everything all right here?"

"What's happening?" Tyler asked. "Are we going to crash?"

"There is no reason to be alarmed," the flight attendant said. "It's just some minor turbulence."

"It doesn't feel minor," Tyler said.

Another bumpy wave of gut-churning turbulence hit, sending Tyler reaching for the airsick bag in the seat pocket in front of him. Ashley stroked his hair, brows knitted with concern.

"Believe me, I've been doing this for almost ten years," Claire said. "And no matter how bumpy a flight might get, in the end it gets us where we are going just the same."

"Thank you, miss," Ashley said. "Any idea how long this turbulence will last?"

"I'm fine, really," Tyler said, looking green and miserable and anything but fine. "Just…"

The rest of his sentence was buried in a second bout of retching.

"I'll see if I can get some kind of estimate from the pilot, okay?" the flight attendant said. "I'll be back with some bottled water. Hang in there."

Ashley nodded, immensely grateful and feeling more than a little guilty about not taking Tyler's fear of flying seriously. Still, this was probably the worst of it. Soon things would smooth out and in no time they would be home with Esperanza and Cookie and Ace, and everything would be back to normal. There was really nothing to worry about.

Three Gs was doing great, feeling amazingly calm and centered, despite the turbulence. He had the reading light above him switched on and illuminating him like a spotlight. He glanced around to make sure that some of the other passengers nearby could see him talking to the rich blonde, Mercedes she'd said her name was, doing his thing, acting smooth and unruffled, despite the bumpy ride. Cool as Antarctica.

"So," he continued. "I have to pay attention to everything from finding the right accountant to making sure that I look fit and fine, because keeping my sexy right is part of the business too.

And, if you don't mind my saying, it looks like you keep your sexy very *very* right."

"It's a full time job looking this good," Mercedes replied. "Did you know I am actually a corporation?" She smiled. "Mercedes Inc. No really, it's true. It was Daddy's idea. Some kind of tax thing. Anyway, I have sixteen full-time employees including a stylist, a hair dresser, a manicurist, a makeup artist, an esthetician, a dermatologist, a personal trainer, a masseuse, a nutritionist and a personal chef."

"Is that right?" Three Gs responded. "Have you ever done any acting? Because you'd be great in one of my pool party videos."

"How fun!" Mercedes squealed. "Mitzi and Celeste will just die when I tell them." She frowned suddenly, overly groomed blonde eyebrows knitting on her flawless forehead. "Wait a minute, who are you with?"

"Who am I with?" Three Gs frowned. "You mean a girl?"

Mercedes laughed. "No silly. What record label?"

"LaFace. Why?"

"Oooooooh. That's just not gonna work."

"What?"

"LaFace is owned by Sony," Mercedes explained.

"So?" Three Gs asked. "You got something against the Japanese?"

"No," Mercedes said. "It's nothing like that. It's just that Daddy owns stock in Interscope. Now if you were with Shady Records like that 50 Cent guy, then it would be a different story, but Daddy would so totally lose it if I was, like, publicly consorting with the enemy." She touched his arm with her long French nails. "Privately, I can do what I like, of course."

Three Gs clenched his jaw, skin crawling where she had touched him. He reassured himself that she was clean, that it was no problem, but he couldn't help remembering a news story about a fight to ban acrylic nails on pediatric nurses because of the amount of germs that breed underneath them. He swallowed, dry throat clenching.

"Are your nails real?" he asked, battling to keep his voice calm and steady.

"My nails?" She lifted her slender hand to examine them. "Of course! Those awful fake ones are so thick and tacky, ugh. Let me tell you, I eat so much calcium I sometimes think I'm gonna grow a shell like a snail, but my nails are just that important. Why?"

"They look so pretty, is all," he said, and then winced at how stupid that sounded.

"Why thank you," she said with a smile. "Most men don't notice little details like that. Honestly, I spend more on my nails every year than I did on my boobs, and most guys could totally care less unless my nails are around their you-know-what."

Three Gs was just starting to get his heartbeat back to normal when a chihuahua popped its head out of her purse and leapt up into her lap. Its brown eyes looked runny and gross, and it shook like it was sick or something.

"Oh," he said, cringing back and away from the tiny dog.

"Don't be scared," Mercedes said, laughing. "She won't bite."

"Is it sick?" Three Gs asked before he could stop himself.

"She," Mercedes corrected him. "Not it. This is Mary-Kate. Mary-Kate, meet Three Gs. He's a famous rap star." She dropped her voice to a stage whisper. "But he's with LaFace so don't tell Daddy."

She held up the dog's tiny paw as if wanting him to shake it. The dog's nails were painted bright bubblegum pink. There was no way in hell he was gonna touch a dog's foot. He wanted desperately to go wash his hands, but Mercedes and the little dog were in the aisle seat, blocking him in.

"She's not sick, is she?" Three Gs asked again.

Why couldn't he just shut the fuck up and chill? He started talking to this dumb bitch in the first place to prove he was cool, and here he was ready to lose it all over again.

"She's not sick," Mercedes said. "She's just fine, aren't you, sugarbaby?" She was still holding the little paw. "Mary-Kate has her own manicurist, you know. Today she's wearing the new Dior Addict nail color in Cosmic Rose."

"Nice," Three Gs managed to say. "You must… give her baths and stuff right?"

"Every day," Mercedes said. "She gets her special honeysuckle and shea butter moisturizing spa treatment, plus an antibacterial peppermint and tea-tree rinse and a little spritz of whatever perfume she likes best each season. Last summer she was all about Escada's Sexy Graffiti. But she just hate hate hates that awful hippie one they debuted this summer, so for fall, she's going back to

Chanel's Coco Mademoiselle. I, of course, only wear No 5. Just like Marilyn Monroe."

The word antibacterial made Three Gs's heart slow to something closer to normal and he didn't hear another word after that. He still wasn't gonna touch the damn dog, but at least it wouldn't make him sick.

The little dog suddenly started barking frantically at Mercedes's Fendi handbag on the floor between her feet. No one but Mary-Kate saw the brilliant red and brown banded tail slither and disappear inside the purse.

"Excuse me," Mercedes said. "She just wants a treat." She picked up the overstuffed bag and thrust her hand inside, feeling around in her search for the treats. Unable to find them, she gave the bag a violent shake. "I can never find anything in here. I'm just not one of those organized people with all their lipsticks alphabetized and a special pocket for their breath mints. That's what I pay Alana for."

She finally found the little Ziploc bag of dog treats. They looked disgusting to Three Gs, greasy brown lumps that left a thin cloudy film on the plastic. The smell when she opened the bag was rich and livery and nauseating.

"What are they?" Three Gs asked, his nose wrinkling as Mercedes picked out a treat with her long nails.

"They are free range chicken with sweet potato and flax seed, organic of course," Mercedes replied. "I don't believe in all that genetically modified food and stuff, because its, like, against nature."

The dog did not want the treat. She continued to bark at the handbag. Three Gs could feel the constricting bands of a monster headache forming around his skull.

"She's bipolar," Mercedes explained. "That's what her psychiatrist says, but you know, now I think that she may just be suffering the residual effects from the trauma of her childhood in the puppy mill. Do you know about these places? Puppymills?"

Three Gs shook his head.

"They're, like, totally awful and dark," Mercedes said with the tone of a child telling a ghost story. "And all the poor dogs live in these tiny cages with germs and filth. They don't even have any place to go potty except *right there*."

Three Gs felt his throat constricting down to a pinhole, heart skittering frantically inside his chest as if it wanted out. He looked back at the little dog and imagined its fur crawling with invisible germs. How could you wash away something like that? You couldn't. There wasn't enough soap in the universe.

Mercedes was still going on and on about things so horrible that Three Gs was overwhelmed with an urge to punch her in the face, just to get her to shut the fuck up. Once the thought of punching her popped into his head, he felt suddenly terrified that he really would hit her, that he would not be able to stop himself. He clenched his fists in his lap, gripped with wave after wave of uncontrollable panic.

Troy suddenly leapt up from his seat across the aisle and spat out a half-swallowed curse, nearly causing Three Gs to keel over dead from a heart attack.

"I came this close to beating the last level!" Troy said sheepishly, holding up his PSP.

"You and your goddamn games," Leroy said, shaking his head. "You playing them or they playing you?"

Three Gs could not stand it any longer. He mumbled an excuse to Mercedes and pushed past her into the aisle. Not running to the bathroom in the rear of the plane took every ounce of willpower he had, but when he finally got there the damn thing was occupied.

"Sir," an older flight attendant said. "I'm sorry, but I'll have to ask you to return to your seat. The captain is expecting more turbulence."

"I just…" Three Gs said, yanking frantically on the locked restroom door. "I need…"

"Hey," the flight attendant said, voice calm and gentle. "It's okay. There's nothing to worry about, I assure you."

"But I need to wash my hands," Three Gs said, horrified to realize that he was close to crying. Shame nearly overwhelmed the panic as he turned his face away, wishing that he would just have a damn heart attack and get it over with already.

"Well, why didn't you say so?" the flight attendant said softly. "Here." She handed him a bottle of hand sanitizer from her apron pocket.

"Thanks," he said, dumping more than half of the little bottle into one palm. "Thank you. Thank you very much."

"No problem," she said. After a thoughtful pause, she continued. "You know, I really enjoyed your latest album, "Introspective." Some of the earlier stuff about butts and big dicks and all that was funny and clever but kinda... well you know, silly. This new album is a quantum leap for you as an artist. It's darker, more real, and your dexterity with words never ceases to amaze me."

Three Gs looked at her with a lopsided smile, rubbing the cool gel over his hands and feeling its healing chill spread throughout his body, calming him. "You know, I never would have made you for a hip hop fan."

The flight attendant shrugged and returned his smile. "What can I say? I have teenage sons. Anytime they want a CD that has one of those parental advisory stickers on it, I like to give it a listen first and make my own decision. By the way, my name is Grace. Just let me know if you need anything else during the flight."

"Listen, Grace," Three Gs said, handing the bottle of hand sanitizer back to her. "I know I need to go sit back down, but would it be a big deal if I just stand here for a another minute or two?"

Grace smiled at him and tucked the little bottle back into her apron pocket. "I won't tell if you won't," she said. "But only for a minute, okay? We're coming into heavy turbulence and I don't want to have to tell my kids that Three Gs suffered a traumatic brain injury because I didn't make him sit down and buckle up."

"One minute," he replied. "I promise."

FIFTEEN

Captain McKeon squinted at the schematics of the fuselage with a penlight between his teeth while Arch fought the yoke, buffeted by the extreme weather. The digital displays remained ominously blank.

McKeon put the light back in his breast pocket and pried open a trap door in the flight deck floor.

The musical beeping of someone punching in their cabin key code sounded in the claustrophobic space and when the door popped open, McKeon saw that it was Claire, looking beautiful and anxious.

"Any idea when we'll climb over?"

She paused, words trailing into nothing as she stared open-mouthed at the dead control panel.

"Oh my God," she said softly.

"We just lost the board," McKeon told her. "I gotta recycle the breakers."

He took the light from his pocket again, clicked it on and carefully lowered himself through the trapdoor and into the avionics hatchway beneath.

The thin, narrow beam of light flitted through the forest of wires and cables, casting harsh, jittering shadows. It had all looked so neat and simple on the schematic, but things were far more chaotic in three dimensions. McKeon searched for several seconds before finally locating the electronics compartment, and once he found it, he stuck the penlight between his teeth again and set to work unscrewing the panel. Just as the last screw came loose, he heard an odd sound, a sharp hiss like some kind of hydraulics. He thought it was curious, but as he pulled the panel loose and shone his light into the compartment, there was nothing there.

McKeon quickly discerned three circuit breakers in the off position. Squirming deeper inside, he reached for the first of the breakers. His fingers stretched, reaching, and finally hit their mark as he reset the first breaker.

"Okay, Cap," Arch hollered from the mouth of the hatchway. "They're coming back up."

McKeon reached further to hit the next breaker and his finger brushed some sort of thick cable that almost seemed to move out of the way of his questing fingers. He flipped the second and third breaker and heard a raucous cowboy whoop from the deck.

"That's it old man!" Arch cried. "We are back in fucking business!"

McKeon smiled, hot, shaky relief flooding through his body. He closed his eyes and rubbed their inner corners with his thumb and forefinger, letting out a long breath. When he opened his eyes again and looked back at the breakers, he saw something so odd that for a second, he could not quite register what he was seeing.

There was a snake inside the electronics panel. It was beautiful, a rich golden brown with black-ringed, leaf-shaped spots like chestnut-colored eyes all down its back and sides. Its triangular head was raised up, showing a pale throat, and its cold, alien gaze was locked on McKeon.

McKeon stared, mesmerized and frozen with a sick, drowsy fear, until that hiss he had heard earlier came again. There was no question of where it was coming from. Paralysis abruptly broken, he started crabbing frantically backwards, away from the angry reptile. The snake struck out, sinking its fangs into McKeon's inner thigh, scant inches from his crotch. McKeon gave a startled yelp and twisted away, feeling hot tendrils of pain coiling out from the bite as a huge swell of paralyzing fear washed over him. He felt a stinging slap on the back of his head, just like when he was a kid and his older brother would let him have it for saying something stupid.

It bit my head, he thought. Son of a bitch bit me in my fucking head!

The massive, killing pain that buried him like a mountain of scrap iron and broken glass eclipsed everything else as his consciousness was chewed down to red ragged scraps, then finally swallowed by merciful darkness.

* * *

"Captain?" Claire called into the hatchway. "Sam, are you okay?" She had heard the startled yelp and now all she could see was McKeon's cap laying upside-down beside his unmoving hand. "Arch! Something's wrong. The captain isn't moving."

"Now, don't go getting all hysterical on me, little lady," Arch said, punching the auto-pilot. "Step aside and let me have a looksee." He called down into the hatchway. "Sam? What the hell are you doing in there?"

Claire bristled with hostile fury. Why did Arch always have to be so condescending? She wasn't being hysterical, she was just pointing out...

Her eyes went huge as Arch cursed and jumped down into the hatchway, hauling McKeon's limp, unmoving body up into the cockpit.

"Christ!" Arch said. "He must have had a heart attack or something."

"A heart attack?" Claire said, struggling to remain calm and not prove Arch right about women by becoming hysterical. "Okay, give me a minute."

She threw open the deck door and called across the First Class seats. "Agent Flynn," she said, voice steady. "Could I see you for a moment?"

Flynn's brows drew together and he shot a glance at his partner. "Stay put, kid," he said to the boy as he unfastened his seatbelt and nodded to his partner, who did the same.

Claire stepped aside for the two agents to enter the cockpit.

Flynn dropped to one knee beside the prone Captain. He was very obviously dead, eyes slitted and rolled up, tongue thick and protruding between bluish, swollen lips, but Flynn felt for a pulse anyway. He looked at Sanders, then at Arch and Claire and shook his head.

"Jesus," Arch said, sounding subdued and genuine for the first time in all the years that Claire had known him. "I flew with him for ten years."

"What happened?" Claire asked. "Was it a heart attack?"

Flynn lifted McKeon's lifeless head, fingers questing over the back of the captain's scalp. "There's some swelling on the back of his head under the hair," Flynn replied, examining fingers wet with blood. "And blood. He may have hit his head at some point but that doesn't explain why his heart stopped." Flynn pulled a cotton handkerchief from an inner pocket and wiped the blood away. "Honestly, I'm no doctor. I really don't know what to make of it. All I can tell you for sure is that he is dead."

Sanders frowned at the body. "Shouldn't we head back to Honolulu?"

Arch shook his head. "We're past the point of no return. It would take us longer to get back to Honolulu than to continue on to Los Angeles."

A startling one-two punch of turbulence rocked the aircraft and everyone staggered, hands out to steady themselves.

"Claire," Arch said. "Go and make sure everyone is strapped in." He turned away and spoke into his headset. "LAX tower," he said. "Hula one-two-one, distress. Pilot in command has suffered a fatal heart attack."

His head cocked back to Claire and he made a little shooing motion. She narrowed her eyes at him and turned to leave, while the two FBI agents lifted McKeon's body and placed him on a small bunk at the back of the deck, covering him with a blanket.

Claire made her way down the Coach cabin aisle with catlike grace, long legs bending and compensating fluidly as the aircraft rocked and rolled around her. Her mind was awash with anxiety, but she kept her face cool and reassuringly calm as she bent down beside Tommy and Curtis, the two young boys on their very first flight without their parents.

"You guys doing okay?" she asked.

"Tommy is scared," Curtis told her.

"Am not!" Tommy replied.

It was obvious that they were both very scared and Claire really felt for the two of them. Clearly there was something going on in their lives with their recently divorced parents and this trip was making them very anxious and uncertain even without bumps and turbulence.

"Do you think Mr Wong is scared in his part of the plane?" Tommy asked, big brown eyes wide and worried. "I bet he is."

"And who is Mr Wong?" Claire asked.

"Mr Wong is my cat," Tommy said. "He's the same age as me, only in cat years that's actually not a kid age at all, but a grown up cat age."

"Is that right?" Claire asked.

"Can I go visit his part of the plane and make sure he's okay?" Tommy asked. "I think I better do that."

"I'm sorry, honey," Claire said. "But there's no safe way to get from our part of the plane to his part of the plane while the plane is in the air. Not unless you're only six inches tall and can crawl through the air vents."

"I'm fifty-one inches tall," Tommy said, looking crestfallen.

"Don't worry," Claire said. "I'm sure Mr Wong is just fine. I think we'll be glad to get to Los Angeles."

"I won't," Tommy said suddenly. "I want to go back to Hawaii."

"Shut up," Curtis said. "Baby!"

"Hey, come on, you guys, it's okay," Claire said. "But think about it for a second. How do you know you won't be glad to get to Los Angeles if you've never been there before?"

Tommy shrugged and Curtis looked away, out the black, rain-streaked window. The plane took a sudden vertiginous plunge and the two boys locked white-knuckled hands, disagreement forgotten.

"Just think of it like a roller coaster ride, okay," Claire told the boys. "You like roller coaster rides?"

"No," Curtis said. "Not really."

"Yeah," Claire sighed. "I guess I don't really like them either."

"I'm too short for the grownup rides," Tommy said.

"I tell you what," Claire said. "This is what you're going to do. You're going to close your eyes and count slowly to ten. When you get to ten you open your eyes and then you make the funniest face you can at each other. Whoever laughs first loses."

The two boys nodded, momentarily distracted.

"Best out of five wins," she said. "I'll be back in a few minutes to check on the score."

She forced her cheek muscles to pull her lips into a smile, but her brain kept on running worst case scenarios, laughing at her pathetic attempts to distract the kids from impending doom. The two boys closed their eyes to begin the game and Claire turned away before her brittle smile had a chance to shatter.

Vi had been trying to concentrate on her dilemma, going back and forth on whether or not to leave her husband, when the combined influence of her pleasant satisfied drowsiness, the dim, humming quiet of the cabin and the single white Russian she had ordered suddenly ganged up on her all at once and she drifted off into gauzy, erotic dreams. She had always been a very heavy sleeper and never noticed the turbulence or the flickering lights. She also didn't notice the three-foot long Mozambique Spitting Cobra making its careful way up under her sarong, into her lap and up between her massive breasts.

Todd Velance had thought it would be way harder to get away with murder. They make it seem so tough in the movies. There's always some nosy guy vacuuming up dandruff and pulling shreds of DNA out of the waffles of your sneakers. But somehow, against all the odds, Todd had gotten away with it. It wasn't even as if he was some genius criminal mastermind. He'd just decided it would be for the best to get rid of Beryl.

Of course, stealing all the rich ladies' jewelry from the hotel where Beryl worked had been his idea from the get go. Beryl was the night manager at a big luxury resort on Maui and had the keys to everything. She was beautiful, tall, thin and hungry with legs for days and a good girl gone bad kind of smile that made everything easy for her. Problem was, she wasn't too smart. Problem for her, that was, not for him.

It never even occurred to her that the cops would suspect her right off the bat. After all, she had the access. It had been his plan at the beginning to just ditch her and let her take the fall, but it soon became clear that that wouldn't be good enough. After all, she would rat on him in a minute, once she realized she'd been had. Nope, there was only one way to make this work, to make a clean break, as his mother always used to say.

He thought it would be harder, more upsetting. He thought that it would make him feel bad, because that's how everyone always said a person ought to feel about killing someone. The truth was, it was much less of a pain in the ass than trying to get the bitch off. He just put a pillow on her face while she was sleeping and BANG. End of problem.

She peed though, when he shot her, and that was a little gross. But it wasn't his bed anyway so what did he care? Besides, all that blood from her head was bound to make a much worse stain than a little pee. She, her sheets and all her stains were no longer his problem.

As he packed up the big sparkly tangle of necklaces and things, and headed for the airport, he kept expecting someone to try to stop him, some cop or something to dive out of the bushes and wrestle him to the ground, but it just never happened. He bought a ticket with cash and showed the fat lady behind the ticket counter a fake ID. She didn't even blink, just smiled her big soft cow-smile and told him to have a nice trip.

So far, Todd was having a very nice trip. It was quiet, uncrowded and no one around him even gave him a second glance. To them, he was just another tourist, a little rushed, a little tired, but looking forward to getting home. When that weird lady wigged out just before takeoff, he'd had a sudden fear that she was going to single him out, to point right at him and say: "Murderer!" Lucky for him, it never happened. Crazy bitch got the bum's rush along with her wimpy husband and the plane just took off without a hitch.

Todd really had no idea what he was going to do with himself when he arrived in Los Angeles. Presumably he would need to find someone disreputable to turn the pretty baubles into folding cash and then maybe he would go check out that Hollywood sign. Maybe buy some kind of cool car and zip around up in the hills with a hot blonde giving him a blowjob while he drove. Check out Rodeo Drive and get himself some fancy shoes and sunglasses. Maybe get discovered and do some acting where he could pretend to be a crook. How great would that be? Have all the cops in Hawaii searching for a guy who was off in Hollywood pretending to steal things for money. That would be awesome.

He thought he felt something sliding over his foot and pulled it up, startled. He hit the light above his seat. It didn't illuminate the floor by his feet very well, and he didn't see anything down there but his shoes, which he had slipped off when the plane first took off. He shrugged and wiggled his toes in his dark socks, stretching them and telling himself not to be paranoid. He looked up at the in-flight movie playing on the watery screen above their heads. There was a dark-haired, handsome guy putting the moves on one of the lead blondes. He was a sort of tough guy type, but with a little softness around the mouth that made the broads all crazy wet. Todd figured he was at least as good-looking as that guy. He wouldn't mind doing a romantic love scene with some famous hottie like Jessica Alba in between the criminal roles, just for variety. Women went for him; they always had. A man had to use his skills in life.

While Todd lost himself in pleasant fantasies of Jessica Alba, several banded kraits were twining around his empty shoes, waiting for the return of his feet.

SIXTEEN

Of course, Eddie Kim couldn't sleep. He was far too wound up to do anything but pace back and forth, waiting for word from his man at LAX. He was actually thrilled when one of his lieutenants reported that the midnight deadline for a minor debt had come and gone, and the dumbass loser deadbeat who owed Kim three grand had basically blown the lieutenant off, telling him that he'd get around to it in the morning.

The lieutenant had been very surprised when Kim decided he needed to pay the deadbeat a personal visit. Normally this kind of piddly-ass shit was beneath him, but he felt like he really needed something to do with his hands. Anything to take his mind off South Pacific Air Flight 121 and Alexander Gong's visit, and how much was riding on this whole Sean Jones business.

The story of the deadbeat went like this: the guy, Brandon or Brian or something like that, was writing a script about Asian gangs. Brandon-or-Brian himself was a blond, blue-eyed actor/model/whatever from Missouri and thought Chiang Kai-Shek was an appetizer that came with the five dollar lunch special. He had it in his mind that he himself would star in this brilliant epic, along with a wacky Asian sidekick and a hot Asian love interest like Lucy Liu or Chiaki Kuriyama. Most importantly, he wanted it to be "real." Not like this other phony Hollywood bullshit. His movie was going to be the real deal—raw, unflinching and honest.

So he contacted Eddie Kim. Apparently he had some rich older woman that was "financing" him, no doubt in exchange for occasional Viagra-fueled service calls. He said he would pay Kim fifteen hundred dollars to "pick his brain" and wanted to be able to list Kim as a "consultant" to sell how "real" this project was. Brandon-or-Brian really seemed to like that word. "Real." He must have used it a hundred times at their meeting at the Formosa Café. He even wanted Kim to play a cameo in the film.

Kim was amused at first. The kid clearly had no clue whatsoever, but he had balls and totally unwarranted confidence that all of Hollywood would be beating down his door to make this "real" movie of his. Because Kim had been amused by the whole thing, he hadn't asked for the cash up-front. Really it was more his own fault than anything else. When the meeting ended, the kid had hemmed and hawed and told Kim he would need to have his assistant cut a check. Kim had explained that he didn't want a check. He wanted cash, and he wanted it by midnight that night. If that was too soon for Brandon-or-Brian, it was no big deal. Kim would be happy to wait until the end of the week. Of course, the usual interest would apply.

The way the kid smiled and slapped Kim's shoulder and told him that his people would call Kim's people told Kim that all the consulting in the world wouldn't help this guy. He clearly had absolutely no understanding whatsoever of what he had gotten himself into.

So the week had passed without payment, without any word at all from Brandon-or-Brian or his mythical assistant. Kim had more pressing matters to think of and he relegated the whole foolishness to one of his lesser lieutenants. By lucky coincidence, the midnight deadline happened to fall on the night of the whole South Pacific Air Flight 121 business. Kim figured a little visit with Brandon-or-Brian would be just the kind of simple distraction he needed.

Shaking his surveillance was never easy for Kim, especially with the upcoming trial, but he was creative and determined and was eventually able to surreptitiously switch cars in a Barnes and Noble parking structure, sending his FBI tail off after the decoy while he and four of his men headed up into the hills in a battered brown Toyota covered with colorful hippie bumper stickers that said things like "Go Vegan" and "What part of 'Love thy Neighbor' don't you understand?"

Brandon-or-Brian lived at the far end of Woodrow Wilson Drive, a twisty little street that wound through the hills above the Cahuenga pass. His house was a tawdry little stucco box built in the sixties that looked like something a fast food hamburger would have come in back in the unenlightened days before recycling. It balanced on the edge of the road as if tossed from a moving car, dark except for a dim, flickering glow in the plate glass window on the far end. Brandon-or-Brian's black Magnum was there, parked out front, and there was another car too, a low-end BMW. Clearly Kim was interrupting a casting call. That thought made him smile as he watched his men split up and surround the little house—Danny, T Bone, and Fei Chai heading around the back while Xiao Li stepped up to slip the Mickey Mouse lock on the front door.

Inside, Kim and Xiao Li followed the sounds of cooing and moaning that issued from the living room. The place was all done up with Asian-modern furniture that looked as if it had been bought cheap after a suburban P F Chang's China Bistro went out of business. Every surface was crowded with tons of faux-Chinese junk featuring irrelevant nonsensical hanzi characters that said things like "Strong Tranquility," "Hot Fever Temperature" or "Open." There was some god-awful smarmy Canto-Pop drooling from the expensive speakers and Kim could see bits and pieces of a tiny Asian girl pinned to a leather sofa beneath Brandon-or-Brian's large, hairy bulk.

By that time, Danny had joined them after entering through the back door, leaving the burly T Bone and Sumo-sized Fei Chai to keep watch outside. Danny was by far the youngest of Kim's men and cracked a huge grin when he saw what was going on. Kim placed a cigarette between his lips and pulled a Zippo from the inner pocket of his Armani suit jacket.

"Is this a bad time?" Kim asked, sparking the lighter and dipping the tip of his cigarette into the flame.

Brandon-or-Brian leapt up off the woman with a surprised grunt and promptly tripped, ankles trapped in his bunched-up pants. Xiao Li helped him up with the barrel of a .45 pressed beneath his chin. The girl on the sofa reached for a handful of sheer, lacy clothing to cover herself and Kim told her in quiet Chinese to stay put and keep her legs open. She seemed to understand what was happening far better than her erstwhile gwailo boyfriend and did what Kim said instantly and without protest.

"Well what do you know," Kim said to Brandon-or-Brian, eyeing his exposed and swiftly shrinking genitals. "I guess what they say about white guys being so much better hung than us Asians is just a myth, huh?"

"Are you crazy?" Brandon-or-Brian asked.

"I think that's probably a pretty fair assessment of my mental state," Kim replied. "Runs in the family, you know. But enough about me. Let's talk about my money."

"Is that what this is about?" Brandon-or-Brian asked, combing his fingers nervously through his hair. "Money? I said I would handle it in the morning."

"And I say you'll handle it now," Kim said. "Do you have it or not?"

"Of course not!" Brandon-or-Brian whined. "I don't carry fifteen hundred dollars around in cash."

"It's three grand now, cowboy," Kim said, taking a deep drag of the cigarette. "Interest."

"Interest?" Brandon-or-Brian said. "You're kidding."

"I may be crazy," Kim said, smiling. "But I'm never kidding."

He nodded to Danny, and the younger man grabbed Brandon-or-Brian's arms, pinning them behind his back. Kim put out one hand and Xiao Li put a roll of duct tape in Kim's palm.

"All right Mr Hollywood Filmmaker," Kim said, pulling out about a foot of duct tape with a loud, ripping sound. "I want you to pay very careful attention. You're gonna want to remember this scene so that you can write it into your movie."

"Don't... I..."

Whatever else Brandon-or-Brian was going to say was neatly cut off as Kim started wrapping the duct tape around his blond head, covering his mouth.

"Hold him good," Kim said. "It's time for some serious realism."

Danny wrapped one muscular arm around both of Brandon-or-Brian's arms and used his other hand to grab a fistful of greasy blond hair. Xiao Li stepped in and pressed the .45 against Brandon-or-Brian's temple just in case he thought of trying anything funny. Brandon-or-Brian froze, eyes huge in his dead-white face.

Kim took the cigarette from between his lips and held it less than an inch from Brandon-or-Brian's right eye.

"Lesson number one," Kim said. "When you owe money, you pay it."

He touched the glowing tip of the cigarette to Brandon-or-Brian's pale eyelashes, singing them down to the root one by one. Brandon-or-Brian screamed beneath the tape, the sound reduced to a muffled squeak. Kim took another drag off the cigarette and, disgusted by the taste of burnt hair, he spat on the carpet and then ground the cigarette out in the inner corner of Brandon-or-Brian's right eye.

Even with the tape over his mouth, Brandon-or-Brian was making so much noise that Kim almost didn't hear his cellphone ring. Gesturing to Xiao Li to shut Brandon-or-Brian up, Kim took the tiny phone from his pocket and smiled at the caller ID.

"Yeah?" he said into the phone while Xiao Li pressed the mouth of his .45 against Brandon-or-Brian's good eye.

"Pilot in command on South Pacific Air Flight 121 has suffered what was reported as a fatal heart attack," the voice on the other end of the line told Kim. "Things are looking up."

"Outstanding," Kim said, flipping his phone closed.

Kim looked back at Brandon-or-Brian. He was crying, snot running in silvery rivers over the duct tape. His right eye had swollen completely shut and looked like a woman's lipsticked mouth, puckered up for a kiss. Kim was pretty much done with him, but just for good measure, he pulled out a slender stiletto and neatly slit both of Brandon-or-Brian's nostrils all the way up to the bridge of his ugly, Caucasian nose.

"You guys finish up here," Kim said to Danny and Xiao Li. "I feel like celebrating." He nodded to the naked girl. "Get dressed. It's time for a date with a real man."

Kim took the girl and Brandon-or-Brian's Magnum and headed up to Mullholand Drive.

SEVENTEEN

Arch was squinting into the lashing rain and thinking about how his rising to the occasion and saving everyone on this flight was going to get him more pussy than he could shake a stick at when he suddenly spotted a flash of yellowy-green movement in the crevice between the yoke shaft and the housing. The two FBI agents had returned to the cabin and alone in the flight deck, Arch could not believe what he was seeing. Wriggling out of the crevice and up the shaft towards Arch's hands were several gracile scaly bodies, each no more than six or seven inches in length and each topped with a wide, triangular head and big, anime green eyes fringed by what looked like thick chunky eyelashes.

"Snakes?" Arch said, incredulous. "Well I'll be…"

He snatched his hand away as one of the slender reptiles struck at the spot where his fingers had been only seconds before.

"Son of a bitch!" Arch spat, grabbing a thick flight manual and swatting at one of the darting heads.

The heavy book hit its mark, squashing the little snake's upper third into a bloody pulp. Its companions disappeared back inside the instrument panel and the circuit sparked, shorting out suddenly. A piercing alarm went off, followed by a series of warning lights.

"Aw, shit," Arch said, Texas drawl stretching the curse into two long juicy syllables.

In the main cabin, the overhead lights came on and the movie abruptly stopped. Jennifer pulled out one of her ear buds, annoyed at this sudden development. but her hand froze halfway to pressing the call button for the flight attendant when oxygen masks suddenly popped out to dangle above the seats. At first, she could not figure out why the clear plastic masks were decorated with colorful streamers that swung beside them, wrapped around them and through the straps. Then the "streamers" started to move, coiling and stretching towards the upturned faces of the terrified passengers. The mask above Jennifer's seat had two "streamers" dangling on either side of it, both patterned in warm autumn browns and reds, and she realized suddenly that they weren't just oxygen masks that dropped down from the ceiling.

They were *snakes*.

Dozens and dozens of snakes descended like some kind of awful practical joke where fake snakes pop out of a tin of candy, only these snakes were real, with bright, malevolent eyes and thin questing tongues hissing with cold, alien fury. Jennifer pulled her hand away from the call button, but she was too slow. The snakes dangling inches from her face reacted simultaneously. One clamped down and chewed viciously on the fleshy web between her right index finger and thumb. The other struck at her face. She felt the snake's long, thin fangs punch through the cartilage of her nose and she could smell the hot acidic stench of burning venom as it coated her vulnerable sinuses, making her choke and sneeze like when you laugh while trying to drink a Dr Pepper and it goes up your nose, only a billion times worse.

Flailing and striking blindly out at her reptilian attackers, she half jumped and half fell into the aisle, dizzy and disoriented, drowning in caustic pain. The plane lurched abruptly and she felt an avalanche of carry-on luggage slam down on top of her from the overhead bin, snapping her neck and caving in the back of her skull. As a wave of numb blackness swallowed her pain, she felt nothing but a kind of hollow gratitude.

Vi woke with a sudden start, ill-defined sensuous images from her lingering dream giving way to a most peculiar sensation of something thick, muscular and strong sliding between her breasts. At first she thought it was part of her dream, until she looked down into her cleavage and saw a tawny brown and black head with round beady eyes glaring back at her.

She let out a shrill scream and the snake between her breasts reared up, hissing viciously and spreading a narrow hood inches from her nose. Then, like some porno-Freudian nightmare come to life, the snake opened its mouth wide and let loose a jetting spray of toxic venom directly into her eyes.

Lisa screamed when the snakes dropped from the ceiling, throwing herself down on the floor between the seats with her hands wrapped protectively across her belly. She just could not understand how this could be happening. How could live snakes get on the plane? It just didn't make sense. But sense or no, it was happening, and Lisa had never been so scared in her whole life, not just for herself, but for her baby. Her little tiny vulnerable baby that could do nothing to defend itself. Would the venom from a snake kill her baby? She had no idea but had no plans to stick around and find out.

She had seen some stairs leading up, presumably to the first class cabin. If she could make it to those stairs, she could get away from all this. Crawling down the aisle on her belly while people screamed and flailed and fell over all around her, Lisa kept the image of the stairs firmly in her mind. If she could just make it to the stairs.

Then someone fell right on top of her, a man with vomit on his shirt, and she wanted to scream again, but couldn't with his huge heavy weight pressing down on her, crushing her and crushing her baby.

"Get… off… me!" she said, fighting to free herself from beneath the lolling semi-conscious bulk. "Godammit!"

When she looked up, there was a fat tan rattlesnake inches from her nose. It shook its rattling tail at her, its hostile gaze pinning her down as surely as the man on top of her was. She tried to pull in all her limbs, to hide herself under the dying man, praying silently, just a kind of desperate wordless plea. But whoever is supposed to answer the prayers of terrified pregnant girls must have been out to lunch because the snake struck at her, fanged mouth gaping pink and awful. At first it hit the man above her and she thought maybe she would be okay, but the snake seemed unsatisfied with the unresisting flesh in its jaws and coiled back for a second strike. Several others turned towards her at that moment, hissing and cocking back as bite after bite clamped down on every exposed part of her body. Lisa felt like she was screaming when the rattlesnake struck again, but there was no air left inside her and the snake's fangs sank into her eye, pumping hot venom directly into her brain. Her convulsions were instantaneous and involuntarily achieved what all her conscious will could not. As her body was wracked with spasms, her spine arched and flexed, tossing the dead weight of the man above her to one side. Her death was quick, heart seizing up and then surrendering inside her chest. The baby lived for several seconds longer in its bath of blood and venom, but quickly joined its mother as the poison dissolved its budding organs and soft, unformed bones, reducing it to just another gob of scarlet muck inside the quickly disintegrating vessel that had once been Lisa.

When the oxygen masks dropped down, Tyler struggled to focus on the one dangling directly above his seat, thinking that he had probably taken too many Xanax. The pills had mingled with several tiny bottles of bourbon in his belly and, while he finally felt calm, he also felt a sort of thin sugary glaze over all his senses, making everything seem shiny and slow. There seemed to be a real emergency happening, but for some reason, he couldn't really get that upset about it. He mostly just felt annoyed at Ashley for screaming in his ear and waking him up out of his pleasant nap. He reached out to grab the oxygen mask and pull it towards his face, but instead found himself holding something totally different. It was pale and wide and cool and seemed to twist and flex like a bodybuilder's arm. Suddenly it slammed onto his face, covering his mouth and nose. He wondered for a befuddled second if the oxygen masks were automatic or something, but there was a terrible smell inside that thing, a meaty, acidic sort of smell. It popped off and Ashley was shaking him, screaming and suddenly pain erupted across his face, digging hot needles into his eyes and squeezing his throat closed in a slick fist of nausea. He reached for Ashley but he couldn't seem to see where she was. He wanted to say her name, but his tongue seemed way too big and just flopped around in his numb, drooling mouth. Someone was pulling him, dragging him down out of his seat, and he really hoped it was her because the fear had finally broken through his drugged out haze, surfing in on the waves of pain. He had been right all along. Something terrible really was happening and that knowledge brought him no satisfaction whatsoever.

Claire heard the screaming and ran back into the rear cabin, only to be stopped dead in her tracks by the sight of dozens of twisting scaly bodies dangling from the ceiling along with the deployed oxygen masks.

"Please," she said, gripping the seat backs to hold herself steady as her mouth seemed to move on autopilot. "Please remain in your seats with your seatbelts securely fastened."

"Fuck that!" a young man replied, pushing past her and making a run for the front cabin.

"Please remain calm…"

Before she could finish her sentence, another jolt of turbulence tossed her like a rag doll. She stumbled and fell into the lap of a screaming fat lady whose swollen sticky eyes wept thick milky pus as she clawed and tore at Claire's blouse. Several other overhead compartments dropped open. Shopping bags, briefcases, jackets and laptop computers rained down on the panicked passengers. A cute pink leather tote bag dumped down onto the shrieking fat lady, showering her with cosmetics, crumpled tissues and bobby pins. Claire was finally able to pull free, struggling futilely to straighten her torn blouse. She was struck by a totally ridiculous thought that she should have worn a nicer bra, instead of the plain white cotton one that was now exposed by a long vertical rip. She thought of her thin, chic and bitchy mom who always used to warn Claire that she better have on pretty underthings all the time, just in case she ever got in a car accident. Claire wouldn't want to miss out on such a fortuitous opportunity to hook a handsome, rich doctor. In that moment, she hated her mother for still being there like an unquiet spirit inside her mind.

Todd pushed his way past the brunette stewardess, making a mad dash for the front of the plane with his carry-on gym bag full of diamonds clutched to his chest like a baby. She was on crack if she thought Todd was just gonna sit there and let snakes bite him. This was like some kind of crazy nightmare. He had imagined all kinds of bad things happening to him after he killed Beryl, but snakes? Was this some weird kind of *Twilight Zone* retribution?

Just before they'd decided to pull this job, Beryl had a little too much to drink and dragged Todd into a tattoo parlor. She had decided impulsively that she needed a tattoo, a snake wrapped around her slender ankle, and wanted him to hold her hand while the guy did it. It was the last thing he wanted to do that night, but he had to admit that the cute expressions of pain she was making while the guy drilled ink into her skin and the little kittenish noises that slipped out of her as she struggled to hold still had really turned him on. The tattooed snake hadn't come out so good and was kind of crooked and blurry, but she seemed to like it. That little snake on her ankle was the last thing he'd looked at before turning and leaving her dead and cold in her stuffy apartment.

Now there were snakes everywhere, real live poisonous snakes, and people were bitten, dying. It was almost like Beryl had somehow wished this fate on him from beyond the grave as punishment for taking her life. It just wasn't possible that something like this could happen. They had all that security and stuff. They wouldn't let poisonous snakes on a plane. Not after 9/11. He had to be asleep in his seat, caught in some kind of guilt-induced nightmare. That was the only logical explanation. He'd thought all this time that he didn't feel bad about killing Beryl, but meanwhile the guilt was all storing up inside his brain, waiting to spring this horrible nightmare on him when he least expected it.

Having realized that none of this was really real, Todd felt much more relaxed. He stopped shoving people out of his way and concentrated on waking himself up.

"Wake up," he said.

Nothing happened. On the seat back to his left, a fat triangular head raised up out of a massive coiled pile of gleaming black and gray scales. It didn't look anything like the snake on Beryl's ankle and it seemed to be staring right at him.

"You aren't real," Todd told the snake. "None of this is real."

The snake didn't argue. It just bit him.

Todd couldn't believe how much it hurt. How could something hurt that much if it was all just inside his head? The snake's fangs left burning bloody holes in the side of Todd's neck and he felt suddenly dizzy and sick. A jolt of sudden turbulence threw him to the ground and more than a dozen other snakes were there to greet him, crawling over him, biting him again and again.

"Not real…" he whispered as his tongue began to swell and grow unwieldy inside his mouth.

People who he had shoved out of his way were now stepping on him, hard feet kicking him and trampling his arms and legs, but it was getting harder and harder to feel anything at all. He wished that he would just wake up, but instead of waking up, he was swallowed up by hot, swirling blackness that was kind of like sleep, but not. And after that, nothing.

Arch turned to the door as Tiffany plunged into the flight deck, breathless and terrified, blue eyes huge and ringed all around with too much white. She really was a hot little number, with them cute itty bitty titties of hers, and she was definitely looking like she could use a little masculine reassurance.

"Sorry about the bumpy ride, doll," Arch said. "But you are not going to believe what came out of the instrument panel. Take a look at this." He held up the tiny dead snake with its squashed head dangling crooked and useless. "Have you ever in your life seen anything like that?"

"I..." Tiffany sputtered. "I... uh..."

"I sure took care of that little sucker," Arch said, tossing the slain enemy on the floor. "Don't you worry, little missy. When his buddies show up, they'll get more of the same."

"Snakes..." Tiffany said.

"I know, honey," Arch said. "I told you I'll take care of them other ones just as soon as they show their pointy little heads."

Tiffany was making more incoherent noises and pointing and stuttering and Arch sighed with frustration. Seemed like even Lassie was better at letting everyone know what was what than a hysterical woman.

"Look," Arch said finally. "Either spit it out or let me get back to flying this bird."

Tiffany's eyes rolled up into her head and she fainted prettily into a blonde, crumpled heap.

"What the hell is going on down there?" Sean asked, voice pinched and anxious. "Is there a bomb or something?"

"Flynn," Sanders said. "Stay with the kid."

His partner nodded and Sanders bolted from his seat, moving swiftly down the aisle towards the spiral stairway and the noisy chaos below. He could hear screaming and scuffling and people calling to each other in the madness. He had his gun drawn and pointed cautiously towards the carpeted floor as he started down the staircase.

Then he heard another sound, one so horribly familiar that it froze Sanders in his tracks, broadsided by an overwhelming crush of nauseous terror. It was the bone-dry warning rattle of an angry rattlesnake.

The snake was there on the second step, staring up at him with that cold, unblinking desert gaze. A huge diamondback, dusty sand-colored with the black and white banded tail raised up high, rattling furiously. Sanders's mouth flooded with metallic saliva and he could almost taste that horrible rubbery toxic flavor that had coated his tongue that day, back when he was just five years old and playing in his back yard in Tucson, Arizona.

On that day almost thirty-five years ago, Johnny Sanders had been trying to play knights with his best friend Dave Taylor. His little sister Sheila, who had just turned four years old and was always following him everywhere, kept on ruining everything. She would not leave them alone and their mom had said that they had to play with Sheila too because it wasn't fair not to include her. Sheila said she wanted to be a knight instead of a fair maiden, but didn't even know how to pretend to be dead after she lost a sword fight and kept on asking all kinds of stupid questions. Finally he made Sheila go look for the dragon in the rock pile on the far side of the yard while Johnny and Dave had a big sword battle with sticks.

Sheila had called across the yard that she had found the dragon. Johnny, who was winning the sword fight, called distractedly over his shoulder and told her to stab the dragon with her sword.

That's when he heard that sound, that horrible dry sound like death's chattering teeth. Sheila screamed and Johnny ran to her and found her clutching one chubby sunburned leg with two red, puffy holes just above the knee. She was pointing and wailing that the dragon had bit her, and when he looked into the pile of red rocks, he saw the snake.

It had its black and white tail held high, shaking it really fast to make that rattling sound with a tan stack of hollow scales on the tip. Its eyes were the same color as the rest of it and there were ridges over each one that looked like angry eyebrows. The snake was coiled back into a depression in the rocks and there was nowhere for it to go except right past them. Sheila was choking on her sobs, gasping and hiccupping as she fell back on her butt in the dust. The snake suddenly struck out at her again with its mouth wide open. In what felt like horribly drawn-out slow motion, Johnny acted without thinking and reached across to pull his sister away from the furious reptile. He felt the powerful jaws clamp down on his arm and at first it just felt like when his mom would grab his arm if she was mad in the supermarket or something. He looked down at his forearm, just above the wrist, and saw two holes, just like the two holes on his sister's leg. Thin, watery blood was oozing from the holes and a burning pain seemed to ignite inside them, spreading quickly up his arm and down to his fingers. And that taste, that strange dry and unnatural taste in his mouth, like he had licked a dirty car tire, or chewed the used and blackened eraser on a pencil.

Dave ran to get their mother. Johnny wanted to help his sister, but he felt like he was going to throw up and had to sit down on the ground as waves of dizziness washed over him. He was terrified that the snake was still there, but he couldn't see it anywhere he looked. He turned to Sheila, who was lying on her back with her eyes barely open and her breathing much too fast, loud and desperate in the afternoon hush, and Johnny was sure that he had killed her. A policeman came into the yard in a tan uniform and for a delirious second, Johnny thought he was going to be arrested for telling Sheila to poke the snake with a stick.

"She said it was a dragon!" Johnny told the policeman when he knelt down beside Sheila.

"Now just take it easy, son," said the policeman. "Try and stay calm, okay?"

"But it hurts," Johnny said. The inside of his mouth felt numb and tingly. It was hard to talk.

"I know, son," the policeman said. "But it's important."

Their mom was there in her pretty blue dress, ruining the knees of her tan pantyhose on the scattered gravel, sobbing and clutching Sheila's limp, sweaty hand.

"You were supposed to be watching her!" his mother spat, and Johnny recoiled from this accusation, wracked with an overwhelming guilt more painful than the venom racing like magma through his veins.

He must have blacked out, but his mother's angry words were still echoing in his mind when he woke up later in the hospital. There was a nice doctor with a friendly cowboy face who told Johnny that he was going to be okay. The friendly doctor explained how lucky Johnny was that the snake had used up most of its venom before it bit him. Sheila, on the other hand, was not so lucky.

Sheila was in a coma for three days before she finally died. Johnny's mother held him and kissed his hair and told him that it was not his fault, that she had just been scared and angry when she said those things and of course she still loved him, but Johnny knew in his heart that it really *was* his fault. He hadn't wanted to play with Sheila. He had wanted to get rid of the annoying little brat the whole time and he was sure that somehow he really must have told her to poke the snake on purpose.

That guilt never really left him and every time he saved a life in the line of duty, he felt a cold, melancholy depression as he found himself thinking that it didn't matter. Nothing would ever make up for not being able to save Sheila.

The other thing that had never left him was his nearly incapacitating fear of snakes.

He had been able to successfully hide his phobia for years, but an encounter with a suspect who kept pet snakes had caused Sanders's boss to require mandatory counseling. Since then, Sanders had been working on it with a Bureau shrink and was making what he felt was serious progress. He still could not stand to actually touch a snake, but he was getting better with photos and video. He had even been able to stay in the same room with a guy from the zoo holding an albino corn snake for almost five whole minutes. Rattlesnakes, on the other hand, were a whole different story. He could not even hear a recording of their rattle without coming close to vomiting. He reacted to rattling noises like a Nam vet reacts to firecrackers. Even looking at a photograph was still totally out of the question.

Now here he was, on a critical mission to transport and protect a witness in one of the most important cases of his career, and there was a rattlesnake on the plane. Terrorists, mad bombers, or other human menaces of any kind would be no problem for Sanders, so why this? His mind could not even attempt to analyze and understand, locked as it was in a primal fear so deep and profound that he felt as if his heart would stop.

The rattlesnake on the step turned its rough-scaled and sinewy body around and slithered down beneath the steps of the staircase. That was when it registered that there was not just one snake.

The rear Coach cabin was crawling with sleek, serpentine bodies of all sizes and colors. People were screaming, panicking as they were bitten again and again. Beneath the screams was a white-noise gush of constant multilayered hissing as more and more aggressive, angry snakes filled the cabin. Sanders was utterly paralyzed with terror. Even in his worst nightmares, he could not have conceived of a hell so perfectly tailored to fit his own fears. They were on a plane, flying above the Pacific Ocean.

A plane full of venomous snakes. There was no way to get away. Nowhere to run. They were all going to die. Just like Sheila.

Flynn was suddenly beside him, hand on Sanders's numb arm and eyes wide.

"Goddamn!" Flynn said, taking in the chaos.

"She said it was a dragon!" Sanders whispered.

"John," Flynn was saying. "John, come on, snap out of it."

Flynn pulled Sanders back up the stairs as more snakes twined around the banisters, tasting the air with flickering black tongues and reaching for him.

"Ever since I was a kid," Sanders was saying. "Since Sheila... I..."

"I know, man," Flynn said. "Hang in there."

"Ophidi..." Sanders whispered, feeling his throat close down, strangling his words. "Ophidia-phobia."

"Fear of snakes," Flynn said. "I know."

"I can't..." Sanders trailed off, wiping his dry lips with the back of his gun hand. "I..."

"Just sit tight," Flynn said. "I'll handle this."

EIGHTEEN

When snakes fell out of the ceiling, Curtis and Tommy tried to hide in the narrow space between two seats where feet normally go. Curtis was really too tall to completely fit so he tried to squeeze himself into as small a space as possible. He could feel Tommy's body pressed up against his back, shivering. Curtis could see a guy lying on the ground in the aisle not more than a foot away and though he couldn't be completely sure, Curtis thought maybe the guy was dead. Not dead like in the movies where he would just get up and go have some coffee as soon as the director said cut, but really forever dead like Grandma Cooper and Tommy's goldfish and Tupac Shakur. There was also a lady throwing up in the seat across the aisle. A snake had bitten her on the neck just like Dracula and she was puking all over herself and banged her head on the wall, the window and the seat in front of her. Her face swelled up fatter and fatter, turning smoky dark purple like a bruise. Curtis was glad Tommy was behind him and couldn't see any of these terrible things. Curtis liked horror movies and gory video games and considered himself pretty jaded when it came to gross stuff, but even he felt sick looking at the puking lady. Tommy was way more sensitive. He couldn't watch nature shows because he felt sorry for the gazelles when the lions ate them. He even felt bad when villains died on TV and not just the big boss villains but the henchmen too. In short, Tommy was a big pussy, but as much as Curtis liked to tease him about it, Dad had told Curtis to protect his little brother. Curtis was supposed to be the man when Dad wasn't there, and it was his job to make sure Tommy wasn't hurt or scared.

Curtis wanted very badly to cover his eyes and so he wouldn't have to look at the puking lady, who had started shaking all over like that epileptic kid back in kindergarten who'd had a fit in the playground and the teacher had to put her comb in his mouth so he wouldn't swallow his tongue. Nobody was helping her or putting anything in her mouth to make sure she didn't swallow her tongue. Mostly everybody was running around screaming and swatting at snakes. Even stepping on the guy who was probably dead. Curtis wished he could close his eyes, but he needed to watch out for that snake that had bitten the puking lady, in case it was still around and tried to bite him or Tommy.

That was when Curtis saw a different snake, crawling in the aisle between the probably dead guy and Curtis's sneakers. The snake that had bit the puking lady was a kind of pretty brown and gray pattern and much smaller. This one was black and huge, longer than Curtis was tall and had a round white ring like an eye just below its head. Curtis thought maybe it didn't see him until Tommy suddenly tried to stand up.

"Mr Wong!" Tommy cried. "We have to find Mr Wong!"

As soon as Tommy moved, the snake did something that made Curtis recognize it instantly. Something that made the fear he had been feeling minutes before seem like nothing at all. First the snake hissed and raised its head up until it was tall enough to look at Curtis eye-to-eye as he crouched down between the seats, and then it spread open a wide flat hood just below its head. The underside of its neck was white with some black stripes. There was no mistaking this kind of snake. It was a cobra.

Curtis felt Tommy go stiff and frozen behind him, eyes locked on the angry snake. Curtis thought suddenly of *Rikki Tikki Tavi*, that animated movie that he had seen when he was little. There were these two cobras, a male and a female, and the mongoose Rikki Tikki Tavi had killed the male somehow but the female, the dead snake's wife, was angry and wanted revenge. Curtis remembered a scene where Nagina, the female cobra, was in the kitchen, just inches from the little boy's leg, and she said, "If you move, I strike. And if you do not move, I strike."

That scene had scared the pants off Curtis back then, so much so that it had given him nightmares for a week. And now here was a real live cobra right in front of him and he couldn't remember how Rikki Tikki Tavi had saved the boy in the movie. He thought maybe it had something to do with her egg, but that wouldn't help Curtis now. He had to think fast, to save Tommy.

The laminated sheet that tells you what to do in an emergency on the plane (no information about snakes though, Curtis thought, a lot of good that does now) had fallen out of the seat pocket and was on the blue carpet about an inch from the tips of Curtis's right index finger. He thought of snake charmers, a show he had seen once on the Discovery Channel. Snakes are deaf, the show had said. They don't get charmed by the music; it's the movement of the flute and the basket lids that holds their attention.

The snake was looking right at him, meeting his gaze just like a person, and its mean little black eyes seemed much smarter than you'd think a snake would be. Curtis had never been so scared in his whole entire life, but he had to do something. He had to take care of Tommy like he'd promised.

He grabbed the white laminated card and held it up, waving it the way those snake charmers waved the lids of their baskets. The snake's eyes instantly moved from Curtis to the swaying white card, and it raised itself up a little higher, hissing angrily.

"Look over here," Curtis said, waving the card back and forth. "Come on, snake, look at this."

The snake lunged at the card but didn't bite it and Curtis nearly had a heart attack, but he kept on waving the card. His wrist was starting to get pretty tired.

"Tommy," Curtis said out of the corner of his mouth.

His brother didn't answer; he just kept on making little whimpering noises, wide eyes never leaving the swaying cobra.

"Tommy," Curtis repeated. "Tommy, listen to me. I want you to climb up over the seat."

"What?" Tommy asked, his voice sounding small and distant.

"Move real slow and I'll keep on distracting the snake," Curtis said. "Hurry! Go on!"

"I can't!" Tommy wailed, pressing his face into Curtis' back. "I'm scared!"

"I know," Curtis said. "But you have to."

"No!" Tommy said. "I can't!"

Curtis wanted to yell at Tommy and tell him to quit being a big baby but the swaying snake had inched closer to his hand. He couldn't keep waving the card forever. He wished that he was brave and cool like that snake hunter guy on TV who could just grab a snake behind its head and hold it up for the camera.

"Okay," Curtis said. "Then I'll…" He jumped a little when the snake lunged towards the card again and he had to swallow hard to keep talking. "I'll go with you. Stay behind me, okay?"

"Okay," Tommy said in a tiny voice.

"Ready?" Curtis asked.

"Ready," Tommy replied.

"Stay behind me," Curtis said.

Curtis very slowly got his legs under his body and started inching upward, keeping the card moving back and forth in the same spot. The snake was still gazing furiously at the card as Curtis slid first one butt cheek then the other up onto the seat. He had never concentrated so hard on anything in his life. It was like the hardest, most important test he'd ever taken and nothing existed except him and the snake. His arm was fully extended, aching and tense as he started to bring the waving card over towards the armrest, preparing to make the move up over the back of the seat, when he saw out of the corner of his eye that Tommy had not stayed behind him. In fact, Tommy had not moved at all. He was still crouched in the space between the seats, staring at the snake.

"Tommy," Curtis whispered. "What are you doing? Get up on the seat."

"I…" Tommy squeezed his eyes shut. "I can't."

"You have to," Curtis said. "Move, NOW!"

Tommy reached out to put one arm on the seat and the snake's deadly focus shifted from the card to Tommy's arm.

"No!" Curtis cried, franticly waving the safety card. "Look here!"

"He's looking at me!" Tommy whispered. "Make him stop looking at me, Curtis!"

"Come on," Curtis said. "Stupid snake, look over here."

Curtis smacked the snake in the nose with the card. The snake hissed and struck at the card but missed. Tommy let out a terrified yelp and tried to clamber up onto the seat.

Then Curtis could barely follow the sequence of events. First, a lightning-quick strike as the cobra's sleek little head darted in and its mouth clamped down on Tommy's arm. Tommy screamed and Curtis screamed and the snake was just gone, disappearing beneath the seat in a blink of an eye, leaving Curtis holding the stupid safety card in one hand and his brother's rapidly swelling wrist in the other.

"Tommy!" Curtis said.

"He bit me!" Tommy said. "You told me to climb on the seat and then he bit me."

Tommy's words started to get all mushy and his eyelids drooped down like he was sleepy. Curtis looked at the two tiny round holes in Tommy's skinny arm and wondered if he should do something; try to suck out the poison or something like that.

"Tommy!" Curtis grabbed his brother and hauled him up onto the seat. "Hang on, Tommy. You're gonna be okay. Come on, we need to get out of here."

"Mmmsshter Wong," Tommy said, slurry voice almost too soft to hear. "We gotta... find Mishter... Wong."

Three Gs saw the snakes and the screaming madness in the cabin in front of him. He started yanking frantically on the bathroom door again. All other thoughts had vanished from his mind and nothing else existed but the problem of the locked bathroom door. If only he could get inside the bathroom, everything would be okay. The flight attendant who had been cool and sweet to him and given him the hand sanitizer was nowhere to be found, and what the hell was this person doing in the damn bathroom for so long anyway? There was a long, dark-brown snake slithering down the aisle, headed right for him. Three Gs put his shoulder to the flimsy door twice, three times and then finally, the hinges in the center that caused the door to fold in two snapped and half of the door fell away, crashing down onto the snake.

A teenage kid's body tumbled out of the bathroom, flopping against the toes of Three G's green suede Gucci Firenze sneakers. It made him leap back in horror and disgust. The dead kid's face was purplish-black and swollen like bread dough. There was thin yellow puke oozing from his nose and mouth, crusted in his bloody dreads, and his boxer shorts were half down, bunched up midway down his thighs. Beyond him was the crumpled corpse of a barely dressed white girl with bleach-blonde hair stained crimson with clotting blood. Homeboy obviously got nailed by a snake just as he was about to get busy, but all Three Gs could think about was how long they had been dead and how long it took for germs and diseases to breed inside a dead body. He quickly kicked off his shoes before the germs from the corpse could creep up onto his legs and pressed himself back into the galley, socked feet icy cold against the chilly floor.

Flynn had to physically drag the frozen Sanders back up the steps and out of danger. He could barely get a hold on his partner's sweat-slick arms and he finally just shoved Sanders aside and unholstered his Glock. With his other hand, Flynn pulled a stun gun from a Velcroed case on his belt and after a single deep, calming breath, he waded down into the bedlam.

Fighting through the chaos, he glanced back over his shoulder at the front cabin. About half of the oxygen masks had dropped down, but no snakes that he could see.

"Claire!" he called, zapping a questing snake head with the stun gun and swatting another aside with the butt of his Glock. "Move people towards the front. The *front!*"

The pretty brunette flight attendant turned to his voice, eyes huge and blouse torn open, revealing a distracting V of pale skin dusted with charcoal freckles. When she moved, the blouse gaped wider to reveal one thin white cotton bra cup. Flynn quickly looked away, but not fast enough to avoid catching a glimpse of a large dark nipple poking up through the flimsy fabric of her bra.

"All right," she said. "Everyone!" She paused, steadying her voice. "Please move towards the front of the aircraft at this time."

Flynn looked back at Claire, surrounded by deadly reptiles and terrified passengers yet just as cool and calm as if she was pointing to the locations of the emergency exits. The sick and frightened passengers turned to her without hesitation, desperate for leadership. Flynn couldn't help but think that she would have made a great agent.

* * *

When the shit with the snakes started going down, the first thing that Troy felt was a kind of hollow panic. Not for himself, but for his boss. Where the hell was G? He had seen his boss dash off to the bathroom several minutes earlier and knew full well that unless they were in a truly dangerous situation, G never liked having anyone anywhere near the door while he was in the bathroom. The ride was a little bumpy but basically uneventful. There was nobody on the flight that Troy had clocked as a potential problem, so he'd just been killing time, playing *Death Jr* on his PSP and watching with half an eye for his boss to amble back down the aisle.

Now that all hell had broken loose, Troy had only one thing on his mind, and that was to make it back to the rear bathroom and get G out of danger. Leroy was beside him, steady, eyes narrow and ready for anything as they surveyed the squirming snakes and panicking passengers all around them. Troy ripped loose one of the tray tables and tossed it to Leroy, then tore off another and used it to whack the nearest snake.

"Go," Troy commanded. "Head back to the rear."

Swatting snakes and squeezing past stumbling, bitten victims gasping for breath, Troy and Leroy moved in easy sync, holding the tray tables like shields and moving steadily against the flow until they reached the rear galley.

Troy spotted Three Gs jammed back in the corner. He had no shoes on and was staring at a pair of bloated, stinking corpses in the tiny bathroom.

"G!" Troy called, but Three Gs just kept staring, hand over his mouth. "G, come on man, we need to get you the hell out of here."

"Uh huh…" Three Gs said quietly, but made no move towards Troy.

Troy found himself remembering being in sixth grade back at PS 98 with G, only he'd been plain old Clarence Dewey back then. Clarence's mama died that year and he had his first real panic attack less than a week later. Troy and Clarence had been in the boy's bathroom on the second floor when some sick kid puked in the doorway, unable to make it to the toilet. Even though the janitor came and cleaned up and sprayed Lysol and everything, Clarence flatly refused to leave the bathroom, because it would mean walking over the spot where the sick kid had thrown up. In the end, Troy had to give Clarence a piggy back ride over the "contaminated" spot in order to get him out. Clarence had begged Troy not to tell the teacher why they had been gone so long and they both wound up getting detention. Although they had been casual friends since first grade, that strange day would somehow cement their relationship and define Troy's lifelong job of making sure no one knew about his friend's obsessive compulsive disorder. He remembered the smell of Lysol burning in his nostrils and the feel of Clarence's skinny body bouncing against his back, hardly weighing anything at all. And here they were again, Three Gs refusing to budge and only one way to get him out of there.

"Get up," Troy said, turning his back and patting a broad shoulder. "Come on, I'm gonna get you out of here."

Three Gs reluctantly let Troy pull him up onto his wide back. As soon as his boss's sock feet left the floor, Troy signaled Leroy to go. Together, they bullied their way up towards the front cabin, Leroy knocking snakes aside as they went, dodging falling luggage and dying passengers.

Mercedes regained consciousness to find herself wedged between the seats in the rear of the plane. The cute rapper guy was gone and worse, so was Mary-Kate. Her Fendi purse was gone too, which wasn't all that much of a loss, since it was from last season, but she wished she had the Ziploc bag of treats to shake to call Mary-Kate.

"Mary-Kate!" she called softly. "Sugarbaby, where are you?"

She thought she heard whimpering a few seats up ahead. All these horrible snakes all over the place were biting people left and right. Tiny Mary-Kate didn't stand a chance. Mercedes was the first to admit that she was pretty selfish. Her entire life was basically all about me, me, me, but still, she had become really attached to Mary-Kate. At first it had been a kind of Paris Hilton, trendy thing to have a cute little dog in her purse all the time, but petting Mary-Kate was better than Valium when Mercedes was stressed out and it always made her laugh the way Mary-Kate would nose her way under the covers at night and then turn around and stick her head out on the pillow, just like a tiny person sleeping. The thought of anything bad happening to Mary-Kate made Mercedes feel sick to her stomach but she was afraid to move, afraid of being bitten.

"Mary-Kate," she whispered. "Sugar, sugar, sugar! Where's my baby girl? Come on, sugarbaby. Come to mama!"

Mercedes struggled to rise and as soon as she moved, all the snakes within eyeshot turned towards her, thin forked tongues licking towards her like sleazy guys in some nightclub. Heart pounding in her chest, she reached up to grab the seat beside her and pull herself up when a hideously swollen dead face rolled towards her, flopping over the edge and drooling blood and yellow vomit. Mercedes shoved herself back, gagging on the horrible smell of spoiled meat and melted rubber and rust. She kicked frantically back at the leering corpse.

"Help!" she cried. "Somebody help me!"

But everyone else was panicking and acting like they were the stars of a disaster movie, which was just totally wrong since she was obviously the one in the most danger. She climbed up over the soft dead body and stood up on two armrests, straddling the aisle and struggling to balance on only one high-heeled shoe. Tears were making a runny mess of her eye makeup as the snakes closed in around her, draping from seat backs and dangling from overhead compartments.

A thick, brownish-black snake suddenly lunged at her face and she screamed. Out of nowhere a hand shot out and grabbed the horrible creature right out of the air. She turned and saw that hunky Asian guy from three rows up, holding the snake just below its head while the snake's body twisted around frantically and it opened its pink mouth up wide, clear fangs stretching out and dripping gross yellowy stuff that was probably horrible poison. She watched in shock and amazement as the Asian guy put the snake's head against the lip of the overhead compartment and slammed it, severing the snake's head like a guillotine. Blood spray-painted the ceiling as he tossed its limp body aside and took Mercedes by the hand.

"Are you all right?" he asked.

She looked up at him then back down at the dead snake and started crying. "I can't..." she spluttered. "I... my dog..."

"Look at me," the guy said softly, holding Mercedes's face between the palms of his big hands. "It's going to be all right. We'll go together. Come on. I'll carry you up the aisle."

"Mary-Kate!" she said. "My little dog. I have to find her."

"Come on," he said, lifting Mercedes like she weighed nothing at all. "We'll find her."

"Wait, there's my bag!" she said, reaching down to grab her lost Fendi purse off a seat as they passed.

A snake struck at the spot where her bag had been only seconds before. Mercedes let out a tiny shriek, clutching the purse to her chest as she was carried down the aisle.

If I find Mary-Kate alive, she told herself, I'll let her have the whole bag of treats.

Ashley couldn't pull Tyler anymore. She had always considered herself to be cool in a crisis, but her brain seemed barely able to function, folding up tighter and tighter on itself like crazy origami. Why did she have to pick Hawaii? Why hadn't she taken Tyler's fear of flying more seriously? Why couldn't they have just gotten married on the beach in Malibu and spent the week in some cozy little oceanfront condo like Tyler had wanted? If she hadn't been so selfish, none of this would be happening.

Then, out of nowhere, a big black man in a black suit was right there, throwing Tyler's loose, unconscious arm over his thick shoulders and helping Ashley to her feet.

"Come on," the man said. "We need to get up to the front of the plane. Was he bitten?"

Ashley nodded, eyes filling with tears. Tyler, her beloved Doggy Daddy, who put up with her and all her rescued dogs, who loved her and wanted her to have the Hawaiian wedding she dreamed of no matter what—he was dying now, dying because of her. How could this be happening? How could... *snakes* have gotten onto the plane?

She saw an Asian guy go down the other aisle with a flailing Mercedes tossed over his shoulder like a sack of potatoes. She did not see the chihuahua. That was when a sound cut through all of Ashley's fear and confusion. It was the soft whimper of a terrified little dog and it was very close.

"Mary-Kate?" Ashley said, suddenly sharply focused.

The black man holding Tyler looked at Ashley like she was out of her mind, but she just gestured for him to get Tyler up to safety. She squatted down and whistled softly.

"Mary-Kate, come!" she called, peering down under the seat.

She could see the tiny dog cowering beneath a seat three rows down, ears pinned flat to her head and her whole body shivering, making a disco ball shimmer across the carpet as her diamond collar twinkled in the flickering lights. Worse, there was a long brown snake headed down the aisle, tongue flickering out towards the terrified and bite-sized Mary-Kate as if it could taste her fear.

"Oh no, you don't," Ashley cried.

Without hesitation she whipped off her new Hawaiian-patterned shirt and threw it over the advancing snake. Topless but for her pink cami-bra, she dived down under the seat where Mary-Kate was hiding and grabbed the chihuahua while the snake thrashed beneath the colorful fabric, twisting and tangled and searching for a way out. Ashley ran, clutching Mary-Kate protectively to her chest.

"Ashley's got you, Mary-Kate," she said. "I've got you now, honey. You're safe."

Suddenly the complete absurdity of the situation struck Ashley. Mary-Kate and Ashley, just like those Olsen twins that were always in the tabloids. She let out what had to be a completely crazy laugh as she made a mad dash for the front cabin.

Mercedes was there with that Asian guy in the front when Ashley came through with the dog. Mercedes let out a stifled sob and threw her arms around Ashley, gently taking the terrified Mary-Kate from Ashley's arms.

"Thank you," Mercedes said. "Oh my God, thank you so much." She pressed her face into the fur behind Mary-Kate's neck. "If we get out of this alive, sugarbaby," Mercedes said, "I swear I'll donate a million dollars to Chihuahua Rescue. Ten million. Please just let us get out of this alive."

Ashley thought of little Esperanza, waiting for her back home with Cookie and Ace, and added a silent prayer of agreement. Please let them get out of this alive.

Flynn laid the unconscious man in a nearby seat and started gathering up spilled luggage and carry-on items, motioning to the male flight attendant to assist, building a makeshift wall to block off the snake-infested rear cabin.

"We need to block both aisles," Flynn said. "Form a barrier to keep the snakes in the rear of the plane."

"I never thought I'd hear myself saying this," the male flight attendant said, "but we need more carry-on luggage!"

Even with emptying every garbage can and pulling bags out from under every seat, there wasn't anything close to enough to block both aisles. The left side was close to solid but the right was less than half full. They had no choice but to go back in and grab more from the rear cabin.

Flynn spotted the rapper hunched in a nearby seat with his two bodyguards hovering nervously over him. The rapper himself was clearly close to useless, but the two guards were able bodied and well trained. Flynn called out to them.

"You two," he said. "Come with me."

The better looking of the two threw an anxious glance back over his shoulder at his employer. The older female flight attendant came up behind the two guards and placed a hand on each of their shoulders.

"Go on," she said. "I'll stay with him."

"All right," Flynn said, gesturing to the two guards. "Stick close and keep your eyes open."

"You a cop?" the good looking one asked.

"FBI," Flynn responded, zapping a nearby snake and motioning for them to follow. "Name's Neville Flynn. You?"

"I'm Troy McDaniel," the guard replied. "This here is Leroy DuBois."

"Charmed," Leroy said, swatting a snake with the broken tray table.

"Okay, Troy, Leroy," Flynn said. "Here's how it's gonna go. We go row by row. I'll keep back the reptiles and you two collect bags and toss 'em back. Got it?"

"Got it," Troy said.

Flynn used the stun gun to fight back the army of angry snakes, the cabin filling with the thin, acrid stench of burning scales as the two body-guards flung bag after bag onto the pile. As they moved forward, Leroy opened the next overhead bin to the left and Troy the right. Flynn spun, stun gun ready, when Leroy suddenly cried out, batting a long slender thing that had fallen from the over-head compartment and wrapped around his neck. He ripped it loose and threw it to the floor, stomping it and smashing it with the tray.

"Good job, slick," Troy said, smirking as he lifted another duffle bag and tossed it back into the pile. "You killed a stocking."

Leroy lifted the dark object between two fingers. Troy was right—it was a sheer, seamed woman's stocking. Leroy shrugged, sheepish, when suddenly he yelped and clutched his right buttock.

"Shit!" he cried. "Get it off me! Get it off me!"

There was a brilliant blue-green and black snake latched furiously to Leroy's ass.

"Damn!" Troy grabbed the snake's muscular, coiling length and ripping it loose, throwing it to the ground and stomping furiously on its head. "Motherfucker!"

"Son of a bitch!" Leroy said, lower lip clenched between his teeth and chubby face drawn with genuine fear. "Goddamn that hurts!"

"Go," Flynn said. "Get him back up front."

Troy helped Leroy, and Flynn followed, grabbing a few more pieces of luggage and zapping snakes until the charge in his stun gun died. Emboldened snakes surged forward as Flynn dived through the barricade, jamming the last pieces of luggage in place just in time.

NINETEEN

Claire was fighting down panic as she went row by row, checking to see who had made it up to the front cabin and more importantly, searching for the two little boys who had been flying alone. She had checked the seats in the rear cabin where they had been sitting, but they were empty except for the two little backpacks, one red and one blue, still stuffed under the seat. It was unsafe back there, crawling with deadly snakes, and she had no choice but to make a run for the front cabin and hope the two boys had done the same.

When Flynn's large hands suddenly gripped her arm, she flinched, a small noise escaping before she could stop it.

"It's okay," Flynn said. "It's me."

She bit down hard on her lower lip, fighting to stay calm and losing. "I can't find those two little boys. The unaccompanied minors. I looked every-where and…"

"It's okay," Flynn repeated. "We'll find them." He raised his voice, addressing the terrified sur-vivors. "Has anyone seen two little boys?"

"They were in twenty-seven A and B," Claire said.

The huddled passengers who were still con-scious and unharmed all shook their heads and dropped their eyes.

"We have to go back and look for them!" Claire said, clenching her fists and frowning at the barri-cade of luggage.

"It's not safe, Claire," Flynn said firmly. "There's nobody alive back there."

"You don't know that," Claire said, her voice rising in panic in spite of her desperate need to stay cool. "They… They could be under the seats… or…"

"Hey mister…" a young voice called from the forward galley.

Claire's head whipped around at the sound of that voice, an unconscious trill of relieved laughter bubbling up out of her. She ran down the aisle to the galley and Flynn followed close behind. They found Curtis and Tommy huddled together by the beverage cart. Tommy was barely conscious, his arm obscenely swollen.

"My brother," Curtis said. "He got bit."

"Oh my God," Claire said, gingerly examining Tommy's arm and touching a palm to his burning forehead. She turned to Flynn. "What should we do?"

"Well, we all learned the basics. Drain the venom, clean the wounds, immobilize the bitten area and keep it lower than the heart where possible. Most importantly, remain calm."

Claire pushed a sweat-dark lock of blond hair back from Tommy's heavy-lidded eyes and then put a hand on Curtis's arm.

"I was supposed to be the man," Curtis said, eyes shiny with unshed tears. "I was supposed to take care of him."

"You're taking care of him now," Claire said softly.

"It's too late now," Curtis said, tears spilling down his cheeks. "Look at him. It's my fault he got bit."

"That's not true, honey," Claire said. "You brought him up here where it's safe, didn't you?"

Curtis nodded, looking back at his semi-conscious brother.

"See, that was very brave," Claire said. "You probably saved him by getting him out of there."

"Is he going to die?" Curtis asked, small face grim and serious.

"No," Claire said, hoping it was true. "But he really needs you to keep on being brave now, okay?"

"Okay," Curtis said, pressing his lips together and trying so hard to be brave that it nearly brought tears to Claire's eyes.

Grace was with Leroy, holding his sweaty hand and telling him to stay cool, when she heard the faint sound of a baby crying in the rear cabin. She was struck with an instant clear and awful image of Maria and her baby Isabella trapped back there, surrounded by deadly snakes.

"Oh God," she whispered, dropping Leroy's hand and spinning to face the barricade of luggage.

There was no time to think, no room for hesitation. She pulled aside enough bags to squeeze through and then quickly replaced them behind her.

The rear cabin was dim and stuffy, sporadically lit by showers of sparks and flickering No Smoking and Seatbelt signs. Corpses lay draped over seats and sprawled in the aisles. All around her was the stealthy, slithering movement and sibilant hiss of writhing snakes.

It took her eyes a second to adjust to the darkness as she scanned the hellish scene around her, searching for signs of the baby and her mother. One of the slumped figures Grace had mistaken for a corpse suddenly began to stir, hands clutching at a bloody blonde head as a querulous voice called out.

"My baby…"

"Maria," Grace whispered, touching the young mother's hand. "I'm here."

Maria did not appear to have been bitten, but she had a large, nasty contusion just above her right eye and her face was sticky with clotting blood.

"Isabella!" Maria said, voice twisting up into the higher octaves of panic. "Where's my baby?"

Grace scanned the shadowy cabin, ear cocked to the soft whimpering of the infant. It sounded low and to the left, somewhere in the center row of seats.

"Stay put, Maria," Grace said. "I'll find her."

Following the sound of the feeble cries, Grace spotted a colorful twist of blanket sticking out from between the seats in the center row. It was the infant, Isabella, on her belly on the floor, crumpled blanket trailing into the aisle and tiny feet kicking. Grace was about to reach out and grab the baby when she heard an ominous dry rattling sound that stopped her heart. Her eyes tried to look everywhere at once, every shadow and shape taking on malevolent purpose, but she could not spot the threatening snake. That was when Isabella arched her spine and rolled over onto her back, revealing the bright green and yellow-striped plastic rattle pinned to the sleeve of her romper. She shook her little fists and the rattle sounded again, and Grace let out her held breath in a shaky sigh of relief.

Before Grace could take another breath, there was another rattling sound, this one slightly higher in pitch and further back. To Grace's utter horror and alarm, an enormous, black-banded timber rattlesnake slithered swiftly from beneath the seat, sliding over the infant's narrow chest with its thin forked tongue flickering out towards the plastic rattle.

Paralyzed with fear and icy dread, Grace clenched her fists, nails digging into the meat of her palms. If she tried to grab the baby now, there was a very good chance she would be bitten, or worse, Isabella would be bitten. But if she did nothing, the baby might still be bitten. Torn and tortured and unsure, Grace silently willed the unknowing infant to stay still. Strangely, the infant seemed calm, not at all frightened by the slick alien weight sliding over her tiny body. Innocent and docile, she had no idea of the deadly danger she was in.

Grace made an indecisive move towards the infant and the rattlesnake reared up, hissing and rattling as its blunt head cocked back on its coiled neck, eyes locked on Grace. One of the snake's muscular coils pushed across the tiny bridge of Isabella's upturned nose and she started to cry.

"No!" Grace screamed as the snake's attention shifted to the infant beneath it.

"Isabella!" Maria called, voice torn to anguished rags.

Grace reached out, waving her arms to distract the snake from the baby. "Here. Look here!"

The snake rattled again, and seeing that its warning was going unheeded, it suddenly struck out at Grace with a suckerpunch, strong jaw gripping her side just above her waist as if trying to pinch an inch.

In that instant, just when Grace felt sure that all was lost, a hand shot out of the darkness, grabbing the rattlesnake and pulling it up and away from Grace and the howling baby. Wide eyed and incredulous, Grace saw the blond FBI agent wrenching the twisting and furious snake away from them as it bit him again and again in the shoulder and chest.

"Go," the blond agent said. "Get the little girl out of here."

Despite the burning pain in her side, Grace lifted the terrified infant and turned to half run, half stagger down the aisle to the sobbing Maria.

"Oh my God," Maria said, clutching the baby tightly to her chest. "Is she okay? Was she bitten?"

"No," Grace answered, feeling waves of nausea and cold sweat washing over her. "She's fine."

"Thank you," Maria said, tears running freely down her cheeks. "Thank you, thank you."

"Don't thank me," Grace said and then trailed off, looking back over her shoulder where the blond man was hunkered down over the armrest of a seat. "Go up to the front," she said instead. "Get Isabella to safety."

"But where are you..." Maria frowned, eyebrows drawn together.

"Quickly now," Grace said. "I'll be right behind you."

She gave the anxious young mother a light shove towards the barricade of luggage and then turned back, dodging snakes on both sides as she made her way back to the blond agent.

"Come on," she said, grabbing him by the wrist. "Let's get out of here."

He turned his sweat-slick, pale face towards her voice, and she was horrified by how bad he looked. He had clearly been bitten several times by other snakes even before he grabbed the rattler.

"I'm dying," he said. "But I did it. I saved her."

"You sure did," Grace said. "Now come with me. You can die much better up front where there are no snakes."

He gave her a thin shadow of a smile and did not resist her as she hauled him to his feet and dragged him up to the front of the plane.

When Flynn saw Grace coming through the barricade with Sanders, it took a second for him to register what he was seeing. He'd thought Sanders was still upstairs with Sean.

"Sanders!" Flynn called, taking his partner's arm and helping him into a nearby seat while Claire tended to Grace. "Man, are you crazy? I thought you were afraid of snakes."

Sanders looked up at Flynn as Flynn tore open his partner's shirt to examine the bites. Sander's chest was lumpy and swollen, mottled with black patches of extreme tissue death. The muscles twitched and writhed like living things trying to escape the confines of his skin. Sanders's eyes were slits, his gaze unfocused.

"I saved her," he said to Flynn, his voice barely audible. "I saved Sheila."

"You did good, John," Flynn said, but his partner was already before Flynn could finish saying his name.

Sanders, the bad cop, the tough guy, Flynn's straight man and best friend, he was really dead. Sanders, who had no sense of humor, but knew every word to every bad eighties pop song ever written and used to torment Flynn by singing out loud and off key on long drives. Sanders, who had gotten so drunk the night he signed his divorce papers that he tried to hit on a very obvious drag queen and Flynn had to physically carry him back into his apartment. Sanders, who used to say that he was just too damn stubborn to die.

It was Kim. Kim was the cause of all this. It was totally insane, showy and foolish, an act of lunatic terrorism, perpetrated with total disregard for the innocent lives of the other passengers. Only a sadistic madman like Kim would think to fill their plane with venomous snakes. Even if Flynn could protect Sean from being bitten, the pilot had already been killed and clearly it was no heart attack. Could the copilot be next? Would they be trapped in a flying tomb full of corpses and snakes, waiting to see if they would all succumb to the deadly venom before they ran out of fuel and perished in a fiery crash?

"Flynn!" It was Sean, calling from upstairs. "Flynn, come on up here a second."

Flynn pulled himself together and reached out to shut his partner's eyes. He pulled one of the scratchy blue blankets from the overhead compartment and used it to cover Sanders, feeling the greasy weight of loss in his belly like a bad meal, waiting to assault him later, when this was over and he was home alone in his bed, wondering how he could have done things differently. Assuming, of course, that he lived long enough to make it to later.

He headed up the spiral stairs to see the copilot and Sean hunched over Tiffany, the blonde flight attendant, who was lolling, groggy and disoriented, in one of the seats.

"I'm fine," she was saying. "Fine."

"Poor little thing just went and fainted dead away," Arch said.

"Are you sure you're okay?" Sean asked, face drawn with genuine concern. "I could get you a soda or something."

Tiffany smiled. "That's my job, silly. I should be getting you a soda."

"Flynn," Arch said. "There are goddamn snakes in the flight deck. Aggressive little bastards too. This kid tells me there are more, that passengers are being bitten. You want to tell me what the hell is going on here?"

Flynn told him. Tiffany held Sean's hand, blue eyes wide. Arch frowned, stunned as the enormity of the situation started to dawn on him.

"So that's where we stand," Flynn said. "Now we need to figure out what we are going to do."

"With all due respect," Arch said, "I already know what I need to do. See, in case you might have forgotten, we happen to be inside a two hundred foot aluminum tube hurtling through rough skies thirty thousand feet above the Pacific Ocean. Any one of those scaly little sons of bitches can trip a circuit, a relay system or a hydraulic and this bird goes down faster than a Thai hooker with a fist full of thousand Baht bills. So my job is to keep LAX up to date on how totally screwed we are, then find some way to avoid getting bitten while keeping our asses out of the water for another two hours. So y'all feel free to stay here and figure whatever it is you want to figure. I've gotta go fly the plane."

Flynn watched the copilot turn on his boot heel and head back up to the flight deck, slamming the door behind him. Sean looked up at Flynn with his eyebrows drawn together and Tiffany struggled to her feet.

"Hey," Sean said softly.

"Honestly, honey," she said, touching Sean's shoulder and then his cheek. "I'm fine. I better get my little butt downstairs. I have passengers who need help."

"Okay," Sean said to her as she turned and walked away, a little wobbly at first, but recovering her saucy swing by the time she got to the spiral staircase.

"I better talk to Harris," Flynn said.

"Huh?" Sean turned back from the hypnotic swaying of Tiffany's toy-sized backside with a big dumb grin on his face.

"Never mind," Flynn said, shaking his head.

Teenagers. Even faced with a dozen types of horrible, agonizing death, they can still be distracted by a woman's ass. Unbidden, Flynn found himself struck by an image of Claire's direct and unflinching gaze as she watched him pour coffee in the rear galley, what felt like a million years ago. Of Claire standing in the midst of all the mayhem and madness, calm and cool with her blouse torn open. Her ass beneath her plain uniform skirt was not quite as tiny as Tiffany's, but she was no J-Lo either, that was for sure. Yet there was something about her that just wouldn't leave Flynn alone.

Wiping his dry mouth on the back of his hand, he headed up the aisle to the air-phone.

Harris was eyeing his eBay auctions when a call came through from Flynn.

"Now what?" Harris asked into the phone. "I'm kind of busy right now."

"Sanders is dead," Flynn said.

For a handful of heartbeats, Harris couldn't wrap his brain around what Flynn had just said. "Dead?"

"You know all those damn security scenarios we ran?" Flynn asked. "Well, we didn't run this one."

"What the hell are you talking about?" Harris asked.

"That son of a bitch Kim," Flynn said. "He somehow loaded the plane with deadly snakes."

"I'm sorry," Harris said frowning and clicking off eBay, spinning in his chair. "I think we have a bad connection or something. I thought you said *snakes*."

"You heard right," Flynn said. "Snakes. You know, long, skinny poisonous reptiles with fangs. They killed Sanders, the pilot and several passengers. Several more have been bitten and might not make it to LAX. Sean is fine, but we've got a pretty dire situation up here."

"Snakes?" Harris frowned. "What kind of insane plan is that? Kim can't possibly guarantee a snake will get to Sean."

"He doesn't have to guarantee it if he brings the whole plane down."

Harris silently considered this. It was crazy, but so was Kim. And Flynn was right. This situation was very, very bad.

"All right," Harris said. "Do what you can and for God's sake, don't let anything happen to that damn kid. I'll get things rolling on the ground."

"All right," Flynn echoed, and the connection was severed.

Harris slowly put the phone down and motioned to the two agents standing by in the doorway. Agent Jeremiah Fisk was a younger white man with a boyish, clean-shaven face and thinning dark hair whose deceptively mild appearance hid a whole lot of bad-ass, not to mention a sharp, biting sarcasm and graveyard sense of humor. Agent Darnell Lawson was large and black, built like a rhino and just as tough. He had to have all his suits custom made to fit his massive frame, but unlike the standard big guy cliché, he was also fiercely intelligent and meticulous in nature, with a real gift for playing dumb just long enough to give a suspect enough rope to hang himself. Fisk and Lawson were the only men, other than Flynn and Sanders, that Harris knew he could trust with something this critical, this impossible.

"All right, boys, listen up," Harris said. "I want a crisis team at LAX a-sap and by that I mean yesterday. Fisk, I need the cargo manifest for every scrap of freight on that flight. Lawson, I can't believe I'm saying this, but I need the best poisonous snake expert in this time zone and I need him by my side or in my ear in twenty minutes or less."

"Venomous," Lawson said.

"What?" Harris frowned.

"Snakes are venomous, not poisonous," Lawson said.

"Fine, whatever," Harris said. "Just make it happen."

The two agents nodded and went to work. Harris grabbed a walkie-talkie off the desk and spoke to the surveillance team at Kim's house. "Whatever you do, do NOT let Kim out of your sight."

Down in the front cabin, the passengers who had not been bitten were tense and angry. Paul more so than any of them. In fact, he was livid. How the hell could something like this have been allowed to happen? He should have gone with his gut and turned right around and marched off the plane as soon as the bullshit with first class happened. He'd be eating a room service roast beef sandwich and calling an escort from an airport hotel room paid for by the airline instead of being trapped up here with deadly snakes.

"Please, everyone," the bitchy brunette flight attendant was saying—Claire, he remembered her name was. "Let's all try to stay calm and work together to get through this."

"Can someone please explain to me," Paul was asking, raising his voice to be heard over the cacophony, "how and why you imbeciles allowed somebody to transport venomous snakes on a passenger flight?"

"We really ought to go back, don't you think?" the plain blonde yuppie woman was whining, clutching her bloody and wheezing husband.

"We are closer to LA now," Claire started to say.

"You know what they call that?" Paul asked. "They call that past the point of no return."

"I don't want to die!" yelled the bimbo with the chihuahua.

"Look," Claire said. "You're not helping anyone here, sir."

The rich guy got to his sock feet, fists clenching and unclenching. "So the game plan is what?" he asked, voice tight with anxiety. "Stand around here and wait to get bit?"

"Take it easy, G," the older flight attendant said, putting a hand on his arm.

"DON'T…" He pulled his arm away from her, teeth bared. "Godammit!"

"EVERYONE CALM DOWN!" Claire said, cutting through the shouting.

Silence, broken only by the rumble of the engines. Paul crossed his arms and looked away.

"We are doing the best we can," Claire said.

The passengers all remained silent, cowed. Paul fumed wordlessly.

"Now," Claire said. "There's supposed to be a doctor on board."

She grabbed the passenger manifest, eyes scanning the list until she found what she was looking for.

"He was in row twenty-eight, seat C," she said. "A Dr Robert Foster."

"Twenty-eight?" the older flight attendant asked. "That's in the rear cabin."

All heads turned toward the barriers of luggage blocking the aisles.

"If he's back there," the blonde flight attendant said, "he must be…"

"We'd better check," Claire said.

Paul watched her creep up to the barrier and curiosity got the better of him. Watching as she carefully pried loose a green and red backpack from the pile, he tried to pretend he wasn't looking.

"Can you see him?" the blonde flight attendant asked.

"Dr Foster?" Claire called.

Paul saw her turn away, horror and disgust twisting her features as she shook her head in an endless negative, hand over her mouth. She staggered away and Paul stepped in behind her, helpfully picking up the red and green backpack and raising it up to replace it in the barrier. But before he slid the bag back into the slot, he could not resist peering into the flickering hell of the rear cabin.

Snakes were everywhere, sliding over every surface, coiling around corpses and dangling from the overhead compartments. Down on the left was seat twenty-eight C. The occupant of that seat, Dr Robert Foster, was very obviously dead. His face was a ghoulish mask of greenish-purple and lurid red, his white polo shirt stained crimson with blood. What at first looked like a thick swollen tongue protruding from his gaping mouth began to move, twisting from side to side as it lengthened and stretched. It was the wet, bloody-slick and scaly body of a snake, pushing its way out of the dead doctor's mouth.

Sickened, Paul jammed the backpack into the gap, blocking out the view of the nightmare scene. He was unable to block it from his mind.

Troy and Tiffany stood with the sweating, shivering Leroy. Leroy could not sit because of the pain and had to kind of half lean over the seat, clutching the arm rest and baring gritted teeth. Troy was helping Leroy unbuckle his pants and peel them down slowly over the bitten area. His pale blue and green boxer shorts were wet with watery blood.

"We been through some shit together," Troy said quietly, pushing up the left leg of Leroy's loosefitting boxers to reveal the swollen and oozing bite. "But I got to tell you I never expected to be getting all up close and personal like this with your fat black ass."

"Just don't be getting no weird ideas back there, all right?" Leroy said, humor stretching tight and thin over his jagged anxiety.

"Jesus," Tiffany said softly, peering at the gruesome punctures.

"Jesus?" Leroy said. "Jesus what? What's wrong?"

"Don't you have to suck out the poison or something?" Tiffany asked.

"No way, uh-uh," Troy said. "I ain't sucking nothing. I love you like a brother, man, but I just don't swing that way."

Ken was standing in the aisle a few rows down beside Grace. He arched an eyebrow at Tiffany. "Don't look at me, honey. I'm in a monogamous long term relationship now."

"Look," Leroy said. "There'll be no ass sucking by nobody, thank you very much. Can't you just put some shit on it like... like ointment or something?"

"Not going there," Ken said, throwing up both hands and turning to back to Grace.

"Let me go get the first aid kit," Tiffany said. "Hang in there, Leroy. We're gonna take care of you, okay?"

Tiffany found Claire over in the galley with the two boys. She had the first aid kit and was sorting through the antibiotic ointment, adhesive tape and aspirin, trying to find something, anything that would help Tommy.

"We're going to take care of this," she said, more to herself than to Tommy. "Don't worry."

In the first row, Maria sat holding her baby. Across from her were Mercedes and Ashley, watching over Ashley's comatose husband and petting the tiny chihuahua. Tiffany saw the young mother stand and ask the pale and tearful Ashley to hold little Isabella. Ashley took the infant gingerly with the overly cautious body language of someone unused to babies.

"Forget about that," Maria said, stepping into the galley and gesturing to the first aid kit. "Do you have any olive oil on the plane?"

"Olive oil?" Claire asked.

"I don't think so," Tiffany replied. "But I can check."

Tiffany scoured every compartment of the galley. All the meals were pre-made and pre-packaged on the ground, so while they did have little packets of salt, pepper, mustard and other condiments, there was no plain olive oil.

"There's these little containers of low fat Italian salad dressing," Tiffany said, doubtfully eyeing a small single serve cup of dressing capped with foil. "But that's it."

"Olive oil?" Mercedes said suddenly. "Oh my God, I have olive oil." She dug around, searching inside her handbag. "I've been doing the Hasher-Daylander diet for six weeks now," she said. "You know, the one with the citrus enzymes? Then I heard about this hot new diet where you can eat whatever you like, within reason of course, but you have to drink a teaspoon of extra virgin olive oil with every meal."

"Fantastic," Maria said, removing one of her earrings. "When I was a kid, whenever my dad took us hiking, we always carried olive oil and a razor blade in case of snake bites."

Baby Isabella made a funny, high pitched hooting noise, as if approving of this idea. Ashley smiled down at her and then at Maria.

"I think she likes you," Maria said.

Mercedes finally pulled out a small bottle of very expensive, boutique extra virgin olive oil from Dean and Deluca. "Ta da! It's super good for the skin, too."

"Okay, perfect," Maria said, opening the bottle of olive oil. "You're supposed to swish it around in your mouth to seal it from the poison." She turned back to Tiffany. "And I'll need something to spit into."

She knelt down beside Tommy, earring in one hand and oil in the other. "Tommy."

The little boy turned his head towards the sound of his name but did not reply. His eyes were unfocused slits, his pale face dripping with sweat. His brother sat beside him, silent, hugging his own knees and staring at the far wall.

"Tommy, honey," Maria said, "I'm gonna do something to help you now."

The boy nodded almost imperceptibly.

"Can you look at Claire?" Maria said. "See her there? Look at her, honey."

Tommy's eyes shifted to Claire where she stood behind Maria.

"Hurts…" he whispered.

"I know it does, Tommy," Claire said. "Look at me, okay."

Maria used the sharp back of her earring to make a small incision next to the two puffy, swollen punctures. Quickly swishing the olive oil around in her mouth, she bent and put her lips to the wound. Tommy made a small whimpering sound. Tiffany put a plastic cup in Maria's outstretched hand and she spat a bloody mouthful into it.

"You are being so good, Tommy," Claire said, looking a little green.

"Wow!" Mercedes said. "Gross."

Maria repeated the process, swigging the oil and then sucking and spitting. Tiffany turned away to see Leroy in the aisle behind her, watching Maria with wide eyes, mesmerized.

"Now that's what I'm talking about!" Leroy said. "Can I be next?"

Flynn returned to the First Class cabin to find Sean standing at the top of the spiral staircase, face blotchy red and furious.

"Dude," he said. "You want to tell me what in the hell…"

Flynn cut him off. "Look, just sit tight."

"Sit tight?" Sean asked. "Are you crazy? I can't just sit tight. Is this your idea of the right choice? You told me things were going to be all right and now everything is totally out of control."

From downstairs, there was a sudden scuffle and panicked swearing. Sean's eyes went wide. He was inches from losing it.

"Do you remember the first thing I ever told you?" Flynn asked.

"I know what you said," Sean replied, "but—"

"What's the first thing I ever told you?" Flynn asked again.

"Things are different now," Sean said. "You have a whole plane full of—"

"What. Is the first thing. I ever told you?"

Sean paused, narrowing his eyes. "You said, 'do as I say and you'll live,'" Sean answered.

"Very good," Flynn said. "I need your help now. I need you right here, by that air-phone. As soon as Agent Harris comes on the line, you come get me. Got it?"

"I'm not a little kid," Sean said.

"I never said you were," Flynn replied. "But that doesn't change what I need you to do right now. Can you do that for me?"

"I…" Sean looked back over his shoulder at the air-phone. "I guess."

"Okay then," Flynn said.

Chen was watching over the left-hand luggage barrier when he noticed a brown leather handbag sliding forward out of the pile. He put out his foot, using his toe to wedge it back into place, and felt muscular resistance push back from the other side. He felt the resistance subside for several seconds until a neighboring backpack started inching forward. To his horror, he noticed that the backpack was not the only thing moving. All throughout the pile, purses and bags slowly began working themselves loose. He spotted dark, slender heads squeezing through the cracks, some head high, some down near the floor.

"They're trying to get through!" he cried, stomping a nearby head that had been stealthily questing towards his shoe.

Chen heard the distinct sound of the quick, well-trained exhale that accompanied a decisive punch or kick and spun, instinctively defensive. Behind him was the fey male flight attendant. The guy had just thrown a surgically perfect, head-high kick, smashing the head of a striking snake that would have nailed Chen in the back of the neck. The flight attendant was also holding a pot of coffee and had delivered the kick without spilling a single drop. Chen could not help but be impressed. He had seriously underestimated this guy. He might be all queeny and fey, but he clearly knew his shit.

"Thanks," Chen said.

"Heads up," the guy said, hand on Chen's shoulder as he stepped in front of Chen. "Taste this, you bitches!"

He threw the scalding coffee on the area where the most snake heads were pushing through. They hissed and retreated, redoubling their efforts on the other side. Behind Chen and the flight attendant, the bald black guy who had been sizing

Chen up earlier appeared holding a fire extinguisher.

He let the snakes have it with a blast of fire-retardant foam, then tossed the extinguisher to Chen.

"Don't let those bastards through," he said.

Chen nodded and trained the nozzle on the barricade.

Flynn ran back to the galley. He rummaged through the lemon-scented towelettes and packets of sugar and napkins and cocktail straws in a desperate search for anything that could be used as a weapon. Claire appeared in the doorway, dark eyebrows drawn with concern.

"We need weapons," Flynn told her. "Where's the silverware?"

"There are real utensils up in First," she said. "But down here, we just have these."

She held up a clear plastic packet that contained a napkin, a little paper envelope full of salt and an envelope of pepper, and a single white plastic utensil that gave Flynn sudden vivid and awful flashbacks to the grade school lunchroom.

"Sporks?" he said, eyeing the blunt toothy spoon.

"Sporks," Claire said, nodding.

"That just won't do," Flynn said. "What else do we have down here?"

She grabbed one of the mini bottles of champagne that had been set aside for her little going away party, a million years ago, before all this madness. Holding it up to the light for a brief moment, she brought it down sharply against the edge of the counter like a tough girl in a bar fight. The cheap champagne fizzed up and formed a foamy puddle on the floor, leaving her holding the neck of the bottle, snapped off in a jagged and deadly edge.

"Now that's more like it," Flynn said.

He watched for a moment as Ken joined them and started helping Claire smash bottle after bottle, stealing occasional sips.

"We can't let it all go to waste," Ken told Claire.

Flynn could not allow himself to be mesmerized by the beautiful determination in Claire's strong jaw and fierce eyes as she lined up the broken bottles, or the way that several glossy corkscrews of black hair had come free from the clip and tumbled down over her forehead. He needed to stay focused on the task at hand.

Turning away, he noticed a pickup stick jumble of golf clubs in a half-open storage closet. The bag they had been inside was gone, carted off as part of the barrier, no doubt, but the clubs themselves would be excellent weapons. They could use medical tape from the first aid kits to attach the broken bottles to the clubs to form spears.

That was when he heard a soft sobbing coming from one of the seats near the galley. When he turned around, he spotted the woman with the short blonde hair whose brand new husband had been bitten. The one who'd saved the little dog. She was crying hopelessly, her arms wrapped around herself and her head pressed against the seat in front of her.

"Hey," Flynn said. "You okay?"

"No," she said, almost too quietly to hear over the drone of the engines and the sound of breaking glass. "No, I'm not. I'm not."

Her husband was in the seat beside her, strapped in and lolling. If it weren't for the rapid rise and fall of his narrow chest, Flynn would have sworn he was already dead. She was facing away from him, eyes bleak and rimmed with red.

"Hang in there, okay?" Flynn said, unsure of what else to say. "We're all gonna make it."

"I never put him first," she said softly.

"Excuse me?" Flynn asked.

"He put up with fosters that weren't house-trained," she said. "And me leaving in the middle of my own birthday dinner that he had cooked himself to go pick up an owner surrender in Santa Ana. He never complained about the money I spent on rescues and never put his foot down and told me there was no room for one more. He loved me that much and I always put the dogs first. Always."

"But you saved him," Flynn said. "He must outweigh you by fifty pounds and you pulled him out of there."

"I knew he was afraid of flying," she continued as if she hadn't heard Flynn. "I knew it, but I didn't take it seriously. If I'd only listened to him, just this once, we would be home with our dogs right now." She pressed her forehead back against the seat again. "Now it's too late," she whispered. "Too late."

"Just try to keep it together," Flynn said, feeling awkward and wishing he could think of something comforting to say. "We'll be in Los Angeles soon."

"Too late," she said again and again, lost in her own guilt and remorse. "Too late, too late, too late."

TWENTY

Dr Stephen Price was a professor of herpetology at UCLA. He was forty-two, tall and skinny with tousled dark hair and intense blue eyes that blazed with a passion bordering on the fantatical whenever he spoke about his beloved reptiles, or "herps" as he liked to call them. He looked much younger than he was and was frequently mistaken for one of his own students.

A little over two years ago, he had been featured on an episode of *Herp Patrol*, a reality show that dealt with the smuggling and illegal sale of dangerous herps, from endangered poison dart frogs to leucisitic crocodiles and of course, snakes. Price's debut episode featured some genius who'd tried to bring six juvenile *Lachesis melanocephala*, also known as the blackhead bushmaster, into the States, hidden inside his acoustic guitar. Two curious customs agents had been bitten, although only one of the bites had actually involved envenomation. Dr Price had done his dissertation on this rare and fascinating Costa Rican pit viper, and the producers of the show had approached him to do a talking head segment, backed up with some footage of Price's own prized adult *melanocephala* named Lalo and some of the institute's other bushmasters, including the darker *stenophrys* and their enormous record breaking twelve-foot *muta muta*, currently the longest viper ever found.

In retrospect, Dr Price had to admit he let being on television go to his head a little. Okay, well maybe a lot. He bought a vintage Mustang with a vanity plate that said "SNKMAN" and dumped his loyal, geeky girlfriend for a younger woman, an actress named Camden with fake tits and a snake tattoo who thought snakes were "rad." He did three other spots for *Herp Patrol* and was contacted by US Customs to work with them on some real cases. He was approached by more than one network to do his own show, pumped full of cappuccino and empty promises in meeting after meeting, but his new happening Hollywood lifestyle was starting to feel empty. He was getting behind on his papers, missing out on critical matings and hatchings, and generally spending too much time with humans and not enough with herps.

He was in the lab very late that night, watching over a clutch of endangered Antiguan racer eggs that would be the first ever hatched in captivity, when his cellphone rang.

"Stee-eve!" It was Camden, her valley accent drawing out the vowel into a whiny sort of cat-call. "Where are you?"

"Cam," Dr Price said, sighing. He could hear her pouting over the phone. "I've got those Racer eggs…"

"Steve," she said. "Do you even care what day it is?"

"I'm sorry," he said, looking up at the calendar above his desk. The only thing written in that day's square was *racers* with a large question mark beneath it. "What day is it?"

She made an exasperated sound. "It's our anniversary!"

Dr Price squeezed his eyes shut and covered them with one hand. "Oh," he said pointlessly, knowing he was in for it no matter what.

"Oh?" Camden replied. "Oh? Is that all you can think of to say? Maybe I ought to paint some scales on my body. Then maybe you would notice me once in a while."

"Cam, honey…" he said.

"Don't you 'Cam honey' me," she said. "A relationship is about two people being together. Building a life together. *Together*."

"Of course…" he said, eyeing the Racer eggs over one shoulder.

"Steve, am I a priority in your life or not?" she asked.

Dr Price, who would rather milk a cranky Taipan than deal with a woman asking questions like that, made some vague, noncommittal noises and then turned towards the sound of the lab door opening.

It was not Sanjay, his intern. It was three very serious-looking men in sober suits with Fed written all over them.

"Dr Steven Price?" said the older man who was clearly in charge of the group.

"Some men just walked into my office, Cam," Dr Price said into his cellphone. "They look very official. I'm gonna have to call you back."

"If you hang up this phone, Steven," Camden said, "you can forget about coming by later."

"I'll call you back," Dr Price said.

"Don't bother!" Camden said. "Because I WON'T BE HOME!"

Dr Price heard the click of the severed connection and breathed a sigh of relief. He folded the phone closed, slipped it into his pocket and turned to face his visitors.

"What can I do for you gentlemen?" Dr Price asked.

Twenty minutes later Dr Price was sitting in the back of a speeding van, clutching his laptop case like a life preserver and feeling more than a little queasy as he attempted to wrap his brain around what he'd been told.

"Okay," he said. "Okay, let me just say this out loud and make sure I'm understanding what you're telling me." He paused, frowning. "You have an unknown number of venomous snakes loose on a plane. Several passengers, one of your agents and the pilot have already died and others have been envenomated but are still alive. They are still two hours out of Los Angeles, currently somewhere over the Pacific Ocean. Am I getting this right? Because frankly, it sounds more than a little crazy."

The older agent who had introduced himself as Harris nodded. "Based on the information we have received from our man on the aircraft, that is our assessment of the situation at this time."

Dr Price pulled out his cellphone and dialed the National Poison Control Center from memory.

"We've already contacted the local ERs," Harris said.

Dr Price looked up at Harris, narrowing his eyes. "The local ERs? If the situation you described is real, then I don't think you understand the magnitude of what we are dealing with here."

He unlatched his case and pulled out his laptop, balancing it on his knees and booting it up. He could see the fed's nose wrinkle as several gruesome close-up photos of necrotic snakebites appeared on the screen.

"Los Angeles County ERs can handle the occasional envenomation from one of our local rattlers," Dr Price said. "But a 747 full of snake bites from species unknown is beyond the capacity of even the best facilities in the area."

He could hear his call connect, ringing on the other end.

"I'm calling the National Poison Control Center to alert every ER in the Tri-County area and order every available helicopter crew to be prepped and ready. We've got less than two hours to mobilize an army."

A smooth female voice picked up on the other end of the line and Dr Price held up a finger to Harris.

"Yes, hello," Dr Price said into the cellphone. "This is Dr Steven Price. My priority emergency ID number is 5213478... No you will *not* put me on hold..."

Claire stood with Ken beside Grace, who was slumped in one of the seats, wrapped in three blankets but still shivering, teeth chattering like castanets.

"The passengers are right," Grace said between her chattering teeth. "These seats are really uncomfortable."

"Gracie," Ken said softly, taking Grace's hand. "Hang in there, mama."

"Ken," Grace said. "When are you going to buy Kitty a ring?"

"We were thinking about going shopping together this weekend," Ken said. "You know, go scare all the nice normal couples at Robbins Brothers. Pick out diamond rings that match. You know me, I'm not gonna let her hog all the sparkle."

"Of course not," Grace said. She paused, coiling in on herself and riding out an awful wave of pain before letting out her breath and continuing. "Have you... set a date?"

"Well, I want June, of course," Ken said. "But Kitty's mom and her partner are both college professors and June is finals and graduation and all that so I'm thinking that's probably not going to work. As for my so-called family, as much as I would love to see the look on their hypocritical white-trash faces when they find out their unnatural heathen pervert of a son is actually getting married to a genetic female, they are absolutely *not* invited."

"What about us?" Grace asked, squeezing Ken's hand with a weak grip. "We're your family too, you know."

Tears filled Ken's eyes and he brought Grace's sweat-slick hand to his lips.

"Of course you are invited, Gracie," Ken said. "Claire and Tiff too. You've always been like a mom to me, more so than that narrow-minded bigot who still thinks she took home the wrong baby from the hospital. You guys have to come, Grace, otherwise my side of the church will be empty except for a few bitchy, bitter old drag queens dishing on the bridesmaid dresses and the flowers and the decor."

Grace tried to smile, but her body was suddenly wracked with spasms, a trickle of yellow bile dribbling from the corner of her mouth.

"Shit!" Claire said. "She's going into shock."

"Don't do this to me, Gracie," Ken said. "I need you to be there. Don't you dare die on me, you hear me? Don't you dare."

Claire turned away, filled with a thousand jagged emotions, and saw Flynn standing down the aisle. Their eyes locked and Claire could feel something pass between them, although she couldn't have explained what that might be.

"Flynn," the young boy, Sean, called from the foot of the stairs. "They got a snake guy on the phone."

Flynn moved immediately to hustle Sean back up the steps to safety and Claire saw the nasty businessman exchange a glance with the anxious rapper.

"Who the hell was that?" the businessman asked.

"Agent Flynn?" Dr Price said, trying to hold Harris's satellite phone between his shoulder and ear while calling up a chart on his laptop entitled "Effectiveness of Monovalent and Polyvalent Antivenins in the Treatment of Ophitoxaemia." "Dr Steven Price here. I understand you have a very unusual situation up there."

"That's one way to put it," said the deep voice on the static-filled line.

"Okay," Dr Price said. "First things first. I understand there have been fatalities. How many people are bitten and still alive? Any under the age of twelve?"

"Three adults, two males and one female. One of the men has been bitten in the face and is currently unconscious, possibly comatose," Flynn replied. "There is also one seven year-old male, bitten on the forearm."

"Right," Dr Price said. "And what steps, if any, have been taken in the way of first aid?"

"One of the passengers tried to suck the poison from the child's arm," Flynn said. "But it's hard to tell if it helped or not."

"Unfortunately," Dr Price said, "I would say that it probably did not. It has been scientifically established that venom absorption takes place almost instantly after a bite occurs, but the use of suction to remove venom is still a topic of heated debate in the medical community. However, especially in the case of the child, I definitely would advise the use of a tourniquet, not too tight, between the wound and the heart. Make sure it is loose enough to slip one finger easily between the bandage and the limb. And most importantly, encourage the victims to stay calm."

"That's gonna be tough," Flynn said. "We've got dozens of killer snakes fighting to get through the barricade and attack us."

"I'm sorry," Dr Price said, frowning. "Did you say the snakes are going out of their way to attack people?"

"I've dealt with homicidal meth-heads that were more laid back than these snakes," Flynn replied.

"Look," Dr Price said. "That just doesn't make any sense."

"You think I'm making this up?" Flynn asked. "These bastards are out for blood. They're pushing through the barricades right now to try and get to us. We're under siege up here."

"But snakes don't attack humans unless they are provoked," Dr Price said. "I mean, sure, some species, especially the various cobras, can be pretty bitchy sometimes, but even they are not going to randomly attack a large group of people for no reason. Most snakes in an unfamiliar and threatening situation would prefer to get away and hide. That's the whole point of threat displays like the rattle or the hood, to scare enemies away without having to resort to a bite. Venom is precious and it takes time to make more, so snakes don't want to waste their venom on something too big to eat unless they have no other choice."

"That's all well and good in theory," Flynn said. "And if I was sitting in a cozy library somewhere listening to a goddamn herpetology lecture, maybe I might be convinced. But I'm on a plane with a dead pilot, dead civilians, and a soon-to-be dead little boy and I'm telling you that these snakes are going out of their way to attack us."

"Okay, okay," Dr Price said. "It could possibly be a pheromone. That's what female animals release to trigger mating behavior. It can also provoke serious hyper-aggression, like some kind of drug."

"Great," Flynn said. "Snakes on crack."

Arch scowled grimly out at the lashing rain, fighting the turbulence and trying not to think of the million and one ways this situation could go to hell in a hand basket. Suddenly, a particularly large jolt knocked a pen from the flight desk. It rolled across the floor and bumped into Arch's boot. He was reaching down to retrieve it when he spotted a smooth scaly tail wrapping around the base of his seat.

He dropped the pen, which rolled away and fell into the still-open avionics hatch. Rotating in his chair, his eyes followed the snake's dark brown body, searching for the business end, until he was suddenly face-to-face with a rearing, pissed Taipan, poised and ready to strike.

"Jesus H Christ!" Arch hollered, raising his hand defensively to protect his face as the snake struck out at him.

The snake latched on to the meaty part of Arch's right hand, just below the pinkie. Arch lurched up out of his chair, trailing nearly seven feet of flailing, coiling and pissed off snake. He shook his arm like it was on fire, whipping the snake back and forth in a desperate attempt to get the damn thing to let go. He took a wild, dancing step backward and tumbled down into the open avionics hatch.

Silence on the flight deck, broken only by the hum of engines and the gentle swish of rain streaming over the glass. Then another volley of turbulence hit, jiggling the yoke and causing it to inch slowly forward. In turn, the aircraft itself began to descend ever so slightly through the churning clouds.

"Listen," Dr Price told Flynn. "There are nineteen species of venomous snakes in North America, nearly five hundred worldwide, each with its own unique toxic cocktail. Some can kill you in two minutes, others in two days, while others are no more deadly than a bee sting. You have to realize that administering the wrong antivenin can have serious consequences. Paralysis, coma and even death. It is absolutely critical that you identify the particular species responsible for each individual bite."

"Man," Flynn replied. "I'm no zoologist. I have no idea what kinds of snakes these are. I mean, I saw one that could have been a copperhead, and there are definitely some rattlesnakes of various kinds…"

"You're going to have to be more specific that that," Dr Price said.

"Shit," Flynn said. "All right, we'll see about rounding up all the dead ones we can find."

"That's a good start," Dr Price said. "Also see about getting detailed descriptions from those who have been bitten, or witnessed a bite taking place."

"All right," Flynn said. "I'll call you back."

"And make it fast," Dr Price said. "Time is tissue."

Paul decided he had finally had it with this horse-shit when the bossy black Fed who was acting like he was in charge of everyone came down from First Class and started handing out orders. He told the Asian guy and the bodyguard who hadn't been bitten to collect up all the dead snakes they could find. He told Claire to get detailed descriptions of the snakes that bit Tommy, Grace and Leroy. Just like that, everyone did what he said, obeying like good little boys and girls, while he disappeared back up into the exclusive cushy safety of First Class.

Paul exchanged a look with the rapper, his mouth a tight, angry line.

"You thinking what I'm thinking?" the rapper asked.

Paul nodded. Together the two of them grabbed their broken bottle spears and headed over to the stairs.

"I'm sorry," the blonde flight attendant said. "You can't go up there."

"Watch us," the rapper said.

"Out of the way," Paul said, brandishing the spear.

"Please," the blonde said.

"Move, girl!" the rapper said.

The blonde flight attendant meekly hung her head as Paul and the rapper shoved her aside and stormed the up the spiral stairs.

Upstairs, First Class was nearly empty, clean and safe. No wonder the black fed was keeping it all to himself. He and his little surfer-butt boy sidekick, both of whom were now standing in the aisle, staring him and the rapper down.

"Why exactly," Paul said, "are there snakes on this plane?"

"I'm sorry, Flynn," the breathless blonde flight attendant said, appearing at the top of the stairs. "I tried to stop them."

"It's all right, Tiffany," Flynn said. "I'll handle this."

"Handle it?" the rapper asked. "My boy is dying down there. We could be next. You call that handling it?"

"I have no time to explain," Flynn replied.

"Make the damn time," Paul said. "You put us all at risk, and now you're gonna tell us why."

"What I'm gonna tell you is to go back downstairs," Flynn said. "*Now*."

"Who the hell do you think you are?" the rapper asked.

Tension inside the cabin ratcheted higher and higher. Paul wrapped his fists tighter around the handle of his makeshift spear and refused to back down.

"Listen," the surfer kid said suddenly.

"Sean," Flynn said with a warning tone.

The boy ignored him. "The snakes are on the plane because of me. Because I'm supposed to testify against Eddie Kim."

There was a long, drawn out beat of silence.

"Jesus Christ," Paul finally said. "We're all gonna die."

"Not me," Flynn said quietly.

All heads turned to the black fed.

"Now look," Flynn continued. "We can stand around here and do this whole panicked angry mob thing. Get all worked up blaming me and him and the government and everybody's parents. We can do that if you like. But think about it for a second. What do you think you're gonna gain from that? So I tell you what, why don't we just skip it?"

Another pause, silence, no one with a word to say. This Flynn guy had everyone's attention.

"People," he said. "My job is to handle life and death situations on a daily basis. It's what I do, and I do it very well. So if we want to survive this, we are going to have to stop wasting energy and start working together."

As much as he wanted to, Paul couldn't find a crack in the guy's argument. As much as he hated to admit it, the guy had a point. Paul slowly let the air out of his lungs and lowered the spear.

"If you guys want to do something constructive," Flynn said, "go help Troy and Chen gather up dead snakes. We need as many as we can find so that the doctors on the ground will know what kind of antivenin we'll need. Whatever you can find, bring them back up here to me. But be careful."

There was no way Paul was going to touch any snakes, dead or alive.

"I'll help," Sean said.

"Not you," Flynn said. "I need you to stay up here."

"I can't just sit here and do nothing," Sean said.

"You can and you will," Flynn said.

"Remember when you said we all have choices to make?" Sean asked. "Well, I'm making one. Don't treat me like a prisoner."

"I'm sorry, Sean," Flynn said, "but I need you to stay up here."

"Why?" Sean asked, clearly exasperated.

"Because," Flynn replied, voice calm and even. "If you die, then this is all for nothing."

Sean frowned, but before he had a chance to respond, a voice called up the stairs.

"Yo, we got us some dead snakes."

The bodyguard and the Asian guy came up the stairs. Each had a gory pile of dead snakes wrapped up in bundles made from discarded shirts. The bodyguard was also brandishing one blue-green snake in his fist.

"I think this here is the bitch that bit Leroy," he said.

Claire ran back to where Tommy and Curtis were huddled in the galley. Tommy was barely conscious, his breath fast and labored. Curtis was sucking his thumb, his eyes wide and vacant.

"Curtis," Claire said. "Honey, can I talk to you for a second?"

He looked up at her with a thousand-yard stare but did not speak.

"Do you think you can remember the snake that bit your brother?" Claire asked.

Curtis looked away, thumb still in his mouth, and shook his head. Claire let out a long deep breath, crushing down her mounting frustration. She wanted to shake the kid and make him speak, but he was clearly shutting down, traumatized and regressing because of the stress and fear. Claire was no child psychologist. She had no idea how to deal with a situation like this, especially when another child's life was depending on it.

"Curtis," she said, fighting to keep her voice low and even. "I know you don't want to think about that right now, but the doctors need to know exactly what the snake looked like in order to save Tommy's life. Can you maybe remember what color it was?"

He shook his head again, still not meeting Claire's gaze.

"It's really, really important that you remember," Claire said, feeling like she was going to scream. "Please, Curtis."

Curtis neither moved nor spoke. He just sucked his thumb, staring at nothing.

"It's okay," Maria said, coming over to sit beside them with her baby dozing on her shoulder. "You don't have to talk right now if you don't want to." She raised her eyes to Claire.

"Troy and Chen collected up a bunch of dead ones. Maybe they found the one that bit Tommy."

"I really hope so," Claire said quietly.

Curtis continued to suck his thumb, silent.

Claire climbed the stairs to the first class cabin to find Flynn back on the phone with the snake guy.

"Well," Flynn said, eyeing the limp deceased reptile draped over his left hand, "it's kind of bluey-green."

"It's teal!" Ken offered helpfully. "Like that sort of horrendous Eighties spandex club-trash kind of teal that you would wear with a poodle perm and big geometric earrings."

"Yeah, thanks," Flynn said. "It's teal with black markings on the back and white underneath."

"This is ridiculous," Paul said, crossing his arms. "We're screwed."

"How the hell am I supposed to know if the thing's anal plate is divided or not?" Flynn asked. "We never had a chance to be properly introduced."

"Listen," Mercedes said. "Why don't we just take pictures of them?"

"Parietal what?" Flynn said into the phone, frowning down at the dead snake.

"Brilliant," Paul replied. "We can just drop them off at the nearest Jiffy Photo when we land and we're all frickin' dead. Great idea. Why didn't I think of that?"

"Haven't you ever heard of email?" Mercedes asked.

Flynn glanced at Claire, eyebrows raised, and then back over at Mercedes.

"Perfect," Claire said. "All we need is a digital camera with a cord to plug it in to someone's laptop and a wireless connection."

"Or this," Mercedes said, holding up her Treo. "It's got email and takes photos too."

"Damn," Flynn said. "I'll never make another blonde joke as long as I live." He spoke back into the phone. "Dr Price, we're going to be emailing you some photos."

Claire turned her head towards Sean's now-empty soda can. As she watched, the can slid, slowly at first, then gaining speed until it fell off the tray table. The plane was descending sharply, far more so than it ought to be. Heart in her throat, Claire turned away from the flash as Mercedes snapped photos of each of the dead snakes and quickly headed up to the flight deck door.

She punched in her access code and then slowly pushed the door open. "Arch?" she called.

The dim, silent flight deck was deserted. The two empty seats were turned away from each other and the abandoned yoke trembled as the huge unmanned aircraft slowly descended toward the ocean.

She heard Sean's voice from the first class cabin behind her.

"Are we landing? I don't see any lights out there."

Then Flynn, deep voice as cool and commanding as always. "Buckle up," he said. "Right now."

Claire placed a palm against the wall to steady herself and crept towards the gaping black maw of the avionics hatch.

"Arch?" she called again, hating how tentative her voice sounded. She didn't want Arch to hear and tease her for being a girly girl, so she took a deep breath and made her voice low and steady. "Arch, where are you?"

No answer, but she could feel the plane's trajectory become steeper, its descent growing more and more severe. She made her slow, rocky way over to the avionics hatch, bent down and peered over the edge into the darkness.

She let out a startled yelp as an enormous brown snake burst up from the hatch, its obscene pink mouth gaping and fangs dripping toxic venom. It struck at her, missing her by less than an inch as she stumbled back and away, losing her balance.

Desperate and terrified, she kicked at the hatch door, trying to slam it down on the snake's writhing body, but it was too fast, slithering up and out into the flight deck before the hatch clicked into place.

Suddenly a staticky voice spoke from a speaker in the vast instrument panel.

"Hula one-two-one," the voice said. "You are descending through twenty-four thousand feet. You are losing altitude, do you copy?"

She made a grab for the radio and the vicious snake reared up, hissing and blocking her reach. She snatched her hand back and scrambled away, looking everywhere for anything sharp or heavy, anything that could be used as a weapon.

"Hula one two one," the voice repeated. "Do you copy? Come in Hula one-two-one."

Claire's gaze settled on a bright red fire ax in a narrow glass cabinet beside the flight desk.

Ken called up the stairs to Flynn. "The barricade!" he cried. "It's coming down!"

Troy and Chen dropped their burden of dead and bloody snakes and tore down the steps with Flynn close behind. In the cabin below, the luggage wall was beginning to topple, aggressive snake heads pushing through every slot and crevice as jolting turbulence shook the aircraft like a dog with a chew-toy. Ken strapped the barely-conscious Grace into her seat, told Tiffany to help Leroy and then called out to Ashley to help him get the two little boys out of the galley and belted in.

Mercedes was clutching the little dog, chanting in a low monotonous voice, "We're gonna crash, we're gonna crash, we're gonna crash."

"I hafta…" Tommy was saying as Ken set him into a seat and buckled the belt across his lap, "throw up."

Ken was barely able to dodge a volley of hot yellow bile that splattered the seat in front of Tommy. Ken, who never felt really comfortable around children, did his best to comfort the poor kid.

"I'm sorry," Tommy said, tears streaming down his cheeks.

"It's okay," Ken said, patting his hand. "You and your brother stay right here."

"Mister…" Tommy was saying, head lolling back against the seat. "Mister Wong."

In spite of Chen, Flynn and Troy's best efforts, the two barricades were swiftly deteriorating. They were both so infested with writhing snakes that it was impossible to get close enough to make repairs, and when the plane was hit by another barrage of turbulence, both sides simultaneously burst open and scattered to bits, luggage and snakes tumbling everywhere. Panicked passengers frantically unbuckled their safety belts and leapt out of their seats, only to be slammed and bashed into walls, seats and each other.

The plane's descent towards the ocean was increasing exponentially. Flynn had no choice but to head up to the cockpit and find out what the hell was going on. Dodging luggage and stomping on snakes, Flynn dived for the stairs, taking them two at a time.

In the first class cabin, Sean staggered into Flynn the moment he hit the top of the stairs. Flynn caught the kid and steadied him, holding him firmly by both shoulders.

"What the hell do you think you are doing?" Flynn asked. "Why are you up and running all over the place? For the last time, keep your ass in that seat."

Flynn sat Sean firmly down like a naughty schoolboy and then struggled off towards the cockpit.

Claire kicked out at the glass case that held the fire ax. The glass shattered violently, glittering shards raining down all around her as she reached in and grabbed the ax off its clips just in time to swing it around, blocking an advance from the vicious snake, still coiled between her and the pilot's chair.

"Hula one-two-one," the tinny voice through the speaker called out again. "You are now descending through eighteen thousand feet. Do you copy?"

"Godammit!" Claire said, jabbing at the hostile snake with the ax, fear and frustration chewing her up inside. "Move, you stupid shit!"

The snake dodged the blade and hissed angrily, striking out at her left foot. She danced aside, nearly falling back into the hatch, as the snake slithered past her and coiled by the door. Claire could see that the door to the flight deck had not latched and hung slightly ajar. Enough for that skinny bastard to squeeze through and go after Sean. She couldn't let that happen.

Letting out a crazy, madwoman's howl, she raised the ax above her head and brought it down with all her strength.

Flynn made his way towards the partially open cockpit door, growing more and more alarmed. When he pulled the door open, only his finely honed instincts allowed him to leap back and avoid getting his head bisected by a falling ax. He watched, speechless, as the blade came whooshing down and neatly severed the top two feet of a huge Taipan from the remaining five feet of body. The uneven halves flopped madly around on the floor of the flight deck, spraying thick gouts of blood.

"Not that I don't appreciate the effort," Flynn said, "but I haven't needed a haircut in years."

Claire smiled, still holding the bloody ax and still managing to look painfully beautiful.

"My God," Dr Price said, staring at the screen of a mobile data terminal displaying the first of the photos sent down from the passenger's Treo.

"What?" Harris asked, peering over his shoulder at the screen. "Do you recognize it?"

For a few seconds, it was difficult for Dr Price to speak. The snake in the photo was a stunningly beautiful female Ceylonese palm viper, one of the largest, if not the largest he had ever seen. Her triangular head was crushed into a bloody rag. It physically hurt him to see such a rare and gorgeous specimen laying there butchered, a victim of human evil. That son of a bitch Kim was using rare, exotic and endangered snakes as kamikaze killers, hopped up on some horrible drug and sent out to do dirty work they had no way of understanding. A snake like her belonged in a safe place where she could be studied and appreciated, or better yet, living in her own natural environment as a part of her native rainforest ecosystem. But there was nothing he could say to express this feeling of loss and outrage to Harris and the others, who were only concerned for human life. He had to bury those emotions and concentrate on the job he had been given, the job of saving those people's lives.

More photos were coming in. Boomslangs and taipans and kraits and mambas. It was impossible. Utterly impossible.

"I…" Dr Price stuttered. "These… these are not North American species…"

Another photo came up, a battered and bloody *Crotalus horridus*, also know as the canebrake rattlesnake.

"Okay, well some are, but these here…" He gestured to the veritable who's who of venomous snakes appearing one after the other on the screen. "These are Asian, Australian, African…"

"Does it matter?" Harris asked. "Let's just make a list and get the anti-venom."

"*Antivenin*," Dr Price said. "And anyway you don't understand. These snakes aren't even from this continent. They come from all over the globe. Only a few hospitals even have foreign antivenins and those are mostly for exotics that are common in the pet trade."

"You mean people actually keep venomous snakes as pets?" Harris asked. "What sort of sicko would do that?"

Dr Price was about to come back with something snappy when a new photo opened. It was an enormous Russell's viper.

"Jesus," Dr Price said softly. "Russell's? Jesus, this is bad."

"Yeah," Harris said. "It's bad. How long?"

Dr Price looked up at him, frowning. "How long what?" he asked.

"How long will it take to get the anti-venom—I mean antivenin—for all these foreign species?"

"Could take as long as twenty-four hours," Dr Price said. "Maybe forty-eight."

"So what do we do?" Harris asked.

"At this point," Dr Price replied, "I don't know that there is anything we can do."

Chen and Ken were fighting a losing battle, trying to keep the snakes from pushing apart the barricades as the increasing turbulence knocked the baggage around, weakening the entire structure. There was a distinct feeling of descent as ears popped and stomachs lurched and all the loosened luggage was beginning to slide towards the front of the plane. Chen and Ken worked in silent, furious tandem, triaging the worst holes and tossing carry-ons across the center seats as Chen worked the left barricade and Ken the right. They had a brief moment of hope, when the plane seemed to level off and the relentless attack of the tireless reptiles hit a mysterious lull. Chen looked across the row of seats and met Ken's exhausted and shell-shocked gaze and nodded almost imperceptibly. They'd done it. They'd won.

Of course, it couldn't last. The plane dropped like a stone as renewed turbulence rocked them viciously from side to side. The two barriers exploded simultaneously, luggage and snakes flying everywhere as Chen threw himself down on his belly in the aisle.

All around him, people unbuckled themselves in a panic, desperate to get away from the snakes. As soon as they left their seats, the turbulence tossed them like toy soldiers, bashing them into the bulkhead and each other. Airborne and terrified snakes flew through the air like deadly party streamers on New Years Eve in Hell, wrapping around necks and limbs and biting again and again. Chaos and panic reigned as Chen fought to stand and find Mercedes, to make sure that she and her little dog were all right.

Upstairs in the First Class cabin, Sean must have stood up and sat down and stood back up again a hundred times. He had never felt so scared in his entire life. He wanted to trust Flynn, to believe that he would protect Sean just like he'd promised, but there wasn't much he could do to protect Sean from a plane crash. You couldn't shoot the Pacific Ocean. Even if he somehow survived the snakes and the crash and didn't drown or get eaten by sharks, he would be stuck out in the middle of the ocean at night with no fresh water.

He hated being stuck up here like some little kid who had been punished, sitting around with nothing to do but imagine various horrible ways to die. It was his fault that they were in this crazy mess in the first place. The least he could do was help get them out of it.

He thought of Tiffany, the pretty blonde flight attendant. He was pretty sure that she was into him, although it was always hard for him to tell with girls unless they came right out and said so. She had amazing legs and a pretty smile, and the way she touched his arm while they were talking made him feel all hot with his heart beating way too fast. She was downstairs trying to help people and Sean could hear terrible sounds coming from the lower cabin—screaming and crashes and all kinds of chaos. He couldn't stand the thought of anything happening to Tiffany, even if she wasn't really into him like he thought. That was it. He could not sit up here and let her be killed, bitten or crushed beneath fallen luggage. There were other people who needed help too, people who were dying all because of him. He had no choice.

Galvanized by a new chorus of terrified screams, Sean unbuckled his seatbelt and stood, fighting the turbulence as he made his way towards the stairs.

He was halfway down, clinging to the railing and fighting the G-forces and searching through the chaos for blonde heads, when he spotted Tiffany in the left hand aisle. Her long hair was all wild and hanging in her face and her blue eyes were wide and bright with panic. She had lost one of her shoes and her big toe was poking through a large hole in her sheer stocking. Laddered runs ran up her muscular leg, showing narrow stripes of her slightly paler skin beneath the tan nylon. She looked scared and beautiful.

Behind her, one of the beverage carts had come loose from the galley. The aircraft hit a particularly strong series of bumps and to Sean's amazement, the heavy cart went airborne, ice and straws and napkins flying in its wake.

"Tiffany!" Sean hollered. "Watch out!"

She turned towards the flying cart, staring with shock and awe. Without wasting a second to think, Sean dived from the stairs onto Tiffany's back, knocking her sprawling beneath him on the carpet. The flying cart sailed over them, wheels mere inches from the back of Sean's tucked-down head, before crashing dramatically into the wall.

For a few seconds, he was afraid to move. Then, as the seconds seemed to elongate into hours, he started to become painfully aware of the feel of Tiffany's body beneath him. His leg was between her legs and her firm little butt was right under his crotch. His face was pressed into the blonde tangle of her hair and he could smell her shampoo, a clean flowery smell with the smell of her skin beneath it. This was the worst possible time for those kinds of thoughts, but he just couldn't help it. He pushed himself up on his elbows, embarrassed, and then quickly stood before she had a chance to feel what was starting to happen beneath his shorts.

She looked up at him with those blue eyes all ringed in smeared black makeup and reached a hand out to him. He took it and helped her to her feet.

"Thanks," she said, brushing ice cubes and lime wedges from her clothes.

"No problem," Sean said, trying not to look at her wet blouse.

Ashley was still buckled into her seat when the beverage cart came hurtling through the air directly at her. She ripped off her seatbelt and was able to throw herself to the floor so the cart only clipped the back of her head as it smashed into the seat where she had been only seconds earlier. She lay, dazed and stunned with her cheek pressed against the rough blue and yellow carpet for what might have been either a few seconds or a year while her body weighed the pros and cons of unconsciousness. Apparently it decided against passing out and she was able to struggle slowly to her knees. Her hand went to her temple and came away bloody. She had to battle down a crushing wave of dizzy nausea as the sweet, sticky spray from punctured soda cans showered her with a fine mist of flavored droplets. That was when a single word flashed bright and screamingly urgent in her mind. It was her husband's name.

Tyler. Where was Tyler?

She turned back to the wreckage of the beverage cart and saw Tyler's tan legs and brand new sandals sticking out from underneath. Blood mingled with orange juice and iced tea, soaking a scatter of South Pacific Air napkins. Ashley screamed Tyler's name and started yanking futilely at the impossibly heavy cart. She could feel one of her fingernails peel off in a bright bloody starburst of pain as she wrenched at the twisted frame. Suddenly the big black guy Troy, who was with that rapper, was there beside her, telling her to step back. He and the Chinese guy pulled the cart off Tyler and then they both turned their faces away, mouths set in tight grim lines.

"Let's go," Troy said, keeping his body between her and Tyler. "We need to get you out of here."

"Tyler," Ashley screamed, pushing against the immovable wall of Troy's massive chest. "I can't leave my husband, he's been bitten. He's afraid of flying!"

"Please," Troy said softly as Chen gripped her other arm. "Let's just go now."

"No!" she cried. "Tyler!"

"Listen to me," Chen said softly. "There is nothing you can do for Tyler now. He did not make it, do you understand? You can't help him. You need to take care of yourself."

Ashley let out an anguished sob and covered her mouth, leaning into Chen as if her legs had suddenly forgotten how to work. This could not be happening. It must just be some kind of horrible nightmare.

"Oh God," she whispered into her hand, tears streaming down her face. "Doggy Daddy!"

Suddenly Mercedes was there beside her with Chen, manicured hand on her arm and holding Mary-Kate against her chest.

"Ashley," Mercedes said. "Come on now. Esperanza needs you. All the little rescue dogs need your help. You need to pull yourself together now. Come on."

Mercedes held Mary-Kate out to Ashley. "Mary-Kate is scared. Will you hold her while I go help Leroy?"

Ashley looked down at the tiny dog and then back up at Mercedes. Troy was still blocking her view of the seat and her dead husband. She bit her lower lip and then nodded, holding out her hands. Mercedes placed the little dog in Ashley's arms and she pressed her face into Mary-Kate's soft, sweet-smelling fur.

Up in the cockpit, Flynn and Claire battled the G-forces to make their way across the flight deck towards the pilot and copilot seats.

"Do you know how to fly this thing?" Claire asked, reaching out and grabbing the back of the copilot's seat.

"I was hoping maybe you did," Flynn replied, steadying himself against the desk.

"Me?" Claire hauled herself into the seat. "Are you kidding? I can show you how a seatbelt works and point to the emergency exits but that's pretty much the extent of my knowledge of aviation."

"Come on," Flynn said, grabbing the pilot's seat with one hand and gesturing to the vast and complex wall of instruments and dials and switches. "How hard can it be?"

Claire shot him a quick flash of sardonic smile and then looked out through the rain streaked window at the vast black skin of the ocean, hurtling towards them at terrifying speed. Her smile dried up, replaced by tense, pale fear.

"Hula one two one," cried the crackly voice from the tiny speaker. "Pull up! Pull up!"

"No problem," Claire said. "We'll get right on it. Now, anyone want to tell us exactly how the hell we do that?"

"I'm guessing it would be something like this," Flynn said, throwing himself into the pilot's seat and grabbing the yoke.

Planting his feet, Flynn pulled the yoke towards him with all his strength.

"Come on," he said. "Grab the other one. We need to pull together."

Claire copied Flynn, grabbing her own steering apparatus in front of the copilot's seat and pulling it towards her. It felt like battling a living thing and she could feel it fighting her, resisting, as if it was straining towards the beckoning ocean below.

"It's not working!" she cried.

"Pull harder," Flynn replied, voice still cool and calm. "NOW!"

Claire gave it every ounce of strength she had, a deep, primal sound welling up inside her chest and forcing its way out through her clenched teeth. She thought of Grace, of the two little boys, of all the people counting on her in this moment. She thought of the rest of her life: law school, buying her own home, planting a kitchen garden with fresh herbs and a bird bath. Adopting two cats, building bookshelves for all her law books and novels and yes, maybe even finding a way to finally connect with someone for more than a night or two. All the things that she had dreamed of. The things that lived in that hazy, indefinite future world of someday. All the things that would die in the cold embrace of the Pacific Ocean tonight if she didn't find just a little more strength. A little more determination. She had to make it, to survive and make it to her own private someday, if for no other reason than to prove her mother wrong. Her mother who said becoming a flight attendant was a terrible idea, that Claire would die in a crash and never amount to anything in life. She just couldn't let that happen.

"Everybody," Sean called, waving his arms. "Hey listen up everyone! We all need to get up to the first class cabin, okay?"

Tiffany stood beside him, kicking back snakes and waving everyone towards the stairs. "Come on," she said, helping the shaken passengers mount the spiral staircase. "One at a time. Keep moving."

Everyone was so busy trying to keep their footing and help those who had been bitten that no one seemed to notice the enormous, serpentine silhouette undulating inside the Plexiglas light fixture spanning the bulkhead near the stairwell. The opaque sheet began to shudder as the coiling shadow continued to pile up behind the glass, bowing it outward and down under the immense weight until...

SMASH!

The Plexiglas shattered into a million tiny fragments, showering the terrified passengers like frozen raindrops as a gargantuan twenty-foot Burmese python crashed to the floor in the center of the aisle.

Its head was the size of a greyhound's, its muscular girth thicker than a body builder's thigh. It coiled into a mottled brown and tan pile the size of a large coffee table, its pale, striped eye regarding the crowd with cold, alien appraisal.

At that point, any semblance of civilized behavior vanished under a wave of primal panic and a deep instinctual fear that went all the way back to the days when humans were few and voracious predators were many. People stormed the stairs in a mad frenzy, pushing and shoving each other aside in a blind rush to get away at all costs. As more and more people crammed themselves up the gracile staircase, it began to shiver and groan under the unaccustomed weight and there was a squeal of protesting metal as the railing began to separate from its mountings.

Ashley and Mercedes struggled to make it to the stairs, with Ashley clutching Mary-Kate and Mercedes trying her best not to scream, but Paul shoved them both aside, grabbing for the railing to pull himself up. The railing came away in his grip and he fell backwards, tumbling into the two women, and the three of them collapsed into a crumpled heap less than six feet away from the enormous reptile.

Paul tried to stand, but the second he raised himself up to his knees, the python's huge head whipped around to face him, tongue out and tasting the air as it began to move swiftly towards him.

"Shit," Paul said, looking around in a panic.

His eyes fell on Ashley, crouching protectively over the little dog as Mercedes tried to help her up. To everyone's surprise and horror, Paul swiftly ripped the little dog out of Ashley's arms and tossed it at the advancing snake.

Ashley let out a howl of anguish, echoed by Mercedes as Mary-Kate bounced awkwardly off the carpet inches from the snake's questing head, yelping pitifully as she hit and tumbled against the shining coils. In the blink of an eye, the snake turned and struck, slamming like a truck into the hapless chihuahua with its jaws wide, gripping Mary-Kate's skinny ribcage like a vice. The little dog made a horrible sound, like the shriek of an infant dipped in scalding water, and the snake corkscrewed swiftly around her, spinning coil after coil around her struggling body.

"Oh my God," Ashley screamed. "Do something!"

"It's killing her!" Mercedes cried.

Blood began to bubble from Mary-Kate's nostrils, eyes bulging hideously from her tiny apple head as the muscular grip of the serpentine death machine tightened around her. Within seconds, the chihuahua shuddered and went still and the snake relaxed its grip, nosing almost sensuously around in Mary-Kate's bloody wet fur. Mercedes let out a choking sob, hands flying up to cover her mouth, but Ashley just stared with a kind of unplugged hollow expression as the snake unhinged its jaw around Mary-Kate's head and deftly swallowed the little dog whole.

"What's it doing now?" Tiffany whispered, clutching Sean's arm.

The snake had begun to do a strange, S-shaped undulation of its neck, head weaving rhythmically from side to side. Suddenly its huge pink mouth gaped wide and a dribble of yellow liquid drooled from its chin as it regurgitated a sticky cascade of sparkle. It was Mary-Kate's diamond necklace, webbed with gore and digestive juices. The necklace landed on the carpet at Mercedes's feet and her face flushed a deep, furious crimson as she turned to Paul.

"You animal!" she cried. "How could you?"

All eyes turned to Paul, utterly aghast and horrified.

He shrugged, eyes cutting down and away. "Oh come on," he said. "It's only a dog. You all would have done the same thing."

Silence in the cabin.

"It's a frickin' dog, people," Paul said.

Mercedes turned away, sobbing inconsolably, but Ashley, who up until that moment had been staring dully at the bile-slick necklace on the carpet, suddenly let out a mad, kamikaze shriek and swung out at Paul with a wide, angry hay-maker. It was the last thing on earth he expected to happen and he caught her fist square in the nose. Blood exploded from his nostrils and he staggered back, tripping on the python's coils and falling directly into its killing embrace.

The snake struck at Paul's neck, jaws grasping him under the chin and clamping down on his windpipe, throttling the desperate curse that squeezed from his gaping mouth as his body quickly disappeared beneath loop after loop of glossy coils. Only one spasming hand and his expensive loafers were visible as the snake relentlessly crushed his bones and closed his airways.

"Come on!" Sean called, snapping everyone out of their dull, mesmerized fascination. "Hurry! We need to get upstairs NOW!"

Ken carried the barely conscious Grace. Maria carried her baby, holding shell-shocked Curtis's hand and helping him mount the stairs. Chen had already made it to the top with little Tommy in his arms. Mercedes and Ashley helped each other, pale, tear-streaked faces blank and overloaded with stress, fear and anguish. Troy and Three Gs supported Leroy as he struggled and limped over to the wobbly stairs. Sean went last, ushering Tiffany ahead of him.

The broken and battered stairs groaned and protested beneath far too much weight as Troy, Leroy and Three Gs moved up together ahead of Sean and Tiffany. Then, just as Tiffany reached the top, another powerful wave of turbulence hit and the stairs finally gave out.

Tiffany made a grab for the lip of the upper floor, but Sean was too low and tumbled back, landing painfully in a pile of jagged stair fragments.

Sean sat up, dazed and shaking his head. Above him, Tiffany dangled precariously, legs swinging above his head. He realized that he could see right up her skirt. She was wearing two separate stockings, not pantyhose, and tiny black g-string underwear, but there was no time to appreciate that fact because the huge snake didn't even bother trying to eat the bloody rag that was left of Paul. It just let go of him and started stretching upward, forked tongue flicking out towards the bottom of Tiffany's swinging foot.

"Leave her alone, you fucker!" he shouted, leaping to his feet and waving his arms like a maniac. "Come get me! Come get me, you big ugly bastard!"

The snake's huge head swung towards Sean, emotionless eyes locking on his. Sean suddenly realized he had absolutely no idea whatsoever what to do.

He looked frantically around him for something, anything that could be used as a weapon. Above him, someone was pulling Tiffany to safety, but Sean was screwed if he didn't find a way to beat this killer python. He thought of Flynn, who had saved his life and told him he had to live, or else all this was for nothing. Failure wasn't an option. He couldn't let Flynn down and he couldn't let Eddie Kim win.

The snake's paler chin and belly were smeared with clotting blood and its gore-slick coils left long crimson smears on the blue and yellow carpet as it moved sinuously towards Sean. Taking a crooked step backwards, he remembered that the big python was not the only snake in the cabin. There were dozens of smaller snakes all around him, draped over seat backs and slithering between the rows. He spotted a discarded golf club with a broken bottle taped to its head, but there was a fat rattlesnake between him and it. Before he had time to think, he pulled the in-flight magazine, the one with the article on Bali, from a nearby seat pocket and threw it at the rattler. The magazine landed open, forming a tent over the rattler's head, and Sean reached out and grabbed the golf club before the confused snake could get its bearings.

Sean turned, wielding the glass-tipped golf club just in time to meet a powerful strike from the huge python. It was more luck than design, but he somehow miraculously managed to get the club up and level with the striking jaws. The snake impaled itself on the jagged glass, the broken bottle slashing deeply into the vulnerable pink meat inside its mouth. The snake reared back, wrenching the club from Sean's grasp. It was stuck fast inside the beast's bleeding maw.

With astonishing strength, the snake flung itself around the cabin in wild, agonized death throes.

Sean made a run for the hole where the stairs had been when a flailing section of coil slammed into his ribs like a baseball bat wrapped in steak, knocking the wind from his lungs. He barely dodged a strike from another snake near his feet as he staggered and just caught himself from falling into a coiling nest of small vipers between two seats.

He heard Tiffany call his name and when he looked up, he saw her pretty face looking down from the hole where the stairs had been. Beside her, Troy held a twisted, knotted rope that had been quickly made from several shirts.

"Grab hold," Troy called, "and I'll pull you up!"

Sean didn't need to be asked twice. He did not want to die down here with all the snakes and corpses. He leapt at the dangling rope, gripping the end, a blue shirt that looked kind of familiar. Troy hauled him easily up through the hole, massive arms straining and bulging as his weight rose effortlessly through the air. He had never been so happy in his life when hands grabbed onto his arms and T-shirt and dragged him up.

Tiffany threw her arms around him and that's when he realized that she was just wearing a lacy black sort of camisole thing that was pretty much totally see-through. It had been her blue uniform shirt that was the last one on the rope. He figured he must have the biggest, dopiest smile of all time on his face at that moment, but he could not make himself care. He had never been so happy to be alive.

As if by some kind of benign magic, he suddenly felt the plane start to level off and smooth out. He let out an exuberant cheer and pulled the smiling Tiffany close again.

"Don't be cheering and shit just yet," Troy said, stomping on a snake head that came slithering up from the hole. "We need something to block this hole."

"I have an idea!" Tiffany said, pointing to something square and yellow stowed on the wall near the cockpit door. "We can use that."

"What is it?" Sean asked, looking closer.

She ran to it and yanked it off the wall. When she returned, Sean could read the stenciled letters on the bulky yellow object.

"LIFE RAFT."

"Great," Sean said. "How does it work?"

"Help me," she said, grabbing one end.

Sean grabbed the other end and helped her lower the raft into the hole. When it was more or less wedged in, she motioned for everyone to step back.

"I always wanted to do this!" she said, and then yanked the rip-cord.

There was a loud rapport like a shot and the raft exploded into shape, forming a fat, bloated seal that completely blocked the hole.

There was a moment of relative quiet. Everyone stared at the raft. Nothing happened. Then, they could hear the sound of hissing and slick bodies sliding and pushing against the underside of the raft.

"It's supposed to be shark proof," Tiffany said, blue eyes wide and fixed on the raft.

"About now," Troy replied, "sharks are sounding pretty damn good."

"Speak for yourself, dude," Sean said.

On the flight deck, Claire watched with amazement as the dark ocean receded beneath them.

"We did it," she said.

"I never doubted you for a minute," Flynn said, holding up a massive hand for her to high five.

She giggled like a child and picked up the radio mic. It took her several seconds to make sure it was on before she spoke into it.

"Um, hello?" she said, thinking there was probably some sort of code or cool slang she was supposed to say like "roger" and "copy" and that sort of thing, but she just couldn't think of how to work it in. "Can anyone hear me?"

"We copy you, Hula one two one," the staticky voice from the speaker replied. "But that sure doesn't sound like Arch."

"This is flight attendant Claire Miller speaking," she said. "I have Agent Neville Flynn here in the cockpit with me."

"Roger that, Ms Miller," the voice said. "You want to fill us in on what the hell is going on up there?"

"We've lost our…"

She spun around as the avionics hatch sprang suddenly open. She dropped the mic and tried to stomp the hatch back down when Arch's juicy drawl issued from beneath the hatch.

"What the hell are you doing?" he cried. "Are you crazy?"

"Oh," she said, eyes wide as the ragged, bruised and battered figure of the copilot appeared like an abused jack-in-the-box in the open hatchway. His face was dead white and glistening with fat droplets of sweat, eyes sticky red slits and hair plastered to his damp forehead. He had a fat, purple lump on his left cheekbone and a crusty gash above his left eye.

"Jesus H Christ!" Arch said. "When y'all are done gawking at me like I just showed up butt-naked in church, I could sure use a little help here."

Flynn grabbed Arch's outstretched hand and helped him up out of the hatchway. That was when Claire saw Arch's other hand.

The hand itself was swollen up like a grotesque, pink fleshy mitten with a peeling red and black mess beneath the bloated pinky finger. Two suppurating holes leaked yellow and cloudy pink goo, and the whole thing had a powerful stink like spoiled chicken livers and bile and blood on hot asphalt. His sleeve was torn up to the armpit and the arm beneath was the size of a leg, skin stretched taut and shiny and streaked with mottled red stripes.

"Oh my God," Claire said softly.

"Claire," Flynn said. "Give me your scarf."

Claire removed her South Pacific Air logo patterned scarf and handed it wordlessly to Flynn. Flynn wrapped the scarf twice around Arch's arm just below the shoulder.

"The bastard got me good, didn't he?" Arch asked, smiling gamely but still looking green and deathly ill.

"Are you going to be all right?" Claire asked anxiously. "Can you fly with one hand?"

"Sweetheart," Arch replied, "you'd be amazed what a man can do with one hand. Now get. I got work to do here."

Flynn handed him the fire ax and nodded.

"You need anything, just let me know," Claire said.

"You bet," Arch said, laying the ax across his lap and donning his radio headset. "LAX tower, Hula one-two-one. Y'all want to hear a funny story?"

Flynn motioned for Claire to go ahead of him as the two of them moved out of the cockpit.

"Hey," Flynn said. "If law school doesn't work out, you're pretty good with that ax."

Claire smiled, feeling near delirious after everything they'd been through. "Yeah. You think you've forgotten how to fight giant snakes but then it all comes back to you."

They both stopped short at the sight of every living passenger on the plane huddled together around the large rubber raft blocking the hole where the stairs had once been.

"Flynn," Sean said. "We had no choice. The snakes... they got through the barricades. They were everywhere."

"Yeah, all right," Flynn said. "You did what you had to do."

"So now what?" Tiffany asked.

"Now," Flynn said, "we try and survive the rest of the flight."

TWENTY-ONE

"What about zoos?" Harris asked Dr Price as they sped through the night in the back of the FBI van. "They have all those foreign snakes. Don't they have antivenin? What if a zookeeper gets bitten?"

"Sure," Dr Price said. "But zoos will only have the antivenins for the species they have currently on exhibit. And these photos we've received from the passengers on board that flight are only of individual snakes unlucky enough to get caught. Who knows what other species are there on that plane but have avoided capture? What we really need is a detailed list of every single species, exact numbers, everything. An exotic shipment that size would have to come through a dealer. Not just any dealer, but someone who would be not only willing to traffic in dangerous, illegal and endangered herps but also willing to do business with an underworld criminal like Eddie Kim."

"Okay," Harris said. "So who in Hawaii would fit the bill?"

"No," Price said. "They wouldn't be in Hawaii. Hawaii is too strict about non-indigenous species."

Harris narrowed his eyes, wheels turning. "Wait a minute," he said. "Eddie Kim lives here in Los Angeles. Could he have shopped locally?"

"Of course he could have," Dr Price said, not liking where this train of thought was taking him. "And there's only one person in Los Angeles who knows all the dirt on every two bit herp smuggler on the west coast."

"Well," Harris said, "we better go talk to him."

"Her," Dr Price said, pinching the bridge of his nose between his thumb and forefinger. "Dr Anabelle Bennet, Curator of Reptiles at the Los Angeles Zoo."

It was just after five o' clock in the morning, but of course Belle would be in the nursery, fussing over the latest hatchlings. She suffered from never-ending insomnia, just like Dr Price. It was one of many things they had in common.

Dr Price tried phoning her but she did not believe in cell phones and was not picking up in her office. They had no choice but to go down to the Zoo and talk to her in person, something Dr Price had been studiously avoiding for nearly two years.

Oscar, the graveyard shift guard at the gate, gave Dr Price a big, gap-tooth grin when he pulled up in the FBI van.

"'Sup Dr Price?" Oscar said with a knowing wink. "You here to see Dr Belle?"

"Yes," Dr Price said, as Harris held his FBI identification out the window for Oscar to see. "We have an emergency situation of the utmost urgency."

"You remember where to find her, don't you?" Oscar said, opening the gate so they could drive in.

"Yes, thank you," Dr Price replied, blushing.

Harris looked at him quizzically as the large black agent behind the wheel pulled through the gate.

"Dr Bennet and I…" Dr Price said, "had… well, we were… involved at one time."

Boy, that didn't even come close to covering everything he'd been through with Belle. And here he was, following the twisting roads though the darkened park, roads he still knew like the back of his hand, back to the reptile nursery. He and Belle had spent so many amazing nights lost in delirious geek ecstasy over the hatching of a previously unknown color morph of the rare *Chrysopelea pelias* or enthusing over a newly gravid death adder. He remembered the first time he'd met Belle, at a conference on identification and management of herp diseases in Tampa, Florida. They were out by the pool in the con hotel and he'd spotted her standing there, with her mile-long legs all coltish and awkward, big chunky glasses that kept on slipping down her nose and freckles on her plain librarian's face. She'd had a big floppy hat and a terrible bathing suit that looked like something donated to the Goodwill after some fat great aunt had passed away. Loud orange and yellow flowers with a little skirt that hung loose and unflattering on her skinny hips. She had a bit of a sunburn and was talking passionately with a colleague by the bar, waving her arms around and making wide, exaggerated shapes with her hands. She had just returned from a field trip to Madagascar and was bubbling with childlike enthusiasm and excitement over her observations and encounters with the bizarre and unusual Madagascar leaf nosed snake. Dr Price was halfway in love with her before he ever met her. She was stubborn and lacking in social graces and could be infuriating at times, but she was so like him in so many ways it was almost scary. Truth be told, she was the best thing that had ever happened to him, and he broke her heart for a pair of fake tits and a more photogenic smile.

Dr Price was not ready for the emotional suckerpunch of seeing her again, even under the best of circumstances. In the midst of this madness with the plane and everything, it seemed to hit him even harder.

She was dressed in her usual Zoo T-shirt and jeans and had her mousy brown hair pulled back away from her pale face. When he knocked on the partially-open door, she spun and her blue eyes lit up behind her glasses.

"Is it the racers?" she asked, voice breathless with barely contained excitement. "Did they hatch?"

He looked down and shook his head. "Not yet, Belle."

"Well who's watching the clutch now?" she asked, eyes turning hard. "Camden?"

"Sanjay is with them," Dr Price said.

"Ah," she said, turning back to the bright yellow tangle of newly hatched green tree boas in the tank beside her. "And how is Miss September?"

"She's..." Dr Price stuttered. "We'll..."

Harris, Lawson and Fisk pushed past Dr Price to enter the room. Belle registered the feds with an arch of her eyebrow.

"Dr Bennet," Harris said. "I'm afraid we are dealing with a ticking clock here. We have an unprecedented emergency situation that requires your assistance."

"Belle," Dr Price said, "I think you better sit down."

Toward the front of the first class cabin, Maria sat across the aisle from Tommy and Curtis. Isabella dozed, heavy and warm on her shoulder. Tommy was whimpering softly and moving fitfully in his aisle seat, but Maria was also very worried about Curtis. The older boy sat icy pale and silent by the window, still sucking his thumb with dull eyes staring at nothing. He let Maria sit him down in the seat beside his brother and buckle him in with no more resistance than a big flexible doll.

"Hey, Curtis," she said softly. "I have a fun idea."

The boy did not look at her or acknowledge that she had spoken. She sighed and reached into her purse for a small notebook she had been using as a baby diary. She carefully tore out a few sheets and dug around for a pen. When she found one, she laid the paper and pen on the tray table in front of Curtis.

"If you get bored," Maria said, "you can draw some pictures."

Curtis's eyes slowly dropped to the sheets of paper.

"Do you like to draw?" Maria asked, encouraged by this tiny shadow of animation in the boy's face.

Curtis nodded very slowly and then reached for the pen.

"That's great," she said. "Why don't you draw a picture for your mom?"

He did not respond, but he had put the pen to the first blank sheet and began to draw a long skinny shape. Maria felt hugely relieved to have made even this tiny bit of progress. She just kept on thanking God that little Isabella was probably too young to remember any of this when she grew up. She rubbed her palm over her baby's tiny back and closed her eyes.

Tommy let out a stronger whimper and then something that might have been a word, but was too soft and slurred for Maria to understand. Troy, who had been sitting right behind them with the rapper Three Gs, stood and came around beside the young boy.

"How is he?" Troy asked Maria.

"I don't know," Maria said. "The same, I guess."

Troy hunkered down over the boy, massive shoulders hunched and head bent down low.

"Hey there, little man," Troy said. "How you doing?"

Tommy said something that sounded kind of like *wrong*.

Troy held up his PSP. "I bet you could give me some tips on how to get this guy to dunk," Troy said.

Tommy's sticky slits of eyes suddenly seemed to clear a little and he looked up at the big body-guard. "Are you Three Gs?"

Troy smiled. "Nah. I'm just his bodyguard."

"My brother likes Three Gs," Tommy said. "But my dad doesn't think he's 'propriate."

Troy laughed and shook his head. "Yeah, I guess you could say that."

"What's your name?" Tommy asked.

"I'm Troy," the bodyguard said. "And you're Tommy, right?"

"Right." Tommy paused, his face screwing up with pain as he clutched his stomach.

"You okay?" Troy asked.

"I feel really terrible," Tommy said. "Like I want to throw up all the time but I don't have anything left inside me."

"Just hang in there, kid," Troy said. "We're gonna be in LA real soon."

"My cat is on the plane, too," Tommy said. "His name is Mr Wong. Do you think he's okay? You don't think the snakes got him, do you?"

Troy's face went grim and hard. "I don't know, kid. I hope not."

"I hope not too," Tommy said.

There was a long moment of quiet, and Tommy turned his eyes to his brother's drawing and then back up to Troy. "Troy?"

"Yeah?"

"How much do you get paid to bodyguard Three Gs?"

"Plenty. Why? You thinking of becoming a bodyguard when you grow up?"

"I was thinking maybe you could bodyguard me and my brother too," Tommy said. "I have twenty dollars that my dad gave me, but it's in my backpack downstairs. I could give it to you later though, when we get to Los Angeles."

A big grin bloomed across Troy's face and he put a gentle hand on Tommy's skinny shoulder. "Deal. I got your back, kid."

"Do you have Curtis's back too?" Tommy asked.

"Definitely," Troy said. "You just try and rest for a little while, okay?"

"Okay," Tommy replied, eyes already sliding shut.

"Kraitler," Dr Bennet told Harris and Dr Price. "No two ways about it, Reginald Kraitler is your man."

"Kraitler?" Dr Price said. "That can't possibly be a real name. Does he specialize in kraits and rattlers?"

"I have no idea if that's the name he was born with," Dr Bennet said. "But I do know that he's a sleazy, unethical, meth-head scumbag who would sell his own mom for the right price. Lives out in the desert near Palmdale and experiments with chemicals and radiation and crossbreeding. Weird Frankenstein shit."

Harris's eyes lit up. "Do you think he could have some sort of chemical, some process or something that could make snakes turn hyper-aggressive?"

"If anyone could," Dr Bennet said, "it would be Kraitler."

"Okay," Harris said, beckoning to one of his agents. "Fisk, run a check on this Kraitler guy. Lawson, get us a chopper a-sap. Looks like we're off to scenic Palmdale." Harris strode out of the room without another word.

Dr Price shrugged and pointed to the door. "I better... Well, I mean..."

Dr Bennet nodded and wrapped her bony arms around herself. "Sure, right," she said, looking away.

"Well," Dr Price said again, pointlessly. "Goodbye then."

"Steve," she said softly.

"What?" he asked.

"Email me a live head count and some photos when the Racers hatch, okay?" she said, not meeting his gaze.

"You bet," he replied, trying on an ill-fitting smile.

"Dr Price," Harris called from the hallway. "Patch it up on your own time, willya? Time is tissue, remember?"

"Okay then," Dr Price said, pointing to the door.

"Bye," Dr Bennet said.

He turned to go before he could embarrass himself any further.

* * *

Three Gs was sure it was getting warmer up in the first class cabin. Not just warmer, but stuffier too. It was as if he could feel billions and billons of hot, crawling germs sailing through the stale air like malignant snowflakes, bumping against his eyes and filling every pore of his skin. The little kid who'd been bit had puked twice since they'd been up there, effectively creating an impassible barrier between Three Gs and the bathroom. There was nowhere to sit that wasn't close to someone else. He didn't want to be anywhere near Leroy, who seemed to be getting worse and worse. Even though Three Gs knew that the venom from a snake bite wasn't contagious, he just couldn't stand to look at Leroy.

The rich blonde that he'd been talking to back before this whole nightmare started had been crying nonstop since they got up here, clutching the Ziploc bag of gross dog treats and making a dull, monotonous keening that felt like fingernails dragging across the raw, frayed ends of Three Gs's shattered nerves. There was clear snot on her upper lip and smeary streaks of mascara under her red, sticky eyes. The other blonde with the short hair was trying to comfort her, but it didn't seem to be doing any good because she kept breaking down and bawling too. Both of them kept on sniffling and wiping their runny noses on the backs of their hands and then touching things—the seat backs, the arm rests, everything near where they were sitting, and no one stopped them.

Grace, the nice flight attendant who'd given him the hand sanitizer, looked like she was dying, and

Troy was off talking to the two kids, and it was definitely getting hotter, no doubt about it. The cabin was filling with a thick, nauseating miasma of armpits and bad breath and anxious sweat that was making it harder and harder to breathe.

Just when Three Gs thought it couldn't possibly get any worse, his nostrils were assailed with a sharp, horrendous stench that could be only one thing. He stood and took several steps back, hand pressed over his nose and mouth, only to be treated to the disgusting and appalling sight of the young mother changing her baby on a seat across the aisle, mopping up sticky clots of greenish shit from between the infant's chubby legs and dropping the filthy wipes into a clear plastic bag. He turned away, squeezing his eyes shut, but he could still picture hoards of E coli bacteria swarming around the baby and the seat beneath it, creeping across the aisle like something out of a horror movie.

If only he could make it to the bathroom and wash his hands, everything would be okay. He stood beside the yellow raft that sealed the hole where the stairs had been, listening to the hissing and slithering of the snakes below and tapping his index finger against his thigh in increasingly complex patterns that didn't seem to do any good at all. He didn't know how much longer he was going to be able to take this.

Claire sat on the armrest beside the fading Grace. Ken had found a small, emergency oxygen mask and placed it over Grace's drawn and greenish face, but it did not really seem to be helping her harsh, labored breathing. She was dying and they all knew it, though none of them wanted to acknowledge that fact.

Grace flapped a weak hand near her mouth, gesturing for Claire to remove the mask.

"Last month," Grace whispered, her voice breathless and nearly lost under the rumble of the engines, "they offered me… early retirement." She paused and took another hit off the mask. "But no… This dumb broad… just had to take… another tour of duty."

"Don't try to talk," Claire said softly, trying to replace the mask, but Grace brushed it away.

"You guys are like… family to me," Grace said, her breathing becoming more and more labored.

"We know," Ken said over Claire's shoulder. "We love you too, Gracie. Just try to hang in there, okay?"

"Couldn't just…" Grace whispered, "Leave you…"

"You're not leaving us," Claire said. "You're gonna be fine."

"Isabella…" Grace said. "I want to see… Isabella."

Ken hustled down the aisle to where Maria sat with her baby. Claire saw him whisper to her and she stood, heading back towards them.

"Hey," Maria said softly.

"Hi angel," Grace said when she saw the infant. "Look at that… pretty angel."

The sleepy baby yawned and then smiled, reaching out with tiny trembling hands.

"Yeah," Grace said, reaching up to touch the baby's fingers. "I'm tired, too." Her eyes started to drift closed. "I think I'll just... have a little rest..." Her voice became slurred, airless and almost inaudible. "Goodnight, angel."

Maria took Grace's slack hand and squeezed it. Grace's fingers were limp, her breath shallow and fast. Claire touched the spot just beneath Grace's ear and felt her pulse, speedy and erratic beneath her hot skin.

"Will she be all right?" Maria asked anxiously.

Claire looked up at the little baby in Maria's arms. The child was still smiling, amazingly calm and content in the midst of all this fear and death.

"I just don't know," Claire said.

"She saved Isabella," Maria said, eyes welling up with tears. "That's why she got bit, to save my little girl."

Claire, Ken and Maria said nothing for what felt like a century. Finally, Claire spoke without lifting her eyes. "We have to make it. We have to make it out of this alive, for Grace. Otherwise, she got bit for nothing."

Sean pulled up the front of his T-shirt to wipe sweat from his face. "Is it me," he asked Flynn, "or is it getting kinda hot in here?"

The big man looked up from checking his handgun. "This is nothing. You ought to try ghetto August in Atlanta."

Sean reached up to the little round nipple-like nozzle above his seat. He twisted the outer ring one way and then the other, but there was no flush of cooling air. He stood and put his hand in front of an air vent near the ceiling. Nothing.

"Check it out," Sean said, trying some of the other little fan nozzles over some of the other seats. "There's no air flow. Nothing."

Tiffany was standing several rows down and turned her head towards Sean. Much to his disappointment, she had untied her blue uniform blouse from the shirt-rope and put it back on. She too raised her hand to several vents and nodded.

"He's right," she said.

"Something is wrong," Claire said. "If the air recycling system is down, it's gonna get very hard to breathe in here."

"Shit," Sean said, futilely twisting the nozzles, testing each one and still getting nothing. "What should we do?"

"Stay cool," Flynn said. "I'll go talk to the cowboy."

Flynn checked the tourniquet around Arch's stinking, swollen arm. The skin of his hand and forearm was starting to peel off in sheets around the blackened, mushy and necrotic bite. He looked even worse, if that was possible, like he had just woken up facedown in a puddle of piss and vomit after a week-long Sterno and Nyquil bender. His eyes were over-bright, sunken and more than a little manic.

"You think I don't know it's hot as hell in here?" Arch asked. "I also got abnormal vibration in engines one and two. I had no choice but to throttle back."

"Throttle back?" Flynn said. "You mean you're slowing down?"

"Well," Arch said, wiping sweat from his eyes with his good hand, "it was either that or option B."

"And that is–?" Flynn asked.

"Option B," Arch said with that hot, crazy gleam in his eye, "is I go faster, push the engines till they seize up on me and then we eventually plummet into the ocean and experience a variety of horrible deaths, including but not limited to: fiery explosion, drowning, hypothermia and/or shark attack. Me, I might not even make it to the shark attack portion of our show if things keep going like they been going but regardless, it's safe to say that there will be no survivors. The Coast Guard will spend the next year identifying femurs."

"Okay," Flynn said. "Let's stick with option A then."

"I thought you might see it my way."

"So meanwhile," Flynn continued, "how can I fix the air conditioning?"

"Looks like we lost power to the outflow valve motor. It needs to be reset manually. The good news is it's pretty simple—just find the breaker panel and flip the switches."

"Fine. So where's the breaker panel?"

"That's the bad news," Arch replied. "To get to it, you'll need to go down through the cargo hold." He grinned and wiped sweat from his eyes again. "Sucks to be you right now, man."

At that moment, Ken burst in through the cockpit door. "Oh my God, Flynn!" he said. "We need you back here right away!"

* * *

When Flynn returned with Ken to the first class cabin, Three Gs was standing in the center of the aisle with way too much white around his eyes, like a spooked horse about to bolt.

"I said get away," Three Gs said, arms windmilling wildly. "Don't fucking touch me!"

"Please," Tiffany said, showing her palms. "No one is going to touch you. Just try and relax, okay?"

"You relax!" Three Gs spat. "Can't you feel how disgusting it is in here? I need to get out of here. I NEED TO GET OUT OF HERE!"

He suddenly threw himself at the raft blocking the hole where the stairs had been, yanking and twisting the supple yellow rubber.

"G!" Troy said, stepping in front of Tiffany. "What the hell are you doing? You want to let those snakes up here?"

"I need to…" Three Gs kept tugging on the raft. "I need…"

"Easy, bro," Flynn said, coming around to stand beside Three Gs. "You really need to try and stop and think for a second."

"Don't touch me," Three Gs said, crouching back and defensive.

"I'm not going to touch you," Flynn said, hands up and open. "We're just going to talk, all right?"

Three Gs eyed Flynn suspiciously but seemed willing to listen, when suddenly the plane hit a rocky spot of turbulence. Flynn staggered forward and Three Gs stumbled into him. The next series of events was almost too quick to follow.

"I said DON'T FUCKING TOUCH ME!" Three Gs cried.

He was holding Flynn's handgun.

"Back up!" Three Gs said. "Now!"

Flynn's hand went instinctively to his now empty shoulder holster, eyes narrow.

Troy leaned over and whispered to Claire. Claire nodded and ran to where Grace was buckled in, barely breathing.

"Clarence," Troy said softly. "Come on now, dog. This ain't you. Waving a gun at women and children. See that little boy over there..." He pointed to a wide-eyed Curtis, who was peering anxiously over the back of the seat. "He's a big fan. He wanted to meet you so bad and now this is how you wanna act in front of your fans?"

Flynn could see hesitation in Three Gs's body language, the heavy Glock starting to waver in his grip. It would be no problem to take the gun away from him and break one of his arms, but the bodyguard's words were obviously cutting right through Three Gs. Better to handle the situation without violence if at all possible. There had been enough violence already on this damned flight.

Claire appeared behind Troy and handed him something. Troy nodded and held the object out to Three Gs. It was the bottle of hand sanitizer from Grace's apron pocket.

"Here," Troy said. "Why don't you put that gun down and get cleaned up?"

Three Gs sank into a nearby seat, letting the Glock drop heavily to the carpet. Flynn retrieved it immediately and stashed it back in its holster while Troy came forward and handed his shaken boss the bottle of hand sanitizer.

That was when the lights went out.

"Shit," Flynn said, turning in the sudden darkness. "Now what?"

The aisle was dimly illuminated by a strip of emergency floor lights along either side.

"There are some flashlights in here," Claire called from the galley. "Go talk to Arch and find out what's going on."

"The cabin lights are down," Flynn told Arch, pushing open the cockpit door.

"I know, I know," Arch said. "Can't do nothing about that now. I got bigger fish to fry, like trying not to pass out or die before we land. If you like you can fix it when you head down to fix the air."

"Gotcha," Flynn said.

"Did the gals find the flashlights?" Arch asked. "They're in the utility closet in the galley."

"Claire is getting them," Flynn said.

"It'll be light soon," Arch said. "I don't think I've ever been as happy as I'm gonna be to see that dawn."

"I know what you mean, man," Flynn said.

Claire sat with Grace, holding her cool, rigid hand and trying very hard not to cry. Her bones ached with stress and exhaustion. The flashlight that she held was not pointed at Grace's twisted face, but at the carpet at her feet. All around the dark cabin, little moving puddles of yellow light illuminated bits and pieces of anxious passengers, fearful eyes and nervous limbs. It was still unbearably stuffy and close and she could hear the slither and rustle of snakes inside the walls, in the vents, pressing up against the raft, all around them, searching for any breach, any way in.

Claire was pretty sure that Grace was dead. Claire hadn't checked for a pulse for several minutes, but Grace was stiff and still and her hand was almost the same temperature as the armrest. Claire felt a kind of childish, superstitious certainty that if she did not check for a pulse, she wouldn't have to not feel one, and as long as she did not officially confirm that Grace was dead, then she might still somehow be alive.

"Hey," said a low voice from the aisle.

Claire raised her flashlight to reveal Three Gs. He was holding the bottle of hand sanitizer.

"Is she...?" Three Gs asked, brows drawn together.

Claire swallowed hard and nodded. "I think so."

Three Gs looked down at the hand sanitizer, a sheen of unshed tears in his dark eyes. "Shit," he said softly.

A moment passed in awkward silence.

"Hey, listen," Three Gs said. "I'm real sorry about... well, about before."

"It's okay," Claire said. "We're all scared and stressed out and anxious right now."

"I know," Three Gs said. "But that's no excuse."

Claire nodded. "We all just need to try and stay calm and work together to make it out of this in one piece," she said, removing the oxygen mask from Grace's dead face and turning off the flow. "I think maybe Tommy could use this now."

"Can I ask you something?" Three Gs said, stepping aside to let her stand.

"Sure," Claire said.

"You think that little kid would still talk to me?" Three Gs asked. "If I went over and said what's up?"

"He has hardly spoken since his brother got bitten," Claire said. "Anything that might get his mind off what happened could be worthwhile."

Three Gs nodded thoughtfully.

"Come on," Claire said, carrying the small oxygen tank over to where the two little boys sat.

Three Gs followed her and as she bent to tend to the unconscious Tommy, he spoke over the top of the seat to Curtis. "Hey there."

Claire watched out of the corner of her eye as Curtis looked up at Three Gs. The boy didn't say anything, but just the eye contact alone seemed like a big improvement.

"Sorry I was tripping like that before," Three Gs said. "See, I got this problem with anxiety." He paused and looked away. "I ain't never told nobody about it. It's kinda embarrassing, but I'll tell you what. If I get out of this in one piece, I'm going right to the doctor and seeing if I can't find some way to get on top of this thing."

Curtis still hadn't spoken, but he was clearly listening.

"Guess you won't be buying any more of my albums," Three Gs said. "Now that you found out what a big baby I really am, huh?"

"I like 'Freakasaurus Rex,'" Curtis said.

"You do?" Three Gs said, letting out a short shaky laugh. "That's one of my favorites too."

"You should do more songs like that," Curtis said.

"If I do, will you buy the album?" Three Gs asked.

Curtis nodded.

"Then you're still my biggest fan?" Three Gs asked.

Curtis nodded again.

"Everybody feels like a baby sometimes when scary things happen," Curtis said. "It's not really a big deal."

Claire smiled to herself as Maria came over to check on Tommy.

"Will you stay with him for a while?" Claire asked Maria.

Maria nodded and put a hand on Tommy's sweaty forehead. Curtis and Three Gs were talking about music. It almost seemed like they would make it.

Then, as Claire stood, her flashlight beam swept the aisle and caught the toe of Grace's ugly, comfortable shoe sticking out from her seat. They always used to tease her about those awful shoes. Ken called them "Granny Chic for the Shuffleboard Set" or "Orthoclodhoppers." Grace claimed that she wore them as protection against unwanted advances from ardent foot fetishists and actually owned three identical pairs so she always had back ups.

Suddenly it seemed to hit Claire all over again that even if they did make it to LAX, it was too late for Grace. Too late for Tyler and for all the other passengers who had died, whose bodies lay scattered down below in the Coach cabin, contorted in the agony of painful death and crawling with snakes. It might be too late for Tommy. It all seemed like more than she could bear.

She forced her legs to move, to carry her stone-heavy and weary body down the aisle to the galley. She had no idea how long she stood there, palm against the bulkhead and eyes staring unseeing past the darting flashlight beams and shadows and flickering glimpses of sweaty skin and hollow, shell-shocked faces, but she realized that her cheeks were wet with tears. She did not hear Flynn behind her until he spoke.

"Claire," he said, his deep voice low and intimate.

She did not turn to face the big man, just kept on staring, feeling numb and disconnected. Nothing seemed real. Not even her own tears.

"Claire," Flynn said again, reaching out to touch her shoulder.

Suddenly, everything felt far too real. Especially the warmth of that large, calloused hand against her skin. She turned, raising a hand to wipe the moisture from beneath her eyes.

Standing so close to him, she could not help but be impressed, intimidated and even a little bit flustered by not just his physical size, but by his sheer presence in the narrow confines of the galley. His cool, dark gaze locked with hers and she felt a flicker of inexplicable intimacy that seemed utterly out of place in all this madness. He had removed his jacket and tie in the airless swelter and she could smell him, the overtly masculine tang of his sweat and skin that had her suddenly wondering what it would be like with him, to wake up in the morning with that smell in her hair and her sheets.

She was grateful for the dark, because it hid the furious blush that stained her cheeks as she looked away, breaking the eye contact. He read this shift of gaze as sadness and gently squeezed her shoulder.

"I'm sorry about Grace," he said.

Claire nodded but said nothing, feeling that hopeless emptiness wash over her again.

"I know what you're feeling," Flynn continued. "I do."

"I don't even know what I'm feeling," Claire said, feeling suddenly reckless. "I feel different every five minutes. Sad, scared, angry, hopeless. A second ago, I was feeling like I wanted to sleep with you." She let out a dry, humorless laugh. "Crazy."

She could see that he was taken aback by her unvarnished honesty, but he recovered well. It actually made her smile to think that she was able to ruffle his professional cool just a little bit.

"Everything you're feeling is totally normal for a high stress situation like this," he said. "Except for wanting to sleep with someone like me, which is totally insane and I suggest you seek professional help immediately."

Claire laughed and shook her head. "Believe it or not," she said, "I kinda wanted to sleep with you before the whole high stress situation thing."

"That makes the need for professional help even more urgent," Flynn replied. "Just ask my ex-wife."

"Honestly, Flynn," Claire said, looking back over the rows of seats. "I'm scared to death. I want to be strong, to be there for Tommy and Leroy and everyone who needs me, but I just don't know how much more of this I can take. I feel like my brain is just going to fly into a million jagged pieces and I'll start screaming and never be able to stop."

"I think you are a lot stronger than you realize," Flynn said. "You know, I spend every day dealing with people who do terrible things to one another and that kind of shit wears away my faith in the human race. But I'll tell you, Claire. I have faith in you."

"I think you're the one who needs professional help," Claire said, a half smile curling in the corner of her mouth.

Flynn shook his head. "I've got my money on you, kid," he said. "And I'm never wrong."

"Never, huh?" Claire asked.

"Never," he replied. "Now how about it? Let's you and me get these people some air."

Claire looked up at him and nodded. "Okay," she said.

"Ready?" Flynn asked over his shoulder.

Behind him, Troy and Chen stood by with glass-tipped golf clubs while Claire trained a flashlight on the door to the dumbwaiter that ran from the first class galley to the cargo hold below.

"Ready," Troy said.

"Ready," Chen repeated.

"Do it," Claire said.

"On three," Flynn said. "One... Two..."

He reached out and gripped the handle on the dumbwaiter door, fingers flexing and then tightening.

"THREE!" he cried, yanking the door open.

Coiled inside the dumbwaiter were two puff adders, fat, almost heart-shaped heads whipping around to hiss viscously at Flynn. Before they had a chance to strike, Troy and Chen, acting in smooth tandem, skewered the angry reptiles with their makeshift spears. Without missing a beat, Claire stuck the flashlight between her thighs and held up a lighter taped to a can of hairspray, releasing a jet of flame to crisp the flailing snakes. The galley filled with a stench of burnt scales and hot sizzling meat as Troy and Chen pulled the blackened remains of the two adders from the dumbwaiters.

"Impressive," Flynn said, eyeing Claire appreciatively.

"I went through a pyromaniac phase as a kid," she said, shrugging.

"Who didn't?" Flynn said. Then he paused, frowning slightly. "Anything else I ought to know about you?"

A silent moment passed between them and Flynn could see Troy and Chen exchange a bemused look. Claire didn't seem to notice. She was looking intensely up at Flynn in a way that was making it difficult to pay attention to anything else. He forced himself to look away.

"Troy, Chen?" he said.

The two men cocked their heads, curious.

"Yeah?" Troy replied.

"Do me a favor," Flynn asked.

"Sure," Troy said.

"Anything," Chen replied.

"It seems relatively safe up here for now," Flynn said. "But no matter what happens, don't let anything happen to the kid. If we lose Sean, then the fucker who did this to us wins, understand."

"You got it," Chen said.

"No problem," Troy said.

"Let me come with you," Claire said suddenly. "You don't know your way around down there."

"I need you up here," he said, turning back to her and pressing a two-way radio into her hand. "Be my eyes and ears."

Although he did not come out and say it, he knew that she still heard him loud and clear. If anything happened to him, he was counting on her to take care of things. With Sanders dead, she was the only one he knew he could count on to have the cool head and strength of leadership needed to keep everyone together.

She handed him the hairspray can and he looked down at it, shaking his head.

"I thought you couldn't bring a lighter on the plane anymore," he said.

"You're not supposed to, but they cut us stews a little slack," she said. "Who knew that my nasty nicotine habit would actually do someone some good?"

"It's a filthy habit," Flynn agreed. "I've quit six times."

"This is round seven for me," Claire laughed. "But if we get out of this alive, I'm going to buy some of those expensive French boutique cigarettes and chain smoke the whole pack down to the filter one after the other."

"Save one for me," Flynn said, slowly folding his long limbs into the cramped space of the dumbwaiter. "I'll be back as soon as I get the air up and running."

"You better," Claire said, her hazel eyes narrow and serious.

Flynn nodded, took a deep breath and then slammed the dumbwaiter door closed, stabbed a button and started the wobbly descent into the snake-infested cargo hold.

TWENTY-TWO

Alone at the far end of a barely-there dirt road twisting through miles of barren nothingness, Kraitler's compound was a rundown collection of trailers and aluminum prefab buildings. Harris and his men had debated choppering in to Edwards Air Force Base and coming in from the ground to maintain some element of surprise, but there was no time for subtlety. They would have to set down in the guy's backyard and come out swinging. From the description they had received from Belle, it seemed to be a fair assumption that this man would be armed and dangerous. Dr Price, who had been in a few fairly hairy situations on collection trips in various war-torn countries around the globe, still considered himself a pacifist who avoided violent interpersonal confrontations at all costs. He was fearless when it came to handling some of the deadliest creatures on the planet, but when it came to aggressive behavior on the part of his fellow human beings, he was utterly intimidated.

Harris, on the other hand, was like a little kid on Christmas morning. His eyes were shining as he checked and rechecked his sidearm, raring to go and ready for action.

"We're glad to have you back in the field, Hank," Agent Lawson shouted over the thunder of the rotors.

"I'm glad to have me back in the field," Harris replied, grinning hugely as the chopper banked over Kraitler's compound.

On the ground below, the door to one of the trailers flew open, disgorging a scrawny, wild-eyed man. He was as thin and dark as beef jerky, his leathery skin a deep, well-done brown that went far beyond tan. His nearly waist-length blond hair was sunbleached almost pure white and his wide, crazy eyes were faded like jeans to a pale chalky blue around tiny pinprick pupils. His sharp, prominent hipbones and a rattlesnake belt were the only things keeping his worn leather pants from falling down his pipe-cleaner legs. He was shirtless, his long bony torso an anatomy lesson in the details of the human skeletal structure. He was holding a shotgun.

He looked up at the approaching helicopter, hair whipping around his knife blade cheekbones, and then bolted for a nearby barn-like structure.

Harris motioned to the pilot to take it down, and Dr Price felt his stomach lurch as the chopper veered frighteningly close to the ground.

"What are you doing?" Dr Price asked, holding on for dear life.

"My job!" replied Harris, letting out a child's unselfconscious rebel yell as he bailed from the moving helicopter. He rolled as he hit the hard-packed desert ground and came up with his gun drawn and ready to fire.

"FBI!" Harris shouted over the thunder of the helicopter blades. "Freeze!"

The man, Kraitler presumably, whirled around and yelled out some sort of obscenity that was lost in the roar as he fired the shotgun at Harris. A scattered explosion of dust and gravel erupted inches from where Harris had been standing seconds before.

Harris returned fire as Kraitler made a mad dash for the barn, slipping in through the partially-open door. Harris pressed himself flat against the wall by the door.

"Let's go, Doc," Agent Fisk said, taking Dr Price by the arm and helping him to the ground the second the helicopter set down.

"Shouldn't we wait here?" Dr Price asked, alarmed.

"We need you," Agent Fisk said. "Don't worry. You just handle the snakes. We'll handle the humans."

Dr Price turned and watched the helicopter take off again, leaving them to their own devices about a hundred miles from anywhere. He really was not so sure about all this, but he sure didn't want to wait out in the open all by himself, so it seemed like he had no choice but to follow the two agents into the aluminum building.

* * *

In the First Class cabin, Tiffany was handing out bottles of water to the overheated passengers. Sean watched her slender silhouette move through the cabin, feeble light reflecting off the water as she held the bottles out. Wordless, he stood.

"Here," he said, taking a few of the bottles from her arms. "Let me help you."

She smiled at him, her eyes tired and anxious but that smile still so pretty and sweet in spite of everything.

"Thanks," she said.

He couldn't help but notice that her blouse was wet from the condensation on the bottles. He turned away before she noticed him noticing and handed a bottle to Troy. The big bodyguard was hunched over his friend, anxious as a mother.

"How is he?" Sean asked.

"I don't know, man," Troy said. "He's in a lot of pain."

"I'm fine," Leroy said, voice rough and feeble. "This ain't nothing compared to the genital warts your mama gave me for Christmas last year."

"Yeah," Troy replied with a smile. "When your mama kissed me under the mistletoe, I had to get a rabies shot."

"Well," Leroy said with a skinny rind of a smile on his lips, "I would rather get bit by a hundred more snakes than get another kiss from your mama, 'cause they don't make no anti-venom for that bitch."

Troy laughed and shook his head. Sean had no idea why they were saying such awful things about each other's mothers but if Leroy was smiling, he must be doing okay.

"Drink this," Troy said, uncapping the water and handing it to Leroy.

"What, no Courvoisier?" Leroy said. "I thought we was in First Class."

"You need water," Troy said. "You're getting dehydrated from fever."

"Man," Leroy said softly. "I don't know. My stomach is jacked. I'm afraid I'll puke it up again."

"Just have a little bit," Troy said, holding the bottle up to Leroy's lips. "Come on man, you need fluids."

"I feel like a damn baby," Leroy said, taking a tiny sip and then another. "Fluids. Fuck, man, I got some fluids for your mama."

Sean handed another bottle to Troy and left the two bodyguards talking trash about each other's mothers. Two rows down, Three Gs was sitting, talking over the seat to the older of the two little boys.

"Want some water?" Sean asked, still a little leery of the rapper after his previous outburst.

"Sure," Three Gs said. "Thanks."

Sean handed over the water and Three Gs took out a packet of tissues from his pocket to clean off the neck of the bottle before opening it and draining the whole thing without letting the bottle touch his lips.

"Hey listen, kid," Three Gs said. "I guess I was kind of an ass…" He cast a glance back at the little boy and swiftly corrected his language. "A jerk, back before."

"It's not his fault," the boy said solemnly. "He has anxiety."

Three Gs smiled sheepishly and shrugged. "Anyway, sorry for acting like that," he said. "There's no excuse for waving a gun around like a damn fool."

"That's okay," Sean said. "No hard feelings." He turned back to the kid. "What about you? You want some water?"

"Can I have a root beer?" the boy asked.

"Let me go ask Tiffany," Sean said. "They must have root beer in First Class, right?"

The kid nodded with a little half smile.

"Do you think your brother could try and drink some water?" Sean asked, glancing at the unconscious younger boy.

"He won't wake up anymore," Curtis said, frowning and anxious.

Maria, who sat across the aisle with her baby, reached out to Sean.

"Give the water to me," Maria said. "I'll try to get him to drink some."

"You want one for yourself?" Sean asked.

"Sure," she said, shifting the dozy baby to her other shoulder and accepting a second bottle.

"Does..." Sean frowned at the baby. "Does the baby need water too?"

Maria smiled and shook her head.

"She's still breastfeeding," Maria said.

Sean blushed deeply at the mention of breasts and tried very hard not to look down at the ones in question, which were quite large, although the idea of them being full of baby milk was actually pretty gross. Even though that's what they were for in the first place, it still kind of weirded Sean out.

Feeling conflicted and uncomfortable, Sean made a mumbling excuse about the root beer and went to find Tiffany with her cute, perky little breasts that had nothing to do with babies.

Crammed into the claustrophobic moving coffin of the dumbwaiter, Flynn concentrated on his breathing, keeping it slow and even and trying not to think about what would happen if the electricity suddenly cut out, trapping him inside this airless box with no way out. He tried not to think about the way the roof of the dumbwaiter pressed down on the back of his hunched-over head and his slumped shoulders, or the fact that his long legs were folded up to his ears with no place to go, no way to unbend no matter how cramped and uncomfortable he got. He definitely did not want to think about the little open hatch in the top of the dumbwaiter, just big enough for a healthy snake to wriggle through. The ride down to the cargo hold was less than a minute, but it felt like forever to Flynn as he made his shaky, vibrating descent through the narrow shaft.

As he felt the little elevator slowing, he readied the can of hairspray Claire had given him. When the dumbwaiter came to rest at the bottom of the shaft, Flynn kicked open the door and let out a blast of flame, sweeping the area directly outside the door. A beat of silence passed and Flynn cautiously unfolded his cramped limbs from the dumbwaiter, scanning the dim hold around him. He tucked the hairspray into his hip pocket and pulled out a flashlight, clicking it on and surveying his surroundings. He appeared to be in galley storage, a section of the plane filled with instant coffee and boxes of extra napkins. One of the boxes had broken open, releasing a spill of jaunty red and white straws across the floor, but Flynn did not see any snakes.

"Okay," he said into the two-way radio. "I'm here."

"Good," Claire's warm voice replied, cutting though the static. "The EAP panel is to your right."

"I see it," Flynn said, squatting down beside the panel and peering at the wing nuts holding it in place. "Hang on a sec."

He put the radio down and deftly unscrewed the wing nuts, trying to look all around him at once. Carefully removing the dusty panel, he set it aside and shone the flashlight into the blackness beyond, revealing a crawlspace that was maybe two inches wider than Flynn's shoulders. He thought of the cowboy copilot's recent quip.

Sucks to be you right now.

Man, he had that right. This sucked about as badly as it was possible for something to suck. With people, no matter how big and bad, Flynn could always easily anticipate their every move. He had a knack. His instinctive understanding of the workings of the criminal mind had always given him an edge in his dealings with humans both good and bad that he came across in his average work day, but in this situation, all that knowledge and understanding just didn't apply. Who knew what the hell was going on in all those cold-blooded reptile brains. Even someone like Dr Price, who supposedly did understand these ancient and mysterious creatures, didn't understand why these particular snakes were acting the way they were acting. Flynn was totally on his own here, completely off script with no idea what would happen next. He was alone, except...

"You still there, Flynn?" Claire's voice called out from the radio. "Talk to me."

Flynn smiled and picked up the radio. "Hey," he said. "What are you wearing, baby?"

Claire laughed. "Did you get the access panel open?" she asked.

"It's open," Flynn replied, eyeing the dark maw of the open crawlspace. "It's gonna be a tight fit, but I'm going in."

"Be careful," she said.

The inside of the cavernous aluminum building on Kraitler's Palmdale ranch was weirdly hushed and uncomfortably hot, thick with the all too familiar metallic scent of snake shit baking under heat lamps, mixed with an underlying stench of death and decay. There was a partially-open door at the far end of the room where Harris and Kraitler must have gone. Along the walls around them, hatchling racks and white plastic herp tanks were stacked to the cathedral ceiling with a rolling ladder to reach the higher levels. On the bottom level were several sofa-sized enclosures containing truly spectacular giants. Reticulated and Burmese pythons and anacondas, all well over twenty feet and crammed into habitats far too small for their enormous bulk.

Dr Price bent to peer in at a massive, thirty-foot female anaconda on his left. She had no water in her enclosure, just a little crumpled newspaper, and her scales looked dry and rough, her colors dull. Above her in the next level up was a row of stunningly beautiful *Bothrops*. A fer-de-lance on the end had a terrible case of *necrotic stomatitis*, commonly known as mouth rot. His neighbor, a large Costa Rican terciopelo, was striking at the glass monotonously over and over. One of her fangs had broken off and was stuck to the glass in a smear of sticky venom.

Every snake he saw seemed almost psychotically agitated, exhibiting bizarre behaviors and unnatural movements. In several cages, he noticed dead, envenomated but uneaten prey, often more than one. White rats and rabbits, bloated and frozen in the throes of agonized and painful death, but not devoured. It seemed to make no sense. A snake that is ill and off its feed will not even bother to strike at offered prey. Dr Price did not feed live prey, because he did not want to take the chance of one of his precious and exotic beauties getting injured by a feisty rat and also because he liked to load the dead prey animals with vitamin and mineral supplements and medications if needed. There were far too many times that a snake was not interested in feeding and Dr Price had the fun job off removing the dead prey from the tanks before they spoiled under the heat lamps.

So what the hell was going on here? Why were all these snakes killing prey animals again and again but not eating them? He thought of his

conversation with Agent Flynn on the snake-
infested plane, how Flynn had claimed the
unnaturally aggressive snakes were attacking them
continually. It seemed almost as if this guy Kraitler
was somehow training the reptiles to kill for
pleasure rather than for sustenance.

"Something is very wrong here," Dr Price whispered to Agent Fisk.

That was when the tank beside Dr Price's head
shattered as a bullet smashed through the Plexiglas, dumping a startled and pissed off rhino viper
at Dr Price's feet.

"Holy shit!" Fisk cried, dancing away from the
hissing snake while drawing his gun and returning
fire.

Dr Price had only a fleeting glimpse of a possibly
female figure in the far doorway before instinct
kicked in and he put the flying bullets out of his
mind, concentrating solely on the viper coiled less
than six inches from his feet.

There was a pair of very nice Gentle Giant snake
tongs on a hook to his left and he quickly snatched
them up and spun around to grip the viper about
a third of the way down its length. To Dr Price's
amazement, the viper twisted and struggled with
almost unnatural power, nearly wrenching the
tongs out of his hand. Most first timers are afraid
of handling the "hot" or venomous species, but
experienced handlers like Dr Price will tell you
that, other than the danger of envenomation, the
venomous snakes are normally much easier to
handle than their non-venomous relatives.
Because they pack a deadly bite, they don't need

to be nearly as physically strong. Handling a cranky constrictor who wants to give you a hard time can feel like arm-wrestling a body-builder, but on the whole, the venomous snakes are much easier to overpower.

But not this one. Not only were these snakes abnormally aggressive, they were abnormally strong as well. The rhino viper was giving Dr Price a hell of a battle, squirming and flailing with the strength of a python twice its size. Before the snake could break free, Dr Price quickly dumped it into a large plastic garbage can and slapped the lid down tight.

"Jesus," Dr Price said, but when he turned, he realized that he was alone.

He could hear gunshots and crashing and shrieking coming from the other side of the far doorway. It was probably a good idea to just stay put and let the professionals handle the humans like Fisk had said, but curiosity got the better of Dr Price and he inched towards the door, still holding the snake tongs out in front of him like a weapon.

The room on the other side of the doorway was a large, brightly lit laboratory. There were several things going on at once, but Dr Price's eye was drawn to the steel table in the center of the room. There in the center of the table was a huge black Mamba, partially dissected and stinking. Beside the table there was something that made Dr Price feel genuinely sick to his stomach. Rows and rows of tiny hatchlings, every imaginable species, all immobilized side by side with their heads trapped inside clear Plexiglas tubes. Above them was a complex IV drip system and each hatchling had a fat needle inserted through a hole in the Plexiglas tube and into the spot just behind its head, dumping a steady dose of who knew what horrible drug directly into their newborn brains.

When he was able to pull his gaze away from this unnatural horror, he started to register the human events unfolding in the lab. At the far side of the room, Harris and Lawson had wrestled Kraitler to the ground amid smashed equipment and broken glass. Harris was struggling to cuff the wildly struggling Kraitler while Lawson held him down. Closer to Dr Price, Fisk was spinning around and around with a tiny, mostly naked female clinging like a rabid monkey to his back. The girl had a messy, dyed red bob haircut and the physique of an under-developed thirteen year-old boy, clad in nothing but red cowboy boots and a pair of yellow and blue underwear that read "SUPERSTAR" on the back in ugly, Seventies-style lettering. She would have looked underage, except that her tiny, triangular face was wizened and deeply wrinkled like the preserved and shrunken head of a Japanese anime character. Her enormous lemur-like green eyes were glittering with bright, drug-induced mania. Several of her front teeth were missing and the ones that remained were gray and crooked. Her wiry arms were crusted with scabs and she was screeching at the top of her lungs, pounding on Fisk's head and shoulders with small, ineffectual fists.

"Get this crazy bitch off me!" Fisk roared.

Dr Price looked down at the snake tongs in his hand and back at the manic waltz of Fisk and the half-naked girl. He tried to think of a way to help, but nothing came to mind. Seconds later, Fisk backed up into a row of holding tanks on the far wall, smashing the girl into the twisted racks and broken glass. The girl let go of Fisk and tumbled to the ground as a rain of glass and injured snakes fell onto her upturned, screaming face.

As Dr Price and Fisk watched, the girl raised her hand to cover her face but not quickly enough to prevent a strike to the cheek from a fat death adder. On the other side of the room, Kraitler, finally cuffed and dragged to his feet between Harris and Lawson, howled out, "Ronnie!"

The girl leapt to her feet and bolted towards Kraitler, but she only got three steps before she staggered to her knees, eyelids drooping with ptosis as she wretched and spit on the concrete floor, her bitten cheek bulging like she had a mouthful of chaw. Like a struck mouse, she fell over on one side, breathing rapidly, eyes bulging and teeth clenched as rapid paralysis seized her contorted body.

The adder slid across the concrete towards her and Dr Price neatly caught it with the tongs, dumping it into a nearby plastic holding tank. Several other gravely wounded snakes, including a deadly inland taipan, were making their crippled way towards Dr Price, wanting to attack him, even though they were mortally injured. It was horrible, what Kraitler was doing here. Even if there had never been snakes aboard South Pacific Air Flight 121, this atrocity needed to be stopped. All these beautiful animals would have to be euthanized.

They could not be safely kept after Kraitler's regiment of drugs and unnatural conditioning. As Dr Price grabbed the advancing Taipan with the tongs, it made a crazy attempt to bite the tongs several times and then shuddered and died in his grip.

"Kraitler," Harris said as Fisk swiftly handcuffed the sick woman on the floor. "Looks like your girlfriend got herself a hell of a nasty bite."

"Ronnie!" Kraitler called, fighting against Lawson's patient grip. "Baby!"

"I sure hope you have antivenin here," Harris said. "Or else your baby is in a whole lot of trouble, isn't she? What kind of snake was that, Dr Price?"

"*Acanthophis antarcticus*," Dr Price said with out looking away from the long, black-tailed rattler gripped in his tongs. "That's the common death adder."

"Death adder?" Harris said. "Ooooooh, that sounds pretty bad."

"One of the top ten most venomous snakes in the world," Dr Price replied, piling the rattler into a holding tank and sliding the lid closed.

"Top ten, huh?" Harris said. "Bummer."

"Please," Kraitler begged. "Help her."

"No problem," Harris said. "We'll help her. But first we want a full list of every snake you sold to Eddie Kim,"

Kraitler's eyes went wide and he let out a volley of inventive profanity.

"Now, while I generally agree that one should always be free to express one's anger, rather than just keeping all that hostility all bottled up inside,"

Harris said, "you better tell me where that list is. Time is tissue, isn't that right, Dr Price?"

"Oh yeah," Dr Price said over his shoulder, chasing down the last escapee, a mainland Tiger Snake. "Especially..." He stuck the tongs between two rows of tanks and deftly nabbed the Tiger. "When you're talking..." He put the snake in the last free holding tank. "Envenomation of the torso or head."

Kraitler hung his head. "There," he said, gesturing with his chin to a large black binder on the table beside the eviscerated mamba. "It's the last entry in that book."

"Outstanding," Harris said, reaching out and leafing through the binder. "And now, how about that antivenin?"

"In the fridge," Kraitler said, shoulders slumped, defeated.

"Price," Harris called. "You want to dose the girl? I'll call for an ambulance."

"Sure," Dr Price replied, heading for the stainless-steel fridge.

He pulled the door open and was treated to the glorious sight of row after row of color-coded bottles of antivenin.

"Looks like they are reverse alphabetized by the Latin," Dr Price said, mostly to himself as he sorted quickly though the vials. "What kind of psycho reverse alphabetizes things?"

"Yeah!" Harris said, gratuitously cuffing Kraitler on the back of the head. "What the hell is wrong with you?"

"Ow!" Kraitler yelped. "Fucking fascist!"

"That's for alphabetizing things backwards," Harris said, smacking Kraitler again. "Freak."

"You see this?" Kraitler said to Lawson. "This is blatant harassment."

"If you didn't want to be harassed," Lawson replied, "you probably shouldn't have tried to shoot him."

"Okay, let's see here," Dr Price said, trying to stay focused on the task at hand. "Here's the As. *Azemiops, Atropoides, Atheris, Aspidelaps, Agkistrodon*. Here we go, *Acanthophis*."

Dr Price tended quickly and quietly to the stricken girl while Harris radioed the chopper for pickup. Kraitler sat handcuffed on the floor, all the fight gone out of him, while Fisk went through the list of snakes that had been sold to Eddie Kim and put the antivenin for each species into a red plastic cooler. Dr Price found it hard to believe that they had actually won. They'd beaten the odds, found the antivenin and the list of species. Now all they had to do was make it back to LAX and hope that South Pacific Air Flight 121 could do the same.

In the First Class cabin, things were getting steadily more and more unbearable. The narrow space was dark and humid as a wrestler's armpit, humming with suppressed tension and fear. The muggy, airless heat, the thick funk of fear-sweat, the acidic tang of vomit and the gassy, necrotic stink of dying tissue around suppurating snakebites all mingled to form a viscous miasma that made it extremely difficult to breathe. Three

Gs was sitting by a window, alone, clearly trying very hard to keep it together and losing the battle.

Maria was trying to comfort her hot, fussy baby and trying to keep from letting the two little boys see how scared she really was.

Leroy had stopped making jokes about Troy's mother and was leaning over a seat with his swollen and still bleeding ass in the air, looking painfully humiliated and near tears as the sweat rolled down his tightly clenched jaw line and soaked through his gold and black FUBU T-shirt, making the fabric cling to his skin like wet plastic wrap. Troy stood silent beside him, mopping sweat from his face with a black bandana and watching Sean.

Chen sat with Mercedes and Ashley, trying to offer some sort of comfort to the tearful pair and feeling painfully inadequate. He also had his eye on Sean.

Sean stood with Tiffany, the two of them talking softly to the inconsolable Ken, who sat beside Grace's blanket-covered corpse and cried silently into his hands.

It seemed to be getting hotter and more airless with each passing minute, and everyone's mind kept returning with varying degrees of hope and desperation to Agent Flynn. Flynn, fighting through the army of deadly reptiles, searching for the breaker panel that would give them the air they needed.

Anyone with even a passing proclivity for religion prayed to any deity who might be listening. Those who didn't tried to put their faith in the resourceful Flynn, to believe he could be strong enough, tough enough and quick enough to save them. Everyone had to find a way to believe in something, to fight back the despair, the weary resignation that wore away at their hope with the tireless strength of the ocean.

Claire believed in Flynn. His calm, unshakable confidence. His big steady hands and level gaze. She knew he could do it and tried to silently beam her support through the tiny radio in her hand, to surround him with a mental force field of invisible protection.

"Flynn?" she said into the radio, looking down at the flight manual and turning to a page of complex schematics and diagrams of the holds below. "You still with me?"

"Looks like someone jammed an access door open," said Flynn's staticky, disembodied voice. "A fast and dirty job, just to make sure the snakes were able to make it out of the pressurized cargo bay."

"Be careful," Claire said.

"If I was careful," Flynn said, "I'd be in a different line of work. Now, which way is the outflow breaker panel?"

Below, in the pressurized cargo hold that lay beyond galley storage, Flynn made his way past a scatter of exotic orchids, their fragrant and brightly-colored blossoms crushed and broken beneath the bellies of crawling snakes. "The outflow breaker panel is in the next compartment," Claire's voice told him. "Keep moving towards the rear of the plane."

He peered past a tipped pet carrier and spotted an aluminum cargo container partially blocking a small hatchway.

"Okay," he said into the radio. "Hang on a second."

He muscled the container out of the way and then paused, ear to the door. He could hear the stealthy slithering of reptilian bodies on the other side. The door was hinged to open towards him, a distinct disadvantage in dealing with whatever was on the other side.

"Claire," he said into the radio. "I'm gonna need two hands for this. I'll radio when I'm on the other side."

"Okay," Claire replied. "Don't get killed, or I'm going to be really pissed."

"Wouldn't dream of it," Flynn said before clicking the radio off and swapping it for the hairspray torch in his hip pocket.

He took a deep breath, unhooked the latch and then pulled the door open an inch, releasing a blast of flame into the space beyond.

He listened again and this time heard only the thrum of the engines. Cautiously, he opened the door the rest of the way and shone his flashlight into the compartment beyond.

This area seemed to be an oversized baggage hold, cluttered with surfboards and odd-sized packages and other unwieldy items. Laying on the ground directly on the other side of the door was a smoldering lump of burning snake meat. Apparently that had been enough to back his brothers up. There were no other reptiles in evidence at the moment.

"Okay," Flynn said, pulling the radio out again. "I'm in the next compartment. Now what?"

"Stand with your back to the door you just came through and the panel should be at about eleven o'clock on the far wall."

"Got it," Flynn replied, clocking the length of the far wall. "Looks like some stuff got tossed around in the turbulence. There's a bunch of junk cluttered up on that side, but it's gotta be back there somewhere."

To be honest, Flynn was not really looking forward to poking around behind things, knowing there had to be more snakes somewhere in this room. Plus he did not want to use the makeshift flame-thrower in the direction of the panel, for fear of roasting the delicate electronics. Casting the beam of his flash light over the strange and inexplicably sinister shapes around him, he spotted a massive mesh bag with the PADI logo and a reflective tag bearing the familiar symbol for diver down, a horizontal red rectangle with a white diagonal stripe.

The bag had broken open on one side, spilling out a cluster of items.

Flynn crouched over the spill, searching for anything to use as a weapon.

His fingers sorted quickly through masks and musty-smelling wet suits and fins and other useless things before he found a small, sturdy dive knife with a glowing compass set in the handle. Not great, but better than nothing.

"Okay then," he said, more to himself than Claire.

He made his cautious way across the cluttered hold, skirting a huge, breathtakingly tacky reproduction of Michelangelo's David shrouded in transparent bubble wrap and lying prone as if sleeping. Instead of white marble, this version was painted a hideous peachy, fake Caucasian skin tone, complete with dark brown hair both on his head and worse, on his tiny genitals as well. Flynn couldn't conceive of anyone wanting this atrocity in the first place, let alone paying God knew how much to ship it somewhere as luggage on a passenger plane.

Distracted for only a second by the surreal and awful statue, Flynn almost missed the large, dark-brown snake coiled at David's head.

Pure instinct was all that saved him, an instinct honed by years of training that moved his body out of danger the second his eye caught the first flicker of movement. In a smooth, unthinking motion, Flynn ducked to the right, dodged the strike and followed through with his left hand, grabbed the striking snake as it overshot past him and then brought the knife down in the center of the snake's narrow head, pinning it against the floor.

The snake thrashed violently, its body whipping against Flynn's arms and chest with bruising strength, but its struggles quickly weakened and it shuddered and then went limp. Flynn pulled the knife from the snake's skull and wiped both sides against the leg of his trousers.

He shook his head and let his breath out slowly, then put his shoulder to a bulky aluminum cargo container blocking the area where the outflow breaker panel should be. He shoved hard and then leapt back, ready with the knife in case anything was waiting back there to surprise him. There were no snakes, no stealthy attackers. There was, however, a small, rectangular breaker panel on the other side. He could see that a switch marked "air flow" had been jammed down in the "off" position and subsequently bent by the force of the container slamming into it.

"Shit," he said, digging the point of the dive knife up under the switch and trying to get enough leverage to bully it up to the "on" position. No dice.

Even though she could not have heard him, Claire's voice spoke up from his hip pocket like some weird magic trick. "Flynn?" she said. "What's going on?"

He pulled the radio from his pocket. "This goddamn lever is stuck," he said. "It just needs a little muscle."

He slipped the radio back into his pocket, put both hands on the knife and levered it against the bent switch with all his strength. He could feel it slowly giving in and loosening up when a flicker of shadowy movement danced in the corner of his eye. He spun to face a gang of oncoming snakes, several species approaching from several directions, and all with the same thought in their tiny reptilian minds. He drew the hairspray can like a six-gun and, back to the delicate electronic panel, he let the aggressive snakes have it with a blast of flame, sweeping the can back and forth like a fire extinguisher until the hairspray ran dry.

"Flynn?" Claire's muffled voice called from his pocket. "Did you get it?"

The flame sputtered and died, revealing no less than seven barbequed snakes cooked to various degrees of doneness. One medium rare viper was still squirming, and Flynn quickly put an end to its suffering with the heel of his shoe.

"Flynn?" Claire repeated, he voice tight and anxious. "Hey Flynn, is everything okay down there? Talk to me!"

Flynn took out the radio. "So," he said, turning back to the air flow panel and pushing up on the stubborn lever as hard as he could. "Why law school?"

Finally, as he strained against it with all his strength, the lever snapped into the "on" position. The outflow motor began to cycle up, humming to itself.

"Is now really the time for this?" Claire asked.

Before he could answer, a jolt of turbulence hit and he staggered back against the bulkhead, dropping both the knife and the radio. The knife skittered away across the floor while the radio tumbled against a nearby cargo container. As he reached for the fallen knife, an enormous flat black and white hooded head popped up between him and the dive knife, mouth agape and fangs dripping with deadly venom.

Flynn leapt back, dropping to a defensive crouch, hands searching desperately for some other weapon. His fingers found the radio and he spoke casually into it, eyes never leaving the menacing cobra.

"Sure," he said, voice calm and even. "No better time than the present."

The cobra lunged at him and he dodged nimbly back, letting the radio clatter to the floor. Claire's disembodied voice spoke up from the fallen radio as Flynn threw various bulky items into the snake's path.

"It's all my dad's fault I guess," Claire said. "He... well, he died just before I turned twenty-one..."

Flynn reached out for another thing to throw to block the advancing serpent and his hands hit the open diving bag, grasping a long cylindrical shape that his fingers identified seconds before his brain.

A gun. Not an ordinary gun, but a spear gun. That was good enough for Flynn.

"He was never around when I was growing up," Claire's voice continued. "Looking back now, I know that was partly because my mom was such a bitch on wheels, but it was also because he worked so tirelessly to help people. Poor, disadvantaged people with nowhere else to turn."

Flynn raised the spear gun, steadying the barrel. The snake was a difficult target, narrow and swift-moving, but Flynn was good. He let all the air slowly out of his lungs and squeezed the trigger with a smooth, even pressure. The spear shot out from the barrel and nailed the cobra right in the center of the widest part of the hood, just below the head. The snake flew back from the force of the hit and the spear through its neck thudded into a standing surfboard, pinning the snake against the colorful fiberglass.

"He was my hero," Claire said, oblivious to the continuing drama in the hold. "I pretty much worshiped him growing up and lived for the rare days when he would take me to the big library with him. He would be reading some two hundred pound legal textbook while I sat next to him reading *Charlie and the Chocolate Factory* or *Charlotte's Web* and feeling all mature and cool in the quiet, grown up part of the library. Then on the ride home, he would tell me about his cases. They were just like fairy tales, full of poor Cinderellas and heartless wicked stepsisters. I always thought of my dad as this knight in shining armor, fighting these horrible corporate dragons to save the humble villagers. I knew even then that when I grew up, I wanted be like him, to help people. To be a knight in shinning armor just like him."

Flynn kicked aside a smoking snake carcass and picked up the radio again. "Okay," Flynn said, voice still calm and unruffled. "So then why did you run off and become a flight attendant? Why didn't you just go to law school straight out of college?"

Three more snakes suddenly appeared from inside a tipped cargo container, these all green and smaller and disturbingly quick, all poised between Flynn and the hatchway leading back to galley storage.

"Well that's just great," he muttered, rolling his eyes.

Up in the First Class galley, Claire leaned against the bulkhead, wiping sweat from her face with a

South Pacific Air cocktail napkin and staring down at the radio. Why hadn't she just gone straight to law school? There was really no easy answer to that one. She had fully intended to do that, to just have a normal, linear life that went from point A to B to C and so on. Then, when her father died, killed instantly by a stroke as if struck by lightning, she went a little crazy. She remembered so clearly standing there at his funeral, wearing some black dress she'd bought in a rush at the last minute and didn't even really like all that much, feeling a curious, slow and not entirely unpleasant madness creeping up the back of her neck and sinking into her grieving brain.

Everything she thought she knew about herself suddenly seemed like nothing but a construct, a concept, a blueprint for a house she wasn't even sure she wanted to live in. In the weeks after she watched them lower her father's coffin into the ground, she couldn't stand to be home. She drank too much, partied too much, slept around with abandon and didn't want to think about the future. Then she woke up one morning with this idea, this burning need to travel all over the world before she settled into whatever sort of a life she would eventually decide to lead. It seemed to be the perfect choice, the only choice.

But how could she put that strange, stormy and headlong madness she had gone through into words, words to share with a man she barely knew?

"After my dad died," Claire said into the radio, "I kind of had to rethink everything about my life.

Things got even worse between my mom and me. She remarried right away and I'm pretty sure she had that rich chump waiting in the wings even before my father passed away. I guess you could say that I became a flight attendant partially to piss her off. She always thought of stewardesses as cheap and easy, basically one step above prostitutes. The day I left for my first flight, she told me not to come crying to her when I was a used up old spinster with more mileage than a '61 Buick and nothing to show for it." Claire laughed softly, shaking her head at the memory.

"Since then," she continued, "I've visited over twenty different countries, learned to speak three different languages and crossed the international date line more often than most people cross their own state line. I've seen the Pyramids of Egypt and stood on the Great Wall of China. I trekked through the Amazon rainforest, across the Australian outback, and across the glaciers of Alaska. I've eaten blowfish sushi in Tokyo and goat eye tacos in Mexico City. I've had lovers who didn't speak English. I once fooled around with a museum guard at the Louvre who snuck me in after hours to do nasty things in front of the Mona Lisa." She waited to see if that little confession would illicit a comment from Flynn but when it did not, she continued.

"Anyway," she said. "A few days before my father died, he and I were sitting together out on the porch. It was one of the last really hot days of the summer, but at the time it seemed like the heat would go on and on forever. He was going over some papers and

I was reading a magazine. He paused for a second and reached for his glass of iced tea and while he was reaching, he glanced over at what I was reading. It was some article about Peru, the ruins and things, and he just kind of sighed. He told me that he loved his life, that he loved his work and the satisfaction of helping people, but that he regretted never taking time to travel, to see the world outside his little office. He said that he was planning to take some time off in the coming year and thought maybe we could go see the Grand Canyon." She paused, throat tight. "Needless to say, it never happened for him. I suppose in a way, you could say that I wanted to see the world for him. To live the life he'd always wanted, before I settled down and followed in the footsteps of the life he actually led. I went and saw the Grand Canyon, and standing there on the cool green lip and looking down into that incredible hot red gash in the skin of the earth, I had this feeling like he was there with me." She bit her lip. "God, it sounds so corny, so new age silly to say something like that out loud, but that's how I felt." She paused and looked down at the radio. "I can't believe I'm telling you all this. You must think I'm a total whackjob."

Silence. No sarcastic, deadpan comment, nothing at all, just silence.

"Flynn?" she said into the radio.

Still nothing. Her heart clenched, suddenly double-timing inside her chest.

"Flynn?" she said again. "Come on Flynn, don't mess with me. Don't make me come down there and kick your ass!"

Her anxious attempt at humor sounded tense and desperate in the stuffy galley. Sean and Tiffany heard the fear in her voice and turned towards her, concern on their faces.

"Flynn, please," she said. "Answer me!"

Then, suddenly, Mercedes called out from her seat near the hole where the stairs had been.

"Do you hear that?" she cried. "Listen!"

Claire stopped calling for Flynn and turned her head to face a small air vent across the galley as a deep whooshing sound resonated through the cabin. It was a beautiful sound, the sound of cool, fresh air gushing through the vents. The passengers leaned their sweaty faces into the vents, laughing and drinking in the oxygen, but Claire could not bring herself to smile. Flynn still had not answered her. He had fixed the air and saved their lives, but at what cost? Claire continued to say his name over and over like some kind of mantra, feeling the tiny flame of hope inside her diminishing as the radio gave back nothing but silence minute after endless minute.

Then, another sound. Not from the radio or the air vents, but a deep rumble inside the shaft of the dumbwaiter. It was getting louder, rising up from galley storage. Unless snakes recently figured out how to push buttons, that could mean only one thing.

The door to the dumbwaiter flew open, revealing a cramped and sweaty Flynn. He unbent his long legs and climbed down out of the tiny box, smiling and rumpled and very much alive.

"Sorry," he said. "Snake ate my radio."

Claire laughed and threw her arms around him. "I thought you were dead!" she whispered, gripping him tightly.

"Wow, hey," he said softly, big hands gently touching the small of her back. "I ought to come back from the dead more often."

She looked up at him and there was a hot, tense moment when she was pretty sure she was going to kiss him, but then the passengers all burst into cheers and whistles and joyful spontaneous applause and his lips twisted up into a funny little half-smile.

"Hey, Flynn!" Sean called, holding out the airphone. "I hate to interrupt, but that FBI guy is on the phone again."

Flynn gave Sean's shoulder a paternal squeeze and then took the phone. Claire could not hear what he was saying, but she saw his eyes light up, seconds before a huge grin spread across his face. He nodded, hung up the phone and then turned to the passengers.

"Everyone, listen up," he said. "They're gonna have the antivenin for every single species of snake on this plane waiting for us at LAX."

More cheers sounded in the cabin. Mercedes and Ashley hugged each other and then pulled a shy but smiling Chen into the embrace. Maria squeezed her baby tight, kissing the top of the infant's head and saying a small, grateful prayer. Leroy rallied the strength to high-five Troy and Three Gs did a funny impromptu dance in the aisle that made Curtis giggle into his hands. Tiffany hugged Sean and kissed his cheek, leaving him with the biggest, dumbest grin on his face. Ken came forward and took Claire's hand, still mourning Grace but glad to be alive. Claire put a gentle hand on the back of Ken's neck, but her eyes were still on Flynn. He was leaning over Tommy and Curtis.

"Tommy," Flynn said, touching the boy's arm. "You're gonna be fine. There's medicine waiting for you at the airport in Los Angeles. All you got to do is just make it to the airport. Can you do that?"

Tommy did not speak, but his eyes opened a little and seemed to focus on Flynn for a precious second before sliding closed again.

"The medicine will fix him, right?" Curtis asked, clutching his folded drawing to his chest.

"Good as new," Flynn replied.

"Leroy too?" Curtis asked.

"Leroy too," Flynn said.

"Okay," Curtis said.

Flynn turned back to Claire and Ken. "It's all up to your pilot now."

Claire nodded, squeezing Ken's hand. "I'll go tell Arch the good news."

Outside the round windows, a warm pink flush was painting the purple clouds as the plane flew eastward into dawn.

TWENTY-THREE

When the chopper landed in the center of Kraitler's compound for the second time, the wind was tossing the spindly mechanical dragonfly viciously from side to side. By the time Harris, Dr Price, Fisk and Lawson, with the surly handcuffed Kraitler in tow, were all piled in and the chopper lifted off, the gritty desert winds had gone from a minor annoyance to a serious impediment. They barely made it back to nearby Edwards Air Force base before their chopper pilot had no choice but to set down and wait it out. Harris was livid, but the pilot just shrugged and parked a cigarette in one corner of his unshaven mouth, telling them to go get some coffee. There would no taking off into this mess for at least another hour, possibly longer. When Harris tried to make the urgency of the situation a little clearer, the pilot just smirked and told Harris to take it up with God.

Needless to say, they didn't have an hour or possibly longer. Flight 121 would be coming in to LAX at eight thirty am and like Price said, time is tissue. Passengers would be sick, dying, and every second counted. They didn't stand a chance without the exotic antivenins obtained from Kraitler. There was no choice but to drive.

Harris turned Kraitler over to the local authorities and told them they would need to take the woman Ronnie into custody as well, as soon as she regained consciousness of course. Paperwork signed off and dealt with, Harris, his agents, and the exhausted snake guy hit the road in an unmarked black Crown Victoria with the red cooler full of antivenin strapped down inside the trunk.

Shreds of trash and dry rattling palm fronds smacked against the Crown Vic's windshield, whipped away into the swirling dust as Lawson wrestled the wheel, fighting the wind down the 14 freeway at one hundred and ten miles per hour through the Antelope Valley. Price was snoring lightly in the seat beside Harris, clearly spent and unused to this kind of mad excitement. Harris, on the other hand, finally felt alive again. The stress, the ticking clock, the lives in the balance, and the on-the-fly problem solving; it all felt like some kind of essential vitamin his body had been deprived of while cooped up behind that desk, infusing him with a clear sense of purpose and drive. He felt more awake than ever, sharp and ready for anything.

Anything, that is, except Los Angeles morning rush hour.

The 5 Freeway was not too bad and it was still relatively early, but by the time they hit the 405 things began to clog up. Just a little at first, then more and more until they hit a dead snarl just before the junction with the 101. There was an overturned semi sprawled across the road, blocking all but one lane, and its cargo of live chickens were running and flapping all over the place, bringing traffic in both directions to a near standstill.

"Hop off!" Fisk said, pointing to the upcoming Sherman Way exit. "Take Sepulveda."

Dr Price rubbed his eyes and sat up, suddenly awake and very interested in the conversation. "Sepulveda? You're crazy. It'll be a parking lot. You might as well just stay on the freeway."

"How about Coldwater?" Fisk asked.

"Too far east," Dr Price said.

"Somebody decide something!" Lawson said, pulling up to a red light at the bottom of the Sherman Way ramp. He was from DC like Harris, and like Harris, Lawson still couldn't figure out the sprawling endless suburban patchwork stitched with freeways that composed greater Los Angeles County.

"Left," Fisk and Dr Price said at the same time.

"Okay," Lawson said, hitting his turn signal.

"Kanan-Dume?" Fisk asked.

"Hell yeah," Dr Price said. "Right. Kanan-Dume. Definitely the way to go."

"Get on the 101 West," Fisk said.

"If you say so," Lawson replied. "I'm so lost at this point I might as well be on Mars."

"You're in beautiful Van Nuys, California," Fisk said, gesturing around at the shabby donut shops, industrial buildings and warehouses. "Smut capital of the United States. Something like seventy five percent of the dirty movies made in the states come out of the San Fernando Valley."

"Figures you'd know that," Lawson said. "Which way?"

"Right," Fisk said, "at this next light."

"I hate to be a party pooper," Harris said, "but how about injecting a little urgency into the matter and saving the tour bus chit chat for a day when little kids aren't dying from deadly snake bites?"

"Sorry, boss," Fisk said.

The 101 North was nearly empty and they were able to hit the Kanan Road exit in mere minutes. However, once on the desolate, stomach-churning, white knuckle twists of the tiny canyon road, Harris found himself regretting the amount of coffee he'd had in the past four hours.

"Are you sure about this?" Lawson asked, bullying the unwieldy Crown Vic into a tight hairpin turn without touching the break.

"Sure I'm sure," Fisk said.

"It's really beautiful out here," Dr Price said wistfully. "In these canyons, you'll find California kings, gopher snakes..." He looked off out the window. "And Pacific rattlers of course."

"If this road really goes to the airport," Lawson asked, "why are we the only ones on it?"

"It doesn't go to the airport," Dr Price said. "It goes to Pacific Coast Highway."

"Pacific Coast Highway goes to Lincoln," Fisk said. "And Lincoln goes to the airport. Besides, us being the only ones on the road is the whole point, now isn't it? Don't tell me you'd rather be back in traffic."

"I just hope you two know what you're talking about," Lawson said, skeptically eyeing the rugged canyon landscape around them.

Harris looked at his watch. Seven fifteen. He pulled his cellphone out of his pocket and flipped it open, scowling at the twirling image of a satellite dish searching for a signal.

"You won't get a signal out here," Dr Price said, smiling. "That's one of the things I like about it. Out here, you can almost pretend the city doesn't exist."

"Shit," Harris said, snapping the phone shut and ignoring the geeky doctor. "Get the lead out, Lawson. Get me out of Wile E Coyote land and back in the real world."

"I got news for you, boss," Lawson said, cranking the wheel into another tight turn. "This is a Crown Vic, not a Lamborghini. I'll do what I can."

"Yeah," Harris said quietly, thinking of Sanders, Flynn and the people who were still alive on that plane, still fighting for their lives. "Do what you can."

Claire found the door to the flight deck closed. She punched in her security code, but it seemed that the electronics were down, rendering the little keypad dark and useless. She knocked.

"Hey Arch!" she called, knocking again. "Open up."

No answer.

"Arch?" Claire put her ear to the door, but couldn't hear anything but the thrum of engines.

Seconds later, Flynn was beside her. She had to shake off the flush of heat she felt at his closeness and instead bit down on her lower lip.

"He's not answering," she told Flynn.

Flynn stepped in front of her, pounding on the door.

"Arch!" he shouted. "Dammit, open this door."

Flynn put his shoulder to the door, but cockpit doors are built tough, deliberately made to keep people out, and this one was no exception. Flynn was clearly doing more damage to his shoulder than the door.

"Shit," Flynn said, casting around for anything to use to break the lock.

Claire picked up one of the glass-tipped golf clubs and was about to hand it to Flynn when the little keypad flashed several times in quick succession and then stayed lit. Claire quickly dropped the golf club and started punching in her code. She only got halfway before the keypad started flashing again. Frustrated, she slammed her fist into the door, which hurt way more than she'd expected.

"Don't worry," Flynn said, picking up the golf club. "I've got the key."

Claire stepped back as Flynn had at the door. The glass shattered and the shaft twisted but the door remained unaffected.

"God DAMN these doors are tough," Flynn said.

"It's because of terrorists," Claire said, shrugging sheepishly.

"Fuck terrorists," Flynn said, ready to take another swing when the keypad suddenly lit up again.

"Wait!" Claire cried and punched in her code as fast as she could.

Miraculously the lock clicked and released and the door popped open. As the door swung wide, Arch's stiff, twisted body tumbled out, falling loosely against Flynn before flopping to the ground at his feet. Arch's face was horribly swollen and blackened, almost unrecognizable, like a cheap Halloween mask someone had left out in the sun.

Claire covered her mouth, trapping a scream inside. Sean came swiftly up behind her and his eyes went huge when he saw the prone copilot at Flynn's feet.

"Dude!" he said. "Is he dead?"

Flynn crouched beside Arch on the carpet and felt for a pulse beneath his ear. "Not yet," he said, gripping a wrist and then feeling the other side of his neck. "Well, actually..." He felt the first side again. "Now he is."

"Oh my God," Tiffany said, appearing behind Sean. "Ohmygodohmygodohmygod!"

"Hey," Sean said, taking her hand. "Shhhhh. You'll freak everyone out."

Tiffany looked silently up at Sean, blue eyes huge, and then swallowed hard and nodded.

"Sean," Flynn said. "Give me a hand."

Together Sean and Flynn lifted Arch's body and moved it roughly aside as Claire stepped forward and opened the flight deck door all the way.

Inside, coiled and hissing as they slithered over the controls, four huge green mambas all turned their heads to face Claire, tongues flickering towards her warm flesh. Clearly Arch had managed to hit the automatic pilot before the attacking mambas overwhelmed him, but they were still soundly screwed. The closest of the snakes lunged at Claire and she quickly slammed the door seconds before it reached her. Before the door lock was able to reengage, Flynn slammed the golf club into the key pad, shorting in out in a spray of sparks.

"Jesus!" Claire said, voice tense and constricted.

"What are we gonna do?" Sean asked, holding the fearful Tiffany. "Do you know how to fly a plane?

"Look," Flynn said. "I said I was good at Monopoly but I never said I could fly a 747."

"Okay," said Claire, face set and grim. "Okay, then." She turned and headed back down the aisle into the First Class cabin. "Everyone," she said. "We have a fairly serious situation here."

All those exhausted, hopeful faces turned up to her, all counting on her, and she felt close to some profound breakdown that might be tears or laughter, or maybe both.

"Listen," she said and then paused, unsure of how to continue.

There was just no good way to say what she had to say. No way to soften it or make it less terrifying. This could be the end of the line for all of them and yet she had to bite down on a wild bubble of laughter as she suddenly pictured the scene from that old comedy *Airplane* where the stewardess asks if anyone can fly a plane and all the passengers wig out in preposterous ways. Maybe Mercedes would take her top off.

She had to get a grip. They were obviously counting on her. She couldn't afford to wig out now. Then she felt Flynn's big warm hand on her shoulder as he stepped up silently behind her. She took a deep breath and forced herself to continue.

"Our remaining pilot has been killed," she said. "The plane is currently on autopilot so we are not in any immediate danger, but someone has to land this plane." She paused, looking out over the rows of incredulous faces. "Anyone?"

Silence in the cabin and Claire could feel her heart sinking. Then, Three Gs stood up and stepped into the aisle.

"You?" Claire asked.

"Hell no!" Three Gs said, pointing to Troy. "Him."

Troy looked back at his boss, stunned. "G," Troy said. "Have you finally completely lost whatever was left of your mind?"

"You can do this," Three Gs said, gaze unwavering. "I know you got this in you, Troy. In all these years, you've never let me down. Take us home, dog."

"You're a pilot?" Flynn asked.

Troy stood, shrugging. "I got over two thousand hours," he replied.

"No shit?" Flynn said.

Troy closed his eyes and pressed his fingers to his forehead, seeming to be digging down deep for some kind of strength. "I can do this," he said finally.

"But what about those snakes?" Claire asked Flynn. "We need to get those snakes out of there first. We can't risk losing another pilot."

Flynn looked back at her, dark eyes weighing every option.

"Flynn!" Chen called from the rear of the cabin, near the hole where the stairs had been. "Check this out."

Flynn headed back to the large yellow raft plugging the hole and Claire followed close behind.

"Look," Chen said, toeing the raft. "It's getting softer."

Flynn bent to examine the heavy rubber and found that Chen was right. The raft was flaccid, sagging in the middle. It still held, but Claire could see that it wouldn't last.

"Maybe it got ripped when Three Gs was yanking on it," Chen said. "Or maybe one of the snakes below got a fang into it somehow. Either way, I figure we have maybe ten or fifteen minutes before this thing is soft enough for the snakes to get in around the edges."

"Oh, man," Claire said. "What are we going to do?"

"Well," Flynn said, "I guess it's time to open up some windows."

When Harris, Dr Price, Lawson and Fisk finally hit Pacific Coast Highway, they found it packed with surfers, boards poking out of open-topped Jeeps and strapped to battered Woodys as they hunted up the raddest breaks, fighting to be the first to hit the early morning waves. Also congesting the narrow beach road were balding television producers and movie executives in their mid-life crisis sports cars, screaming into their cellphones on their way to the studios from the precarious mansions they'd just rebuilt after the latest wild fire or slide or other natural disasters that Malibu had used to try to get rid of them.

Lawson pulled the red and white plastic magnetic bubble from the glove box, rolling down his window and setting it up on the roof of the car, tweaking the siren and scooting around pissed off surfers in the breakdown lane. It occasionally got a little exciting, but they made it to Lincoln without incident. Of course, just because they were in the home stretch didn't mean they were there.

They were nearly rear-ended by a cellphone head in a Jaguar when a white haired cop suddenly stepped out into the street, holding up a hand to stop the oncoming traffic.

"It's a shoot," Fisk said. "Great."

"A movie shoot?" Harris frowned out the window at the huge trucks filled with lights and ominous-looking equipment. "You have got to be fucking kidding me."

Flynn watched the flight attendants move swiftly through the First Class cabin, strapping people into their seats and showing them how to brace themselves. Ken was helping Maria strap the mask from the small oxygen tank they had used on Grace and Tommy around baby Isabella's tiny face, and Tiffany was helping Leroy as he struggled to find a comfortable position that still allowed him to be belted in, but if Flynn was honest with himself, he would have to admit that he was really just watching Claire.

She was such a natural leader, all cool, unflappable poise and confidence as she moved through the cabin. Of course she was scared, they all were, but she sucked it up like a pro, taking care of business, no sweat. His already sky-high admiration for her was growing exponentially every minute.

Admiration, a wise-ass voice inside his head said. So that's what you want to call it.

As much as he hated to admit it, he found his brain getting more and more cluttered with totally ridiculous thoughts about this woman he had no business thinking anything about at all. Thoughts like what she would look like with her hair down and wild around her face, and how the thick, curly chaos of it would feel in his hands. Clearly, she'd only been kidding when she made that comment about sleeping with him. Anything else, any sort of underlying heat or inexplicable connection in her warm hazel eyes, was obviously just wishful thinking on his part. Besides, he did not need to be entertaining these sorts of thoughts about some pretty little white girl young enough to be his daughter, no matter what she might have said. What he needed was to hustle all thoughts of that nature right out of his head and stay focused on keeping them all alive. He looked away from Claire where she was hunkered down helping

Curtis tighten his safety belt and concentrated on untangling a yellow nylon safety ladder from its compartment in the galley. Sawing it loose from its mooring with the dive knife, he securely knotted the nylon around the knob of the cockpit door.

"Hey," Claire said, suddenly behind him, as if summoned like a genie by his impure thoughts.

"Hey yourself," he replied, pretending to be checking the strength of the knot on the cockpit door.

"Listen," she said. "When the windows go, we'll lose cabin pressure and oxygen. You and Troy have got to get us down as fast as you can."

"All right," Flynn said, looking over at Troy, who was standing alone and pensive beside Leroy. "No problem."

"I have faith in you," Claire said, smiling. She swiftly stood up on her toes and kissed him on the cheek, close enough to his lips that he felt her lips brush lightly against the corner of his mouth.

It was the last thing he expected, but he tried to play it cool, even though that quick little kiss slipped like a monkey wrench deep into the gears of his clever strategy for not thinking about her anymore.

Having so blithely breached his perimeter, she turned on her heel and walked away and he knew she knew that he was watching her as she went. Watching the shift and sway of her strong legs and hips beneath her tight blue skirt, he made a deal with himself. If they survived this madness, if LAX was real and not just some fantasy they all dreamed up between bouts of fighting for their lives, then as soon as his feet were on the California ground, he would give her his card. Put the ball in court. If she wasn't just playing with him, if she really wanted to put her money where her mouth was, she could call him up and tell him so. And then... well then, he would take it from there.

In the meantime, he needed to survive and make sure everyone else survived along with him.

"Okay, everybody, listen up," he said, stepping forward into the aisle. "It's gonna get pretty crazy in here in a few minutes. Make sure you're strapped in tight. Remember, keep your heads down, protect them with your arms and hold your breath as long as you can."

Flynn surveyed the faces around him: exhausted, beaten and terrified, hanging on to the thinnest shreds of hope. All of them believing in him, trusting him, looking to him to make this eleventh hour miracle happen and suddenly he wasn't so sure. Maybe he was making a terrible mistake, gambling with innocent lives. But he had been over every angle, every option, and this was the only way. The mammals in the cabin would have a hard time, sure, but they were strapped down and warm blooded and they would survive. The reptiles, on the other hand, would be tossed and battered and sucked out into the freezing sky. Those able to hold on would swiftly go torpid or die from the extreme drop in temperature. Then, it would be up to Troy to set this crippled bird down whole.

"Troy," Flynn said softly. "You ready?"

"Been training my whole life for this," the bodyguard replied, sounding firm and determined in spite of the tense anxiety in his posture.

Beside Troy, the feverish Leroy held up a shaky fist. Troy touched his fist to Leroy's, then nodded to Three Gs who smiled and nodded back.

"You got this," Three Gs said. "No sweat."

"What about you?" Troy asked, a line of worry creasing his broad brow. "You gonna be all right, G?"

"Me?" Three Gs shrugged. "I'm fine. Though I'll tell you what, If I live through this shit, I ain't wasting another day sweating the small stuff, you know what I'm saying?"

"I hear that," Troy replied, turning to brace himself in the aisle and gripping the opposite end of the yellow nylon ladder. "Flynn, let's do this."

"Everyone strapped down tight?" Flynn asked, looking around the cabin one more time.

Heads nodded all around. Sean and Tiffany clung together, as did Mercedes and Ashley. Maria clung to her baby and Curtis held on to the unconscious Tommy. Claire sat in her fold-down seat in the forward galley, watching him.

"All right, then," Flynn said, "I've had it with these motherfucking snakes on this motherfucking plane. Flight attendants..." He drew his Glock and thumbed off the safety. "Prepare for landing."

Without further ceremony, Flynn fired the handgun. The sound of the shot was deafening and the baby screamed with fear and alarm as a window burst in the center of the cabin in a row where no one sat. Flynn turned and swiftly followed up with another shot to the window on the opposite side.

The baby's terrified cries were immediately buried in the furious howl of a powerful, sucking wind shrieking through the cabin. Seconds later, the limp life raft tore loose from the hole in the floor, releasing an explosion of writhing snakes and broken-open luggage all vacuumed up and towards the shot-out windows.

The passengers clung grimly to their seats and tried their best to protect their heads from the maelstrom of flying debris and desperate reptiles.

As the icy wind screamed around them, Flynn signaled Troy to pull the nylon ladder and yank open the flight deck door. Troy nodded and put all his muscle into it, ripping the door wide and sending the four green mambas inside the cockpit tumbling end over end towards the open windows.

One of the mambas slapped into Tiffany, trying to hold on by coiling around her neck. To Flynn's amazement, Sean did not hesitate to reach over and grab the snake, tearing it free and flinging its squirming body out the window. That kid was going to be a whole new man by the time he reached LAX. No question about it.

Flynn fought his way up towards the flight deck, deflecting snakes and debris as he moved towards Troy. Once beside the big bodyguard, the two of them worked together to pull themselves closer and closer to the flight deck door.

"Come on, man," Flynn hollered, voice just barely audible above the howling wind. "You can do it."

"Just get me to that chair," Troy said, pulling himself forward another hard won meter.

Flynn reached out and locked his grip around Troy's wrist, helping him make his way into the pilot's chair. Once Troy was safely buckled in, Flynn dragged himself over to the co-pilot's seat and strapped himself in.

Troy was looking at the huge, complex instrument panel with all the excitement of a kid with a brand new toy, snakes and danger forgotten. He pointed to the switch marked "autopilot."

"Flip that switch, Agent Flynn," Troy said.

"Roger that, Captain McDaniels," Flynn said, flipping the switch to the "off" position.

Troy grabbed the yoke and pushed it forward.

"Damn!" he said appreciatively. "That's what I'm talking about."

Mercedes had her head tucked down and was clinging to Ashley's hand when suddenly there was a loud scream and Ashley's grip tightened so hard that Mercedes thought for a second that Ashley might break her fingers. When Mercedes turned to look at her friend, she saw a vision out of a horrific nightmare. Ashley's head had been bashed in by some hunk of flying debris and was all soft and bloody on one side. There was a jaunty red, yellow and black striped snake wrapped around her face like a Tim Burton cartoon accessory. The snake was nosing around in the pulpy wound on the side of Ashley's head, almost like it was trying to get inside her.

"Get it off me!" Ashley shrieked, hands blindly flailing and accidentally smacking Mercedes in the head. "Oh my God GET IT OFF ME!"

The girl that Mercedes used to be probably would have just screamed and screamed and waited for some guy like Chen to come and save Ashley, but that girl had died with Mary-Kate. She really had no idea who this new Mercedes was, but she did not hesitate to rip the colorful snake off Ashley and bash its little head in with her remaining steel-heeled shoe.

"Ashley!" Mercedes cried. "Ashley, are you okay?"

Ashley's fingers flew over the mushy wet mess on the side of her head. "I… I feel…"

Mercedes put a protective arm around Ashley and tried not to look too close at the wound on Ashley's head. There was some soft pink stuff there in the middle of the ghastly red gash and Mercedes was pretty sure that it was Ashley's brains.

"Esperanza…" Ashley said, her voice barely audible over the howling wind.

That was all she said, and then her head lolled back on the seat and all the animation just drained right out of her eyes. Mercedes thought of the little white dog with three legs that Ashley had showed her back in the Honolulu airport. Esperanza, which meant "Hope" in Spanish. That little dog was back in LA waiting for Ashley and Tyler, with no idea that they were never coming back, and that thought made Mercedes feel terribly sad. Her tears nearly froze on her icy cheeks as she buried her face in her arms and waited to die.

In the cockpit, Flynn handed Troy the radio headset. Troy grinned and slipped it onto his head.

"'What's up, y'all?" he said. "This is your new pilot Troy McDaniels speaking. To my left is my main man, brother from another mother, copilot and super fly G-man, Neville Flynn."

"Copy that, Hula one two one," the voice on the radio replied. "What is your current status?"

"Our current status is pretty much fucked," Troy replied. "But we're doing what we can to unfuck the situation and get our asses on the ground in one piece."

"Sir," the voice from the control tower said. "Do you have any experience piloting a jet aircraft?"

"Oh, yeah," Troy replied. "F-15, F-16, A-10, Warthog. Flown all that shit."

"Outstanding, McDaniels," the voice said. "Then we are damn glad to have you up there. What squadron were you with?"

"*Awesome Fighting Aces*," Troy replied with a smirk. "I tell you man, those people got their shit locked down tight."

A beat of staticky silence over the radio and then the tower's incredulous reply: "McDaniels? Are you saying your only flight time is at the controls of a *video game*?"

"It ain't a video game," Troy said, indignant. "It's a flight simulator."

Flynn gaped at Troy in utter amazement. Troy looked over at him and shrugged. "It's got an introduction by Chuck Yeager and everything."

The clouds parted before them to reveal the Southern California coast, bathed in clear, early morning sunshine. Flynn thought it had never looked so beautiful.

"Just give me the VOR numbers and approach vectors," Troy said into the radio. "And I'll be fine."

"Sir," the voice said. "I strongly suggest that you relinquish the pilot's chair to someone more experienced…"

Flynn snatched the headset. "This is special agent Neville Flynn speaking. FBI. I think maybe you are failing to fully grasp the situation up here. We have lost cabin pressure. We have two passengers who will die if they do not receive immediate medical attention and the rest of us will follow suit in under an hour if we don't get out of this flying deathtrap. Mr McDaniels is ten times more qualified to fly this plane than anyone else on board. He is the one and only person with a hope in hell of getting us down alive. Do you understand? There *is* no one else. So I strongly suggest that you give him what he needs and start clearing traffic, got it?"

"Roger that, Agent Flynn," the voice said. "Hold for VOR and approach vectors."

Flynn covered the mic in the headset and turned to Troy.

"You're pretty good at this game, right?"

"Hell, yeah," Troy replied. "No problem… I mean, my older brother Randy did get the high score, but I'm good… Asshole never lets me hear the end of it, though…"

Harris hung his body more than halfway out the open window of the Crown Vic, shouting at the top of his lungs and waving his FBI badge and ID under the noses of every headset-wearing knucklehead dumb enough to get in his way. Several feet away, a group of sleekly groomed actors dressed up as FBI agents gawked at Harris as he suggested several illegal and probably impossible sex acts that the people in headsets could perform on each other. Lawson silently rolled the car forward through the crowd of extras like a rural train gently nudging cows off the track.

Eventually a man who had to be the director came storming over. He was short and red-faced, sporting a patchy full beard and an expensive gray-green cloth baseball hat. "You want to tell me what the hell is going on here?" he asked his army of headsets.

A thickset blonde woman in a headset was trying to steer him away from the Crown Vic, but he was having none of it. He came over to the car.

"Do you have any idea how much money it is costing me just standing here talking to you?" the director said.

"Do you have any idea how much money it will cost your Director's Guild medical insurance to surgically remove my foot from your ass if you don't let us through?" Harris replied. "See this?" He pressed his shield into the cranky director's face. "I didn't get this from some prop house, asshole. This is real FBI business, so get your goddamn make-believe out of my way before I get on the phone and have your shooting permits yanked and you can make the rest of your precious movie in fucking CANADA!"

Cowed, the director took a step back.

"Let them through," he said.

"Let them through," the blonde said into her headset.

"Let them through," echoed the other headset muppets like cult followers of some strange religion.

"We have a Crown Vic coming through," the blonde said, running beside the slow moving car. "Clear the way and then reset. We are going again right away as soon as they are through. Repeat: we are letting them through and then going again right away."

They passed through the center of what looked like a big car chase set up, complete with guys holding big pieces of safety glass and pushing fruit carts. They made several turns and then were quickly hustled through to the other side. As soon as they were free of the barriers surrounding the shoot, Lawson punched it and less than ten minutes later, LAX came into view.

Harris barked orders into his cellphone as a guard waved them through a back gate and onto the airport tarmac. There was already a cluster of emergency vehicles waiting for the arrival of South Pacific Air Flight 121. Lawson had barely stopped the car when Dr Price jumped out, grabbed the cooler full of antivenin and ran for the medical triage that had been set up to receive the envenomated passengers. Harris hung back, watching everything fall into place, and shook his head. It wasn't over till that plane was on the ground, but somehow, they'd done it. They'd made it. The antivenin would be waiting when they landed.

"Well," Harris said to Lawson and Fisk, "looks like that's that."

"Does this mean you're gonna go back to your desk?" Fisk asked. "Now that this mission has been accomplished?"

"Hell no," Harris said, grinning.

"That's what we want to hear, boss," Lawson said grinning. "We're glad to have you back."

"Does that mean I can sleep on your couch when Ana Luisa throws me out?" Harris asked.

"You bet," Lawson said. "I even have one of those fold-out sleeper deals."

Harris put a hand on Lawson's meaty shoulder. "Damn it's good to be back," he said.

On the flight deck, Troy steered the jet towards the flashing runway beacons below, reaching out to lower the massive flaps forty-five degrees. He looked down at the yoke.

"There ain't no L2 button on this thing,"

"Troy," Flynn said. "I hate to be a back seat pilot, but the plane's not level."

"I know," Troy said. "This ain't like piloting with the analog thumbstick!"

"LAX Tower," he said into the mic. "This here is Hula one-two-one heavy requesting clearance for landing."

"We've cleared runway Twenty-Four R for you one-two-one," the voice from the tower replied. "But you've got a strong tailwind. Advise you come around and use runway six Left."

"No, uh-uh, negative," Troy replied. "Can't do that. There's no time to correct for westbound orientation."

"You try to land west to east," the voice said, "and you'll come in too fast to control."

"Then I suggest you clear the east side, too," Troy said. "'Cause like it or not, this bitch is coming in for a landing."

Curtis was starting to think that he would never be scared ever again in his whole life. When all these scary things kept on happening and happening, it just made him want to take a nap. Almost like there was this certain area inside his brain for being scared and when all the seats in that area were taken, that part of his brain just closed the door and put up a sign that said: "SOLD OUT"

Although he found it impossible to keep on being scared, he did feel really chilly. It was freezing cold, way colder than Curtis had ever felt in his whole life. The air around him felt like it was full of shark teeth and his skin hurt from the icy wind blowing so hard in his face. He wished that he was back home in Hawaii, sitting on the beach with the warm friendly water lapping at his toes and the sun warming his back while he poked a stick in the sand, looking for crabs and stuff. He wished that he and Tommy were both on that beach, that Tommy had never been bitten and that mommy was there with them instead of in Los Angeles. Most of all he wanted his daddy. He didn't like his job of being the man. He wanted daddy to be there so Curtis could just go back to being a kid.

But he wasn't, he wouldn't be there for six whole months. Curtis had no choice but to keep on trying, keep on taking care of Tommy. Even though it was hard to move with all the heavy air pushing him down into his seat, Curtis still reached out and took Tommy's hand, in case the big baby was still scared.

Troy was muscling the big bird down, heading into final approach towards the impossibly tiny runway below. Flynn was sweating in spite of the arctic chill in the cockpit, watching the unforgiving ground hurtling towards them and thinking irrelevantly of the Bugs Bunny cartoon where the plane is screaming towards the ground and then stops dead in the air, inches from a crash because they ran out of gas.

A blast of turbulance rocked the plane.

"Ain't no big thing," Troy told Flynn, though it was obvious from his voice that it was, in fact, a very big thing. "I got a shock controller, vibrates whenever there's contact..."

An even bigger jolt shook the fight deck.

"But it don't vibrate THAT much!"

"Just stay cool, man," Flynn said.

"Here we go," Troy said, releasing the landing gear. "Get ready to lean on those brakes."

For a weirdly serene moment, they were flying along at almost ground level, skimming inches from the tarmac. Then the landing gear banged against the ground, sending the massive aircraft leapfrogging at two hundred and fifty miles per hour before the wheels finally locked down with a deafening screech, gripping the earth like some kind of miracle.

Troy wrestled the yoke with everything he had, but the plane was still perilously close to out of control, veering sharply to the left. A jumbo jet parked on a taxi-way loomed up ahead.

"This ain't part of the game," Troy replied, voice pinched and tight with fear.

"How about crashing?" Flynn asked. "Is crashing part of the game?"

"I don't know," Troy said, knucking sweat from his eyes. "I usually just hit reset and start the level over. I should have taken up Golden Tee."

"Watch it, man" Flynn shouted.

Flynn lent his strength to steer the careening aircraft away from the parked jet. Hydraulics shrieked as they barely missed the jet by a half an ass hair and barreled towards a large blue LAX aviation warehouse. Flynn and Troy leaned on the breaks with their full combined weight as the warehouse came closer and closer.

Letting out a string of colorful profanity, Troy finally managed to bring the enormous plane to a lurching, bumpy stop, less than three feet from the warehouse doors.

There was a century of stunned silence as they all sat in their seats and wondered if this was real. If they were really alive and on the ground in Los Angeles. Everyone was almost afraid to believe it. Then, all at once, everyone in the cabin burst into spontaneous, exuberant cheers.

"Yeah!" Troy said. "Oh yeah! Whose house is this? I said whose motherfucking house is this? Troy's house! That's RIGHT! That's what I'm talking about! Fuck your high score, Randy!"

Flynn shared Troy's excitement, but he was quiet and still, body and mind exhausted and deep fried but still utterly glad to be alive.

"Good job, Troy," he said.

"That's right!" Troy replied. "Yeah! Oh ye of little motherfucking faith," he said into the mic. "Hula one two one is ON THE GROUND!"

"Copy that, Hula one two one," the voice from the tower said. "Welcome to Los Angeles."

At that moment, Claire came into the cockpit and unceremoniously flung herself into Flynn's arms. Before he had a chance to register the warm miracle of her body, alive and safe and pressing up against him, she tilted her head up and kissed him.

No peck on the cheek either, this was a full blown, raw and open mouthed kiss that left absolutely nothing to the imagination. His brain might not have known exactly what to make of this turn of events, but his body knew exactly what to do.

After what felt like an eternity of deliciously slow suspension of time, during which he felt sure that there was no one but her in the entire world, Troy loudly cleared his throat.

"Damn, girl!" he said. "How about a little sugar for Captain Troy?"

Claire broke the kiss and laughed, a wonderful, living, breathing noise that sounded like the rest of her life. She reluctantly let go of Flynn and then leaned in and kissed Troy on the cheek.

"You did it," she said. "You saved us."

"Yeah, well..." Troy said, smirking with false modesty.

Then suddenly the door to the flight deck burst open and the tiny space was filled with cheering people, surrounding Troy and slapping his back, hugging him and covering his beaming face with kisses. Claire stepped back to lean against Flynn for another few seconds.

"You know what I was thinking?" she asked.

"I know what I'm thinking," Flynn replied, caressing the taut curve of her waist.

"Well, that too," she said, blushing. "But I mean about my future, law school and all that. Now that it looks like I actually get to have a future."

"Oh yeah," Flynn said. "What were you thinking?"

She slipped her arms around his waist and smiled up at him. "I was thinking that when I graduate, I might apply at Quantico."

"Are you serious?" Flynn asked. "You want to become an FBI agent?"

"I thought I might," she said. "Why, does that surprise you?"

"Not at all," Flynn said. "I think you would make a hell of an agent."

"Hey, you dirty tramp," Ken called from the doorway with a huge grin on his face. "When you're done catting around in there, we could use some help with the slides."

"All right," Claire said, pulling away from Flynn again and leaving the side of his body she had been leaning against feeling cold without her. "We can talk more about this later."

"Later," Flynn repeated. "I love that word. Half an hour ago, I wasn't sure there was ever going to be a later."

"Oh, there's gonna be a whole lot of later," she said with a mischievous smile. "That's a promise."

TWENTY-FOUR

Dr Price stood in the medical triage area and watched the battered but triumphant passengers make their careful ways one by one down the slide. Animal control officers in protective suits were preparing to enter the cargo hold and for a fleeting second, Dr Price almost wished he was one of them. There were some truly amazing and rare species on that list they had gotten from Kraitler and he would love to see them all, if any had survived. Then a Chinese man was running towards him, holding a limp child in his arms. Behind him was a second, older boy and a well dressed black man who looked very familiar, but Dr Price couldn't quite place his face.

"This little boy was bitten," the Chinese man said. "He's unconscious."

A pair of EMTs accepted the boy from the Chinese man's arms and laid him down on a waiting stretcher, slipping an oxygen mask over his small, pale face and starting an intravenous drip. Dr Price examined the boy's wound. It was bad, very swollen and exhibiting a dusky discoloration around the bite. The fang marks were small but deep. There was some sanguineous vesiculation accompanied by dramatic necrosis around the site, with extensive and ugly tissue sloughing.

"Okay," Dr Price said. "Did anyone see the snake that bit this boy?"

"Show 'em," the black man said to the other kid, nodding encouragingly.

The other kid held out a drawing, executed in scratchy ball point pen, but very well done. It pictured several angles of a large, menacing monocellate cobra, meticulously detailed down to the perfect white ring on the back of its hood.

"A cobra?" Dr Price asked. "Like in *Indiana Jones*, right?"

The kid nodded, and then turned his head, suddenly shy.

"Excellent work," Dr Price said. "Maybe when you are older, you might want to come and work for me."

He selected two vials of antivenin for the Naja species and swiftly worked to reconstitute the dry preparation in Lactated Ringers Solution before using a sterile syringe transfer the solution to an intravenous piggyback set-up.

"Okay," Dr Price said. "Watch for signs of anaphylaxis and get him transferred to intensive care right away." He turned back to the older kid. "He's gonna be fine. The medicine to stop the cobra venom is going into his body right now."

"His name is Tommy," the kid said. "He's my brother."

"You saved your brother's life by drawing such a good picture," Dr Price said. "Good job."

"You did good, little man," the black man said. "Gimme that Three Gs handshake I taught you."

Now Dr Price recognized the man. Three Gs. Pump That Rump. Sanjay was always blasting his albums in the hatchery and Dr Price kept telling his student that he was going to cause some sort of deformities by bombarding the eggs with such heavy bass. Besides, since snakes do not have a "rump" per se, they were probably missing out on the deeper underlying meaning of the music anyway. But whenever Dr Price left and came back, Sanjay would be dancing around the lab, singing to a large, freshly inseminated female horned viper in a clear Plexiglas head tube and telling her to get freaky on it, which Dr Price couldn't help but think sounded like a very bad idea.

The kid raised his hand to shake with Three Gs's and then at the last minute before their palms touched, they both slid back as if repelled by an invisible inch wide force field between them.

"You got it," Three Gs said with a smile.

Then suddenly a woman burst through the crowd of emergency personnel. She was beautiful enough to turn heads as she ran, full figured like Jane Russell in mint condition and jiggling in all the right places. She had bleached streaks in her cherry red hair and the low cut neckline of her 1950's style dress revealed a pair of swallow tattoos as well as a whole lot of pale cleavage.

"Oh my God!" she cried as she came running towards the stretcher. "Tommy, oh my God!"

"Mommy!" Curtis cried and threw himself into the buxom woman's arms like a kid half his age.

"Oh honey!" she said, tears drawing black tracks through the perfect wings of eyeliner around her blue eyes as she squeezed Curtis tight, hand cupping the back of his head. "Oh my God, are you okay, baby?"

"I'm fine," Curtis said. He pointed to Three Gs. "This is my friend Three Gs."

The woman nodded a distracted greeting at the rapper and then did a double take, suddenly recognizing him. Before she could register the celebrity caliber of her son's new pal, Curtis blurted out, "I saved Tommy!"

"You did?" Still with one arm around Curtis, she came forward to the stretcher where Tommy lay. "Is he going to be all right?"

"He's received a nasty bite," Dr Price told the woman. "But the antivenin has been administered and is already working to counteract the venom in his body."

On the stretcher, Tommy's sticky red eyes slowly peeled open and he looked up, unfocused at first.

"Tommy," the woman said. "Sweetie, it's mommy. Mommy's here now sweetie-pie."

"Mommy?" Tommy said. "Are you real?"

"Yes, baby," she said, sniffling back tears. "I'm here."

"I need... twenty dollars," Tommy said.

The mother frowned. "What do you need twenty dollars for, honey?"

"For Troy," Tommy said. "For bodyguarding me and Curtis."

Three Gs smiled at this. "Don't worry about it, little man," he said. "This time, it's on me. You can get the next one."

"Okay," Tommy said softly. "Mommy?"

"Yes, baby?"

"Where is Mr Wong?" Tommy asked. "Is he okay?"

The woman's face fell and Curtis looked away.

"Well…" the woman said and then trailed off.

"Who is Mr Wong?" Dr Price asked.

"My son's cat," the woman said. "He was in the cargo hold."

"Oh…" Dr Price said.

An animal much closer to the size of the normal prey species for those snakes would not have stood a chance on that plane. The chances of the cat having survived were pretty much slim to none.

"The snakes got him, didn't they?" Tommy asked.

"I guess the men searching the plane will find out soon," Tommy's mother said. "We'll have to wait and see."

"I hate those snakes!" Tommy wailed. "I HATE them!"

"Shhhhhhh," the mother said, trying to soothe him. "Don't get yourself all whipped up. You need to rest now."

Tommy was crying feebly as the EMTs replaced his oxygen mask. Dr Price watched the mother and Curtis moving alongside the stretcher as they wheeled it to a newly arrived chopper, ready to air-lift Tommy to Cedar Sinai. Dr Price felt his hostility and anger towards Kraitler and this gangster Eddie Kim suddenly renewed, stronger than ever. Idiots like them were the reason so many people hated and feared snakes, why his beloved herps were so misunderstood and maligned in Western society. Kim may not have gotten his intended target with this ridiculous scheme, but he did a bang-up job of reinforcing the negative stereotype of snakes as cold-blooded monsters. Just the news stories alone would bring on a whole new wave of rattlesnake killing and mothers making their teenagers turn over beloved exotic pets.

"Hey," Three Gs said to Dr Price.

"Yes?" Dr Price replied, pulled back from his dark thoughts.

"Can you help my boy next?" Three Gs asked.

"Oh, yes," Dr Price replied, refocusing on the task at hand and looking over at the huge black man laying on his stomach, nearly overflowing off the edges of an extra large stretcher. "Of course."

Ken and Chen stood together at the bottom of the slide. Chen put a hand on Ken's shoulder and reached out to shake his hand.

"If you are really serious about studying Muy Thai," Chen said, taking out his wallet and removing a business card, "why don't you come down and spar with me at my dojo some time? Most guys who are new to it get all hung up on bashing people's heads in and tend to lose sight of the form. Your form is phenomenal, really tight. I think you have a lot of potential."

"Ten years of ballet," Ken replied, smiling. "And ten more in drag. I'm all about form, honey, though I don't mind bashing in a head or two while I'm at it. It's a crazy world out there."

"You got that right," Chen replied.

A young woman came tottering up to them. She had a glossy black pompadour haircut that would have made Elvis green with envy and was dressed in what could only be described as a sort of slutty matador outfit, the fabric of the jacket and tight Capri pants covered with little Mexican Day of the Dead skeletons wearing sombreros and dresses, and walking little skeleton dogs. Her feet were clad in outrageous ten-inch platform heels that made her a good six inches taller than Ken, not including her hair. Glow-in-the-dark skeletons dangled from her earlobes and jangled around her neck.

"Ken Doll!" she cried, wrapping her arms around Ken. "I was worried sick!"

"It's okay, Ghoulita," he said. "Daddy's home now."

He laid a big wet one on her, until they were both covered from nose to chin in her shiny red lipstick. Chen looked on with bemused wonder at this surprisingly hetero display. Looked like Ken really did have a girlfriend after all.

"Chen," Ken said when he finally broke the kiss. "Allow me to introduce the future Mrs Doll. Chen, this is Kitty. Kitty, Chen. Chen is, like, an ass-kicking muy thai champion."

"Oh yeah?" Kitty threw a high, frightening kick with her ten inch spike heeled shoe flying an inch from Ken's nose. "Cool."

"Ken saved my life," Chen said. "You got yourself a good man."

"Don't I know it," Kitty replied, grabbing Ken by the belt and leading him away. "And if you don't mind, I'm gonna take him home now."

"Take care," Chen called after them, but they were already lost in a gush of private nonsense words, heads close together as they walked.

But where was his own girlfriend in all this? Where was Cynthia? She had deserted him at his tournament and was not even here to see if he had survived this ordeal. His heart was heavy as he turned and made his way over to Mercedes, who was sitting alone on a large black suitcase.

Mercedes was silent, watching men lugging body bags with glassy, up-too-late eyes. Her blonde hair was tangled and wild, her shoes gone and her makeup ruined, but she still managed to look beautiful. She seemed light-years away from the silly, self-centered piece of wealthy fluff she had been when she boarded the plane. Her face was harder, more genuine somehow.

"Are you all right?" Chen asked.

"I don't know," Mercedes replied. "I feel like I've forgotten what that means, to be 'all right.' Everything is so strange now. I have no idea how to just... go back to my regular life. How can I, after this?"

"I don't know either," Chen said. "But I do know that I'm glad to be alive."

She smiled. "Daddy's probably flipping out right now. Trying to sue the airline."

Chen shook his head and smiled back. "My car is in long term parking. Can I give you a lift somewhere?"

"Sure," Mercedes said, taking Chen's arm. "Anywhere but here. But first..." She paused, fishing Ashley's card out of her purse. "I have a little dog named Esperanza to pick up."

The media had discovered Three Gs and were swarming around him while Troy fought to keep them back.

"Oh, man, come on!" Leroy hollered from his stretcher. "Don't let those vultures put my ass on the *Six O'Clock News*."

"Sir," Dr Price said, adding the antivenin for the Ceylonese palm viper to Leroy's IV drip. "Try and remain calm." He raised his voice. "Will somebody please get those cameras away from my patient?"

Several burly security men came forward and hustled the cameras away.

Leroy smirked at Troy. "It's pretty weird to be on the other side of security for once."

"Hang in there, man," Troy said. "We're gonna get you out of here."

"Dr Price's gonna hook you up," Three Gs said. "You'll be back to shoving cameramen yourself in no time."

The EMTs prepared to move Leroy out and Dr Price sheepishly held a pen and a torn medical history form out to Three Gs.

"Could I get your autograph?" Dr Price asked. "For my intern. He's a huge fan."

"Sure thing, Doc," Three Gs said, taking the pen and paper. "What's his name?"

"Sanjay," Dr Price said. "S-A-N..."

"Got it," Three Gs said. "He's Indian, right?"

"Right," Dr Price said, surprised that the rapper would know something like that.

"Here you go," Three Gs said, handing the pen and paper back to Dr Price. "And thanks for taking care of Leroy."

"No problem," Dr Price replied. "It was a pleasure to meet you."

"Cool," Three Gs replied. "Later."

Dr Price watched the two men walking alongside their prone friend on the stretcher and then looked down at the torn piece of paper in his hand.

"DJ San-J," it read. "Keep it real." Then under that: "But do me a favor and keep them snakes in their cages from now on."

Beneath that was a wide, extravagant scrawl that might have been a number three and a G or maybe just sort of cockeyed Picasso doodle. Then, as if by magic, Dr Price's cellphone lit up with the number of the lab. Sanjay. It could only be the Racers.

"Yes?" he said excitedly into the little phone.

"Six out so far," Sanjay said. "Two more still fighting through the shells."

Dr Price let out a happy shout and did a little dance on the tarmac, much to the amusement of the emergency personnel around him. "Did you get it on video?" Dr Price asked.

"All but the very first breakthrough," Sanjay replied. "But Doctor, when are you coming back?"

"I'm on the way!" Dr Price replied. "As soon as I confirm that no other envenomations have occurred here."

He ended the call and was about to put the phone back in his pocket when he paused, looking down at it for several seconds. Then, he took a deep breath and dialed the number of the herpetology office at the LA Zoo.

The machine picked up, of course. Dr Price sighed and waited through the recorded greeting before pushing the number one key to leave a message for Dr Anabelle Bennet.

"Belle," he said. "It's... uh... it's me, Steve. The racers..."

"Hello?" Belle's breathless voice said on the other end of the line. "How many?"

"Eight. Two still working their way out."

She let out a sweet, girlish squeal like a teenager who had just received a kiss from her favorite pop star. "I'll be right over!"

"But..."

She had already hung up. Dr Price looked down at the phone, frowning. He had no idea what to say to her when she got to the lab, but he knew there would be no stopping her from coming. It had been one of the longest, strangest nights of his life and it was about to get stranger, but he found that he was all right with that. He carefully packed up the remaining antivenins and went to catch a taxi back to his lab, where he belonged.

* * *

Sean and Flynn were the last to leave the aircraft. After the surrounding area had been swept and checked, and confirmed safe by Harris and his men, Flynn led Sean over to the lip of the slide. Sean could see that Flynn was still anxious, eyes trying to look everywhere at once, but then Sean got distracted watching Tiffany at the bottom, helping people and not even worrying about herself, still looking amazing in spite of everything she'd been through. Sean was wondering if it would be weird to ask her out, and if he would even be allowed to go on a date while he was waiting for the trial; wondering if she really did actually like him, or if she was just acting that way because of the snakes and all; wondering how she would look naked and what sort of things she liked guys to do to her. All this pleasant speculation was rudely obliterated when a huge brown taipan shot out from behind a broken seat and latched onto Sean's chest.

Arms windmilling wildly, Sean flailed out at the attached creature, but before Flynn could reach him, Sean tumbled backwards, somersaulting ass over end down the slide.

Sean landed upside-down at the bottom with a bone-crunching thud, the furious reptile still attached like it was trying to nurse, thick tail whipping back and forth and slamming into Sean's aching ribs. When Sean was able to focus his eyes back up at the top of the slide, he saw something that made his mouth drop open.

Flynn had pulled his Glock from its shoulder holster and was drawing a bead on the snake. Or more specifically, on Sean's chest. Sean, who felt he had come to know Flynn pretty well over the past twenty-four hours, never thought he would find himself on the other end of that deadpan bad-ass, staring down the barrel of a loaded gun.

"Are you...?"

Sean didn't have a chance to say the word "crazy" because there was a loud, flat crack and he suddenly felt as if he had been punched in the chest by Mike Tyson. Blood splattered in his eyes, blinding him, and his hands flew up to his chest. He was horrified by the wet ragged mess he felt there. He sucked in a huge, painful breath and then suddenly Flynn was there beside him, hauling him to his feet, and the wet bloody mess on his chest fell to the ground beside him. It was the snake, dead and blown into ragged pieces.

"Now," Flynn said. "Aren't you glad I made you leave that vest on?"

The vest. The Kevlar vest. Sean had completely forgotten about it in all the craziness and chaos.

"Jeez, Flynn," Sean said, touching the dent in the stiff fabric of the bulletproof vest. "You scared the crap out of me."

"Sorry, kid," Flynn said.

"Man," Sean said, stretching his shoulder joint. "That still hurt like hell."

"Not as much as a taipan bite," Flynn replied.

Tiffany came running over, calling his name. When he turned to her, she nearly tackled him, devouring him in a deep dish kiss that seemed to last forever. When she stopped, he realized that he had forgotten all about the bruisy ache in his right pec. He just grinned like a big old goofball while she grabbed his hand and wrote her phone number on his palm.

"I think I'm gonna like LA," Sean said.

"Nice shooting, Flynn," Claire said, stepping up beside Flynn.

"Thanks," Flynn replied, armpitting the Glock. "Tell me something."

"Depends on what you want to know," Claire replied with an arched brow.

"You meant what you said about Quantico?" Flynn asked.

"Why not?" Claire said. "It would be a way to help people and still travel all over. The best of both worlds."

"Well," Flynn said, "there is the whole bad guys trying to kill you on a daily basis thing."

"My dad used to get death threats all the time in his little office," Claire said. "So staying in one place your whole life is no guarantee either. Besides," she winked, "I'm pretty tough."

"I'll say," Flynn replied. "The test to get in is pretty challenging, though."

"You saying I don't have what it takes?" Claire asked.

"Not at all," Flynn said. "I'm just saying maybe you might be able to use a little help, kinda like a tutorial."

"Oh yeah?" Claire said.

"I don't normally offer this service, you know," Flynn said. "Only for someone with your... potential."

"Uh huh," Claire said grinning wickedly. "I got news for you, old dog. I think I might be able to teach you a trick or two."

Looking down into her bright, mischievous eyes, he knew that she was right.

"I'm starving," she said suddenly. "How about you?"

"I could eat," he said.

"There's something about almost being killed by venomous snakes and narrowly avoiding a fiery plane crash that makes me want a big plate of pancakes," she said. "With extra bacon. I know a great diner just around the corner from my house."

"Oh yeah?" Flynn said, more about the "just around the corner from my house" part than about the restaurant.

"Yeah," she replied, clearly answering what he had been thinking.

And just like that, slick as shifting gears in a well-maintained sports car, they were going to sleep together. All the teasing possibilities, the double entendre, the nature show mating dance— it was over. There was no more question of if, there was only when.

Then, Harris, like a benign fairy godfather, appeared with Sean at Flynn's elbow, backed up by Lawson and Fisk.

"Agent Flynn," Harris said. "I am officially relieving you of duty for the next twenty-four hours. Lawson and Fisk here will cover the witness." He eyed Claire with her torn blouse and cat-like grin. "And try to get some rest, willya?"

"You gonna be okay?" Flynn asked Sean.

The kid grinned. "I'll be fine," Sean said. "I'll see you tomorrow. Bring the Monopoly board."

"You bet," Flynn replied, letting Claire take his hand and gently lead him away.

In the hold of the battered 747, Animal Control officers Addison and Gonzales swept through the area in a meticulous grid, capturing and bagging any remaining live snakes, and tossing dead ones into a large plastic container. The two men were the main herp specialists in the LA County Department of Animal Services and most of their calls consisted of housewives reporting rattlesnakes in the pool or teenagers whose exotic pet had gone AWOL. Phil Addison was an older man, originally from Arizona, white-haired and deadpan with a steady hand and a calm, unflappable personality. Tito Gonzales was a former student of Dr Price and a little too handsome for his own good. He considered it a natural part of his job to "comfort" the frightened housewives once the offending reptile had been safely contained.

The snakes that were still alive were all uniformly vicious and hostile, no matter how severe their injuries. It was not easy to contain them and there were several hairy moments when they surprised wounded snakes hidden in the crevices between crates and luggage. More than one was so aggressive that the men were given no choice but to kill them. It was clear that something was very wrong with these snakes and it would be up to Dr Price and the rest of his staff to find out exactly what that might be.

Addison and Gonzales had nearly completed the sweep when Gonzales discovered a beige plastic pet carrier hidden under several other pieces of luggage. It was still latched but inside towards the back, he could see a narrow, scaly tail laying very still. He thought it might be dead so he leapt back, startled and readying his snake-stick, when he heard a fierce hiss from the dark interior of the tipped-over carrier. Much to his surprise, a huge, fat Siamese cat launched itself at the bars, paws reaching through the grid to rake the thick sleeve of his uniform.

The cat's chocolate-brown face was matted with blood, as were both front paws. Its crossed blue eyes were wild and glittering. Shining his light into the crate, Gonzales saw that the scaly tail was only one of several gory, severed chunks of fer-de-lance littered around the interior of the carrier.

"Damn," Gonzales said. "You are one lucky cat."

The cat took another swipe at him through the bars.

"Why you gotta be like that with me, kitty?" Gonzales asked. "I'm here to get your furry ass out of this dump."

The cat turned away from Gonzales, dismissively washing the clotted blood from its whiskers.

"Oh, I get it," Gonzalez said, lifting the carrier by its handle. "It's not luck at all, is it? You're so tough you don't need luck, huh? You're a survivor."

The cat looked at Gonzales as if it couldn't believe how long it had taken the human to understand.

Gonzales smiled. "Hey," he called to Addison. "You're not gonna believe this!"

Tommy had just been moved from intensive care to a bigger, nicer room in the pediatric ward. Curtis refused to leave his bother's side the whole time, even though he was so tired he could barely keep his eyes open. The doctors had said that Tommy was "out of the woods," which basically meant not-gonna-die, but Curtis still could not bring himself to go back to their mom's new apartment. Out of the woods or not, he did not want to let Tommy out of his sight, not even for a second. Tommy in turn held on to Curtis's hand the whole time; even when it seemed like he was sleeping he would wake up and start crying if Curtis pulled his hand away, so Curtis figured he better just stay.

Their mom was on her cellphone a whole lot, sometimes shouting at people, sometimes sort of crying, sometimes with her voice all low and fierce. Then, about twenty minutes ago, she got a call that didn't make her yell or cry. It made her eyes get real big and then she kissed them both and rushed off somewhere, saying she'd be back with a surprise.

Before she could get back with her surprise, there was another big surprise. Curtis had been sitting in a plastic chair by Tommy's bed, staring up at some shiny silver balloons that Three Gs had sent for Tommy and kind of drifting in a half asleep sort of way, when he heard a familiar voice in the doorway.

"Hey, Tiger," the voice said.

Curtis looked up and saw his dad standing there in regular clothes, looking almost as tired as Curtis.

"Daddy!" Curtis cried, flinging himself across the room and into his father's arms.

As soon as Curtis let go of Tommy's hand, Tommy woke up, eyes wide. "Daddy?"

"How you doing, kiddo?" their father asked, coming forward to hug Tommy gently, avoiding his bandaged arm

"A snake bit me," Tommy said, pointing to his arm. "But I'm out of the woods now."

"Oh, is that right?" their father asked, sitting down beside him and pulling Curtis into his lap, and even though Curtis was really too old for that sort of thing, he didn't mind one bit.

"Yeah," Tommy said. "And we met Three Gs and got bodyguarded by his bodyguard, who saved us by landing the plane after snakes ate the pilot."

"Wow," their father said. "I hear you did a fantastic job taking care of your brother, Curtis. I heard you saved his life."

Curtis blushed and looked down. "I tried to stop the snake from biting Tommy," Curtis said. "Honestly I did, but it didn't work."

"I know you did," his father said, hugging him tightly. "And I'm very proud of you."

"But Daddy," Tommy said, eyes big and teary. "Even Troy couldn't save Mr Wong. The snakes ate him too."

"I know, Tiger," their father said, pushing hair back from Tommy's forehead. "And I am so sorry about that."

"Brett?" their mom's voice said from the doorway. "Is that you?"

"Hello Kara," their father said in a way that made Curtis feel weird. He slid off his father's lap.

Then a nurse came into the room all mad and frowning with her hands on her wide hips. "Ma'am," she said, "you can NOT bring any animals into this hospital ward. I'm going to have to ask you to take that cat out of here this instant."

That's when Curtis noticed the cat carrier that his mom was holding. At first he thought maybe his mom had gone out to buy Tommy a new cat, like she'd bought a new fish when Tommy's goldfish had died, but then he heard that gruff, rusty door hinge yowl that only one cat he knew could make.

"MR WONG!" Tommy cried, sitting up in the bed so fast he nearly pulled the IV needle right out of his hand.

"Ma'am—" the nurse said again, but their father stood and cut her off.

"Look, give it a rest, will you?" he said. "Can't you see my son has been through hell?"

"I'm sorry, sir," the nurse said. "Rules are rules. If you refuse, I will have to call security."

"Go ahead," their father said, backing the angry nurse out the door. "You do that."

"Mommy, can I pet him?" Tommy asked.

"Just through the bars for now, honey," their mother said, holding the carrier up so Tommy could look inside.

"Hi there, you big fat kitty!" Tommy said, putting his palm against the bars. "I thought you were dead!"

Mr Wong pushed his face up against the grid, purring loudly. Clearly, he had thought the same thing about Tommy.

TWENTY-FIVE

Eddie Kim had to get the hell out of town. When he got the call from his man at LAX, telling him that the kid hit the ground safe and sound, that Kim's plan to eliminate Sean Jones had failed, he closed the expensive hotel drapes, turned off the lights and began to formulate a plan. Kim had more than one roomy leather go-bag he kept in pay lockers around the Los Angeles area, ready and waiting for just this type of situation. Each one was filled with jewelry, cash, guns and a poker hand of fake IDs. He figured he'd take Brandon-or-Brian's Magnum and then ditch it on the other side of the border. The girl, Susi she had told him her name was when he'd first brought her up to this hotel suite, was either unconscious on the floor by the bed or faking it very well. She was cute as a button, but not very sturdy. The poor thing had really had a busy night. If he hadn't been in such a rush to get out, he would have taken a few more minutes with her. However, word about the Jones kid had probably gotten to Alexander Gong as quickly as it had gotten to Kim. He did not have even a second to waste.

Throwing on last night's crumpled clothes, Kim paused in the bedroom doorway, casting a longing glance at the bruised and splayed Susi. When he turned back, his left temple was abruptly introduced to the butt of a gun.

Knocked stupid but not quite unconscious, Kim tried to fight the drowning tarry pain that choked all his senses. He could feel hands on his body, dragging him and moving his head in a way that made him feel like throwing up. He heard that familiar sharp ripping sound of duct tape being pulled off the roll, and the harsh, gluey smell of it as the tape was pressed against his bleeding mouth.

He must have grayed out, because the next thing he knew he was duct taped to the headboard of the fancy hotel bed, arms spread wide, wrists, elbows, shoulders chest and waist all encircled with tape and tightly bound to the ornate wrought iron curlicues behind him. His legs were bent and folded under in an uncomfortably frog-like position, thighs taped to his calves.

There was a woman kneeling beside Susi, helping the girl to her feet and wrapping one of the hotel's two complementary silk robes around her trembling shoulders. When the woman spoke, telling the girl in soft, husky Chinese to go wait in the other room, a spike of ice punched through Kim's churning belly. He would recognize that throaty, caramel-smooth voice anywhere. It belonged to the last person on earth that Kim wanted to see when he came to and found himself duct taped to a bed. It belonged to Gong's pet assassin, Lulu Fang.

She was squeezed into a black and gray snake-skin dress that probably fit her more tightly than it had fit the snake it once belonged to. Her mouth was slicked with glossy red so deep it looked venomous. Her bob was perfect and her slender hands were clad in clear latex gloves.

"Gong Ao-li tells me that you like playing with snakes," she said, using Alexander's Chinese name. "Do you think there is some underlying Freudian message there?"

Kim could do nothing but mmmph emphatically into the tape.

"I like snakes too," Lulu said. "I was born in the Year of the Snake."

She crawled up on the bed in front of him and he noticed then that she was barefoot, her toenails gleaming an iridescent green. Kim fought viciously against the tape, feeling his skin twist and tear, but he could not get free.

"Don't you just hate detectives?" Lulu asked, a teasing smile in the corner of her mouth. "They ruin all the fun. These days there's hardly anything left that you can do to a person." She leaned into Kim, her mouth so close to him that he could feel her warm, cinnamon-scented breath in the curves of his ear. "I want to bite you," she whispered. "Right here."

When she touched the tender indentation just below and behind his ear with the latex tip of her index finger, he screamed into the tape.

"But those lousy detectives," she said. "They have dentition analysis and all that now. Just one little tooth mark is all they need."

Kim's heart was beating so hard and fast that he thought it would explode in his chest. He knew why she was here; why didn't she just get it over with? Then he thought of every person he had ever tortured, every one of them begging him to end it while he just let it go on and on. There would be no getting this over with. This was karma, brutal retribution for a lifetime of casual cruelty.

Lulu flashed her dangerous smile and pulled something from between her breasts. A glass vial with a rubber top and a small syringe.

"Do you know what this is?" Lulu asked, holding the vial up in front of his face and twirling the thick yellowy liquid inside. "It's venom. Venom from a king cobra."

She uncapped the hypodermic needle and inserted it into the vial through the little rubber cap, drawing the sinister liquid into the syringe. Instead of plunging it into his eye or neck, she just recapped it and set it on the bedside table.

"That's for later," she said with a girlish giggle. "For when you are ready. And believe me, baby, after a few hours with me, you'll be begging for that needle. Remember that."

And over the next few endless hours, Kim discovered just how right she was.

EPILOGUE

Kuta Beach, Bali

"Paddle!" Sean called out to Flynn. "Come on, that's it, you got it!"

That was easy for the kid to say. He seemed like he had been born on a surfboard, body loose and easy, wet hair flying and a big goofy grin on his face. Flynn, on the other hand, was a city boy just past his fifth decade on this earth. Sure he was strong and athletic and kept himself in excellent shape, but surfing, it was a whole different game. The ocean felt like a living thing under Flynn's board and not an entirely friendly one either. There were fish and things swimming around in there. Sharp rocks and coral. Flynn clung to the rental surfboard beneath him like it was a life preserver or a woman. He turned his head and spotted two consecutive waves headed right for him.

"Flynn!" Sean called "You need to duck dive! Duck dive!"

"Duck what?" Flynn called an instant before the second of the two waves bitchslapped him right off the board, spinning him like a sock in a washing machine. Salt water went up his nose and sand went down his shorts.

He came up spluttering and Sean was right there, clapping him on the back.

"Dude!" Sean said, helping Flynn get his feet under him. "That was gnarly."

"Okay, kid," Flynn said. "I think it's time for some girly umbrella drinks. I've had it with this surfing shit."

Sean laughed. "Come on, man. You can't give up now. What was the first thing you said to me?"

"What?" Flynn frowned.

"What was the first thing you said to me?" Sean repeated, smiling. "You remember, don't you?"

Flynn narrowed his eyes at the kid. "Do what I say and you'll live."

"Exactly," Sean said. "And now you have to do what I say if you want to live. And I say one more try."

"Shit," Flynn said. "Who died and made you Yoda?"

"One more," Sean said. "And then you can have all the girly umbrella drinks you can stand."

"All right," Flynn said. "One more, and then you'll get off my case."

"I never said that," Sean said, laughing and paddling away with swift, sure strokes.

Flynn sighed and laid out across the board again, paddling after Sean.

As the sun sank into the ocean in a glorious suicidal splash of crimson, magenta and bloody orange, Flynn could sense the anxiety mounting in his youthful companion. When they'd first checked in to the Bali Hai Resort, they had walked down to Jasper Jones's Surf School, but the girl at the desk said that Jasper had gone up the coast for a few days. So Flynn and Sean were just soaking up the sun, eating too much good food and generally feeling happy to be alive. Then, as this, their third day in Bali came to a close, it seemed that "a few days" had probably passed. It was time to check back in at the surf school and see if the elusive Jasper Jones had returned.

Sean and Flynn sat together at a small wooden table at the edge of the beach, Sean sipping a strange milky pink mystery beverage out of a plastic bag and Flynn an ice cold Bintang beer.

"What if he doesn't like me?" Sean said. "Maybe I'll just give him bad flashbacks of Mel or something and he'll want nothing to do with me."

"Maybe," Flynn said. "And maybe not. No way to know until you try."

For a long lazy minute, neither of them said a word. Sean watched a pair of pretty native girls in sarongs walk by as he sucked up the rest of his weird soft drink. He walked over to a nearby trash barrel and tossed the plastic bag. When he returned, he sat up on the table top, facing the ocean.

"Flynn," Sean said, looking back at him and then looking out over the water.

"Yeah?" Flynn replied.

"It's weird about Kim, huh?" Sean asked. "I mean, when we were on that plane, fighting every second and scared that we were all done for, I probably wished Kim dead a million times. I would have been thrilled to see that fucker get the death penalty, but man, I wouldn't wish what ended up happening to him on anybody."

"That's the Triads for you," Flynn said. "They take care of their own shit."

"Yeah," Sean said. "Crazy."

There was another long, comfortable silence. Sean watched another group of scantily-clad girls pass by with the riveted intensity of a dog watching someone eat. When he turned back, he looked down at Flynn with a kind of half smile on his face.

"Are you gonna marry Claire?" he asked.

"Marry Claire?" Flynn said, looking down at his beer bottle and the ring of condensation it had formed on the wooden surface of the table. "Christ, I don't think either one of us are even remotely ready for anything like that."

Flynn took a deep swig of beer. How the hell did this kid do it? Flynn never would have admitted it in a million years, but that was exactly what Flynn had been thinking. He was thinking how good it was to be alive and how he wanted to spend the rest of that life next to that complicated and beautiful woman. He had fully expected to just have a little fun with her and walk away with a few good stories, but somehow, much to both of their surprise, that was not how it had turned out. It just kind of snuck up on them while they were not paying attention. Flynn knew that he had finally met someone who really understood him. Being with her would never feel like settling down. You could never get tired of a woman like her. She was fluid, full of secrets. She was a challenge, an equal, totally unlike any woman he had ever met.

"You love her, though, huh?" Sean asked.

"Yeah, I do," Flynn admitted. "She's an incredible woman. She's tough, smart and beautiful. Her only real flaw seems to be her inexplicable attachment to a jaded and cynical old wolf like me."

"Do you think Jasper is married to someone new?" Sean asked, looking back out over the water. "I never saw anything about a wife on the internet, but that doesn't mean he doesn't have one. I might even have half brothers or sisters."

"You might," Flynn said, finishing the beer. "What do you say we go put an end to all these maybes once and for all?"

"Yeah," Sean said quietly. "Yeah, okay."

They didn't talk as they made their way down the beach to the surf school. The sun had slipped away beneath the horizon and the beach was lit up with gaudy neon, tiki torches and strings of colored lights and flashing disco glitter from the beachside bars.

The surf school was just closing up when they arrived. The girl from the day before was pulling down a rusty metal shutter and snapping a fat lock into the hasp when she spotted Sean and smiled at him.

"If you're still looking for Jasper," she told him, "he's down at the Duck."

"The Duck?" Sean echoed, frowning.

The girl pointed to a tiny, ramshackle bar across the street that was little more than a corrugated tin roof on four poles. Out front was a hand-lettered sign that read "BEBEK" and featured a faded cardboard cutout of Donald Duck. The tiny place was jam packed with surfers.

"Okay, thanks," Sean said.

"No problem," the girl said over her shoulder as she sashayed off down the beach. "Maybe I'll see you there later."

Together Sean and Flynn headed down to the little shack the girl had pointed out. Flynn spotted Jasper by the bar seconds before Sean did. He was handsome and animated, obviously right in the midst of telling some hilariously epic story, accompanied by broad, emphatic gestures. Flynn could feel Sean's whole body tense up.

"Be cool, kid," Flynn said, putting a reassuring hand on Sean's tan shoulder.

"I'm cool," Sean replied, offering an anxious smile.

"Take a deep breath," Flynn said. "And remember, he's just a regular guy, just like you. Got it?"

"Got it," Sean said, swallowing hard.

"So go on," Flynn said.

Sean took that deep breath and then began threading his careful way through the sweaty and inebriated crowd. Looking at Jasper and Sean side by side, Flynn could see how much alike they were. There could be no doubt about their common blood. This was going to be interesting, there was no doubt about that.

It was far too noisy for Flynn to hear exactly what Sean was saying to Jasper, but the truth was that he really didn't need to. Jasper's rugged, deeply tan face went through several shades of emotion from surprise to shock to amazement to something almost like awe. Sean put out his hand, face so raw and open and hopeful that it hurt Flynn's heart to watch him. If Jasper blew Sean off, or made him feel bad, Flynn would be forced to break one of the surfer's legs. But as Flynn watched, Jasper reached out and gripped Sean's outstretched hand and after holding it for a second, pulled Sean into a fierce embrace. Flynn turned away with a smile, headed over to the bar and ordered another beer.

About the Author

Born in New York City in 1969, Christa Faust sold her first story in 1994 and her first novel in 1998. She has a fondness for vintage high heels and Mexican wrestling. Her previous novels include *Control Freak, Triads* (with Poppy Z Brite) and *Hoodtown*. Christa Faust is a regular and highly talented contributor towards Black Flame with books such as *A Nightmare on Elm Street: Dreamspawn, The Twilight Zone: Burned/One Night at Mercy* and the *Final Destination 3* movie novelization. Cult movie director Quentin Tarantino is also a huge fan of Faust's pulp fiction...

Also available from Black Flame

FINAL DESTINATION
AN ORIGINAL NOVEL

DEATH OF THE SENSES

An orginal novel by Andy McDermott

Thirteen storeys up, Manhattan was noticeably quieter than down on the street. Jack could still hear car horns below, but the constant rumble of street noise had faded, giving them an odd, distant quality.

Just as Beriev had said, there were two other cops on the roof on the tenement building, but they were keeping well back from the edge, standing near the entrance to the stairs. Looking past them, Jack could see Lonnie, or at least his top half, his back to them. His lower body was hidden behind the parapet.

"Hey, Pete. Who's this?" asked one of the cops with a dubious look at Jack as he and Beriev walked over to join them.

"Reckons he knows our guy over there," Beriev told them. Jack wasn't the least bit surprised that he didn't bother to tell the cops his name, or mention the small fact that he was also the person who'd saved his partner's life the night before. "Thinks he might be able to talk him down. What's he like at the moment?"

"Seems to have quietened down at the moment," said the cop. "Problem is, every time we try to get close he sets off again."

"What kind of things has he been saying?" Jack asked. Both cops looked at him as if waiting for Beriev's permission before deigning to reply. Beriev nodded slightly.

"Crying, mostly," said the second cop, speaking for the first time. "Lot of stuff about how he can't take any more, how he's got nothing to live for. Not very coherent, it usually turns into a screaming rant after a minute or so. I don't think he really cares whether we can make out what he's saying or not, he just wants to get it off his chest."

Beriev regarded Lonnie for a long moment. "You think he's serious about jumping, or he just wants attention?"

"Hard to tell," said the first cop. "There's been a few times when he's let go of the roof completely—puff of wind is all it'd take to send him over."

"Good job it's not windy, I guess," Beriev said, still watching Lonnie. "Okay then, Curtis. See if you can get through to him."

Jack took a deep breath, then walked slowly across the roof.

Amy wasn't quite sure how she'd got suckered into it, but she was now standing on the edge of the top step with a microphone jammed into her face and telling that over-made-up harpy Chelsea Cox everything she knew about Jack. Whatever the blonde's power of persuasion was based on, she was very adept at it.

"A real-life hero despite being homeless," gushed Chelsea, turning to face the camera and at the same time subtly moving across to push Amy towards the edge of the frame, "who follows up saving the life of a police officer one day by attempting to talk a potential suicide down from the roof of a tall building the next. An inspiration to us all. We'll bring you more on this story as it develops. This is Chelsea Cox for WNYK news." She gave the camera her trademark sign-off look, a hint of a pout and a suggestive narrowing of the eyes as she tipped her head slightly, held the pose for a few moments, then clicked her fingers. "And clear. George, you get that?"

"Got it," said George though her earpiece.

"Think you might use it?"

"We could drop it in as a breaking story during the next commercial break—if they guy's still up on the roof, that is."

"Yeah, I know it's not much, but you can cut in some footage of the leaper as well." Chelsea turned and blinked in surprise as she realised Amy was still standing next to her. "Oh, sorry. We're done now, thanks." She turned back to Brad.

"I, uh... oh." Amy felt oddly disappointed at being dismissed so suddenly, and even a little embarrassed about the fact she was still standing there like a dummy. A sudden change in the noise from the crowd made her turn.

"Hey, he's moving," said Brad, quickly aiming the camera skyward.

"Get back! Get back! I warned you, don't come any closer or I'll jump, I'll do it, I'll really do it!"

"Lonnie?" Jack called, cautiously. "Lonnie, it's me."

Lonnie stopped twitching, peering warily back over his shoulder. "Jack?" he asked in a slightly less agitated voice.

"Yeah, it's me."

"What do you want?"

Jack took another couple of careful steps, then came to a stop about six feet from the ice-covered parapet, his hands held up to show Lonnie he wasn't trying to grab him. "I was... I was kind of hoping to get you back onto this roof."

"Don't waste your time, Jack," said Lonnie, starting to twitch again. "I told you last night! I just can't take any more of this, I just can't..." His voice tailed off and he closed his eyes, slowly lowering his head. Jack thought he saw the bead of a tear grow in the corner of his eye. "I went to the shelter last night after I left you, Jack. It was full. So I went to another one. It was full too. And another, and another. You know where I slept last night, Jack?" He opened his eyes again, the tear breaking free and rushing down his cheek. "A kennel. A God-damn kennel! I slept inside a busted-up old doghouse that somebody had put out with the garbage!" His voice cracked as he started to shake, sobbing. "I had to sleep somewhere that people didn't even think was fit for an animal!"

"Lonnie," said Jack, very carefully moving a step closer to him, "listen to me. I know things are pretty bad, but that's no reason to just give up. There's always a chance, there's always hope."

"No, no, you're wrong," Lonnie said, taking one hand off the edge of the parapet to wipe his eyes. Jack winced, freezing in place. "There's no point. This is it, Jack, this is the bottom. There's nowhere else I can go."

"Except up."

"You really believe that?" Lonnie asked, looking over his shoulder at Jack again. "Look at me! Look at what I've turned into—what I'm doin' right now! No, there *is* no chance, there *is* no hope. Not for me, anyway. If all that I've got to look forward to for the rest of my life is more of the same *shit*," he suddenly yelled the word, "that I've had for the last few years, then... then what's the fuckin' point?" He looked away, staring out across the city.

Jack took the opportunity to move another small step closer to him.

"I can see him," Brad suddenly announced. Chelsea and Amy both looked at the monitor. Even at the sharp angle from which they were looking up at the roof, Jack's head was now visible above its edge. That meant he must only be a couple of feet from Lonnie, Amy realized.

"Keep the camera on him," Chelsea ordered. "George, you watching this?"

"I'm not even blinking," the reply crackled through her earpiece.

"Ready to go live if we need to?"

"My finger's on the button."

* * *

Jack could now see enough of the street below to give him a slight feeling of vertigo. He had no idea whether Lonnie was prone to it or not, but he was close enough to see that even in the cold, his friend was sweating.

"A cop told me something this morning," he said, trying to keep his voice as level as possible. "She said that even if people really do mean to kill themselves by jumping, they always scream on the way down. The second they do it, they regret it."

Lonnie said nothing, but Jack could tell by his expression that he was listening.

"It's no way to go out," Jack continued. "Screaming in terror because you realize you've just made the worst mistake of your life and there's nothing you can do to change it." He hoped he wasn't overdoing it, but he was running out of options.

"I've made other mistakes," Lonnie sobbed.

"But there's still a chance you might be able to do something to fix them! I mean, come on, look at how much you helped me. I wouldn't have survived my first couple of months on the streets if I hadn't met you, if you hadn't told me how to keep going. Lonnie, please, let me help you." He made a deliberate move forward, now only one step away from being able to reach out and touch Lonnie. Or grab him.

"Jesus, he's almost there," said Brad, barely breathing.

Chelsea put down the monitor and moved back in front of the camera. Whatever happened, it was going to take place in the next few seconds, and she wanted to be ready.

"Get back on the roof," Jack begged.

"What about them?" Lonnie asked, shooting a look in the direction of the cops. "What'll they do to me?"

"I don't know. They'll probably arrest you, but—" he quickly continued, seeing fear cross Lonnie's face, "believe me, a night in a cell's not so bad. I was in one last night."

"What did you do?" Lonnie asked through his tears.

"I'll tell you... if you get back on the roof. Here." He held out his hand.

Amy tensed, one hand to her mouth. She didn't have to watch the monitor now to see Jack reaching out for Lonnie.

Slowly, shakily, Lonnie took one hand off the parapet... and reached back over it, his trembling fingers touching Jack's.

Jack closed his grip. The two men looked at each other for a moment. Lonnie managed to smile for the first time in days.

"He's got him!" Brad gasped.

Chelsea frowned. A leaper being talked down from a roof as opposed to jumping from it was a third or fourth story, at best.

"Okay, Lonnie," said Jack, "now, really slowly, really carefully, turn around. I've got you. Just turn around and let me pull you back up."

From nowhere, a cold wind sprang up. It wasn't like a normal wind, Jack thought, a continuous force of moving air; this somehow felt more like a snake circling around them, looking for the place to strike...

Lonnie shifted slightly as the wind hit him, one foot on the ledge, the other raised just above it as he prepared to turn around.

Ice cracked under his toes.

Lonnie's foot shot out from the ledge, his unsupported weight instantly dragging Jack forward and slamming him hard against the unforgiving brick of the parapet. Pain ripped across his chest.

But he still had Lonnie's hand—

"Whoa!" Chelsea gasped. Even anticipating the fall hadn't prepared her for it.

But the man wasn't falling, not just yet...

* * *

"Help me!" Jack screamed over his shoulder at the cops, as Lonnie kicked and thrashed in panic on the other side of the parapet. "Help!"

He could hear them charging across the roof, but he couldn't keep his grip. Lonnie's fingers were slipping...

Amy made an indistinct sound of horror somewhere deep in her throat as the struggling man broke free of Jack's grip and plummeted downwards with terrifying speed, his coat caught by the wind and flapping open like wings—wings that could never fly.

"Shit!" exclaimed Chelsea involuntarily, not caring if she was now on a live feed. She watched him drop, whipping past the windows behind him. Whatever happened, however messy things were, she had to be ready to turn to camera and deliver her report...

"No!" Jack yelled, the cops crashing against the parapet, against him, just a fraction of a second too late.

Amy watched, unable to look away, as Lonnie fell and started to scream. Nine floors up, eight, seven six...

Lonnie's flapping coat snagged on one of the phone wires stretching across the street. It should have either torn under his weight or simply slid off as he fell past.

It didn't.

Instead, it wrapped around the cable, not once, but twice. Impossibly.

But impossible or not, it held. Lonnie was jolted to an abrupt, rib-breaking halt just two storeys above the ground.

Tracking Lonnie's fall, Brad was caught by surprise when the plunging figure suddenly stopped, continuing to tilt the camera all the way down to the ground before he realized something had happened. Reacting on cameraman's instinct, he snapped the zoom lens in to cover as wide an area as possible, Chelsea flashing into view as the picture pulled back. The guy was caught on something at the top of the frame...

Lonnie's coat finally ripped and he started to fall again.

Chelsea snapped her head round to look into the camera in amazement. "Did you get that?" she gasped.

The phone wire, freed of the sudden weight that had pulled it down, cracked like a whip, a wave motion rushing along its length towards the other side of the street.

Lonnie hit the ground, injured but still alive.

Amy barely had enough time to register what had just happened when something passed above her, a strange serpentine movement. The phone line...

The wave reached the end of the phone wire where it connected to the building where Amy, Brad and Chelsea were standing on the steps.

Ice had built up on the wall from a leaking pipe, growing one freezing drip at a time to spread like tentacles along the half-dozen lines running into the building. Hanging down below the cold mass were long, pointed icicles, melted and refrozen together over days into top-heavy masses with claw-like points.

The wave hit the heavy ice. Part of the motion was sent back along the wire; the rest was transmitted into the ice as a vibration.

The ice shattered with a sound like breaking glass.

Chelsea instinctively looked up at the unexpected noise directly above her.

It was the last living thing she ever did.

A chunk of ice, two huge icicles melded together with foot-long tips sharp as daggers, hit her in the face. The jagged spikes plunged right through both of her eyes in a wet spray of ruptured eyeball and spurting blood and brain matter. The sheer weight of the ice rammed the tips of the icicles right through the back of her skull before the shock of the impact sheared most of the frozen mass away. It crashed to the ground between Brad and Chelsea's still-standing corpse and exploded into jagged fragments.

Amy turned when she heard the noise, just in time to see the back of Chelsea's head burst open in a slurry of red and gray. The body somehow stayed balanced for a moment, hands twitching, before its knees slowly buckled and it toppled backwards down the steps, long shards of ice still protruding from its gushing eye sockets. Somebody behind Amy shrieked. She would have done so herself if she'd been able to catch her breath.

A voice was yelling in Brad's ear. It took him some time to work out that it was George back at the studio frantically telling him that they were still live and asking him what had happened. The face in his viewfinder wasn't Chelsea but the young Asian cop they'd just interviewed, staring at him in horror.

Had what he'd just seen through his camera been real? He cautiously pulled his head back from the viewfinder and looked down.

It *had* been real.

"Did you get *that*?" he asked, of nobody in particular, before throwing up.

The story continues in

DEATH OF THE SENSES

1-84416-385-7

An orginal novel by Andy McDermott

Available from Black Flame
www.blackflame.com